SCARS
OF THE
RAVEN
QUEEN

For those who never got to say goodbye, or worse yet, "I love you."

Acknowledgements

To my husband. We did it! Our late-night brainstorming sessions have paid off! Thanks for being my forever love story and daily inspiration for all the book boyfriends I am cooking up.

To my girlies: Naomi, Sunny, Jazzy, Sky Sky, Sarah, Mak, and of course, the ENTIRE Cult of Chaos, thank you all for cheering me on daily and being the unhinged found family I never knew I needed but now know I simply can not live without.

Alexandra. Thank you for saving Aidan from The Cousin Debacle, and in turn, thank you for saving me from accidentally writing some weird Jon Snow & Daenerys shit.

Sarah Emmer, my brilliant god-send of an editor: here's to many more exciting projects as a team! Thank you for pouring your heart into SOTRQ.

To my readers. Wow, here is when words fail me. Without each of you, this would not be my reality and I am eternally grateful that you have given Myla your attention for a time. Happy reading!

Content Warnings

This story contains some content which may be triggering, traumatic, or uncomfortable to read.

Listed below are the subjects I believe may be difficult for some readers. I want my readers to always feel safe while experiencing my stories. If a specific trigger seems especially concerning to you, please refer to the smaller text for context clarification. Otherwise, **skip the smaller text as it may be a spoiler to the story.**

Metaphors of R*pe:

Some imagery throughout the story, in moments where control is taken over another person, could be interpreted as, or are intended as metaphors of sexual assault to make a point. Nothing graphic occurs, however, and no actual sexual assault happens to anyone in this story.

Child Death:

The death of a child occurs. It is a central plot point to the story, mostly on the topic of healing from the loss. The reader does not experience the event on page in any way beyond the discovery of the child, which I aimed to write as gently and non-descriptively as possible to avoid unnecessary distress. This event occurs over the course of two chapters- 6 & 8.

Child in Peril:

This story is set during a war, and our protagonists are parents. Their children will experience moments of danger. Beyond the one death mentioned above, all other children are fine.

Woman In Peril:

FMC faces various moments of danger and abuse. She is alright and kicks ass as a "thank you" to those who wronged her.

Mental & Emotional Abuse:

Topics of emotional and mental abuse are confronted.

Murder

Violence, Death & Gore

Sexual Content

Sexism

 # DISCLAIMER:

reading chapters 6-8 while at work, on public transportation, or any public setting whatsoever is strongly discouraged. -signed Kier, at the recommendation of her beta and e-arc readers.

PROLOGUE

ATOP A SPLIT MOUNTAIN, deep within the darkest cavern, the seer writhes with a cursed sight, trembling with cold as the vision consumes her.

Black, like the deepest ink, spills from the angry storm clouds as they rain justice from the Gods. As the droplets near the blood-soaked ground, they transform into swarms of enraged ravens, which land with deadly accuracy to claim souls off the battlefield in the name of revenge—in the name of their queen and her stolen innocence.

She stands on a gruesome precipice of piled bodies, adorned in armor as equally black as the rain, and wearing a crown of black peonies. Though the ravens swarm violently overhead, shredding flesh with their curled and bloodied talons as they approach the woman, their death belongs to the queen. So, her foes crumble at her feet, raising the mountain of death, bringing her closer to the Gods. To the human eye, her form moves with disciplined rage, but through the unfailing sight of the Gods, it is clear their will fuels every fiber of her being.

In her heart, the Spirit Mother drums, giving her longevity against the numbers spilling toward the malevolent shadow. At her spine, the God of Vengeance holds her upright, providing a foundation to her fury. In her stomach, the God of Death reminds her of the mercy she must not show, for all the Gods are hungry.

Blackened beasts with wings as large as land itself cloak the sun from the sky, dragging more darkness with them, and the forests scream for murder.

The seer's eyes fly open, and her body stiffens with dread as she whispers to herself: "*Death is coming to Myrnith.*"

CHAPTER 1

PAST: MYLA, FIFTEEN

WHAT A FINE DAY to feel so utterly miserable.

Myla glances skyward, wondering if the Spirit Mother is laughing down upon her now. A bitter gloom, courtesy of a prolonged spring, drenches the city. If the new blademaster were to lower his broadsword upon Myla's head, and cut her brain in half, he would find the contents to be equally gloomy.

The torrential downpour casts an ethereal glisten off the rooftops and across a vast stretch of New Falkmere. Rain patters and ricochets off the sharp edges and saturates the moss and ivy blanketing a majority of the city. Myla has never seen it from this vantage point before, but the view *is* breathtaking. Despite her miserable state, she admires the way the city demands respect by simply existing so magnificently.

For the many strong beliefs Myla holds, there is one she is entirely certain of: for as slight, and awkward, and quiet as she is, Myla could never hope to achieve that same scale of magnificence.

A wave of nerves washes through her body, and she follows her father into the Institute of Mystic Arts, as a mere shadow behind his impressive, if not imposing, stature. With every step deeper into the mouth of what feels like her own personal monster, Myla regrets the leftover quail she swiped from the kitchens in her post-breakfast surge of hunger. Her mother says she is growing; Myla simply thinks mealtime portions are too small compared to the platters laid before her father.

The Institute of Mystic Arts is the most prominent structure within the city walls, aside from the palace itself. Enormous stained-glass windows arch in blues, yellows, and greens up from the base floor, past the spiraling staircases outside of the building, and toward the pyre stabbing into the sky. Four towers stand guard at each corner of the establishment, all containing alchemy labs aglow from pupils practicing their craft. Arched bridges jut from each tower, gradually traveling back down to the ground, leading into various parts of the gardens, where sparring and ability testing take place. More than once, Myla has heard of the blademaster who instructs students in the art of the sword from his lair beneath the institute. She has been told that the man is odd, but friendly. His charisma, people say, effectively distracts from his lethal handling of a blade.

I guess I will find out if that's true here shortly.

"Father," Myla whispers, peering from behind his cloaked shoulder to see the large iron double doors swing open before them. A nervous spasm lays claim to her chest; the idea of mingling with the children of Falkmere's finest, as the girl raised in the countryside for fifteen years, sickens her. Though she has been in Falkmere now for almost a year, she still has not established a strong friendship with anyone new. "I don't want to go in here."

"Silence," he hisses, as his cold hand snakes around her slender wrist. "It is a gift from the Gods that you have been allowed a seat here. I shall hear nothing more from you."

Myla swallows hard, averting her gaze from the swarm of students abuzz beyond the entrance. The breeze wafting out is warm and spicy, a thickened air in contrast to the fresh rain, which makes her nauseous. Rebuttals bounce inside the walls of her mind; each excuse to avoid entering seems like a justified one, but before she can find the bravery to speak once more, her father roughly drags her into the massive building. Myla peers down at her smarting wrist, noting how his fingers dig deep into her skin; no doubt more marks will be left.

In every direction, someone of excessive talent, remarkable height, or notable beauty passes, a cacophony of people exerting themselves and excelling within their environment effectively, making Myla feel small and out of place.

As she approaches, Myla observes two curved rows of stairs gradually climbing upwards, meeting directly ahead of them in the center of a room where a balcony overlooks the foyer. A polished gentleman stands in a hunched position over the twisted black railing—the Headmaster, she can only assume. His light hair is slicked neatly behind his ears, curling slightly at the nape of his neck. He is clean-shaven and well-manicured; everything about him oozes immaculate control. Maverick hauls his daughter toward this perfectly refined and intimidating man, taking no notice of her stumbling over her pale blue skirts and her struggle to stay upright as they scale the steps. Myla feels like a prized cow being displayed for the butchers, wondering who will pay the most to kill and consume her.

"Lord Alerys," the gentleman addresses her father in a warm and familiar tone, passing a brief glance over Myla. "I am pleased you have chosen to bring your daughter to us. I believe we will be an asset in her upbringing. Follow me."

Wordlessly, Myla trails behind the two men, watching students mingle as they make their way to various classes. Muttered conversation takes place between her father and the Headmaster, something about her schedule and the hours she must practice to catch up with her peers. Whatever it is they say, Myla allows their mundane words to drift out of focus, regarding instead as the magnificent architecture passes her by, nooks housing studious young men and women while doors creak open and shut with low thuds. Statues of the Gods and

Goddesses, carved of precious gems and crystals, and taller than her, line the halls, catching the light magnificently.

The Institute of Mystic Arts is alive with motion and magic; the very essence of talent is palpable. Were it not for the fact her presence here is the result of her father's insatiable draw to excellence, Myla would allow herself to feel exhilarated. She would bask in the way her soft, blue silk dress harmoniously complements the marble flooring and stained-glass windows. Everything about the establishment feels like magic.

"If you would be so kind as to excuse the disturbance," the headmaster speaks to her now, looking over his broad shoulder down to where she hovers behind. "We have had a blacksmith begin an apprenticeship with our blademaster—his lessons in exchange for the repair of our armory. I am afraid he is polishing today, and it is quite a mess."

Myla groans inwardly as they begin their descent down a steep spiral staircase. *Great, occupied and out of the way for the day in a dreary crypt to practice swordplay with a blacksmith for an audience.* Sensing her displeasure, Maverick allows the headmaster to move a few strides ahead before turning to face her, his severe eyebrows pushed together in an all-too-familiar glower.

"I have paid a fine price to see you established with the most talented in the city, and I won't have you expelled for a nasty attitude." The words are hissed, icy and piercing, with no room for negotiating.

Myla nods, lowering her eyes in submission. "Forgive me, Father."

Below, at the base of the steps, a black door on fine, ornate hinges swings open, revealing a sizable chamber in perfect circular symmetry. Along the walls, weapons of all shapes and sizes hang on iron fittings and torches every several feet illuminate what would otherwise be a completely dark room. The tiles on the floor have been expertly cut, painted, and arranged to depict the ancient maps of Old Falkmere. At its center, a tall and slender man with gray eyes, shoulder-length hair, and a silver mustache stands poised, one leg bracing his body while the other nimbly teases the ground before him, ready to lunge. His large hands wrap firmly around the hilt of a blade—a very real blade which he lowers in a silver flash toward the head of the boy before him.

Myla gasps, instinctively drawing her hands to her mouth to muffle the shriek threatening to echo through the entire room. Her startled entrance causes the young man to flinch, looking momentarily in her direction.

"Ack!" The blademaster's weapon stops a mere inch from the boy's skull. With the flat end, the instructor swings the sword down on his shoulder with a heavy *thump*. "Distraction kills! It does not matter who comes through that door. Do not lose your head because you are *distracted*."

The boy, perhaps a year or so older than her, nods, taking the reprimand with stoicism, though Myla notices the flicker of his light green eyes as they dance in her direction once more, and the corner of his mouth twitches in the ghost of a smile.

"Whom do I have the pleasure of meeting today?" The blademaster, with a brief encouraging smile at his pupil, turns toward Maverick and the headmaster, his gaze assessing Myla in one quick sweep. "Is this Lady Myla Alerys? I have been expecting you."

Myla returns his bow with a deep curtsy. "It is a pleasure to make your acquaintance, Sir..."

"Sir Roderick, at your service."

Myla smiles, thankful to find the man before her carries a friendly tone and the flicker of a smile in his gray eyes. He seems far less severe than she had imagined he might be. Perhaps lessons from him will not be so terrible—if she can avoid distraction. As Maverick and Sir Roderick discuss the details of her training, Myla peeks past the blademaster to where the blacksmith boy is now leaning over a pile of blades which he attentively polishes.

He is clearly not a person of title or position—she would not have needed to know he was a blacksmith to guess it. His clothes are common wear. Evidence of mending is noticeable on his tunic's sleeves, and he wears leather bracers which show signs of warping, perhaps from the high heat at the forge. Scars cross his calloused hands, and ash from a fire streaks up his forearms. He is muscular, clearly no stranger to manual labor. Dark wavy hair falls across his forehead and curls around his ears, giving him a tousled, boyish appearance. She imagines he might look older if he had the more well-groomed style of the royals.

Unexpectedly, amidst her study of him, he glances up, his eyes meeting with hers, and the flash of a grin warms her before her father catches her…distracted.

"Myla," Maverick chides, fingers digging into her upper arm as he yanks her back into the present. "The headmaster is speaking to you."

"Oh." Myla cringes, turning to face the three tall men. She feels impudent and unfit standing here in a day dress and silk slippers, but more than that, she feels silly. Their expectant faces devour her discomfort like a meal which fuels their power. She can sense it—the need to make others small to build themselves up. Well, the headmaster and her father at least. Sir Roderick just looks annoyed, but perhaps not at her. "I apologize," she finally manages, twisting the hem of her sleeve between her thumb and forefinger. "What were you saying, Headmaster?"

"I must implore you to acknowledge the strict nature of this institute. We have little tolerance for anything less than *excellence*. Our students learn and progress with remarkable speed here and often phase out of lessons fast. Do you see yourself as a suitable candidate for this scale of learning?"

Myla swallows, feeling a red flush building in her cheeks. Four pairs of eyes rest on her now, one green set in particular driving discomfort to her middle. While the three men watch for any signs of uncertainty, the blacksmith boy seems tense with anticipation. Slowly, Myla nods. "I am suitable," she says flatly, her attention fixed on the headmaster's, as a black, sticky, soot-like hatred for the deliberately targeted question grows in her. "Thank you for this opportunity," she adds with a small nudge of defiance.

Soon enough, Maverick and the headmaster leave, her father departing with a glare of warning her way. When the door closes behind them, Myla turns to see Sir Roderick moving toward the center of the chamber once more, retrieving his weapon from where it lies.

"Imagine," the blademaster coos, smiling at her and nodding at the space before him, a silent instruction to join. "Having the gumption to question the abilities of a woman when you stand with her in a room full of *swords*. In my experience, that is an excellent way to lose a tongue. Or a *limb.*" His eyes sparkle, and he gestures to the wall lined with blades. "Which one calls to you, Miss Myla?"

I just might like you, Roderick.

Myla giggles, noting the grin spreading across the blacksmith boy's face. "I suppose it doesn't much matter which one I pick as long as it cuts, right?" Myla reaches for a long blade.

Roderick is about to answer when the young man blurts, "You aren't tall enough for that one." He visibly regrets his verbal slip when the blademaster shoots him a discouraging look.

The instructor surprises her when, despite his silent rebuke, he nods toward the boy. "Bryar is right; a blade does matter, cutting or no. You should find a shorter weapon that doesn't compete with your height. You need to be the one swinging the blade, not the other way around."

A coy smile steals over Myla's face as she visualizes a massive blade propelling her steps with its mighty force. "Alright, how about this one?" A smaller broadsword at her fingertips, she looks to where Bryar stands, absently polishing his pile of weapons, watching her selection from beneath his dark brows.

"That would be good," he says.

Roderick nods in agreement and hands his weapon to Bryar. "Polish this one while I give Myla an assessment. We shall resume your training later."

Of all the ways Myla expected her lessons at the institute to begin, foot placements and posture were not what she might have guessed. Alas, she spends an hour with Roderick tapping the space between her shoulders with his blade, nudging her feet half an inch this way and that, and twisting her hips until she stands taller than she ever has. At which point, with a satisfied nod, Roderick sheaths his sword.

"*This* is how you should stand. Sword or no sword in your hand, stand tall, Lady Myla. You have no reason to walk through this world cowering."

Exhilaration rushes through Myla as Roderick continues to instruct her, and she realizes that the lessons this trained killer has in store for her will not be strictly in the wielding of a weapon, but the shaping of her character. In her entire life, no one has ever looked at her and told her to stand taller, to be commanding, to exude confidence. Yet in this one lesson alone, Roderick's words are nothing short of uplifting. When the lesson has ended, disappointment settles over her. At any moment, Maverick will walk through that door to collect her and return her back to their city manor.

They had been living in their family estate, slightly south of New Falkmere near the coast, but earlier in the year, when Myla turned fifteen, her father insisted it was time to bring her out into society and schedule events that might expose her to potential suitors. Myla has never been more miserable. Were it not for her friend Elsa's family also moving to New Falkmere, she would be hopelessly lonely.

With a sigh, Myla returns her heavy blade to its place on the wall and makes her way toward the door to wait for her father in front of the institute, when a flash of red-hot flames catches her eye. Bryar, the blacksmith boy, deflects the swing of Sir Roderick's blade with an impenetrable blast of fire from his palms. His sword lies abandoned at his feet.

"No," Sir Roderick sighs, attempting patience, it would seem. "Your father has not arranged these lessons so you can fight with your magic *still*."

"I know," Bryar responds with an exasperated groan as he leans down to retrieve the weapon. "I'm sorry, it's just second nature to me. Sometimes the flames come even when I don't mean them to." He grips the blade and leans into his footing, facing the instructor with determination, though it is evident he has tried and failed more than once to keep his magic in check.

Myla leans against the door, watching the exchange curiously. She has seen flame wielders before, but the flames Bryar launches seem more spontaneous—not controlled at all. *Perhaps that is why he is here.*

"You are going to burn the hair right off my head, and potentially yours," Sir Roderick says with a hint of a laugh in his voice. "Has your father considered some additional lessons at the institute? Honing your skills might prove helpful."

Bryar shakes his head, digging his feet into the tiles beneath him in preparation for the duel. "He does not want me practicing magic. He wants me to learn how to wield a sword."

"And do *you* want to wield a sword, Bryar?" Sir Roderick asks, his blade slicing the air as it lowers down upon Bryar's, who parries the attack.

With gritted teeth and strained muscles, Bryar deflects two more attacks before answering. "I can't become a king's guard if I don't know how to wield a sword."

CHAPTER 2

PRESENT

"I WILL HAVE HIM *strung up* and eviscerated before I accept that this was simply a hunting *accident.*" Myla smacks two flat palms on the iron table, her gaze traveling across the room to the open-air balcony which overlooks the forest of Old Falkmere. A buildup of heat, a courtesy of their bond, boils within her. A brief glance his way confirms her suspicions: he will reduce the 'hunter' to a sloppy mess of skin and ash before she has the chance to remove any organs.

"No one was hurt," Bryar gives her a pointed look, his fingers drumming the table methodically. "We must treat it as an accident, whether we believe it to be one or not."

Not is spoken in such a way as to validate her feelings. There are too many Raven's Veil Sentinels posted in the woods where the children play for this to be just an accident.

The pitter-patter of small feet and mischievous giggles passing in the hall outside the council room disrupts their conversation. Words of "slow down", and "your lessons aren't half finished", trail after the three young children as Ethstan shuffles behind them, far too old to be chasing them through palace halls day in and day out. He does it anyway.

Myla smiles weakly, as does Bryar, who places a hand on either side of her face, silently commanding her focus. "I will see to it that

Rhyland increases security around the children. And they will not play in the woods anymore. No harm will come to them."

Myla nods, inhaling the crisp spring air deeply. "Alright," she agrees finally. "We will let the man go, but I do not want him hunting in Old Falkmere. He must find deer elsewhere." *Or he can eat poisoned mushrooms.*

"I'll see to that myself," Bryar adds, bending down to press a kiss against her lips. "We have guests arriving shortly. You should take some time for yourself before the *chaos* arrives." He says "chaos" as though it is something to laugh about and not, in fact, a gaggle of fledglings who will no doubt entice their children to more mischief than usual.

"Imogene writes of Aisling…" Myla trails off, avoiding her husband's curious gaze. He watches, waiting for her to share her concerns as she has done many times before. "They just are not getting along. I feel our efforts may be in vain."

Bryar takes a deep breath, releasing a heavy sigh, no doubt visualizing the mischievous grin of their young son. "Aidan is only four, and most children do not get along at that age anyway. We still have time to encourage a connection."

"And if we can't?" Myla asks with trepidation.

"Then we will hope they accept a betrothal between Elenore and Aisling instead—or perhaps Zarek. Elenore is his twin, after all." Bryar stops short and shakes his head, disputing his own suggestion. They both know already that Elenore does not share the abilities of her twin brother. The Ashborn want Aidan to strengthen them.

Myla slumps into a high-back iron chair and reaches for her teacup, taking a long and soothing sip before handing it to Bryar. "It's cold—perhaps we should discuss it with them this evening."

Bryar shakes his head in disagreement as he hovers a palm over her cup until steam rises from it. "If we appear to have given up on Aidan and Aisling already, I am worried that will threaten our alliance with them. It is a risk we cannot afford right now."

Myla snorts in response. "Imogene and Ivan have not been forthcoming about exactly why they were so quick to align with us. Something tells me, betrothal or not, they wouldn't be quick to rid themselves of us."

Not as convinced of the Ashborn's loyalty as his wife, Bryar responds with a grunt and turns to stare out across the expanse of Old Falkmere, listening still to Myla as she continues. "In any case, we must find a way to change Aidan's opinion of Aisling. Like you said, they are young."

At this, Bryar turns, wearing a broad grin. "Change Aidan's mind? On anything? Defeating the Blood Stealer was an easier feat than changing our son's mind on *anything* will ever be."

Myla laughs, extending a hand to him, which he strides forward to take, holding it lovingly to his chest.

"Tell me," she insists with a smile. "Whose idea was it to create tiny replicas of *you and me*? Impossible little things."

"As memory serves," he answers coyly, "I was powerless to you in that circumstance."

Myla stands, laughing slightly before the shrill sound of a playful shriek interrupts their peace. "Off with you then. See to it that so-called 'hunter' is not caught anywhere near our children again. I am going to help Ethstan."

"You do that." Bryar cringes slightly at a loud clamor echoing from the main hall before flashing her a quick, parting grin.

Myla moves quickly toward the door, certain if she does not interfere soon, the children will kill the poor old monk. Stepping out into the hall, she follows the sound of calamity, accompanied by the nostalgia of the last five years, which is the real foundation of their ruins-turned-home.

After the exhausting defeat of Vesperian, and the trying birth of Caspian, all involved were bone-weary, and rest was necessary. Myrnith seemed to sigh in relief, and Myla was eager to fall into the quiet with her new husband and son. It was a season for rejuvenation, not war. Those loyal to her cause, soldiers and friends alike, followed her to the ruins of Old Falkmere. They restored much of the old palace, village, and barracks, making a home for themselves. During the first year, her soldiers remained in her service as volunteers. Their families were safe from the Maverick's torment, and there was peace in the forested settlement. As their town began to thrive and escapees from Maverick's iron reign joined their forces, Myla and Bryar agreed it was time to boost their economic standing. The first steps were generating revenue, funding a treasury, and paying their soldiers.

Rhyland oversaw a mission with the Raven's Veil, and orchestrated an impressive heist of the Falkmere treasury. They reclaimed about a third of Myla's gold—royal riches transferred to her upon the death of King Caius—from her father. Rhyland and the elite force also thoroughly gutted Maverick's old estate, confiscated one of the Imposter King's cargo ships, and burned the remainder of Maverick's fleet. This interrupted many of Maverick's trade deals and left him in violation of many of his agreements. Courtesy of their proximity to the coastline, Old Falkmere began supplying Valyndor with fish and clams in exchange for a decent sum of gold annually. Old Falkmere, now in possession of finer furnishings, clothing, kitchen supplies, and a steady income, was finally a respectable establishment. Now, the restored half of the palace is safe enough for their children to roam and play freely.

Myla enters the main hall. Though the hand-carved arches are chipped from years of abandonment and the destruction of the war, they are still magnificent, bending overhead on both ends and meeting in an ornate design in the center of the ceiling. Amidst the intervals between the arches, faded but expertly painted depictions of the war between the Aetherwing and the Ashborn are shown, once-vibrant colors making the grand room a place of awe. In so many ways, as the tension between herself and her father rises and leads to an inevitable battle for the throne, Myla knows she will miss this place if she is successful. They have the funds and the loyalty to win a war at this point. Maverick does not have the coin nor the support to withstand the near-constant skirmishes much longer. Then she will watch her old, traitorous father kneel at her son's feet.

Myla's attention is violently jerked back into the present when a burst of heat whooshes overhead followed by a rambunctious, "Hah!"

Expertly trained in the art of avoiding her children's play-combat, Myla ducks, her eyes darting to a head of dark curls. His green eyes flare wide, and despite his tiny frame, he is the spitting image of his father. Aidan holds another volley of flames in his palms, no doubt intended for his older brother.

"*Mother*," he quips sheepishly, ignoring the giggles of Caspian and Elenore who stand, one on each side of a sweating Ethstan, held fast by his firm hands on their shoulders.

"What have I said about magic in the palace?" Myla chides, walking toward the boy with her arms crossed. The muscles in her cheeks strain to defy her, to share in the laughter the boy before her clearly fights. Instead, she draws her lips into a thin line. Laughter will wait. "*Playing* with your magic? *Aidan*. You know it drains one's energy too fast to use it needlessly." She gestures toward Ethstan, the singed sleeves of his habit validation enough. "You could hurt someone. You shall help mend Ethstan's habit now. *And* apologize."

Aidan looks up at his mother, a slight sparkle betraying his efforts to appear serious. His little shoulders shrug and his freckled nose scrunches. "But, mother...Caspian said Aisling is better with fireballs than I am."

"And so, you tried to prove him wrong?" Myla asks, daring to glance at Caspian, who presses his lips together tightly to stifle his laughter.

"I did. I pretended the Aetherwing up there was her..." The little boy's side-eye is comical, framed by chubby cheeks and far less stoic than he likely imagines he looks.

Myla sighs, glancing overhead where the depicted face of an ancient dragon rider has been charred. "Did it look more powerful than Aisling's?"

She looks with a slight smile to Caspian, who shakes his head.

"Ah, I see. Well, when Aisling asks about the ruined Aetherwing face tonight, I am sure you can all agree she is not to be told *why* the face is ruined."

At this, Aidan presses hands to his belly in boisterous laughter.

Myla's lips twitch in a smile, and she narrows her gaze on the child. Though he wriggles, trying to mind his mother, he is momentarily distracted as a massively fluffy cat tries to skirt by unnoticed. Its streak of gray blue is unmistakable, and Aidan dips down to catch the cat before it passes, cradling it to his chest reverently. The pet is fondly referred to as Prince Gourdy. Elenore wanted to name him Prince, but the boys wanted to call him Gourd on account of his round and lumbering body reminding them of the autumn harvest. The compromise, which resulted in a fit of laughter for nearly five minutes, was "Prince Gourdy," offered to them by their father. Bryar was clearly pleased with himself, and for days, the name was shouted through the palace simply to evoke that same fit of laughter.

"What am I to do with you?" Myla asks finally, wondering how mothers ever actually disciplined their children when the small faces and silly laughs were so funny.

"Well," Aidan answers quite seriously. "I am hungry."

At this, all composure is lost, and Myla bursts into laughter as she reaches down to tousle her son's hair before leaning and pressing a kiss to his forehead.

Elenore, not even tall enough to reach Ethstan's hip, giggles, pressing two tiny palms to her mouth, and Caspian nudges her in the side, looking down at his sister discouragingly. Myla smiles at the unrefined child, barefoot and unruly. Elenore bears the gift of shared visions. Whatever she sees or whatever her little mind conjures, she can implant in the mind's eye of those she is bonded with. Oftentimes, the children will abruptly begin giggling and it is most assuredly the result of Elenore's shared visions, something that has caused mayhem and mischief more times than Myla can count.

"What did she show you?" Myla asks, refraining from smiling as the three children now fall into a fit of laughter, Aidan's so enthusiastic, he laughs soundlessly. Ethstan sighs and presses two fingers to his temple.

"Did she show you as well?" Myla asks, a nod 'yes' from the monk all the answer she needs. "What was it?"

"It was the young master Aidan, Your Grace, *searing* the tips of Lady Aisling's hair."

Myla looks at Elenore, her eyes narrowing as she extends a hand, calling to the child. Elenore hops over, and Myla lifts her, bracing the little body on her hip.

"Do not encourage him, Elle," she insists. "You must remember to use your gift of vision for goodness and kindness. Do you hear me? It would make you sad if someone burned your hair, so think how Aisling might feel." Myla tugs gently on the end of one corkscrew curl before setting the child down. "Return to your chambers to tidy up. Our guests will arrive in a few hours, and I will not have heathens greeting them." She looks directly at Aidan now. "When you have finished, join your father and me in our chamber." Myla passes Elenore off to Ethstan with his assurance that he will see Aidan delivered to them within the hour.

Myla expects Bryar to return at any time, and she hopes he has the right words to explain to their son how essential his obligations to the Ashborn princess are, but Myla has never possessed the gumption to press it on him with any conviction. Thoughts of her forced marriage to Caius always resurface, halting any words regarding duty or expectation. Deep down, Myla wishes she could have formed an alliance without promising her son to another before he even existed.

Never mind. Bryar will know what to say.

Instead of worrying over things she cannot change, Myla turns to face her reflection, knowing she needs a fresh dress and a comb through her hair before the Ashborn arrive. Elsa should be up in about an hour with clean dresses, so in the meantime, Myla sits at the vanity beside her bed, surprised to find her brush missing. She pictures the ivory brush, with peonies engraved in the handle, and wonders how she could have been so careless with such a precious gift. The door creaks open, and Bryar walks in, unbuttoning his vest and tossing it on the chest by the hearth.

"We won't be seeing the hunter again." His tone is somber as he gazes at the heavily embroidered rug beneath his feet.

He's exhausted.

With a weak smile his way, Myla responds coyly, "I would like to think that is because you *killed* him." She reaches around to touch the back of the vanity drawer in hopes of discovering her brush. It is not there. "I know that is not the case, however," she continues, abandoning the search. "So, what did you do?"

Bryar sits, yanking a tall black boot off his foot, answering with a puff of breath as the second boot slips off, "I threatened him within an inch of his life and asked if he would like a demonstration of how quickly *flesh* melts." He grins boyishly now. "He was more than happy to run as far from Old Falkmere as the realm would allow."

Myla takes a deep breath, releasing a relieved sigh. "Thank you. Now, if there are any more almost-accidental-arrows passing our children's heads, I will kill whoever looses them." Perplexed, her gaze travels to her bare end table. "Have you seen my brush?"

Bryar glances briefly around the bedroom before shaking his head. "I have not."

Myla makes a mental note to ask Elsa when she arrives with the dresses.

When Aidan enters their room a little while later, he looks the part of a polished young prince. He wears a black tunic with a high collar. An intricate red embroidered flame design follows the hems of his sleeves and neckline. His black trousers are uncharacteristically clean and tucked into polished boots. Elsa has clearly taken pains to tame his curly mop of hair.

With a bashful bow, Aidan walks to his mother for assessment. Myla smiles at her son, smoothing a few stray hairs and straightening his tunic.

"Tonight," she says calmly, wearing as reassuring of an expression as possible. "Your betrothal to Aisling will be made public to our people."

Bryar eyes the two of them from where he stands, buttoning the collar of his jacket. Myla wonders when he looks down at his son if he sees how very similar they are, even in this moment. How they stand with identical posture, and the way their eyes scan a room, consuming every detail. Does he see the tiny, dotted freckles beneath his eyes and remember when he had the same faint constellations as a boy?

Myla allows herself a moment of appreciation for the two before her, then continues, "I must implore you to show respect."

Her son's eyes drop to the side as if not acknowledging the responsibility rids him of it entirely. At this, Myla looks at Bryar, a gesture he at once interprets. He sits beside her then takes Aidan's small hands within his own and leans forward, eye-level with the boy. "Have I told you *why* your betrothal is such an honor?"

Aidan shakes his head, brown locks bouncing. His bright green irises seem to seek his father's wisdom.

"Well," Bryar continues, still holding fast to his son. "We have told you—all of you—how Caspian saved us from the Blood Stealer, right?"

Aidan offers another nod in response, and Bryar continues, "You, my son, saved us as well."

"I did?" With skeptical eyes, Aidan's countenance shifts, and his tiny shoulders square.

"You *did*," Myla adds, already beaming at the wisdom of her husband and at his ability to take such a difficult topic and bring comfort and understanding that even a young child can comprehend it.

"That's right. You did," Bryar says, his tone carrying with it the impression of a far-off adventure where only heroes won and lived to tell the tale, exactly the sort of story a four-year-old boy would want to listen to. "We *needed* the power of the Ashborn, a magical bond your mother and I were desperate for if we hoped to win. And do you know who made that happen for us?"

"Me?" Aidan asks, a tiny smile threatening the corners of what previously was a pout.

"Yes, *you*. The Ashborn knew any child of mine and your mother would be *powerful*. You entered this world on the wings of a phoenix, son. You have the blessing of every Ashborn before you. They wanted the guarantee of your friendship, and so they agreed to help us if we agreed that you would become their friend when you were grown."

"Can I be their friend but not Aisling's?"

Myla tries not to smile, thinking of all the reasons Aidan has de-clared he would not marry the girl. *She is too fast. She is too loud. She knows what I am thinking.* And Myla's personal favorite: *She scares me.* Aisling has the gift of knowing a person's thoughts. Even as an adult, it is intimidating. Ivan and Imogene have started taking her to all political engagements. The child has a habit of blurting out the truth the second she catches a person in a lie.

"Believe me, son," Bryar says, not needing to look at his wife to confirm he speaks of women like her. "She is the kind of girl you *want* to be friends with. I promise...if she still scares you in ten years, then we will talk about how to solve this."

"And," Myla adds quickly before Bryar dismisses Aidan. "At the very least, please don't set her on fire this time!"

Aidan snorts, and a little cackle follows him all the way out of his parents' chamber and down the long corridor until they can no longer hear him.

"I felt so good about this conversation until he left," Myla says flatly, staring at the hearth's wavering flames. "He's going to light that poor girl on fire again."

With a nervous puff of breath, Bryar nods slowly. "Good thing they're both fireproof...but...he will sit next to me at the feast tonight."

"Good idea." Myla glances at Bryar as he puts on a gleaming pair of boots, ones not worn riding or in the woods. "What do you mean, 'if he is still scared of her in ten years, you'll talk about how to solve it'?"

Bryar turns away, reaching for a glass of wine and taking a few swallows before facing her, his features somber. "What if he loves someone else by the time they are to wed?"

Her stomach twists, the very thought is one that has haunted her for years. "Or what if he doesn't...but he also does not love *her*?"

"Exactly," Bryar agrees. "Myla. I won't force him to follow through with something *we* promised he'd do before he was even alive. We should not have done it, and we both know it. We both have lived that, and I will not subject my son to anything like what you went through."

The declaration—which should send waves of uncertainty through her—instead brings a smile to her face. Myla stands and walks to her husband, placing a palm on his rough cheek. "I picked an amazing father for my children."

At this, a knock sounds at their door, no doubt Elsa delivering her dress.

"Myla," Bryar interrupts her as she moves to let her friend in. "In the meantime, let's try *really hard* to facilitate at least friendship between the two. I would rather not go to war with my own kind."

But he would. If necessary. Anything for his children. And Myla knows it.

This is why we have so many children. He is temptation walking on two feet.

It is nightfall when the Ashborn procession arrives, first a steady stream of guards, then Ivan and Imogene, looking not a day older than they did when they found her and Bryar in the clearing before Valyndor.

Behind them, a string of their fledglings follows, the final one being a breathtaking child. Wispy platinum hair trails to her waist, flecked with vibrant feathers in hues of red, orange, and yellow. Thick brown eyelashes rim her amber eyes, and her full, pale pink lips purse in a perpetual expression of deep thought. At five years old, Aisling carries herself with a confidence that took Myla nearly thirty years to find. It is a quality in her which both Bryar and Myla admire, and have even commented on.

"Your Grace," Imogene curtsies and Ivan bows, first at Myla and then Bryar.

"What an auspicious occasion," Ivan continues. "I see your children have grown much in this last year."

To their left stands the first prince, Caspian. In so many ways, he could easily be mistaken for Bryar's son as well. His hair is dark and wavy, a trait he inherited from his mother. Freckles dot his tanned skin, just like his brother and sister. His eyes, however, are a dead giveaway to his parentage. They bear an otherworldly blue glow around his pale irises, a light that could be easily seen in a dark room. Standing elbow-high to Myla now, he is on the cusp between small child and the more cognitive level of adolescence. He understands more than the average child of his age. While he is nearly six, his maturity often outweighs his childish moments. Myla sometimes wonders if it has anything to do with the two years he spent suspended in time within her. His soul is slightly older than his body.

Then stands Aidan, a few inches shorter and of stockier build. He looks like he could pummel the older boy beside him. Unknown to most is the fact that he would not hurt a soul unless forced to—save, of course, Aisling, who now watches him. Her warm eyes seem to eat him alive. He stares back, his glare narrowing in judgment, and his lips stretch into a thin line, defiant as always.

Gentle, but defiant. That's my son.

Myla hopes the two children will cease their showdown soon.

Finally, an enormous ray of cheerful sunshine and gleeful giggles is compressed within Elenore's petite frame. The sweet child wiggles back and forth, fidgeting with a small aquamarine bracelet on her wrist—a gift from Bryar for her fourth birthday. Myla's eyes widen as she notes tiny bare toes peeking out from beneath her daughter's long blue dress. *No shoes. Again.* As though feeling her mother's gaze on her, Elenore looks up and smiles, chubby baby cheeks nearly closing around the blue of her eyes. Her mother's eyes, as Bryar likes to remind the girl regularly. Her dark brown hair is curlier than her twin brother's and much longer. The unruly tangles reach the middle of her back. Aidan may look like his father, but Elenore is her mother's child.

Myla is about to speak, taking note of the fledglings when the vision of Aisling running away, dress ablaze, intrudes upon her mind's eye; no doubt a vision intended for Aidan. Myla shoots Elenore a discouraging frown, reaching behind the boys to take the small girl's hand. *Looks like I will keep her close tonight. Curse this man for giving me demons as children.*

Pleasantries are exchanged before the group moves into the great hall where a small feast awaits. The scene might convince any trained eye that nothing is lacking. Music fills the air, and courtiers mingle, each welcoming the nobles with bobbed curtsies, bows, and pleasant smiles. Old Falkmere has the reputation of a woodland retreat. In the years since its partial restoration, they have hosted many nobles who later vie for an invitation back. It is run with the dignity of a fully functioning castle, which houses nobility, and nothing indicates its residents are here because of a stolen throne and a brewing war.

Myla heads the procession with squared shoulders, leading them through the room to a long table at the front. It offers a view of the party and, hopefully, always keeps the children in sight.

"Thank you for your hospitality, Your Grace," Aisling says from across the table once everyone has found a seat.

Aidan sits squarely between Myla and Bryar. Unfortunately, Elenore wiggles free and now sits with Caspian and the other fledglings, no doubt fueling the mischievous side of her big brother.

"It is our pleasure," Myla replies, smiling at the girl. "Did you enjoy the journey here?"

Aisling's eyes sparkle. "I navigated the entire way and flew much faster than mother."

Imogene tilts her chin upward, beaming with pride. "That she did. A queen in the making."

The Ashborn choose their monarchs. When Aisling was born, it is said a great phoenix ushered her into the world, just as it did with Aidan, an ancient mark of favor from the Ashborn's Gods. Since that day, she superseded her older siblings in a chance for the throne.

Aidan shifts, slumping his elbows onto the table, and casting a sidelong glance at his mother as he exudes deep displeasure.

Myla places a light hand on his knee and leans down to whisper, "You do not have to like this moment, but mind your father's words."

The mere mention of his father, paired with a slightly threatening sidelong gaze from the man himself, Aidan straightens and looks across the table to where Aisling sits.

She glares back at him, her small fingers drumming absently on the table.

"We should race," she blurts flatly, a comment which brings Myla's gaze to meet her husband's in trepidation. "Oh, wait—" Aisling responds with a certain unimpressed look passing across her pointed features. "I forgot, you cannot summon your wings yet." Her lips twitch into the hint of a smile before she adds, "Pity."

It is Imogene's turn to look flustered, turning to her husband with a sigh and saying aloud what they are all thinking. "I am beginning to wonder, my dear, if we have betrothed the wrong children."

At this, she glances across the room to where Zarek, Aisling's older brother, balances a small flame in his hand, showing Elenore how he can move the flame from one finger to the next. The girl grins, always entertained by the boy's games, as he is always happy to entertain her.

Myla reaches for her wine glass, taking a long drink before shaking her head. "It is the willful ones we will want to lead our people when we are gone."

Imogene laughs nervously before nodding into a glass of wine. "I suppose you are right there. I am afraid these two will burn the kingdom down before they have a chance to rule it together."

Myla contemplates the circumstances under which the future of the Ashborn kingdom has been laid at Aidan and Aisling's feet, including the careful preparation which has gone into it. Neither Aisling nor Aidan were conceived yet when Myla and Bryar signed the contract which promised them together. When the two children were born so close in age to each other, instead of promising Aidan to one of their older fledglings, it was Aisling who was chosen to bear the weight of her family's future. Watching the young girl's stoicism, Myla is certain they chose well. A glance at Aidan, and Myla hopes that with age, he comes into his own as the rightful Ashborn King. What she is unwilling to do is push her own agenda. The rapidly approaching announcement feels as though she and Bryar teeter dangerously close to the same cliffside of power her father fell from.

No, she reminds herself. *This is different.* Aisling's knowing eyes flicker to hers, and a gentle ringing echoes in the back of Myla's brain. The child is listening to her.

Myla allows her gaze to linger with the girl's, unwilling to be frightened by her. Instead, she pushes her thoughts forward, allowing the girl to impose, uncomfortable as it may be for her young age, it is a lesson she must learn. Memories of the Blood Stealer's last stand fill her mind, a dark and frightful scene shown in vivid detail to the girl.

Though the Gods have given you the gift of knowing all thoughts, it does not mean you should use it on your friends, Aisling.

Aisling soon diverts her gaze, horror washing over her. At this, Myla stands, lifting a goblet of wine with a steady hand, though she feels her body quaking in anticipation.

"Tonight." Her voice is clear, commanding the attention of all. "Is a night I pray the Gods will bless. For this is the evening which I announce with great pleasure *and* pride, the betrothal of my second son, Prince Aidan Alerys of Falkmere, to her Royal Highness, Aisling of Valyndor, future Queen of the Ashborn."

Thunderous applause fills the room, pride swelling across the faces of those in attendance. It is a long-anticipated strategic move, now made public. Were it not for the scowls etched on Aidan and Aisling's faces, Myla would look around the room at the glowing faces of her friends, family, and courtiers and consider the announcement a success. That is until one of Imogene and Ivan's older fledglings, nearly a man now, stands with a furrowed brow, vibrant feathers standing on end in what appears to be disgust.

"You are going through with this?" he spews, looking down upon his parents with no regard to the onlookers around him. He was in training during her time with the Ashborn just before Caspian's birth. Myla can hardly picture that young Ashborn boy now, for before her is a seething young man with dark feathers, ruffled in his distress.

"*Sit* down, Pierre." Ivan hisses, a dismissive wave attempting to brush the uncomfortable confrontation aside.

"I will not," he challenges, his wings appearing as though a flaming ember forms at their edges. "The Alerys rule is in title only. They have nothing to recommend themselves in the way of formidable allies. You will marry my sister off to a *second*-born son and give *him* the title of Ashborn King?"

Imogene grabs her son's fist, her fierce eyes glowing an angry amber as she looks up at him. As always, her tone remains cool but edged with something like poison, a subtle threat. "Careful, my boy. That second son will have the ability to reduce even *you* to ash in a year or so. Jealousy is not your color."

Myla's eyes narrow as the boy glares at her, disregarding his mother's warning. "Do your people *actually* plan to take Falkmere back? Or are we to just allow this betrothal of my sister to go forward with *noble refugees* in hopes that another five years of complacency does not pass?"

Ivan stands now and grips the boy's shoulder. "Sit *down*, you idiot. Silence yourself before you bring more shame upon us."

The damage is done, however. Myla notices the mood change in the room and the discouragement washing over her people. Bryar rises beside her, pressing a reassuring hand to the small of her back.

Collecting herself and willing her voice to be proud and confident, Myla speaks. "What we have accomplished in the face of ruin, devastation, and betrayal these past five years is a feat unlike any other. Against the odds, we have rebuilt this fortress where you so happily feast. My people chose to establish new homes here with a vision and full of *hope* to soon reclaim what is ours. Their faith in me is why we sit here tonight with any semblance of normalcy. We have established profitable trade deals. And we have been biding our time as alliances form with other lords and ladies of the realm. With every skirmish, we weaken my father's forces and drain his pockets."

Pierre now sits, his begrudged gaze resting firmly on his boots, seeming to ignore the growing swell of morale in the room with every word Myla speaks. Her conviction fuels theirs. It is palatable.

"I learned a long time ago that just because someone sees you as *complacent* does not mean that is what is actually happening. The commitment to our cause that I see in all my people's eyes is the very fuel to my flame. It is a sentiment that cannot be fabricated and would not *grow* in the soils of complacency. Our spies have acquired three hundred new recruits to both our army as well as our tradesmen just this year, and the year is young. Not all battles are fought loudly and quickly. Some happen when you are not looking, or in places you simply cannot see. I *will* reclaim my kingdom, and I *will* see my son sit upon the Raven Throne when he is of age."

At this, she looks directly at Pierre. "And I *will* remember who stood beside me when I was not seen as a powerful Queen, but as a *noble refugee*. For those who remain loyal in my times of weakness are the ones I want beside me when I am strong again."

With sleep, the palace quiets, but a maternal call awakens Myla from a deep sleep. With heavy eyelids, and a need to ensure all is well, she slips from the warmth of her bed, braving the chill of the cold stones beneath her bare feet to make her way down the hall. The first door, Elenore's, is ajar. Peeking in, and not in the least bit surprised, Myla finds the bed empty. She continues down the hall to the next door, which is closed. It sticks when opened unless lifted slightly, so Myla leverages the handle, lifting the door in its frame ever so carefully to push it open silently. Inside, one bed is empty. The somewhat larger bed to the left of the room, however, has three children asleep in it, along with Prince Gourdy, who purrs, his enormous fluffy stature stretched across each of their bodies protectively.

Myla smiles and moves closer on tiptoes until she stands just over them. By day, her children are nothing less than feral. Somehow, by night, their messy hair, flushed cheeks, and will to destroy, and riot for the sheer fun of it, fades away, leaving behind what could only be described as angelic tranquility.

Perhaps I was woken by the Spirit Mother so I could see this. Myla rights the blankets, making sure every tiny toe is covered, then gently scoops Elenore from between them. She turns to leave, ensuring the door closes firmly, but before the latch can fall into place, Prince Gourdy leaps from the bed and slips through the narrow opening.

"Goodnight, you menace."

Slumped in her mother's arms, Elenore's eyes flutter open and her small mouth stretches in a sleepy smile.

"Hi, Mama," she whispers as she links her arms around Myla's neck, none the wiser that she is being returned to her bed, as she has already fallen back asleep.

CHAPTER 3

PAST: MYLA, FIFTEEN

"MAVERICK," MYLA'S MOTHER CHIDES, watching in dismay as lady's maids hurry around Myla, cinching her stays and blotting rouge on her cheeks. "You cannot truly mean to take her with us tonight?"

The progress-minded man pays no attention to his wife. Instead, Maverick unboxes a new gown, eyeing it with a certain sort of reverence; the look one might give a prized horse that is relied upon to bring in significant fortune. "She is old enough to attend the King's Masquerade, Lavinia. We shall not hold her back from all that may be at her fingertips should we simply place her in the right room."

Lavinia's brows furrow and her eyes flicker disconcertingly to Myla's as she scrutinizes the irritated young woman before her. "Are you comfortable, dear?"

Myla tugs desperately on the bottom of the corset, hoping to make way for a deep breath, before letting out an exasperated groan. "Not as comfortable as I would be to stay here while you and father attend the Masquerade." Her flippant tone is not lost on anyone. Even the maids exchange wary glances before scurrying from the room.

"You are privileged." Maverick is quick to chastise his daughter, his glare leveling with her own. "How can you not see that the world is opening for you? What shall you do, hide away from it?"

"I do not wish to hide," Myla challenges, yanking at the stiff material of her blue sleeves, now wondering if it is possible to be eaten alive by a dress. "I simply do not like the world that *you* are opening for me."

The bold protest has barely left her lips before it is replaced with a sharp sting, courtesy of the back of her father's hand.

"You will not disobey me!" he snaps, ignoring the gasp which slips from his wife's mouth. Myla pays no heed to the reaction. She will find no comfort there, only the residual effect of years of silencing. Fear has a funny way of paralyzing her mother, even when it comes to her daughter's protection. Bitterness has hardened Myla against feeling much of anything over the matter.

Though Myla tries to cover her face with her hands, her wrists are seized in her parent's angry fists, jerking her to attention. "You will wear the dress *and* a smile, and you will do everything in your power to claim a dance with the king tonight, is that clear?"

Trembling, not from fear but from rage, Myla lifts her chin in defiance and remains silent. Though her bottom lip trembles, she jerks her hands free of her father and meets his fearsome gaze with rebellion. "The king will not dance with anyone," she reminds him. "He waits for his *wife*."

A web of light networks across her skin, threatening to flow.

Maverick scoffs, eyeing the display wearily. He has seen the light which accompanies her anger enough times to know it is not something to risk at present. "He waits on a prophesy written by fools. A young woman such as yourself should have no difficulty turning his head. I will be watching. Mind yourself."

Although her desire to attend the masquerade is less than none, Myla enters the family carriage with little coaxing necessary. They will pass the blacksmith on their way to the palace, and something about that prospect causes her stomach to tighten. Lessons over the last several months have grown increasingly intense. Her body grows stronger, and there is a definition to her arms and midsection that was not there before. Sir Roderick is a challenging tutor, but not unkind. Myla would venture to call him *indulgent* even.

He allows her and Bryar to converse before and after lessons so long as there are no pupils waiting for him. He has even begun answering a few questions wholly unrelated to combat. It has become obvious to Myla that Bryar's education is limited to mathematics and reading. He knows nothing of their history nor the lore which Falkmere is built upon. She and Roderick both seem to have taken a special interest in expanding Bryar's knowledge in that area. Their last lesson proved interesting when discussions of the tiers of magic—as well as King Caius's prophecy—became the primary topic.

Myla's stomach lurches as the carriage creaks into a steady roll forward. Not wanting to raise suspicion, she refrains from drawing back the velvet red curtains, though the small slit between the two provides a peek into the world outside. As the blacksmith shop comes into view, Myla notices the smoke billowing from the forge. *He's there.* Clasping her hands in a ball on her lap, Myla turns her gaze forward facing. The thick head of black waves is hard to miss, curtains or no. The most ridiculous notion, a desire for him to see her gown, taunts the logical functions of her mind, and is quickly dismissed. *Offering to tutor him after lessons was a misstep.*

"Try not to frown so much, darling," Lavinia says, pressing a gentle finger to the furrowed place between Myla's brows. "You will age yourself."

"Perhaps if I were older," she responds with a careless inflection. "I might be able to go or not go as I please."

Maverick scoffs, straightening the cuffs of his fine silk tunic, the black a stark and unbecoming contrast against his milky skin. "You could be seventy, Myla, and I would still own your whereabouts. Myself or your husband."

You don't own them all.

Myla thinks of the educational rendezvous she and Bryar are set to have in two days, an excursion Maverick would both detest and intercept if he knew of it. Rather than give him yet another reason to strike her, she simply lowers her eyes and nods. "Yes, father." Though the words are obedient, her tone is anything but.

The King's Masquerade is an exclusive party. Many spend an entire social season maneuvering their way toward it, seeking an invitation at every table. How the king picks his attendees, Myla has never much wondered about until tonight. Specifically, why is her father invited? What did *he* do to catch the king's attention? Myla assumes the answer to that question will be found inside the linings of Maverick's pockets.

The palace towers above her. Any possible escape from this miserable night is blocked behind by a narrow and currently crowded bridge passing over the thundering falls. The violent waters crash on the cliffs far beneath the palace, and mist rises, cloaking the foliage, which grows in abundance and in every direction surrounding the gardens of the palace until, inevitably, they lead to cliffsides. With only one way to access the palace—the bridge—there is nowhere to go except in.

Upon entering, Myla realizes her gown sets her apart. Most of the attendees are dressed in neutral hues. They look like airy, billowy beings in a painting that might hang in her mother's tearoom—nothing too demanding at a glance, but beautiful, nonetheless. Whereas Myla claims and radiates every drop of color in the room. Her gown sports a full skirt of vibrant blue. Tiny blue sapphire droplets adorning the hem catch the light with every swoosh of her skirt. The bodice calls attention to her slender waist with a subtle pattern of darker blue peonies embroidered along its entirety. A heart-shaped neckline complements her slender neck and prominent collarbone. Complete with slim-fitting sleeves which cuff at the wrists, fastened by sapphire buttons, she is the picture of oceanic mystery. With long, dark curls falling down her laced black and a blue mask to match, more eyes than she knows how to avert with grace lay on her. They feel like a hundred puncture wounds burrowing deeper into her with every step inward. Each pair of eyes either dissects her for her value or her threat. They all seem to ask the same question:

Who is she?

A question quickly answered.

"Lord Maverick Alerys, Lady Lavinia Alerys, and Lady Myla Alerys," the Master of Ceremonies announces their entrance, and at once, Myla's eyes are drawn to the throne where King Caius presides over the room. He is regally perched like a wise owl on a throne too small for his large personality. His otherworldly blue eyes cast an ice over a room that should be warm, given the blazing fires.

This unraveling gaze twists the air in her belly, and warning signs within threaten to attack her nervous system, a voice subconsciously telling her that this is the last man she wants to dance with. For no other reason than the power exuding from his very pores seems to be the mighty lungs of the Gods breathing—no, *heaving* through him. Is he simply a powerful king or is he in fact the embodiment of all the old Gods? Myla was hesitant to wear such a spectacular gown to begin with, but when the king's eyes clamp on her, completely disregarding her parents' entrance, she regrets the choice even more.

Despite the fear-inducing power oozing from his being, he is a considerably handsome man. Of course, she has seen him from a distance before, but as she approaches his throne, ready to sink into a reverent curtsy, she can't help but notice the dark beard framing his sharp jaw. It is speckled with gray. His fierce eyes are brimmed by equally dark eyebrows, and his hair is tucked neatly behind his ears, held in place by the heavy crown atop his head. It is in this moment she notices the almost identical blue of his ornate tunic. Myla doesn't dare cast a knowing glance at her father, but she *knows* the similar color was no coincidence.

With trembling thighs, Myla finds herself lowering into a burning curtsy, her legs bending inhumanly as she puts her reverence on display as the proper lady she is trained to be. Defiance or not, she knows better than to snub a king.

"I am honored by the sight of an unfamiliar face," His Grace speaks, addressing Myla. He hums the greeting as though the vibrations of his voice can strum the invisible string between them and force her to feel something. And she does.

Fear.

For a miserable moment, Myla forgets herself. With a dry mouth, making an impasse for any words that might suggest she is of gentle upbringing, she merely wavers in place atop trembling knees, and wills her face to speak for her in a pleasant smile.

It is not until Maverick clears his throat, subtly gouging an elbow into his daughter's side, that she finds the decorum to speak. "I believe many faces are unfamiliar to you, Your Grace," Myla allows the words to flow, not realizing the insult until her mother gasps, at which point a rectification is required. "I, however, am pleased to see a face we all recognize well." Myla forces a smile, daring to look up at Caius in time to see a smirk stretched across his face.

"Lord Maverick," he addresses her father with a chuckle. "However do you manage such a spirited daughter? You have been withholding her charms, it would seem."

Maverick straightens now that he's been addressed and smiles nervously at the king, and Myla wonders if he will be honest and admit to the king that striking his spirited daughter is his best practiced coping mechanism. Instead, his response is flowery and more of an insult to Myla than any in the room might realize. "Your Grace, it takes the wisdom of the Gods to manage my daughter. I assure you, however, I shall withhold her from this court no longer."

"How reassuring," King Caius chuckles, nodding appreciatively at Lavinia. "Please..." A heavily jeweled hand gestures to a long table. "Sit and enjoy the festivities."

They have been dismissed, but for the entire evening, a permanent chill claims Myla's body, courtesy of the ever-attentive studies of the king, analyzing her from across the room at all times.

Does he see her, or does he see what she hides?

Myla did not dance with the king, and when she collapses into bed as dawn approaches, her aching feet and thudding head are torture enough. She is grateful to have avoided any close contact. The carriage-ride home had been a miserable one. Myla's breath had been slow with a need for sleep, and all she could hear for thirty minutes was Maverick's chastisement. His dissection of her every move, her every word, and found the heart of her failure to be her "ghastly" greeting of the king. According to her red and fuming father, shame was brought upon the Alerys name, and it was all on account of his "unrefined and rebellious daughter." *What is new?* At least a smarting cheek is not a discomfort she can add to her list this evening.

Knock, knock.

Fuck, did I hope too soon?

Myla sits up with a groan, hoping the person on the other side of her door is her lady come to help her out of this suffocating dress and *not* Maverick. Hope does not last long as Lavinia appears, resulting in a less obvious groan and Myla falling backwards once more. The pile of pillows envelops her, breaking the fall and curling around her ears.

Not enough to render her mother soundless, however. "Shall I help you with the laces?" Her timid, kind tone softens the internal cold shell Myla protects herself within. Gentle fingers brush against her wrist, urging her to sit upright. "Come, they look horrifically tight. We can't have you dying in your sleep for lack of breath." There is a hint of humor in her voice, an attempt to reach the dark place her daughter seems to be spiraling into.

Myla can only respond with the anger she feels within. "Gods forbid father's greatest asset dies." A sarcastic snort follows up the statement, but is quickly silenced by her mother.

"*Myla*," Lavinia gasps, turning her daughter's face to hers. "Your father loves you."

"He loves what my gender can offer him." Myla spits the words like venom. "Surely you noticed he dressed me to match the king!"

"A coincidence, darling. Do not conjure things that are not there."

"Father would stand on my neck if it meant he could more easily reach the power he is grasping at," Myla spews in confidence, not averting her eyes, not afraid to see the shock in her mother's expression. For a single moment, Myla will never believe that her father's efforts go unnoticed by her observant mother. "When he strikes me for having an opinion, do you feel the pain too?" Her words are whispers now as she earnestly searches her mother's eyes for some semblance of anger or sympathy, even. Some emotion which may suggest she is an ally.

Lavinia visibly softens, though her eyes droop sadly; the faint smile she wears shines through like a comforting beacon. "We do not live in a world where opinions are ours to have, Myla. I hurt when you hurt. I also hurt when you fight against the path that may very well lead to a place where opinions *are* yours to have."

"You think throwing me into the path of the king will end well for me?" Myla pictures a noose, the same kind many loud wives have met their deaths at the end of. Even now, the string of pearls around her mother's neck mocks Myla, asking if she can feel its phantom strands tightening around her throat with every wayward statement or eye-roll.

"You are the brightest young lady I have ever met." Lavinia's words feel like wind in the sails of a ship stranded on a still ocean. Until she speaks again, and Myla deflates once more. "In time, you will learn to channel your anger into something productive."

"You mean something that does not contradict the men?"

Lavinia sighs, pulling Myla into a standing position and unlacing her dress. "Your father is not your enemy, Myla. If you could only try to see things from his perspective, you might appreciate all he does for you."

With a sharp twist, Myla looks at the tired woman behind her. "I will never appreciate any perspective which concludes that women are as tradable a commodity as a cow. I have seen rare gems go for a higher price than my dowry is set at!" Myla's voice trembles and echoes off the tall ceilings above, threatening to bring the walls down around them.

Lavinia steps back, her hands twisting in an anxious knot at her waist, cringing as her daughter's rage radiates as it has so often before. Even as a toddler, the injustices of the world would ricochet off Myla's body and tremble in the air around her. In recent months, the force of her wrath has grown more and more, a motivating factor for her enrollment in the institute.

"Myla." Her voice is calm. Her face is anything but. She wears a storm, absorbing the tension surrounding them. "I just want you to be safe."

"Then take me to the woods," Myla reaches for her mother, desperation in her voice. "To the caves. Father doesn't know of them, and I would rather be there than here...*waiting*."

"Waiting for what?" Lavinia asks, a heavy breath slipping from her lips.

Myla looks past her mother to the door, which is latched closed. Even still, she feels the need to whisper, as though the dust itself might carry her secrets to her father's desk and find themselves written into a dismal contract meant to punish her insolence. "Something terrible is coming, Mother. If father continues as he is, something *terrible* is coming."

"You will speak the *terrible* into existence, my love. I will not hide you away in the caves; I know you are meant for so much more. Something amazing that simply cannot come to fruition with the pagans, though I wish we could both go there."

The dress falls from Myla's shoulders and soon after, the corset. A weight is released when they are, and she takes a slow, deep breath. "Then at least take me to visit. It has been such a long while and...and I *need* to breathe."

Lavinia collects the dress from the floor and smiles weakly at Myla. "Alright. We shall go a week from today. Your father has an appointment, and our absence will not be noted." Lavinia pauses, leaning forward to tuck a loose strand of hair behind Myla's ear. "You see things differently and in so many ways, I value that. I find myself often wondering what the world around you will look like when you have made something of yourself. I urge you, my girl...do not focus so much on what feels wrong that you lose sight of the beautiful things along the way. Do not forget how to breathe even in the moments that you feel powerless. That is where so many of us lose ourselves, and of all the people I know, I do not want *you* to lose a single drop of whatever it is burning within you. It is the kind of passion that is going to burn that terrible you sense coming to the ground."

CHAPTER 4

PRESENT

SNOW BLANKETS THE GROUND, a late spring storm having descended overnight. A chill in the air makes Myla wish she could snuggle deeper into their bed. The drapes beside the open window billow gently, and the idea of removing herself from the warmth and comfort of their heavy furs to dress and strategize with the council is a miserable one.

"Stop wiggling." A big hand snakes around her middle, pulling her closer to her husband's radiating warmth. "You are letting out the heat," he whispers groggily. The scruff of his jaw rubs against her ear, and she smiles as she burrows her face into his chest, running a hand up his abdomen and imagining just how lovely staying in bed could be this morning.

"I have to get up," Myla reminds him with a groan. "We have a meeting within the hour. Remember? My father will not see another summer in Falkmere Palace." She rolls onto her back, trying to make out Bryar's features in the dark. "Are you sure we are ready for this?"

Eyes still closed and his voice thick with sleep, Bryar begins reciting the details of their carefully plotted ambush. "Your father has been busy making trade deals with Antoin, whom he believes to be a sup-porter of his. He has no idea the trader is our spy. Your father expects Antoin's carrack to dock at Falkmere Bay in a week. When it does, five hundred of our soldiers will spill into Falkmere from the sea. Rhyland will approach from the west with another thousand. Your father no longer has the numbers to hold us off...not to mention he does not have the money to buy swords anymore...which means we will take him hostage. He is cornered."

Bryar's eyes fall open now, and he draws the covers over their heads. "Ivan has agreed to send a company of Ashborn to attack from the sky." His tone shifts from the briefing of a military captain to the slow and syrupy words of a husband with an agenda. "And today is my birthday, so I should like my breakfast in bed this morning."

Myla giggles as his hand moves from her middle downward and is intercepted by her own. Linking her fingers with his, she draws his palm to her waist before returning her hand to his chest where she proceeds to draw slow designs down his belly. Lower and lower, each slight motion a tease to the man tensing beneath her touch until she finds her target, pleased to discover him hard already.

"Did you dream of me?" she asks, teasing a kiss against his jaw, then his mouth.

"Always," Bryar replies breathlessly, digging his fingers into the fullness of her hips, pulling her closer with a groan as Myla's hand moves down his length, coaxing a silent plea from her husband.

"Was I naked?" Myla asks, grinning against his mouth as he parts her lips with his tongue, delving into a slow, thorough kiss before parting to answer.

"Tragically, no. Will you make it up to me now?"

Myla's hand massages him a moment longer before retreating. "*No,*" she whispers slowly against his lips, wrinkling her nose as his stubble brushes roughly against her cheeks. "I am leaving this bed to go learn how and when my father is to be dethroned. You must wake me up earlier if we are to have time for your...other *conquests.*"

Bryar laughs, his arm curling around her as he pulls her in for a hug. "Is it still a conquest if I have already claimed you?"

Reluctantly, Myla sits, shivering as the frigid air rushes between the blankets. "I believe it is merely an occupation then." She reaches for the bellpull, summoning Elsa to come dress her. Most mornings, she would call upon Fern, but when a diplomatic meeting of this magnitude also falls on her husband's birthday, Elsa's expert styling is required.

"Wear the green dress," Bryar says with a sheepish grin from where he still lies, arching his back into a deep stretch. "I like that one."

"Don't move," Myla instructs, her tone equally coy.

"Why?" the warrior-by-day, husband-by-night asks, propping himself up on an elbow to watch her silhouette move across the dim room.

"Because," she playfully responds as she fumbles with a candle, "I'd like to admire you a moment longer before you dress. You are a year older today, and I must look for new silver hairs."

Bryar lets out a deep laugh, running a hand through his mess of curls as if he might feel his advanced age at his fingertips. "I thought you didn't have time for such endeavors this morning—birthday or no."

"Looking takes less time, and its effects last throughout the day." A warm candlelight brings a soft glow across the room to where Bryar now sits, ready to move from the bed. "I shall enjoy watching you in your current state, and you shall enjoy me in my green dress. It is a fair trade. You will have your birthday present tonight once our business is concluded."

"Do I get to know what my present is?" He wears the look of a prowling predator, his eyes devouring her from across the room.

With a seductive bat of her eyes, Myla turns away, allowing him a view of her scantily dressed body before answering, "There would be no fun in spoiling a good surprise."

Before Bryar can respond, his devilish grin is wiped away when a knock sounds at their door—a precaution Elsa has learned the hard way to be a requirement no matter the day nor hour. *"I swear to all the*

Gods, if Bryar is not completely clothed, I will vomit on your floor and make him *clean it up,"* she says through the door.

Myla snickers and retrieves Bryar's tunic from the back of a cushioned chair, tossing it at him and ensuring he is wearing it before opening the door.

"Good morning to you too," Bryar says with a chuckle, pulling boots on and throwing his blue cloak around his shoulders. "I will leave you ladies to it—Elsa, my wife will wear the green dress today." He pauses to kiss Myla's cheek as he passes with a final remark. "And I don't have silver hairs. I am not that old."

Elsa rolls her eyes, casting a knowing look Myla's way. "You have approximately nine months before you will be paying Ethstan an additional allowance to watch an *additional* child." Elsa looks over her shoulder as Bryar passes. "And you *are* that old!"

"We are nearly the same age, Elsa," Bryar taunts with a vague grin before closing the door behind him.

Myla snorts. "I shall not tempt the Gods with another one."

Elsa shivers, drawing her wool shawl tighter around her shoulders. "Elle crawled into my bed again last night."

Myla lets out a sigh, turning to face her friend. "*Truly?* I returned her to her bed twice already!"

"She knew Auntie Elsa would not turn her away." Elsa's voice is light with humor as she retells the event, gently tugging at tangles in Myla's curls. "It does not help that my room is beside the nursery."

"You are the one who insisted you wanted to be close to the children."

"I do," Elsa answers with a smile she fails to hide. "But perhaps we can install a latch on my door."

Myla's brows furrow, and she attempts to turn and look at Elsa, a motion denied by her friend's hand holding her shoulder steady. "Have they...intruded on something?"

Elsa retrieves a long green gown from the wardrobe and nods reassuringly. "Not yet," she answers. "But you never know." Elsa's playful tone shifts, and she redirects the conversation entirely. "I should like to take the children out of the palace today. There will be so much discussion of war, perhaps Ethstan and I may accompany them to the village? There will be dancing and treats, I hear."

Myla nods, ignoring the tinge of fear triggered by the suggestion. The incident with the hunter makes her want to lock the children indoors. What a dull life that would be for them. Elsa has been nothing short of a devoted aunt since Caspian was born. Naturally, tragedy or not, she was always going to be that way. Nevertheless, Myla often wonders if she staunches the pain of Callum's loss with the children. They regularly consume hours of Elsa's days, and Ethstan refers to them as her "balm."

"Yes," she agrees after a moment. "Before you do, please check with Bryar and confirm additional guards accompany the excursion." Myla reaches for Elsa's hand, her eyes finding her friend's. "And Elsa, I will make sure a latch is added to your door...I hope you find use for it."

Ever since Callum's death, Elsa has transformed from a creature of vibrance, and love, and adventure, to a woman of quiet resolve. Any hints at her romantic life are often snuffed out and denied entirely. As far as Myla is aware, Elsa has been completely solitary since the loss of her love. Her private approach to such topics was difficult for Myla to adjust to after such a long history of openness, but she counted it as yet another scar Vesperian left behind.

"Perhaps in time," Elsa answers at last with a weak smile. In her eyes, however, something glimmers. Secrets.

Myla's mouth presses into a thin line as she hides a smile. Secrets give her hope.

In record time, Elsa has styled Myla's hair into a severe twist at the nape of her neck with a few loose curls left down to frame her face. The dress is such a dark green, it is nearly black. A delicate lace collar fastens beneath her chin, creating a false impression of modesty before it plunges dangerously low to the bottom of her sternum, where a twisting design of ivy and thorns is expertly embroidered into her silky bodice. The bodice transitions effortlessly into strategically stitched pleats, which hug her form, loosening only once the material drapes naturally around her knees, creating a perfect silhouette for Myla's natural shape. The sleeves are crafted from the same lace, and a cloak will be required to ward off the chill of the council room.

"What a scandalous choice for plotting the murder of your father," Elsa says while assessing her handiwork. "I believe your foes would not know whether they ought to fight you or fu—"

"Do not finish that sentence," Myla interrupts with a chuckle. "It was my husband's wish, and today is his birthday, so he shall have whatever he wants."

"Disgusting," Elsa says flatly, reaching to fluff a curl at Myla's ear. "I might very well keep myself and the children removed from the palace all day."

Myla grins. "You will do no such thing. There is a celebratory feast tonight. All three of the children must be present and tidy."

With a playfully defiant smirk, Elsa bobs a curtsy. "Yes, Your Grace."

"Stop," Myla insists, returning the smile. "You are the only person who may never treat me like a Queen."

"And yet I always will—are you ready to be one in your own right again?" The serious tone changes, catching Myla off guard. What a question—one that plagues her. Although she has always intended to reclaim Falkmere, her family has comfortably adopted more casual living. Transitioning back into the formality of everyday ruling will be difficult, and something the children have never experienced. Thankfully, Ethstan has made it his personal task to ensure the little princes' and princess' education has been nothing short of a royal's, right down to the manner in which they carry themselves. Admittedly, she and Bryar might have been comfortable allowing their children to grow up with less ceremonial structure were it not for Ethstan's insisting that they must be prepared for the throne, *all of them.*

"I am ready," Myla responds at last, looking down at her vanity and the brush she now borrows from Elsa. Her fingers methodically drum, tapping her rings against the solid furniture one by one. "I am not ready for whatever shall pass between my father and me."

Elsa nods slowly, her light blue eyes seeming darker than they should. "He will not surrender. Being your hostage will only make him angrier."

"I know."

"What do you intend to do then?"

Myla's voice is shaky, but she stands resolute in her response. "Whatever I must. The choice will come down to my children or my father. That is no choice at all. I cannot let a threat to my family continue to draw breath."

"So, you will kill him?" Elsa stares at her friend, her expression grim and uncomfortable. "You plan to kill your father yourself?"

"You know," Myla answers in a soft, pained, reminiscent tone. "Bryar is a father, a good one. He is there to pick his children up when they fall; he is there to dry their tears and solve their problems. Actually, he teaches them *how* to solve their problems. He would never dream of using his children for personal gain. Yes." Crossing her hands before her, she looks directly at her concerned friend. "Bryar is a father. Maverick never has been and never will be *my* father."

Noting the avoidance of her question, Elsa's eyebrows turn upwards, and she nods slowly. "Whoever he is to you, Myla, this does not end with both of you drawing breath."

Ethstan is awake already when Myla passes the library on her way to the council room. The old man stands hunched over a stack of books, scribbling notes onto a roll of parchment.

"Lesson planning?" Myla asks, sparing a moment to say good morning to her trusted friend.

Ethstan looks up with a jump. "You startled me, Your Grace." He gestures to the pile of volumes. "The children have asked for a history of the dragons. We learned of the Aetherwing last week, and so this seems an appropriate follow-up."

Myla nods approvingly. "One tends to accompany the other."

"Precisely," Ethstan agrees. "You are up early, Your Grace." He takes note of the dark outside the window. "It is not half-past four yet."

"War waits for nothing, not even sleep."

"We can feel it." His tone is trepidatious. "Everyone in the palace can sense the shift."

"Well," Myla hums, flipping open the cover of a beautifully illustrated book on lore. "When it shifts from plans to actions, the air grows heavy. Action means death."

"Many deaths, I suppose." He grips the string of beads lying flush against his brown habit. "At every turn, I fear death can be found." The loose skin above his eyes droops, shielding the usually cheerful gaze. It has been a few years since Ethstan completed his vow of silence, and every time Myla hears his old, hoarse voice, she thinks back to the night he spoke of the event which caused his silence in the first place. It was that night when Myla realized the happiest of people can be riddled with undetectable guilt, as is Ethstan's plight.

"Peace is coming," Myla assures finally, allowing her voice to carry conviction, though deep inside, she doubts they are entirely true. Peace has not been her friend for many years.

That doubt increases as she enters the cavernous council room. Today, her council members wear military regalia. As she enters, Bryar nods with approval as he hands a scroll to Lord Thurston. "It's good. Give it to the smithy, enough for the entire army."

Myla's brows furrow, and she offers her husband a questioning look, which he answers with a pleased grin. "You'll see."

"Very well." She accepts his secretiveness, gesturing toward their fully armored bodies. "Is there a battle I am unaware of happening today?"

Bryar's response is solemn. "Rhyland returned this morning. He says Maverick has fallen silent; Falkmere is silent. Rhyland reports fewer troops than ever and some deserters. The Imposter King's cause weakens. There is no better time to strike."

"Deserters? And strike—so we leave today?"

Bryar turns, revealing a full array of black armor. "We must fight someday. It might as well be today."

A thrill surges through her belly, mingling with fear. Weak or not, her father will not be completely defenseless. There will be death soon. "How long will it take to amass our army and march to New Falkmere?"

"They have been ready to march for weeks now. The journey will take one—maybe two days," Bryar answers, his stoic tone easily disguising any familiarity they may share. One could stand in the room now and never know he was her husband. "He will not expect us. We've infiltrated his intel team. The only spy he has reporting back to him is ours, and Antoin is feeding him false information."

A grin spreads across Myla's face. "I have placed my faith and my plans in very capable hands." Her eyes scan her council members beaming faces. Loyal people who have stood beside her since the day she departed Valyndor with a newborn, who stand beside her now, still confident and devoted. "I thank you all, everyone."

At this, Bryar advances toward a topographical mahogany table which reflects the entirety of Myrnith with remarkable accuracy. It was a gift from Rhyland to Caspian on the child's first birthday, carved from Rhyland's own maps.

"We ought to take another day to siphon a host of troops into the city undetected. If they enter through the passageway beneath the barracks at night, with the help of the Raven's Veil, we may be able to hide forty to sixty additional soldiers inside the castle walls. They will be able to stop any sounding alarms and drop the drawbridge for us. I believe there are servicemen within Old Falkmere who would aid in this endeavor."

Myla leans against the table, stunned. "Truly?" She takes a deep breath and looks at the faces around her. Lord Thurston, her Master of Trade, stands, his seafarer's garb freshly pressed and clean for the occasion. He has dark tattoos beneath his eyes, brands he calls them, an indicator of his profession as a trader-by-sea. They each spell something out, though the words are written in an ancient Falkmere dialect, which died out centuries ago, so Myla has never been able to read them. For a titled man, he could be described as rugged. A copper medallion hangs from a rustic chain at his neck and various copper piercings adorn his ears. Half of his straw-colored hair is twisted into braids running along each side of his head while the rest flows freely past his shoulders.

Beside him stands Sir Roderick, the blademaster who taught her how to fight. When they formed this council, Myla believed Roderick's knowledge in combat made him an asset to Bryar, so now he serves as a military advisor. Now, both the Master of Trade and advisor watch her fervently, awaiting a word or a command.

"Send for Ivan and Imogene," Myla commands.

A guard is dispatched to carry out the order.

Myla looks to Bryar. "I believe their attack from the sky is still warranted. I do not wish to descend in confidence and find our luck turns."

Bryar nods in agreement and glances at Lord Thurston. "Can you contribute additional troops to the cause?"

Thurston nods, running a strand of blonde hair between his fingers. "I can contribute them, yes. However, my vessel cannot carry any more bodies than we already have planned. Perhaps Antoin's can accommodate—"

Thurston is interrupted as Rhyland storms in, his tight black curls pulled into a messy half-bun at the top of his head. For a moment, their eyes meet, and something akin to treason crosses over Thurston's face, followed by a half smirk which he is quick to erase.

"Is there any sense in increasing the army which Sir Rhyland will lead?" Thurston stumbles over *Rhyland*, the name barely making it out of his mouth before both men are forced to avert their gaze entirely. Myla feels a warmth flush in her cheeks, realizing now why Rhyland has been absent for so many evenings.

"Perhaps," Bryar remarks with raised eyebrows. Myla's trained eyes take note of the near-invisible smirk he wears as he turns his attention to important matters. "Thurston, get a message to Antoin—he has the Imposter King's ear. I believe it may be in our favor for him to return to Falkmere. There are reports of a gathering taking place in two days. It should not be difficult for him to gain admittance and learn *why* his weakness is suddenly so obvious. Something must have occurred." At this, he passes a subtle, skeptical frown Myla's way, which she acknowledges with pursed lips.

After a wordless nod of approval from Myla, Lord Thurston turns to leave the room, stopped briefly by Rhyland as the two exchange something in whispers, then separate. What might have been a subtle brush of hands is nothing of the sort to Myla and Bryar, who watch intently.

"Rhyland," Myla directs her attention to the tabletop-map. "Does advancing our armies on such short notice change the outcome of the battle in your opinion?"

Now focused, Rhyland grips the edge of the table, chewing his bottom lip intently as he studies. His dress is casual still, so perhaps he has just woken. He wears a faded red tunic with the sleeves rolled up above his elbows, revealing his dark, muscular arms and the runes tattooed to them. "Potentially, Your Grace. We should ascertain the details surrounding the Imposter King's change in position before making any moves. I believe it could be a ruse."

Rhyland voices and validates her and Bryar's unspoken.

"Yes," Myla agrees with a heavy sigh. "It is all rather suspicious. I imagine answers are necessary before we make any potentially fatal moves."

Silence befalls the council for several moments while each member studies the map or a scroll with a few exchanging opinions.

Finally, Roderick speaks, "Might I suggest, Your Grace, that you advance the army to a midway point. Somewhere near enough that they could descend on the palace quickly with the right word but not so close that a retreat is impossible should we discover it is indeed a trap."

Bryar nods, pinching his chin between two large fingers. "Yes," he agrees. "Let us be proactive with our time." Sunlight peeks above the tree line, a few small rays leaking through the opening of the balcony and across the room. Bryar's eyes are slowly drawn to the regal and ravenous silhouette of his wife as the golden light reveals that she has, in fact, worn the green dress. A smirk teases the corner of his mouth as he tears his gaze from her. "Your Grace?" He looks to Myla for confirmation of the plan, his tone anything but formal.

"Proceed then," Myla answers. His examination is not lost on her, nor is the starving flicker in his eyes. "Off with you," she says flatly to her council members, her eyes never once leaving the map before her. "I must prepare to depart the palace this evening. We shall find nothing more to discuss."

One by one, the council files out of the room, Roderick being the last. He closes the door firmly shut and with a thud, and she and Bryar are alone. She keeps her eyes downward, studying the map further despite his warm gaze burning holes in the thin material of her dress. "You should not look at me like that when I am holding council." She attempts a discouraging tone. One that is met with a slight chuckle.

"You should not dress like that when holding council."

Jealousy? Possessiveness? This man has an angle. With a slight side-long gaze, and a failed attempt to hide a smile, Myla responds. "You told me to."

"You listened," he growls, daring a step closer. "Behaving on my birthday? What a *rare* treat. In any case, it *is* my birthday. You had to wear it." At this, he moves to stand behind her, a usually heavy hand now resting with gentle fingertips on her shoulder, brushing her stray hair aside. There, he places a soft kiss. Slow, delicate, tantalizing. A pattern Myla knows well. A pattern she leans into with a sigh as warmth vibrates between them, his magic and hers joining as it has so often before but never losing its electricity.

"You are contradicting yourself," Myla breathlessly retorts, gripping his free hand where it rests on her belly, forcing him closer. "Should I or should I not have worn the dress?" Her head falls back, giving way for his lips to her neck, and she closes her eyes with a tremble as his breath snakes down the sensitive skin of her shoulders.

Lips warm and tender, he presses kisses along her neck and to her jawline, his gloved hands flattening against her stomach and adventuring dangerously low. With a hungry breath in, Bryar spins his wife around, his fingers burying themselves in the back of her thighs to lift her atop the table's edge.

"Right now, you should wear nothing at all."

A giggle slips from her lips, quickly snuffed by her hand against her mouth. "Right now? *Here?*" Lips to her jawline prompt silence, and a low, demanding growl from her husband encourages her body to relax, to surrender, to be claimed. "You know," Myla whispers, bracing back against her arms as Bryar devotes warm kisses to her neck. "If I let you have me in here, you're having the queen, not your wife. It is scandalous, really."

"I won't tell if you don't." His words evoke a genuine laugh, and she nimbly wraps her legs around his waist to draw him closer.

"You've said that to me before."

"Yes," Bryar responds, pausing his *conquest* to meet her gaze. "But that was just for a kiss."

"Well, what are you waiting for? Kiss me again."

"Yes, Your Grace." Obediently, the man leans closer, his eyes flickering hungrily to her lips, full and red with lust, before his savoring gaze trails lower to where the shadows of her breasts whisper through the lace fabric of the dress, taunting him. "I really like this dress," he admits once more before his hands trail carefully up the silhouette of her curves, resting on her neck where the lace collar tickles. "But I like what is beneath it better." In a moment, Bryar pulls the gloves from his large hands before nimbly finding the delicate lace at her neck and tearing it easily. Myla gasps, feeling her body respond in exhilaration as the front of her coveted dress splits, exposing her to her navel.

Like a hungry animal, woken from its winter hibernation with need, Bryar pulls the remainder of the lace from her body, her wrists slipping out of the sleeves, baring her entirely to the waist. His hands claim her breasts, cupping them with passionate reverence as he leans in to silence any response to the destruction she may voice. As the cold against her body is quickly warded off with the heat of her husband, glowing hot with his passion, Myla finds there is a place he is not, which she so desperately needs him. Eagerly, her hands move to the ties of his trousers, which she yanks aggressively until they slip free, loosening the barrier between them and giving way to her endeavor.

"I thought you were going to make me wait," Bryar coos with a satisfied groan as he moves forward with a thrust, burying himself deep inside her aching core.

Myla gasps, bracing her body against the jagged edge of the table, ignoring the pain in her backside, which is greatly counteracted by the immense pleasure swelling inside as Bryar throbs against the nerves in her body. "I can still make you," she assures, her eyes closed as she relishes in his mouth moving to her breast. His tongue grazes across her nipple, willing her to unfold for him.

"No, you can't," he taunts finally, straightening to move closer to her with an intentional thrust, their hips pounding against each other. Breathlessly, Myla laughs and nods in agreement, her cheeks feverish and red, flushed as sweat forms across her exposed abdomen, reflecting the red-hot glow which lights the room off Bryar's body. "Is this enough?" He teases threateningly, slowing the pace and moving to slip out of her.

"Don't you *fucking* dare," Myla gasps angrily as the tension at her core builds, then subsides in a sickening dip of pleasure. She finds his gaze, and within the soft green irises is the savoring of control. The least controlling man in Myrnith, behind the safety of a closed door, commands the queen.

"Then look at me," he instructs. "And come for me." His hand slips beneath her skirt, and as he lunges forward again, his hard length pressing against the divine sensitivity deep within her, his fingers massage the throbbing bundle of nerves between her thighs, wet and dripping on him. Never once breaking their gaze, Myla pants, whimpering as he moves inside her, and a satisfied smile teases the corners of his mouth when, at least, unable to obey, her head falls back and she lets slip a loud cry as her body shudders in ecstatic delight around him.

The victorious conqueror slows his pace, a look of ownership passing over him, and he leans closer, his lips a mere breath from hers. "My good queen," he murmurs, nipping at her lower lip, and as she pants against him, the door, which Myla curses for not barring, swings open.

"Stop," Myla gasps as Bryar pulls her from the table in a fluid motion. Somewhere out of sight, the voice of Elsa cursing under her breath followed by a nervous laugh and instructions for the children to wait sounds. Flushed and still pulsing with a decadence she was far from done with, Myla grins up at her husband as he pulls the blue cloak from his shoulders, draping it over her shoulders, concealing—for the children at least—any traces of indecency. As Bryar moves past her to welcome the children, Myla tugs the cloak around her, nervously grinning as three small heads fly into the room giggling in delight and closely followed by Elsa.

"Oh," Elsa lets out a puff of breath, holding Elenore close to her. "Imagine being me, never knowing what room is safe to walk into." Her bright eyes give Myla a once over before something of approval passes over her face.

"Imagine being me," Bryar mimics Elsa's tone. "Never knowing when someone is going to barge in on me." The two exchange playfully snarky glances, and Bryar reaches down to lift Caspian, grunting beneath his weight.

"I won't be able to lift you much longer, young man."

"I bet I can lift you!" he replies, wiggling free of his father's hold to throw his arms around Bryar's legs. With little huffs, he heaves with all his might, nearly toppling Bryar off balance.

"Whoa!" he exclaims. "I believe you can! Why don't you lift Elle instead?"

"Why?" Caspian asks, grinning up at Elsa and Bryar, who exchange quick insults.

"Because," Bryar defends with a grin. "She is not afraid of heights."

Nor would she have as far to fall should he drop her. Myla thinks, glancing sidelong at Bryar, who examines her, clearly pleased with his handiwork. It is only now that she realizes her neatly done hair has tumbled free and hangs in sweaty locks down her back.

"Anyway—" Elsa remarks with an eye roll Bryar's way before shaking her head at Myla. "I brought the children to say goodbye. We are off to the village for dancing and apples and petting stray dogs." At the latter, the children giggle in excitement, each in turn rolling onto their tiptoes to kiss their parents. Elenore teeters excitedly, bobbing between her brothers before pushing past them entirely to hug her mother.

"Will you finish reading my story before we go?"

Myla grins, kneeling to eye level with the child so she can better right her wild hair and see her cheerful eyes. "Auntie Elsa says the celebration starts soon! How about I read it to you at bedtime?"

"Promise? Can Prince Gourdy listen too?"

Myla nuzzles the girl's nose with her own, coaxing a gleeful squeal. "I promise, and of course he can. We know how much he loves a bedtime story." With a final kiss for each child, they trail out the door and after Elsa. "Have fun!" Myla hollers after, her send-off quickly followed by instructions from Bryar.

"Take Roderick and Ethstan with you!" He then turns his attention back to his partially disrobed wife. "We have unfinished business."

Myla laughs lightly before moving toward the door. "No," she corrects. "*You* have unfinished business. And it shall simply have to wait."

Her statement is met with a smirk. "You cruel woman."

CHAPTER 5

PAST: MYLA, FIFTEEN

ALTHOUGH SHE IS DOING nothing inherently wrong, the pounding in Myla's chest draws a harsh glare on that place within her soul that says otherwise.

The conscience is a bitch. Myla wills her internal voice, the one that cowers at Maverick's feet, to shut the fuck up.

With father busy signing trade deals and mother focused on her coming-of-age celebration, Myla's absence will not be noticed for two or three hours. At least, that is what she is assuming.

At first, Myla had suggested Bryar meet her in the wheat field behind her father's stables. At this time of year, the stems are tall and easy to hide within. Bryar insisted that their meeting elsewhere might be easier to explain, should they be caught by someone *not* of noble blood. As a result, Myla finds herself wearing a simple brown cloak with the hood drawn low. Never in her life has she walked through the village unattended, let alone step foot inside a smithy. Until today.

It is less precise than she expected it to be. The shriek of cold metal people hear from afar presents the idea of distance and *discomfort*. But the blacksmith is warm, and the private room attached is perhaps the most comfortable space she has ever been in. There is nothing that seems too fine to sit on, nothing too breakable to touch. There is a simple set of wooden chairs pushed neatly against an equally simple table. One window catches the afternoon light, casting a golden glow on a shelf of books—mostly agricultural, but a few fables. The bunk bed on the furthest wall supports two tidily made beds with heavy knit blankets. A vase of dry, dead flowers sits covered in a layer of dust atop the hearth and Myla wonders at it, but does not stare long, for the most welcoming and warm part of the room is the boy beside her, nervously scratching the side of his head.

"We cannot study in here." He reaches past her to another door and, when ushered through it, Myla steps into a private garden, fenced off and overgrown with weeds and hanging ivy.

"My father never comes back here," he explains as he pushes a heavy barrel against the door. "But just in case, we will bar it."

Myla smirks, clutching the stack of notes to her chest and casting an eye at the dusty stone floor beneath her. "And if someone tries to come through and finds it barred?"

It is Bryar who grins now, and like a child showing off a prized pet or perhaps some repulsive swampland discovery, he brushes a curtain of ivy to the side, revealing a small opening in the fence. "I cannot sneak out through the smithy; the floorboards creak. So, I broke the fence."

"Despicable," Myla mutters, hiding a slight smile. "What could you possibly need to sneak out for?"

At this, Bryar heaves himself atop the barrel, his long legs draped across it casually and his hands flexing over the wooden rim between them. He shrugs, his broad shoulders closing around the curls at his ears. "I spent some time trying to find out about my mother. That was a few years ago now, and I do not bother looking anymore. But I like the freedom that night brings...so I go for walks."

Though a lady of proper upbringing would never consider straddling a barrel, Myla does, settling into a comfortable position across from Bryar. "What do you find on these walks?"

"Usually, I observe things I do not think I am supposed to see." His lips pinch together as if he is visualizing something distasteful, but then they twitch back into that curious and lazy smile she has become so familiar with. "But sometimes I discover good things that I would never see if I were sleeping here."

"Like what?"

"Like families."

Myla's breath hitches, and she notes the shift in his voice, the way his cheerful disposition dramatically dips into something hinting at sadness or maybe longing, and for some reason, her mind wanders back to the dead flowers.

"But you have a family," he continues. "And I guess that does not seem all that great either."

"I think," Myla whispers, afraid of someone beyond the fence hearing and recognizing her voice. "I think that families, like chains, are rather useless if the links are broken."

Bryar nods slowly, fiddling with a splinter of wood slowly peeling off the barrel. "Or if a link goes missing," he mutters before looking up at her. "And which link in your family is broken?"

"Me, I think." At this, Bryar stands and takes three steps forward. Exactly three. Myla counts them.

One. Has his hair always been that shade—an inky black with caramel brown highlights, only visible in the sun?

Two. Why do his eyes bore so deeply? They cut—no, they are not sharp. They are soft. They *melt*; they melt warm and comforting caverns for a soul to fall into. To be caught in the *softness.*

Three. He has worked all day, his leather vest is scratched and worn, and the laces of his gauntlets are frayed. Why does he look like he has worked so damn hard, but he smells so damn *good?*

"You?" He speaks again, questioning her with furrowed brows. Fearlessly, his eyes in all their soft, intoxicating glory bore into hers as though he will see past the hurt and to the truth. "You are the broken link?" And then he reaches out, snatching the notes from her.

He is all boy once more; with the softness, sincerity, the woody clean fragrance—it is all gone, and he is once again perched on his barrel, reading her notes.

For a moment, Myla believes their conversation has ended. He reclines against the door, flipping through the pages with a lip pinched between his teeth. He appears focused. It is the same expression he wears when their swordplay grows intense. Then he speaks, not looking up from her handwritten papers. To Myla's horror, he is reading her note aloud. *"How can it be that our magic is so taken for granted—an involuntary and inexplicable component to our being? This intrinsically natural gift can only be the result of the Gods' favor. For when I use my magic, I feel the most connected to the Spirit Mother. I do not believe that my lessons are exploring the vast possibilities that these gifts are what makes us entwined with the natural world. They keep us harnessed to nature in a way we would not otherwise be. I believe they ought to humble us, not empower."*

He pauses, then breaks his gaze with her notes to study her. Myla sits with her eyes fixed in embarrassment on the ground, ankles crossed now, slowly rolling the barrel forwards and backwards, creating a rhythmic lull. One she hopes will drown the words out. A note she had not intended to mix with those she is loaning him, something she meant to reflect on personally, is shared with him. He reads them and she listens. Listens to words she did indeed write but feeling them differently when spoken by him. She wonders how her textbooks would sound if read aloud by him.

"You are insightful, Myla. You are not the broken link."

"My father writes receipts and contracts more insightful than that." Myla replies, allowing the flippant tone in her voice to distract from the damn *softness*. Never in her life has Myla met a creature of the male race who was not cold and prickly and condescending. Yet he—this boy—has the audacity to sit there, reading her notes and thinking that what she has to say is insightful. Or worse yet, that something she has to say is worth listening to. It is preposterous.

"Anyone can make a receipt or a contract sound good," Bryar responds. "I doubt your father can bring a sense of passion into it, though. Is he the link? The broken one?"

What a segue. "Fathers aren't broken links."

"Says who?"

"Says my father. Says the headmaster. Says my mother and my governess, and all the other young ladies my age."

Bryar shrugs. "Denial makes good company for ignorance. They perpetuate each other."

With a slight gasp, Myla finds herself clenching her teeth to keep from saying something she does not mean; a defense in the name of Lord Maverick Alerys, an instinctual urge to protect him because that is what proper young ladies do even if he has not earned it. But she does not. She remains silent until the urge passes. Bryar would see right through it, anyway. "You seem to know a lot about the topic?"

"Of broken fathers?"

"Or links. Who is your broken link?"

"I have heard it was my mother. But I have no proof on the matter, so I refuse to cast judgment."

"But she left?"

Bryar's eyes drop, and he lays the pile of paper on his lap. "Yes," he says simply. "She left."

"Mothers are not supposed to do that."

"Yes," Bryar agrees casually. "Yet here *we* are, doing something we are not supposed to be doing. I do not see how it is all that bad. Do you?"

Disbelief runs through Myla's mind. "Are you saying that your mother leaving you was not a bad thing to do?"

He leans forward now, his beautiful green eyes flickering coyly. "I am saying that I am not in the habit of judging someone's motives. People might question why we are sitting here together. Alone. They might assume improper things. That does not make it the truth. The same can be said for my mother—it is easy to assume that she left me because she was a shit excuse for a parent. That does not mean there is any truth in the assumption. I like to lie awake at night and imagine all the good reasons my mother might have left."

Something about what he says makes her uncomfortable. Myla shifts, adjusting her skirts to fully cover her ankles, then she turns her attention to the cuffs of her sleeves, giving each a little tug before looking at him again. "What did you mean by *missing links?*"

His face flattens, and his focus drifts to the ground before he answers. "My stepmother. She died recently. You see, Miss Alerys, while we are not an angry home, we are not a happy one either. Not right now."

Myla's heart sinks, and she grips her hands before her to stay their desire to reach out and hold his hand. "You have lost two mothers then."

"I have," he admits sadly. "I try to imagine, on the days when my father seems like he is one inconvenience away from breaking, that he has experienced heartbreak twice over. I hope to never be able to understand, but *Gods,* his grief can be suffocating sometimes."

"So that's the real reason behind the broken fence." Myla smiles weakly, not daring to meet his gaze as she continues. "I have an aunt who is always sad. Sometimes I think I am glad that I'm only angry. Sad seems so much worse."

He shifts in his seat, curious eyes passing her over and reflecting something akin to reverence. "At least *you* are beautiful, especially when you are angry."

Myla shivers. *He thinks I am beautiful. What would he say if I called him beautiful too?* And yet, all she can think to say in response is, "You are a strange boy."

At this, his curious examination transforms into a satisfied half-smile. "I like you too."

"That is not what I said," Myla retorts, her eyebrows furrowing, causing the freckles on her nose to disappear in the creases of her frown.

Bryar sighs and turns his attention back to the stack of notes he holds. "Maybe not with your words." His response is absent now, his brain clearly beginning to absorb the information on the pages before him. "Your face says things that your mouth does not."

With a little inhale, stunned by his declaration, Myla finds herself pressing two hands to her cheeks, trying, and failing to not notice the way his lips curl in a satisfied grin, though his eyes never leave the page. "Does it?"

"All the time."

CHAPTER 6

PRESENT

"YOUR GRACE!"

Myla twists toward the interruption, ready to reprimand the guard for rudely intruding without even knocking, but the look of distress etched in the young man's features, the sweat of exertion apparent on his skin, and the ash collected in a thick layer over his shoulders stays her words.

"What is it?" Bryar demands, straightening from the missive before him, a hand instinctively finding its place over Myla's.

"You are needed in the village! There was an ambush."

Hindsight is a useless bitch. Myla has often heard it referred to as a beautiful thing, but that is a lie. Hindsight is nothing but guilt disguised as wisdom. Guilt for not asking more questions or showing more concern. Guilt for not hugging someone more or hugging them longer. The shit thing about guilt is that no one ever stops for it. That is why grief exists. To stop the world.

It is not a long way to the village from the palace, perhaps a ten-minute walk if someone is taking their time. Despite running at her fastest pace, the guards surrounding her matching her step for step, and arriving in no more than five minutes, it feels like an hour to Myla. Every breath is enough time to envision harm befalling her children. Myla can only hope that whatever has befallen the village, Bryar flew there in enough time to spare their children.

Shrieks are the first sounds to break the rhythmic thud of her heart within her ears. Shrieks amidst intervals of whooshing, which brings on a trembling underfoot. A charge of energy pools in Myla's palms, and a glint of light catches in her periphery from her pulsing amulet. She and her husband exchange energy already. A cocktail of fear and guilt.

At first, she can make out nothing amidst the blinding smoke. Buildings are swallowed in plumes of curling black, and greedy flames lap at the tree line. Deeper within the smoke, Myla glimpses hazy flashes of blue light, small and sputtering and aimed at the dark shadowy figures which rush in waves toward them. They come from someone weakened or tired with little power behind them to do much damage at all. *They come from someone not yet confident in their abilities.* Desperate wails stand out differently to her ears than those of the panicking serfs calling her. Though the words are inaudible, something instinctual and maternal transforms the wails into meaning.

Help us, Mother.

Myla sucks in a startled gasp. "It's Aidan!"

She turns to look for Bryar in the mayhem, just in time to see the blur of his body launching through the sky as he spirals headlong toward their children's assailants. Already edged with an ember-like light, his silhouette is contrasted when, accompanied by a guttural cry, the blue light warps from within the smoke, illuminating everything in sight for a moment. From within the blue light, two small figures are highlighted. Aidan, bearing down on his knees with palms outstretched and emitting nothing but hot-blue sparks and the occasional flame, while Caspian stands over his brother. Restorer light seeps from his pores, disintegrating enemy warriors who come too close. Myla feels a surge of burning heat stun her arm, almost, but not quite, as tangible as the insatiable rage boiling within her.

Summoning her magic is oftentimes a conscious decision. Yet now, a mercenary hangs before her by his neck, suspended by a strand of her light. Her magic did not require intellect at this moment. No, it obeys her will as she seeks her children. The enemy's head hangs limp in an unnatural way, and his eyes, barely open, have a glassy look to them. With a flick of her wrist and not a second to regret the life before her, he drops to her feet as she allows a second strand to unfurl, its sharp edge embedding itself in the chest of another attacker. As Myla steps over the lifeless lumps of carnage in her path, bodies collapse in every direction, some from the blast of melting-hot flames and others from arrows and plunging blades.

Gods help those who threaten a mother's child.

"Your Grace!" Imogene, crashing in a violent whoosh as her wings allow for a quick descent, intercepts a bulky mercenary at her back. A wave of feathery fire emerges from the Ashborn Queen's hands, the heat melting the face off her foe. "There are swarms of New Falkmere soldiers along the road to the palace!"

The road Rhyland and Lord Thurston are on.

As the attackers before her fall in heaps of broken bones and scorched flesh, Myla advances one step at a time with Imogene along-side her. Ahead, Ivan and Bryar stand, their bodies a barrier between the mercenaries and the young boys. Aidan still attempts to launch little sputters of flames while Caspian heaves for air, his palms pressed into the ground, sending blue ripples along the surface of the earth, each wave vanquishing the corrupt impurities of his foes. As a result of his exhaustive exertion of magic, his little brother is shielded from the dangers of those clearly determined to watch them bleed lifeless.

Elenore is nowhere in sight.

"Imogene," Myla pleads as she gasps for air, smoke from the burning village filling her lungs. "I cannot see my daughter." Her eyes dart incoherently in every direction, desperate to see a head of curls bobbing from the smoke.

Nothing more needs to be said. That natural maternal instinct, which they each share as a mother in her own right, speaks for itself in the way an aching panic creeps into Imogene's eyes. The Ashborn queen takes flight once more, and from overhead can be seen drifting upon the wind, scanning the surrounding forest with falcon-sharp eyesight.

With a path cleared by her soldiers, Myla rushes into the thick of the smoke, taking up Bryar's back. At her feet, her sons, wearing stoic faces, gasp for air and choke, their cheeks smudged with fresh tears and their small bodies braced together, a brotherly and inherent need to lean on each other for survival.

"Have you seen Elenore?" Her voice cracks in a panic as she lithely deflects an arrow, the nasty whizzing point disintegrating against the golden strands from her fingertips.

Her husband's back stiffens against hers and, for the briefest moment, he looks over his shoulder at her. "Is she not with the boys?" He searches for the children, peering beyond the chaos, blood, and smoke, to where only two children huddle together. Anger and panic alike wash over his darkened features. "Get them out of here!" Bryar desperately demands, his voice shaking as he staggers several steps backwards to avoid a volley of hissing black arrows barely missing their huddle. "*Now!*" he growls with a flinch between gritted teeth and a final glance at where Elenore should also be.

Poison sizzles as metal tips fall from the sky and embed in the ground, turning the soil itself black. Another volley of arrows launches, and one embeds itself into a soldier's chest. His armor-clad body tenses as an inky fluid oozes from the wound, consuming the cold steel and the flesh beneath it. The soldier lets out a horrified shriek and crumbles to the ground, clawing at his middle as flesh sizzles into exposed bone. The poison melts like acid.

Bile rises in her throat, and Myla reaches urgently for her sons, allowing a glance at Bryar as sick concern to leave him behind fills her belly. "Stand!" Myla commands hoarsely as smoke fills her lungs.

"*Stand!*" With an arm in each hand, she pulls the limp and gasping boys to their feet, Aidan the weaker of the two. His tiny arms reverberate with the lingering effects of too much magic in a body too small for such endeavors. Blindly, they stumble beyond the thickest waves of smoke to the side of a villager's house where they take shelter from the fray.

"Mama," Caspian chokes, and the strain in his voice brings a burning pang to her chest. His words are thick, and tears etch trails of clean skin across his face like a deepening in the surface of his newly born trauma. "*Elenore.* She is crying!" He sobs now, grappling at his ears and casting a gaze at Aidan, who strains to listen, his small eyes squeezed shut.

"She needs help!" Aidan wails, clawing at Myla's skirt. "Find her, Mama!"

"I cannot hear her!" Myla wheezes, grasping at her throat before falling to her knees to meet the boys' eyes. "*I cannot see her!* Where did she go?"

Aidan covers his ears, letting out a shriek. "She is crying, Mama, she is—" He stops, his eyes glistening, and looks to his mother. He wears a look which far surpasses fear. "She stopped crying..."

Myla darts to her feet, her legs trembling and an agonizing panic tightening around her heart. "Stay here!" she rasps, her feet catching on the thicket of grass beneath them, and yet she staggers forward, stumbling across the uneven ground, back into the horror which is the leveled village.

The village where dancing and treats were supposed to be, but is instead the landscape of murder. Ethstan and Elsa together, entirely incapable of defeating a trained killer, stand nonetheless, their shoulders pressed together, each with daggers desperately trying to find a hold in the thick flesh of the mercenary before them. To her right, the Ashborn Queen, alongside her husband, continue to lose ground as more volleys of poisoned arrows fly at them, pushing them further away from the hub of assault. Buildings in every direction threaten to burn anybody who remains here.

Like flint casting a spark, the Gods breathe into her again for the first time since that bloody battlefield where Vesperian fell.

Every atom in her vibrates, and her skin grows light with the stars of magic, the hot points of rage. Light from the flames, light from the sun overhead, even the light of her amulet collects within her, causing a darkening around her entire vicinity. Myla turns her face to the sky.

I am your vessel. She hums her desperate prayer, letting out an even breath before the power coils in her throat. Like mountains and oceans falling from the sky in a thunderous boom, a scream ripples from her, causing the earth to shudder. The feeble homes aglow with flames crash around her in every direction, sending sparks into the sky only to be consumed by her hungry magic.

The mercenary before Ethstan and Elsa collapses in a staggered heap, his hands clawing ferociously at his ears as though to tear them from his own head to stay the pain. Despite his fine armor and sharp features, something about the way he scampers backwards and away from her looks feral.

It is enough of an assault against the mercenaries for Bryar and Ivan to set the group of archers on fire, their screaming bodies dancing against the darkness of the woods, desperate to be free of the burning agony. Myla lunges forward, burying her fox dagger deep within the skull of a disoriented enemy before he can retrieve his own weapon.

Her cry, their greatest defense, leaves the killers unaware and unable to defend themselves, and though her soldiers also writhe in pain, Bryar and Ivan stand despite it, reducing their enemies to ash.

Very few attackers remain now, half a dozen maybe. With her porcelain-hued cheeks streaked in blood dripping from her ears, Elsa stands behind one holding a dagger to his throat while she offers him to Myla.

"Who sent you!" It is not a question; it is a threat as Bryar grabs the heavily armed warrior by his black hair and throws him like a rag doll at Myla's feet. Soldiers follow suit, collecting the rest of their attackers into a defeated row.

"Who took my daughter?" Myla screams, ignoring the whimpering of villagers behind her who now watch in horror. Her magic tingles and vibrates off the surface of her skin, taunting the prisoner at her feet. She is ready to kill, and he knows it. "The little girl! Who took her?"

Silence is her only answer, averted gazes and rebellious half-smirks. Expressions of men who do not care if they die—it is compassion compared to what their master might do should they betray him. Myla is no stranger to the antics of war. To them, this is just another command. Desperation gurgles from a place deep within and calls upon the darker side of her magic. Thirsty for answers, her hands coil around the pulsating light of her palms, mere beasts waiting for her bidding to be free and mutilate. A command which would be pointless.

Blood bursts from the skull of the first mercenary in the row of apprehended combatants. Bryar's axe has entirely passed through the bone and brain of his prisoner, and his usually calm demeanor is replaced with righteous fury. A ripple of heat radiates off his body, anger incarnate. His dark brows are pushed inward, driving a deep crease on his forehead. His eyes are hooded with darkness. That is not the last man who will die if he is not granted an answer.

"Do you see your comrade's blood?" he bellows. His hands twist the hilt of his weapon aggressively, shoulders rolling and ready for another violent swing. Sweat and blood mat black curls to his forehead, rigid with stress lines. "Your blood will soon mingle with his if I am not appeased! Where is my daughter?"

The axe is now raised and ready to fall on the second enemy soldier. Bryar's eyes meet with equally dark ones, set into deep sockets. The mercenary 's skin is leathery with age, and a gray beard speckles his chiseled jawline. He appears both young and old at once, something Myla might wonder at if it were not for the current circumstances.

"Your metal is a mercy, sir," the man answers, his voice unwavering despite the impending axe to his skull. The brain prompting him to speak, to tilt his eyes upward in defiance, will soon disgrace the earth they stand on. "You will find no man here willing to speak. Each of us honors our vows of secrecy. It is what makes our guild dependable."

His words send chills through Myla, her skin pricking at the thought that these mercenaries were intentionally hired and sent to harm her family. She has little time to reflect on the sentiment. Her husband, with a desperate and violent cry, fueled first with rage and followed with fear, lowers his axe once more. Bones burst from the broken skin with a sickening crack, spraying tissue and fragments of white at Bryar's feet. A scene he clearly does not regret as he kicks the chunk of skull off his boot.

With each step—each advancement driving a deeper panic into Myla—Bryar's body grows more rigid, and the heat exuding from him is more unbearable than that of the burning buildings around them. The amulets upon their chests pulse with life, their energy exchanging quicker than breath is drawn. Her fear is his; his rage is hers.

"I assure you," Bryar speaks again, dropping his axe to the ground. "My methods are kinder than my wife will be should I not receive an answer this time. One of you *shall* speak." It is a promise, not a threat.

The prisoners' heads drop, eyes lowered to the ground, all appearing ill at the sight of their mutilated comrades. A particularly young one at the end lets out a sniff.

Weakness. Let me at the fucker.

Myla descends. Before she is aware of her movements, she finds herself approaching the young man.

"Bring me a chair!" she commands no one in particular. Nonetheless, a crudely made wooden chair is delivered in mere moments. "This one." She looks at several of her soldiers. "Bring him to his feet and *relieve* him of his clothes."

Her instructions, barbaric as they seem, are met with a brief hesitancy and a slightly aghast side-eye from Bryar before she soon finds the young man standing exposed before her, his manhood shriveled in fear no doubt, for it is certainly not cold.

"Tie him to the chair," she spits in disgust.

Villagers, horrified and interested in equal measure, seem torn between watching and turning away.

Bryar moves alongside her and places a hand on her elbow, whispering so only she can hear him. "What exactly are you doing?"

She sucks in a deep breath and kneels before the man, summoning a stinging white light to her fingers. "He shall tell me what he knows, or I shall shave the flesh from his bones little by little until he tells me who took our daughter."

At this, Bryar smirks, gesturing her way with an open palm. "I suppose my metal was a mercy."

Pale eyes before her are squeezed shut as Myla's face levels with his. With a merciless grip, Myla seizes his chin, forcing him to look at her.

"Do you know what human flesh smells like when it has been cauterized?" she asks, her voice is a whisper, barely traveling past the immediate space they occupy.

"I can imagine," he responds, his voice does not hold the same conviction as Bryar's second victim. No, he is quivering and humiliated.

"Oh," Myla laughs, holding her free hand next to his ear and allowing her magic to meander waywardly from her fingertips. A few strands stray dangerously close to his ear, evoking a wince. "You will not have to imagine if you do not tell me. You see, my husband's magic channels through me. Right now, this light is just a sting, a little prick. Should I choose, it will be hotter than any fire you have ever stood beside. It will be hotter than the fires of the Old Falkmere battle, which turned rock to liquid, and it will be hotter than the fires from a dragon's lungs. And all that *unbearable* heat will be slicing through you like butter. When I am done with you, like fat on a spit, the skin of your eyeballs will split and they will fall to the ground where I *assure* you, I will collect them and make you wear them around your neck for the hounds to eat first. Right before they rip your throat from your neck. Imagine meeting your end *naked* and *crying*. No one will sing songs of your valor, and the Gods will turn your shriveled balls away. You will spend your afterlife shamed." Her words now mingle with the whimpers of the young mercenary before her. "So, tell me," she probes. "Where the fuck is my daughter and who has her?"

"I—Madam, I do not know!"

Myla's hand sinks below the mercenary's waist, to the soft droop of flesh between his thighs, a torturous descent, so it would seem, as the man lets out a brief shriek. "It's *Your Grace*," she corrects. "And you do know. Shall we sample what is to come?" Now, a sputter of sparks and white flames combusts into an unruly ball between her fingers. The heat is surely unbearable even now, though it has not yet made contact. "Or do I need to cut *it* off." She glances between his thighs. "I *will* do it, if you fail to answer me, I will cut off your cock, and you can wear *that* around your neck too."

"No! No—" he speaks, his fingers digging into the arms of the chair as he attempts to propel backwards, accomplishing nothing of the sort as two guards stand behind him, holding the chair steady. "I shall speak!"

"Coward!" a fellow sellsword shouts.

"Traitorous bastard!" taunts another.

"Your cock will be no good to you if he finds out you spoke!" A final, angered warning falls on deaf ears before Myla allows the flames to lap at his most prized possession. The mercenary lets out a shriek which might be mistaken as belonging to a young girl given the shrill inflection.

"She—she has been taken to my master's camp! Follow the road to New Falkmere. She is being held hostage, and my master is prepared to negotiate the terms of her release!"

A gasp ripples across the onlooking crowd, and it takes everything within Myla to not waver, now more than ever, resilience is key.

"And who sent you?" Bryar growls, standing beside his wife now, axe ready to deposit vengeance into their captive's skull.

"I cannot tell you who it was. I have told you all I can!"

A jolt of icy anger pulses through Myla. It is not the answer she wants, but it will have to do. "And how many swords can I expect at your master's camp?" She demands, her voice simmering with rage now.

"A dozen, maybe two," the young man responds, prompting a look of angered amusement to pass over Bryar's hardened face. "But you must make haste!"

Myla stands, urging her guards to unhand the chair, ignoring the nagging thought that Aidan could no longer hear nor feel her. With one fluid motion, she kicks the heel of her boot into the gap between the mercenary's thighs, no doubt crushing his manhood in the process. His chair topples backwards, and she turns to face Bryar and her soldiers, many of them wearing a discomforted expression. He's lucky he spoke before she took more extreme measures. No man wants to watch the mutilation of the male member. They are all of them idiots for even carrying the mindless things into battle.

"You should have cut the damn thing off," she says over her shoulder toward the mercenary who lies sprawling in the chair, crying as his spread thighs flash the smoke-filled sky. "Then you could not be tortured with it."

At this, Myla turns her attention to the men before her. "We advance on New Falkmere. Our fastest riders are to move ahead immediately to check on the well-being of Sir Rhyland and Lord Thurston and scope out this so-called 'camp'. I shall take four lances to accompany His Grace and I immediately." With a sidelong glance at Bryar, Myla lowers her voice. "I do not believe we were told the truth. Why would the other mercenaries allow themselves to be killed if this is simply a hostage situation?" She nods briefly at the cluster of mercenaries being chained one to the other by members of the Raven's Veil. "It makes no sense. We must hurry."

No instructions necessary, four lances are formed, a knight, a squire, and an archer in each, sixteen men in total ready to follow wherever Myla leads. Glancing at Imogene with pleading eyes, Myla speaks. "Please take flight and try to get eyes on whoever it is that might have Elenore." Myla's words falter as she finds herself shoulder to shoulder with Bryar. She can feel the sinking of his energy and see the shimmer of tears in his eyes.

He can't feel his daughter either.

CHAPTER 7

PAST: MYLA, FIFTEEN

THE OPEN DOOR TO the study is a mystery. It is usually the one door firmly closed and most often locked. Today, while Maverick hosts his guest, it sits ajar, allowing the low voices to drift out into the drafty hallway where Myla and Elsa stand, their backs pressed to the corner to conceal their presence.

"Your daughter's path is promising."

"Tell me something I do not know, Dante, or leave. My time is precious." The irritated inflection in his voice says, *"Yes, I know my daughter has the potential to make me a richer man. What else?"*

And the sentiment sends a flurry of anger through Myla, bringing an involuntary sputter of sparks to her fingertips and an angry pressure to her chest. She is familiar with the first, but the second concerns her.

Elsa looks sidelong at Myla with one eyebrow rebelliously arched. "Your dad is such an asshole," she whispers.

The remark is met with a sharp elbow to the ribcage. "Shhh," Myla hushes, twisting to lean further into the hall with strained ears.

Dante's visit is peculiar, and eavesdropping is surely the only way she will discover his purpose. Maverick rarely shares details.

"Elsa shows little potential," Dante continues with a forlorn sigh as though whining into the wind will make a difference.

Myla glances back at Elsa as her friend's features droop despairingly. "*Your* dad is such an asshole."

"Tell me something I don't know." Elsa mimics Maverick's earlier tone, and both girls stifle a brief laugh before silencing themselves to listen to the continued conversation.

"At the risk of sounding desperate, I have come in search of a position for my daughter."

Maverick scoffs. "I have no son for your daughter to wed."

"As *your* daughter's lady. It will throw her into the path of more eligible suitors and hopefully rid her of her unscrupulous reputation."

There is a long pause. Both girls turn their attention to one another, and Myla finds her hand entwined with her friend's, a glimmer of hope for them both, it would seem. Finally, Maverick speaks. "I could not support your daughter. What is in it for me?"

"This would be to my family's social gain; and I should compensate you dearly. An annual sum to cover her expenses as well as an additional price in recompense for your troubles. Elsa would, of course, be a marvelous chaperone to all of Myla's social obligations."

"And in return, Elsa has the chance to charm eligible lords?"

"Yes," Dante admits hesitantly. "But Maverick, consider, your daughter will require eyes on her at all times as her calendar fills, which *fill* it may, should your aspirations for her see fruition."

Elsa tugs Myla away, leading her up the creaking mahogany steps to the second level of the manor where her room is. Once the door is securely shut behind them, Elsa presses her back to the door as a deterrent and presses two palms to her mouth.

"Imagine," Myla says with a begrudged sigh. "Even those in our circle know my father's plans for me."

"What *aspirations* does he speak of?"

"Father plans to use me to climb the social ladder."

Elsa chuckles, pushing herself off the door to glide across Myla's room and land with a *huff* in the feathery folds of the bed. "He is acting as if your family is more noble than it is."

Myla shrugs and plops down next to Elsa. "The Alerys lineage can be traced back to the original monarchy. I think some have forgotten just *how* noble we actually are. Not Maverick though..."

Elsa props herself on an elbow, her hot pink dress a stark contrast to the neutral tones of Myla's room. "On the bright side, I will chaperone you right into the arms of the blacksmith if you would like."

Myla gasps, a response far too forced for her liking. "Elsa—that is not what I want. He is a kind boy, nothing more."

Elsa's eyebrows flash upward, a brief disclosure of her sarcastic disapproval. "Whatever you say. I know you did not have me lie to your governess for nothing."

As though summoned by an evil conjuration, a vicious knock at Myla's door is sharp and unmistakable. "Miss Alerys, it is time for your music lessons."

Myla slumps back with an impertinent eyeroll, a dramatic display of defiance, one which evokes an unbecoming snort from Elsa. "I am unwell!" Myla groans, rolling onto her belly in hopes that her protesting might send The Governess away. The notion is quickly erased by another rap on the door.

Elsa answers, peering around the heavy door. "Miss Alerys seems to have eaten something unsettling," she whispers. "I am afraid she is quite indisposed."

"Very well," the haughty woman's voice is muffled, but the departing rustle of her skirts is loud enough to wash a smile across Myla's face.

"Having you as my lady might prove *very beneficial*."

Elsa returns to Myla's side to lay down. "So, this...boy—"

"Bryar."

"—Bryar. He is just a charitable cause?"

Myla glares sidelong at her friend. "I think he needs charity as much as my father needs more coin."

"So why? You realize how dangerous it is for both of you to be sneaking around...even if it is innocent."

"*It is*," Myla insists. "And I think we both know that, but he is hungry to learn, and I can teach him."

"But why not just give him the funds then? You have your charity allowance."

At this, Myla sits upright, a mounting irritation building inside her. "I don't know, Elsa."

"Okay..." Elsa proceeds cautiously. "I do not mean to suggest anything untoward. I just know you, and this is not like you."

"Maybe it is," Myla argues. "Maybe I am sick of my days being filled with endless lessons with no purpose beyond increasing my marriage-market value." Myla gestures toward the wall opposite her bed which is filled with books, every volume read more than once. "I want to feel useful."

"And he makes you feel that? Useful?"

"Something like that."

The sharp blue of Elsa's gaze seems to burrow itself deep into Myla's subconscious. Her friend is not easily fooled.

"Enough of this, I should change for supper."

Elsa flashes one last coy smile and stands to leave. "I wonder what the blacksmith is having for supper."

"What a strange thing to wonder," Myla laughs, pushing her friend through the door and leaving herself to ponder what on earth Elsa was insinuating. A flicker of energy sends a sharp tingle through Myla's fingers, concealed only by the folds of her skirt and disregarded as a nervous response. The flicker continues well into the evening after Elsa has left, and supper is held by candlelight.

Maverick seems to be in rare form, and the goose on his plate takes the brunt of his frustration as it is shredded into large bites by a three-pronged fork. Myla and Lavinia sit opposite one another, exchanging cautious glances, neither daring to watch Maverick at the head of the table for long. Instead, Lavinia tactfully directs the conversation.

"There is to be a Yule celebration at the palace next week." Her cheerful tone catches her husband's attention. "We received an invitation."

"When?" Maverick demands, setting his cutlery down with a little too much force, causing the wine in their glassware to ripple and shudder. Myla's body matches the response, and the tingling in her fingertips feels like an uncontrollable tension beneath the surface of her skin—a tension which seems to pulsate both outward and inward to the center of her chest.

Perhaps this is how Uncle Albert felt before that heart attack took him out.

Lavinia turns her gaze to her plate, seeming not to notice the red-rimmed eyes of her husband boring into her. Myla catches the tensing at her collarbone, a fearful strain disguised as swallowing. "This morning."

Maverick's lips purse inward and his eyebrows sink, casting darkness over his face. "Did you not think it important enough to tell me sooner?"

"Forgive me," Lavinia answers sweetly. "I am afraid we were both so busy with our tasks I simply could not find the time," she expertly redirects before Maverick can spiral into an outburst. "I do think we should discuss having Myla fitted for a new gown. It is to be a spectacular occasion."

Maverick looks as though he is about to speak, the veins in his neck bulge and his fists clench around the knife in his hand. Myla fears he will bury it in the servant's shoulder like last time. Thankfully, Lavinia's suggestion seems to pacify him, and with an exasperated sigh, he replies. "I hope you prove worthy of these costs, daughter. Between your coming-out party and the new *dresses,* I shall spend more than your dowry to see you married well."

A stinging *zap* jabs at a nerve within her elbow, and Myla takes a slow breath to calm the simmering anger. Words, demands, insults of every kind form on the tip of her tongue, but she calls them back, forcing them into their hiding places for tonight. It is not she who would receive the beating, but her mother. "I hope to prove useful to you," is all she can manage before filling her mouth with far too much goose, a gag to stop the words, so it would seem.

"The Headmaster gives splendid reports of your progress at the Institute of Mystic Arts," Lavinia interjects, her smile doing little to hide the nervous quiver in her voice. "I believe you are excelling, my dear."

Maverick peers at both women from above his tumbler of wine. After a long, slow gulp, he joins the conversation. "He told me last week that you seem to have an advantage in both magic and sword-handling."

Myla nods slowly, afraid to bring her hands above the table should they unravel that awful thread of light to strangle the man at the opposite end of the table. "Yes," she replies. "So, I am told."

"I am to assume that you will perform well for the king then—at your aptitude test?"

"Should the Gods see fit."

Maverick pushes his nearly empty plate aside with a glance of disgust at the bare bones scattered in a mess of roasted carrots and potatoes. "They will see fit." With a final mutter of disgust at the meal, Maverick departs the room, leaving a cloud of angst behind. Even the servants who move to clear his space wear expressions of anxiety; fear of making the wrong move or saying the wrong thing extends well beyond the two women still sitting at the table.

"Do not worry yourself," Lavinia says finally, filling Myla's glass with more sweet wine. "Your father puts too much pressure on himself."

Disregarding the statement, Myla brings her hands into view, revealing a deep trembling. "Something is wrong," she whispers, leaning closer so her mother can hear her. "Since this morning, every irritation seems to be prodding at this...this slumbering *beast* within."

Lavinia watches her daughter's hands for a moment, unflinching at the sparks flickering from her fingertips with no indication as to why. "We shall go to the woods tonight. Your nervous system needs a release."

"But father?"

"Let me worry about him."

Their journey to the cave is a quiet one. For nearly an hour, there is nothing but the heavy blanket of darkness and the orchestra of crickets. Lavinia silently guides her daughter deeper into the heart of Falkmere Wood, aware of how the girl's energy builds like pressure, ready to explode. It circles her in involuntary sputters of light like prowling wolves, ready to sink their sharp, luminescent teeth into her soft flesh for a quick kill.

"Calm breaths, darling," she whispers over her shoulder. "We should be there in a quarter of an hour."

Myla stumbles behind, tripping over the heavy blue silk of her skirts. With every step her heartbeat hastens, a war-drum to the mounting ache in her throat. It feels as though she is being strangled by an invisible hand beneath her skin's surface. Swallowing hard, Myla reaches to touch her mother, grabbing her attention. "Something is not right." Her hand glows, the strings of light trembling beneath the surface and tangling with one another, fighting to break free beyond the walls of her resistance. Swallowing again, her breathing labored, Myla lets out a slight whimper before speaking again. "I feel like I shall *burst*."

Lavinia's eyes trail from her daughter's hands to her throat, which she gingerly touches, caressing with a gentleness only known to mothers. "I know, my love. I know."

The final leg of their journey is rocky; a feat Myla has never struggled with before this night. Drums rhythmically pound in the distance, and the mystical hum of song rituals drifts down the side of the mountain, lulling them closer. In the past, these sounds were exhilarating, comforting even. Tonight, they seem nothing more than a song of her impending doom.

Once they reach the rocky base of the mountain, both mother and daughter are weary. A flurry of glowing torches springs through the old trees, catching on the trunks and casting inconsistent bursts of light as their bearers dance around the perimeter of a huge fire. Most are clad in white frocks, while others are completely naked. An old woman sits cross-legged in the shadowy mouth of a cave, holding a flute. The sweet notes she blows are both haunting and relaxing. They bring with them a sense of hope paired with something older—prophesies, perhaps. More people come and go as they please, some guiding sacrificial goats and lambs to set free in the mountain, an offering to the Spirit Mother. Today, their offering, so her mother says, is her.

Myla follows her mother's suit and sheds her layers until she stands barefoot in her thin white shift, a garment which does nothing to protect from the cold. She lets her hair down, and the long brown locks rest gently against her back. An older man speaking the ancient tongue approaches. He wears a string of bones around his neck and carries a crudely carved bowl full of smashed charcoal.

"The Spirit Mother wishes for you to be marked," he says in their native tongue. "She shall guide my hand."

Myla lowers her chin, allowing the man access to her forehead; he immediately begins scrawling markings across her face, his words an incoherent chant.

Behind him, about Myla's age, is a young man with dark skin and curly black hair pulled into a knot at the top of his head, who watches Myla intently. His caramel-brown eyes seem to see deeper into her than she should like.

Once finished with her, he moves on to Lavinia, drawing runes across her brow. They can now enter the circle of worship. Myla nearly collapses within its perimeter, the weight of whatever brews within becoming something primal. It is not a burden she can stand beneath any longer. Her very skin feels as though it is vibrating, and the space between her collarbone and throat feels as though it is being twisted into knots and pulled too taut to withstand.

"Please," Lavinia asks, kneeling before the woman with the flute. "My daughter needs help."

The music ceases, the lights still, and the blurred bodies of the dancing druids appear to tower large over her body, curling overhead and upwards toward the trees and moon. With every breath, Myla's heart struggles to beat against the pressure of air and magic vying for space. Something otherworldly tugs at Myla's limbs, forcing her into an upright position, and her spine arches until it draws her chin to the night sky. Her web of veins turns golden, an interconnecting body of stars speckling her skin, and all at once, spilling forth from every pore in her body.

In unison, the druids shield their eyes, some turning their backs entirely. "The Spirit Mother is here—cast the runes," a voice commands from behind her, followed up by the clattering of runes in the dirt. "What is the Spirit Mother telling us?"

It is her mother's voice which she hears in response. *Her mother* reading runes. "There is anger in her."

"She must release it," the man with the charcoal kneels before Myla, pressing a hand flush against her neck. "Feel how she vibrates; her soul is poisoned with it. You must ask the Gods to help you, child."

There is something that fills the space where fear should be. Lavinia has often told Myla of when those too young experience the full force of their magic, they have paid the price with their lives. With the ground beneath her growing hot and at the mercy of her energy, and the glittering sky overhead, it is not fear Myla feels, but an insatiable need to scream. That anger is laced with the hope that she might release it all right now and annihilate herself, leaving her father with no more tradable goods. And the need to scream becomes less about reacting and more of a primal response beyond her control. Her lungs burn for it; they beg for it.

The Spirit Mother and the Gods beside her will be heard.

The furor coils within Myla's chest, twisting like a deranged beast beneath the surface of her sternum, slithering upwards to her throat. With each twist of magic, the pressure grows, and the *anger* expands. Rage within infuriation, years of condescending words and blatant disregard, all feast inside of her, fed by the will of the Gods.

Behind, a string of gasps can be heard as lightning cracks overhead and the sky itself splits in half, opening into a black abyss. Dust and leaves swirl around Myla, small and controlled at first but quickly growing into a tempest until nature's wrathful embrace encapsulates her. The Gods feel her fury, and they *fuel* it. They fuel it with the angry snarl of wolves within the cave and with the crumbling of rocks down the hillsides. They feed it with the rage of the wind as it whips between the tree trunks, creating a vicious wheezing. Even the earth is livid as it trembles beneath her, shuddering and causing those around her to bend, although she herself is upright and stretched as tall as possible, her fingers reaching for the moon. All her anger flexes in one solitary location, constricting her throat and taunting her until all restraint falls away. Myla's fingers ball into a fist, and with outstretched arms, she is ready to receive whatever the Gods send her way. An incensed scream erupts from her lungs. It is natural at first, her own voice crying for justice, demanding to be *seen*, until it is not so any longer. The anger of nature grows with the long, deep cry falling from the girl, and the light which normally fills her fingers trickles upwards and gathers at her neck, and her natural voice shifts into something deeper. Her voice and the Gods' above mingle into a cacophony.

The company of druids collapse, their foreheads to the ground, and press their hands to their ears, shielding themselves from the horrific release. A torment which feels like an eternity for the girl is but a few seconds.

And then the anger is gone.

The wailing of her lungs and the wind alike subside.

Sinking to her knees, a deep bone-weary fatigue washes over her body and Myla finds she still trembles. It is not magical tremors anymore; it is loneliness. A feeling made worse by the druids clustering together, their eyes wide with fear, some with trickles of blood running from their ears. Whispers break the silence, and they exchange uneasy glances. No one knows whether they ought to approach her and offer comfort or run from her.

If I could crawl out of my own skin and leave the shell behind, I would.

She takes no offense at the hollow, horrified stares.

What concerns her most is now everyone knows one thing for sure: this is the girl the king has been looking for—the girl he will pay dearly for.

This is the girl who is supposed to break the Blood Stealer's curse and free the land of his poison. Anyone in their right mind would run to the king without delay and hand her over.

"My love!" Lavinia pulls herself from the ground, wiping a streak of blood from her cheek, and moves to where her daughter sits cross-legged, watching the stars above, wondering who it is beyond their light that gave her so much power. A power she does not want.

Please. Take it back.

"Myla," Lavinia probes again. "What...what you just did it—it has not happened in centuries..." Her words are chilling. Although they are traced with admiration, there is also fear in them.

Myla looks sidelong at her mother, an emptiness seeping into her veins. "I do not care." And she doesn't. There is no part of her which feels astonished or proud or even fearful of the magic she has just channeled. She feels nothing but loneliness.

Take the anger away and there is no companion for the injustice.

"You should care very much," Lavinia says gently, stroking the top of her daughter's hand while casting weary glances at the cluster of people who watch her daughter still, frozen in shock.

"Why should I care?"

"Because if your father finds out," Lavinia quivers hesitantly, "he shall tell the king."

A sharp expression crosses Myla's otherwise unreadable face. An immediate understanding replaces that loneliness. Realization that she truly does have something the king might want settles into those lonely places and reinstates anger. "You won't let that happen to me."

Lavinia inhales sharply, and slowly releases Myla's hand, looking cautiously at the many witnesses to the phenomenon. None appear disturbed by any means, but each, in their own way, watches Myla with curiosity, some with distrust. "Should your father or the king find out, there will be nothing I can do, Myla."

Across the firelight, partially cloaked in the shadows of the cave, the boy with the caramel-brown eyes stands slowly. His inconspicuous clothing and unassuming air might allow him to go unnoticed, but Myla notices him.

He moves into the cluster of druids, his head tilted with what can only be read as concern. He looks from Myla to her mother, and then again at those around him. There is a sudden chill in the air despite the immense heat of the fire. He lifts his palms, and an iridescent ripple glides from his body like a wave, engulfing the druids around him. Where shock and awe had been, a look of daze takes over, and the Druids each blink slowly, shaking their heads in confusion before returning to their previous activities.

Startled, Myla stands quickly, dusting the skirt of her shift off before turning on her heels and retrieving her dress just outside the firelight. Whatever that boy just did, she forces it from her mind; she does not have time to try to understand.

Lavinia follows closely. "Are you ready to return then?"

"No," Myla responds.

Her voice quivers, but she doesn't dare crack.

There is no room for weakness.

Weakness will be her undoing.

"Then what are you doing?" Lavinia asks, reaching for her own dress, never once taking her eyes off her daughter.

"I'm walking away from you before I say things I shall regret."

Lavinia's expression is one of shock first and then concern. She brushes a stray tendril of graying hair before taking a deep breath. "Whatever could you be cross with me for?"

"For protecting him," Myla hisses, angrily stepping into her gown. "I am angry because you would rather I keep this tremendous secret so you do not have to stand up to Father. You would rather pretend like not telling him of a letter sooner in the day is your fault than stand up to him. You would allow him to strike us both, then serve wine at supper because his sober anger is somehow less tolerable than his *drunken* anger?" The words spill forth freely, and Myla has little control over stopping them. "You allow him to dress me as he pleases and let down my hems a season too soon and tell my lady to do my hair as though I am already a woman. You allowed my lady to report back to him on if I *bled* so he would know when I could marry. You know who he is and what he does, and yet you make no efforts to stop him, and if you do not try to stop him, how can I ever hope to stop him either? Let alone trust *you*."

The clearing has fallen silent now as her words disrupt what should be a peaceful meditation. Across from Myla, her mother's face stiffens with conflict. Though her eyelids are rimmed with glistening tears, the thin line stretching across her mouth is something else entirely. Myla recognizes the expression: loneliness.

"What would you have me do?"

"Leave him."

"It is not that simple," Lavinia replies, bending down to slip into her boots. "And I love your father. Even if leaving were an option, it is not one I would pick. I recommend you learn to appreciate what life can offer you."

Changing her tone and trying to convince Myla that love is the reason or even *a* reason to withstand her father has always been Lavinia's initial response when questioned. On any other night, Myla would bite her lip, lower her eyes, and ignore the weakness. Tonight, something has changed. The Gods spoke through her, and they continue to do so. The anger is not gone. It is still there, simmering and ready to bellow through her again.

Instead of releasing it once more, Myla allows it to make her brave. "I do not appreciate the idea that Father might marry me off to the king without asking me if that is what I want."

Lavinia grabs Myla's wrists firmly with her long, slender fingers, and brings her face closer. "Hear me now, daughter. If your father hears a single word of this, it is not a matter of *if* he tells the king. It is a matter of when. You *are* the woman the king is waiting to find, and I strongly recommend you take your lessons seriously and learn to hide this before it explodes like it did tonight."

Myla jerks her arm free of her mother's grasp and moves through the crowd to leave. She is nearly past the mysterious boy when he steps in her path.

There is something charismatic and lighthearted about him, and when he speaks, the same tone follows. "A girl who bleeds stars. How very uncommon."

"And you are?" Myla asks, glaring through squinted eyes.

"Someone who watched you call upon the Gods tonight."

Myla scoffs and tries to brush past when he reaches for her hand. "Do not fear, Girl Who Bleeds Stars. Your secret is safe for now."

The ground beneath her feet spirals into queasy motion, and the trees seem to turn well before Myla realizes she is the one moving, not them. She is not simply walking away from her mother, she is running, leaving her behind, and the warning and the cryptic boy as well.

Across the rocks and down the slope, through endless turns of trees and brambles, Myla runs until she cannot hear her mother calling after her. She cannot hear the chanting of the druids, nor their flutes and drums. She can only hear her heavy panting and the crunch of her feet against the forest floor. Until the forest thins and gradually becomes farmland, the clearing which yields most of Falkmere's crops and lies just behind the grove where Falkmere itself is built, in the shadow of the mountains and ancient woods. She keeps running, willing her body to carry itself through the fatigue until she makes it home. Only her father's manor is nowhere in sight. She has not run home; she has run right to the door of the smithy.

There is the sound of a low, solemn violin drifting through the open windows. The forge to the side of the smithy glows, nearly out for the night, and the sound of horses whinnying nearby joins the sweet melody from inside, creating an instant sense of peace.

That tranquility is quickly disrupted when Myla is forced to ask herself: *what the fuck am I doing there?*

Beneath her boots, the ground makes a squalling grind as she turns on her heels, not soon enough to miss the door swinging open. Wearing a tunic rolled above his forearms, bracers tinged and scuffed from the forge, and an unbuttoned vest, Bryar wobbles on one leg as he shoves the air-born foot into a tall boot, hollering over his shoulder, "I'll be back in a few hours." The statement is met with a chuckle and something about: *that's what you said last time, goodnight son.*

Wishing she was quick enough to think of some excuse to be standing there at this late hour, there is nothing to greet Bryar but a stupidly shocked look on her face when his gaze lands on her, curls a mess in the breeze and clothing covered in dust.

"Miss Alerys?"

For all the coin poured into lessons on etiquette and social niceties, Myla fears Maverick might have wasted his money and everyone's time. Standing with her mouth agape and that still, awful tension coiling in her chest is nothing short of humiliating.

"Miss Alerys..." Bryar repeats. This time it is not surprise in his voice, but concern. "Are you well?" He is quick to clear the space between them, and when he stands near, Myla can see the crease of his brows, the squint of his eyes. He searches her for outward signs of harm, his face dripping with concern.

"I—" Her words do not cooperate with the thoughts ambushing her mind. Does she tell him? Does she admit that she called lightning and wind from the lungs of the Gods from the sky? No. Instead, the tightness at her throat and the tension at home spring tears to her eyes.

"Myla..." He speaks once more as he raises a hand to her cheek. The touch startles her at first and she flinches, leaning away, but then draws close again, allowing his rough fingertip to trace away the tears. "What has happened?"

"I was in the woods," she offers instead. "I went to see the druids."

"The druids—why? Were you hurt?" There is an aggression which becomes him, and Bryar's voice drops an octave while his green eyes darken, a threat to all nearby: Gods help anyone who dares lay a finger on her, for he would hurt them in return.

Myla wonders what he would do if she named her father.

"No," Myla is quick to clarify, and all at once, the calm vanishes, replaced instead by the shaking once more in both her body and her voice. "*Bryar*—I can't be here right now."

Requiring no explanation, Bryar nods, his jaw set with unease. "Well, you cannot join me looking like that...come."

To her horror, he leads her inside toward the sound of the violin.

Sitting on the bottom bunk with a well-loved instrument nestled beneath his jaw is a man who looks shockingly like his son—or what his son might look like in thirty-some-odd years. He has shoulder-length hair neatly brushed and tucked behind his ears. It used to be jet black but now it is streaked with brilliant strands of silver, peppering the sideburns and along the scalp. He boasts a full beard along his sharp jawline, which might seem severe were it not for the soft smile it envelops. He seems content in solitude, and as a result, equally surprised when his son returns indoors not five minutes after departing. This time, accompanied by a young woman.

"Father." Bryar's tone is apprehensive at first, but with an expression she cannot decipher exchanged between the two, his tone shifts to friendliness. "This is the young woman I have told you about. Myla, this is my father, Caspian."

"The young lady from your lessons?" The older gentleman stands slowly, absently placing his violin on the pillow behind him. "The...*noble* lady?"

Myla must look up at him now as he towers a few heads higher than her. He's taller even than her father. Her stomach twists with uncertainty. Her gaze flicks to his hands, which are folded gently at waist level. They are huge. For a moment, she wonders if Bryar has ever felt the back of them.

Before she can give any more thought to if Caspian is kind or not, Bryar nervously shoves his sleeves above his elbows, watching the space between his father and friend as they size one another up.

Myla clasps her hands before her, not sure if she should curtsy or run out the door. She chooses the former, hoping to maintain some dignity despite the tear-streaked face and wild hair. "Sir," she greets, risking a sidelong glance at Bryar, who appears equally apprehensive. "Apologies for the intrusion."

"It is a pleasure," he finally answers, a cautiously jovial expression bringing light to his green eyes. Eyes which he seems to have passed on to his son. "Though I must apologize for my surprise. It is not often we entertain ladies of society." Grinning at his son briefly, Bryar's father extends his hand. "Please, call me Caspian. And at the risk of sounding rude, can someone explain to me why we have such a fine visitor at this hour?"

Bryar clears his throat and moves toward a chest at the foot of the bunkbeds. "Miss Alerys will be joining me on my walk tonight, but I am afraid she might draw attention in her...current condition."

Bryar lifts the trunk's lid with a ghastly creak, and Myla watches as he retrieves a plain, faded blue dress. "I thought she might borrow this?"

Caspian nods slowly at first, then more assuring with another glance Myla's way. "I suppose a nobleman's daughter in a tavern might catch some attention—I daresay," Caspian says with a start. "Would your father approve?" He looks at Myla. "I do not wish to see you come to any trouble...nor my son." The latter is spoken with a heaviness that can only be interpreted as a plea. *Please do not get my son in trouble.*

"You are most right, sir," Myla agrees, taking a few slow steps backwards. "I am so sorry. I should not have come."

The trunk falls closed with a startling *bang*, and Bryar takes a few swift steps toward her. "No, Myla—"

Caspian glares at his son, the familiarity not going unnoticed.

Bryar quickly clears his throat, pushing loose curls from his brow with a cringe. "*Miss Alerys.* It is all right. I will walk you home. You should not be alone at this hour."

Caspian nods in approval now, casting a half-smile Myla's way. "Please," he offers the dress Bryar abandoned by the chest. "Wear this on your way; it will do no good drawing attention to yourself."

Myla is left alone in the room when both men step outside to offer her privacy. The dress in her hands is rough, crudely spun, but clean and free of stains. Whoever wore it before took care of their belongings. Myla can only assume it belonged to Bryar's stepmother.

She is quick to change and joins them shortly, uncomfortable when it is obvious she has interrupted a serious discussion. Her appearance in the smithy doorway instantly brings a halt to what might be interpreted as a whispered argument before they greet her with forced smiles. No more words are exchanged. Caspian presses a firm hand on his son's shoulder. More cryptic glances are passed between the two—their own language, it might seem—and then with a final pat and a courteous smile her way, Caspian disappears inside.

"Have I made your father cross with you?" Myla asks, fidgeting with the sleeves of the gown.

Bryar conducts a brief examination of her before taking her hand and pulling her into the cover of the smithy, encouraging her to sit on the bench beside the forge. His touch is electric to begin with, hands rough with work wrapped warmly around hers, but it is even more so when he moves to stand beside her, lifting her thick hair away from her warm neck. "My father is never cross with me. It is more like cumbersome words of advice paired with heavy sighs when it turns out he is right, and I am wrong."

Clumsily, he begins alternating thick strands of her hair back and forth, and it takes Myla a moment of confusion to realize he is braiding her hair.

"Where did you learn to do this?" she asks, steadying her breath as his casts warmth on her shoulders while his knuckles lightly graze her back, working downwards toward the long ends of her hair.

"My mother."

"Your mother left you." Myla counters, her words met with a chuckle.

"My stepmother, that is."

"You don't mind me wearing her dress?" she asks, attempting to turn and look at him.

Bryar turns her head to face forward, his lower lip captured in a focused bite between his teeth. "Dead people do not care about such things, so why should I?"

Myla is acutely aware of the way the rough fabric rubs against her skin. Wearing a dead person's dress minimizes the anxiety in her chest. Although she has an asshole for a father and a coward for a mother, at least she is not dead. Things could be worse. "And your father does not mind me wearing his dead wife's dress?"

Two strong hands grasp her shoulders, turning her to face him. "For a noble woman, you have the most impolite way of talking." Bryar flashes half a smile at her, which disappears quickly. He reaches behind her, swiping the braid gently over her shoulder, and for a brief moment, she imagines his hand has lingered a little longer than it does. "My father does not mind. He would rather you not draw attention where it should not be."

"Why the braid?" Myla asks, touching her hair now as though it is more precious than it was a moment ago.

"Because. Wearing a poor woman's dress does not do enough to make you unrecognizable. Your hair..." He touches the end of the braid again before clearing his throat and stepping a respectful distance back. "It is recognizable to anyone, even the drunk."

"I am not worried about drunkards," Myla answers, hugging the finer gown to her chest. "You are only walking me home."

"No," Bryar corrects, turning and walking toward the heart of Falkmere, motioning for her to follow him up the cobblestone street. "I am not." And for the first time, the son defies his father.

It feels like a crime to have never seen the city like this. Falkmere transforms into an entirely different landscape at night. During the day, the stone buildings and streets layered one on top of the other, built upward along the cliffside of the mountain, seem to blend in with the natural world around it. Moss coats almost every stone surface, and ferns plume sporadically, creating a magical wonderland of greenery. But at night, the tiered layout of the city draws the eyes toward the sky, where the lanterns and torches might be mistaken for stars overhead. Admittedly, Myla has never even been to this portion of Falkmere before. This is the deepest part of the city, opposite the palace and even further from where the institute is. It is where paper goods and materials for sewing might be purchased. Any wares and goods found in her home were likely purchased here, just not by her.

There is an inn at the top of the steep incline, which they walk toward. Just as the path curves to climb even higher and deeper into the city, the tall building is set into the edge of the cliff, begging Myla to wonder how long it took the architects to etch buildings into the stone. A swinging sign hangs above the door, creaking rhythmically in the gentle breeze. They pass the inn and move in a hairpin turn upward. To their right now is the edge of the road, which looks directly over the rooftops beneath them. People pass, some in swarms and others alone. Some jovial and moving aimlessly, caught up in their conversations, while others move with purpose, their heads down and their mouths set in serious lines. After walking in silence for ten minutes, Myla glances to her right where Bryar walks, a barrier between herself and the pitiful stone ledge which supposedly serves as a stop between themselves and a steep fall.

While Myla wants to blurt, *This seems like a terrible place for a tavern to let out. I wonder how many drunks have tumbled over…*She asks instead, "Your father allows you to go to taverns alone late at night?"

Bryar shakes his head. "Not exactly." A cart led by a cranky mule moves slowly toward them, and his hand wraps around her shoulder, pulling her out of the way before releasing her. "I am supposed to be meeting with some friends. They are joining the king's guard, and their fathers bought them commissions. I want to join, and my father told me to learn what I could from them tonight and report back to him."

"Isn't that why you are training at the institute?"

"Yes," he replies. "But we can only do so much without a commission. I can be the most skilled swordsman, but it will not do me any good if I do not have the uniform and the letter."

"So, your friends have gathered the information for you? Can't you speak to a recruiter yourself?"

Bryar shakes his head. "Lately, the king is only accepting men of a certain caliber."

"A caliber that you are not?"

Another grin. Bryar smiles at everything, even conversations of status—specifically status that he does not have. How does he smile so much when there is an abundance of terrible things surrounding him? Shitty mothers who leave, wonderful mothers who die, and all the while, Bryar Monroe smiles. "A caliber that the law *says* I am not."

For once, she smiles back.

And sparks something in him, the boyish grin transforms, and he watches her a second too long. His inflection shifts, becoming soft. Soft like his eyes. It is kind. It cares. It does not hold expectations, just the softness. "Why did you come to me tonight?"

Troubled blue eyes analyze the warm space, small as it is, between herself and the safe green ones opposite. At last, she responds. "I could not go anywhere else, and knew for sure that I would find what I needed there."

CHAPTER 8

PRESENT

"THE GODS ARE CRYING," Caspian whispers, holding Aidan close to him as the two brothers shiver in the pelting rain. "It's okay for you to cry, too."

The storm falls in freezing splats now, sending a sizzling steam into the mid-afternoon sky as the last of the fires are drenched. Both boys sit where their mother left them, Elsa and Ethstan standing beside them, wearing solemn expressions. Neither one is quite sure what to do nor how to act. In every direction is chaos. Villagers run in frenzied directions, some with purpose and others in panic.

Myla doubts her legs will carry her to where her sons are, and yet miraculously, they do. With each breath, she strains to listen, hoping she will detect some sign of life from Elenore, but the silence taunts her. The wondering is like a knife in her chest, cutting her heart in half so she can bleed out every single one of her worst nightmares.

"Come." Her voice is cold as metal, wrought with a stone-like strength, unrecognizable to herself. There is no room for tears, the Gods' or her own. There is no time to stand still or worry in one place. She must worry while she rides. "We leave now."

"I cannot hear Elenore," Aidan says again, his eyes swollen with tears which streak down his ash-covered cheeks. He endures a panic all too real for a child of his age. Never in his life has he been separated from his twin until now. Aidan without Elenore is like an ocean without water: simply preposterous. "I keep trying, but I cannot hear her," he continues, tugging at Myla's skirt with concern. "Mama, where is Elenore?"

Caspian grips his brother's hand and pulls the boy up. Both of her sons wear signs of battle. They are covered in smoke and a few red-hot burns. Aidan's hands tremble with the exertion of magic he is far too young to summon, and Caspian slumps beneath the exhaustion of channeling the Restorer's magic. A power she watched drain Caius repeatedly. A divine magic intended to annihilate the grossest of evils and restore goodness in one fell swoop. As a full-grown man, even Caius felt the consequences of carrying a God's abilities. Caspian should never have tried to use it. Though he failed to truly conjure, his body looks slight beneath its lingering effects.

Both boys look to Myla for answers and reassurance she simply cannot give. Instead, she turns to Ethstan and nudges her sons in his direction. "Fetch their cloaks and riding boots. We have a long journey ahead of us."

"I should go—now," Bryar spits angrily, staring in the direction Elenore has presumably gone.

"No," Myla quivers, though everything inside her screams *yes*. She longs to abandon logic, chase the feeling of fear, and search every inch of the forest in a panic. "We do not know who is out there and if they are counting on us thinning ourselves out. We stay together."

It is less than ten minutes later when riders and their horses leave Old Falkmere. There are twenty-six in the company, including the last four of the mercenaries who Bryar has insisted on holding captive until Elenore is found.

Caspian is tucked warmly in front of Myla, his tiny, gloved hands resting on the horn of the saddle just atop hers. He trembles, and she wonders if it is cold or fear. Whatever it is, she too trembles. The night air bites savagely against exposed skin, and it is not kind to them given the speed at which the horses gallop. These woods have always been a place of peace and answers for Myla. But tonight, somewhere against the backdrop of darkness and tangling branches, is her daughter. Not knowing her condition, nor the disposition of her captor, drives surges of panic through Myla's chest, only made worse with the torturous knowledge that none in the family can hear the girl. Her little visions splashing across the brain at inconvenient times and bursts of thoughts and questions originating from the child—once a nuisance at times—are now the only thing Myla longs for. Some thought or vision that might tell her Elenore is alive.

Show me. Where are you, Elle?

But as the minutes pass into hours along the road to New Falkmere, nothing comes.

No sounds.

No visions.

No little voice saying, "Mama."

So, when Imogene returns, her wings drooping in despair, to report that she has found no camp along the road to New Falkmere, urgency dissolves into something more terrible: hopelessness.

"You have lied to me," Myla hisses over her shoulder at the weary row of captives being dragged mercilessly behind the fast-moving horses. "You *will* suffer for your loose and lying tongues."

Nothing but agonizing silence can be heard as the horses slow to a canter, Bryar intently listening as Aidan bounces, limp with sleep, against his chest. With one arm wrapped firmly around his son, and the other gripping the reins, Bryar watches the road ahead. He is fixated on every detail, every flash of motion and snap of branches within the trees; nothing is lost on him. He has shifted from father to warrior now, every instinct within him geared toward surviving and *saving*. With soldiers, friends, and prisoners alike behind them, riding deeper into the darkness of the night, they watch the road ahead, hoping with every passing moment that a little, curly-haired girl will step out onto the path and smile at them.

She would say, "Don't worry, Mama, I was only playing." They would hold her close and thank the Gods she was safe. They would swear to never let her out of their sight again, but of course they would, because she would have a whole life ahead of her. She would have adventures and feasts and love to experience. She would have fights with her brothers and arguments with her parents. She would have a beautiful love story, and maybe she would even have children. Elenore would have a long life. All she would have to do is step onto the road and return to her parents.

But she does not.

And when at last they do see a tall, lumbering figure in the road before them, the earth seems to crack wide beneath their feet, unleashing an angry, grievous cry. The trees curl inward, making the forest seem small and hot and insufferable. Only it is not the trees curling, but their world shattering around them, crumbling on the memory of those little curls and tiny bare feet. It is not the earth crying, and it is certainly not the Gods crying either. It is Myla, weak in the stomach and barely breathing, falling from her horse to run toward the shape of Rhyland.

In his arms is a small, swaddled body.

"Myla," Bryar chokes, quickly dismounting to chase after her. "Stop!" He seizes her, pulling her to a halt, his features full of devastation he is not yet ready to face. Everything in his eyes begs her not to move a muscle, not to confirm anything so that they can exist there together, both stupidly lost in the hope of their daughter's future.

"I cannot," Myla coughs as a sob catches in her throat, gripping his hands. "Our *daughter*, Bryar—"

Rhyland stops several paces away, close enough for the swelling beneath his eyes and the trembling of his mouth to cause a lurch in

Myla's stomach. "I was with my men when I noticed Imogene flying overhead, and I knew something was amiss." He chokes on his words, offering a weak shrug. "So, I realized I had to return immediately and...I found her about a mile back," he manages before his features crumple, swallowed in a thick sob. "I am so sorry."

"What..." Myla stumbles to where he stands, tripping over her skirts as they swish between her legs violently. "No...no, this cannot be—she was supposed to dance and have treats...I promised to read her story." Myla moves to brush the cloak from around the child's body, but Rhyland stays her hand.

"Please do not look, Myla. This is not your daughter anymore." His voice cracks as he reaches beneath the shroud, revealing a tiny hand, blue with an unnatural frost. Her fingertips are peaked with icicles, and around her wrist is an aquamarine bracelet.

Involuntarily, Myla screams, the rasping in her throat feeling like a million angry daggers. Visions of that little hand curled around a hairbrush too big for her hold, or linked in her father's as they walk, and petite fingers wiggling and outstretched as high as they can reach, begging to be held by her mother, all confuse Myla's mind as she tries to recognize the hand and make sense of its purpose now. As her gaze moves from Elenore's hand to the rest of her, shrouded in Rhyland's cloak, anguish grapples at her belly, and Myla sobs as she reaches for the body, pulling Elenore to her breast. She hits the ground with a thud, cradling her daughter, unaware of anything around her. She cannot hear beyond her own wheezing, but behind her, Elsa chokes on a silent sob as she holds Caspian and Aidan to her chest, shielding their eyes.

She cannot hear the angry cries of her husband as he turns, pulling the mercenaries to their knees. She cannot see the way his eyes blur with tears, reflecting the hot blast of vengeful fire which turns his prisoners into puddles of flesh. Exactly like she promised them he would. There is nothing and no one but mother and daughter.

The day Elenore was born, Myla held her to her chest and promised to always keep her safe. Here, she cradles her daughter again, wishing she could have kept that promise.

The sun sets on Old Falkmere with a weight which crushes the hope it is so accustomed to. There is no gentle sunset with hues of pastel orange and purple. The sky churns black, like the bile of hell has reached the heavens and loses its acid on that sacred place.

As independent search parties comprised of Old Falkmere citizens, soldiers, and the family return to the ruins, bearing grief and the body of Elenore, the lack of a sunset is a harsh visualization of the ending which has occurred.

Bryar walks slowly with Elenore cradled in his arms. His head hangs low, his swollen eyes fixed on the frame of his tiny child. If one were to look further beyond his grief, they would see anger churning in his eyes, rage chewing between his teeth, and wrath turning to iron in his jawline. The charred skeletons of the town's structures frame him eerily, and a silence looms over those watching as he carries his daughter home.

Behind, Myla trails on foot, holding the reins of her husband's horse, where Aidan and Caspian sit, both sobbing. Across her skin is a constellation of dim lights. Perhaps it is her magic trying to peek through, to give way for the inexplicable pain within. To those watching, it looks more like her magic is dying along with her child. The lights which flickered so brightly with heavy emotion, now pulse barely visible.

Perhaps, the absence of light is a tribute to the brightest of them all being stolen so violently from a life that should have been hers.

Perhaps a mother's light must travel with her child's soul and see it through the darkness of death.

It is a sad procession, and of all the battles lost over the last few years, this is the most devastating. When even children fall, one must ask themselves if the fight is even worth it. To every mother watching as Myla passes, trudging through the tears of her husband spilled in the dirt before her, the answer is no.

A sister for her brother's throne.

A twin to bury the dagger of a boundless thirst for power.

Whoever is responsible will pay with his head.

CHAPTER 9

PAST: MYLA, FIFTEEN

TAVERNS ARE STRANGE PLACES. Men and women alike seem less concerned with propriety. The surfaces are sticky with ale, and the music is far too loud. The darkest corners move with undulating figures which Myla ignores, and the lantern lights flicker at the center of the room, casting shadows in every direction. As a smiling young woman with much of her bosom exposed brushes a friendly hand across Bryar's shoulder, Myla decides that the barmaids are far too friendly with their patrons.

Nevertheless, Myla loves the energy. It is not simply loose; it is free.

"Don't drink the ale here," Bryar says. "It's too watered down for the price."

Myla grins at him. "The buzz-to-coin-ratio is off?"

Bryar chuckles and takes her hand, pulling her through a crowd of drunk men. "What would a noble girl like yourself know of being tankard?"

"Tankard?" Myla questions, sidestepping a woman carrying a stack of empty glasses nimbly despite the voluptuous jiggle of exposed breasts. *How the fuck do those not wobble her off balance?*

"Drunk as a wheelbarrow," Bryar answers over his shoulder, noting the sheepish grin on Myla's face as she watches the curvy barmaid pass.

"Oh—well, if only you knew Elsa, then you would understand."

"Who is Elsa?"

"She is my best friend. You will probably meet her when my father wants her to spy on me."

Bryar stops, allowing a group to cross their path. "I assume as your best friend, she will do the opposite?"

"I am counting on it." They exchange a knowing glance, and Myla isn't sure if it is the heat of the tavern or her comment, but his cheeks redden.

In a corner booth, two young men sit, clanking metal mugs against one another. The first boy is thin and tan. His rusty-blonde hair hangs in his cheery eyes, which dance across the room already dazed with too much drink. He seems lighthearted—as far from serious as one could get. Myla immediately wonders how such a skinny, cheerful youth would be accepted into the King's Guard.

The second boy has caramel-brown eyes and dark hair pulled into a tight bun. Myla stiffens. He is no longer wearing a simple tunic—he is dressed like his peers now. But he is undoubtedly the young man from the gathering.

He does not address her nor act as though they have met. He does the opposite. Both boys let out a hearty cheer in greeting, standing to slap one another on the backs in some form of friendly hug.

Commoners have the strangest ways of saying hello. If this were a dinner party at her father's estate, bows, curtsies, and a demure "it's a pleasure to see you" would be exchanged.

Myla prefers Bryar's way.

"Myla," he says, looking at her. "These are my friends—Callum." The lighter-haired boy reaches out to shake her hand. Myla accepts with a flustered smile. "—and this is Rhyland."

Rhyland. The boy from the woods. The boy who shakes her hand and acts as though he did not speak to her two hours prior. "You brought a girl," he says instead. "Why is there a girl at our boy's night?"

Though pointed, the question is not asked in an unfriendly way; rather, it is a curiosity for which both of his friends seek an explanation.

Bryar nervously runs a hand through his hair and sits, patting the seat beside him for her to join. Clearly unsure of what excuse to offer, he says, "We go to the institute together—I ran into her on the way here."

Callum reclines lazily. Something about him is so effortless. He nudges Bryar from across the table, offering his mug to share. "See, Bryar, I told you! You wouldn't be the only commoner at the institute!"

Myla grins and, just as Bryar is about to speak, she intercepts, "My father is Maverick Alerys. You may have heard of him; he is the king's head of trade."

"You mean the fucker who traded across the Thalinir Sea one type of fish for the other?" Callum and Rhyland laugh, both shaking their heads in confusion.

"Oh," Rhyland says, stroking his chin while imitating an adult man with a full beard. "Our fish have gotten boring. Let me inflate the prices at the fish market with these less fresh, fancier, smaller fish and further starve out our lower-class population."

Callum belts into laughter, slamming his drink on the table boisterously. "I bet the fellow who agreed to the deal got all sorts of curious looks when he walked in with an ugly cart of week-old fish thinking he had struck a good bargain."

Rhyland nods, oblivious to Myla who sits watching with an unreadable expression. "Imagine, the only thing you have to do in a day is strike terrible bargains and convince people it was a good idea."

"I would die young and unsatisfied," Rhyland agrees before they both notice Bryar's cold gaze and cease the taunting.

With raised eyebrows and an unimpressed look, Myla leans forward, pressing her elbows into the table. "I choked on a fishbone from my father's terrible trade. I *almost* died young and unsatisfied because of him."

There is a silence as the three boys surrounding her are unsure if it is appropriate to react or speak. Then Myla smiles, the coldness of her expression melting away, and the three boys erupt in laughter.

"I like her," Callum admits to Bryar. "She can stay, even though she is of noble birth." He takes a long swallow of his ale, then speaks again. "So, what is a girl like you doing out here—at night nonetheless—with this imbecile?" He gestures toward Bryar, then settles back into his seat, awaiting a response.

Myla glances warily at Rhyland, who conveniently stares into his mug.

He is not going to tell... She is amazed at his silence and concerned in the same hand. Why would he hold on to such a secret? If she were not here, would he be spilling the information to his friends?

"I was out already, and we ran into each other," she says finally, averting her gaze as Rhyland's eyes flick to hers. The exchange does not go unnoticed, and the table shifts awkwardly before Rhyland looks to Callum and redirects the conversation entirely.

Bryar takes advantage of his friends' singular exchange and leans closer, whispering to her. "Did I miss something?"

With a quick nod, Myla stands. "Yes, I am thirsty."

Bryar follows with a dismissive shrug at Callum and Rhyland, who watch her departure. "Wait—what happened?"

Once out of earshot from Callum and Rhyland, who begin conversing with each other, Myla turns. "Your friend. He was at the Druid's Cave tonight."

"Rhyland?"

"Yes."

Bryar shrugs. "Well, that does not surprise me. His family worships the old Gods too..."

"Yes, but—"

"Your family does not openly worship the old Gods?" Bryar guesses, and Myla accepts his suggestion as it is better than telling him the truth. "Rhyland is a trustworthy person, Myla. He also can erase memories...if...anyone saw you there that should not have?"

Realization washes over her.

The iridescent ripple she saw.

His promise that her secret was safe 'for now'.

Gods. He probably thinks that is why I was crying in front of his house. Fucking pathetic. Better than the real reason though.

The corner of Bryar's mouth twitches, pulling her back to the present. "You can trust both of my friends. I would not introduce you to anyone who might harm you. Now will you come sit back down with me?"

"Yes," Myla agrees. "But first, I need a drink."

As Bryar warned, the ale is grossly watered down, but Callum has a flask of something stronger, which he is quick to pour into each mug. Soon enough the party of four is, as Bryar originally put it, completely tankard. Despite the many, many evenings spent in her room with Elsa and too many glasses of port, this is a different sensation entirely. It is the knowledge that her mother is no doubt frantically searching for her and would never think of looking here. The exhilaration, perhaps? Maybe it is the way the room starts to swirl, and the lighthearted conversation carrying her through her bad mood quickly. Or is it the warm, soft, comforting boy sitting next to her, who, at some point in the last hour, has taken hold of her hand, and now sits reclined with her fingers laced between his? Whatever it is, her stomach is a tangle of fluttering.

When, at last, it is time for the group to part ways, Callum and Bryar stand first, and Myla takes advantage of the moment and looks across the table at Rhyland. She finds he is already looking at her.

"Girl Who Bleeds Stars," he whispers. "I made them forget—the druids. They are none the wiser."

"Bryar told me that is what you do," she responds, leaning closer. "I cannot thank you enough...but I must ask one more favor of you. My mother, can you make her forget too?"

Rhyland nods. "If you can arrange an inconspicuous meeting, I can make her forget."

No questions asked.

Although completely out of character, likely attributed to the alcohol, Myla stands as Rhyland does and bends forward to hug him. "I do not think you realize how you have saved me tonight."

The taller boy, startled at first, returns the embrace with a nervous laugh. "The look on your face in the woods was all I needed to know that it was urgent. Maybe someday you will tell me more. For now...uh..." he gestures to Bryar, who seems to be waiting for her. "I think you're at risk of violating his curfew."

"Shit," Myla remembers with a start that Bryar had told his father he was only walking her home.

Rhyland grins and offers a brief wave goodbye, then leaves.

"Ready?" Bryar asks as they reenter the brisk evening. "I want to see you home, so we should hurry."

"I wouldn't dare keep you out any later," Myla insists. "Don't worry about me. I can make my way home."

Bryar shakes his head and starts walking back down the cobblestone street. "That is just it. I do worry about you, and I think you like that. Now, which way to your house?"

What a confounding boy. "This way." Myla strides beside him, and together they make their way down the steep road, which gradually leads back through the farmland and into the noble's neighborhood where they no longer blend in. Instead, they both stand out, and Myla is thankful that most everyone is likely abed at this hour and as a result, aren't liable to see them.

"It is quicker if we cut through this field." She directs him off the main road and over a bridge, which crosses the river to the sea. The light of the street-lanterns fades until there is nothing but moonlight to guide them.

"Tomorrow, will you ask Rhyland to come to our training session? I have asked a favor of him."

"I will see to it," Bryar answers, though his brow furrows in question, he does not probe. It is a courtesy Myla has never been allowed before: her privacy.

"Thank you—for tonight, I mean. I know you did not accomplish what you intended to do tonight."

"It was worth it," he responds. "I can talk to them about commissions tomorrow." He glances sideways at her before clearing his throat. "Will you be in much trouble tonight?"

"Probably about as much as you will be. It is nearly dawn." Myla pauses briefly before allowing the alcohol to overstep once more. "But like you said, it was worth it." She hardly recognizes the tone in her own voice. What *is that?* With a heavy dose of self-loathing and disgust, Myla clasps her hands together, relying on her own restraint far too much. Nothing good could come of wanting this boy the way she does.

Then again, nothing good comes of anything she does *not* want either.

Bryar must see the way she twists her hands nervously, for he stops walking, forcing her to do the same if they are to stay together. "We crossed boundaries tonight. *Social*...boundaries, that is."

Myla sucks in a breath and nods in agreement. He's the smart one, clearly. She braces herself for the letdown. "Yes, I suppose we have."

"Is it such a bad thing?" He is all boy again with his unruly curls and the way his eyebrows tilt almost mischievously.

"Yes," Myla sighs, trying desperately not to smile back at him. "I think it is a really terrible thing." She glances to the side, taking note of the windows in her father's house. No light shines behind them. The house is asleep.

He grins now, taking one step closer to her before shoving his hands in his pockets. His own form of restraint, it would seem. "You are terrible at saying what you are actually thinking. Let's play a game." He pivots on his feet, taller for a moment, then back to his natural height, excitement for the game at hand.

"What game is that?"

"A game where we both say what we are thinking, *honestly*. I will go first." There is a sparkle in his earthy-green eyes as he continues. "I *think* you hide your feelings behind anger and indifference because at home, feeling is dangerous. But I think it is important for you to know that with me, *all* of you is safe. Including your feelings." Another step closer, and he whispers this time. "Your turn."

Myla's breath hitches and her hands loosen, falling helplessly at her side. "How do you expect me to follow that up?" She laughs, all to mask the thud of her heart and the heat rising in her cheeks. He stands much too close now, and it takes every drop of self-control to not reach out and take his hands again.

"Honestly," is his only response.

Honestly.

"Fuck," she whispers now, pressing fingers to her temples. With a deep breath inward, Myla speaks, cursing herself before the words are even out. "Well honestly, I can't *think* of anything right now because all I want to do is kiss you."

The air stills. Criminally. Nature has stopped to listen to her say things proper noblewomen are not supposed to say. A cricket chirps, but she interprets it as a mocking laugh.

But he is not laughing. Smiling? Maybe. Yes, it is a smile, she concludes. But it is not his usual boyish smile. It is warm and inviting. It is safe. His expression welcomes her closer and calls to the neglected pieces inside her to seek refuge in his haven.

So, she steps forward, hesitant at first, unsure of how to navigate such uncharted territory. When his hands, also unsure, take hold of her waist and clumsily pull her toward him, she finds their bodies are pressed flush, one against the other. Close enough to feel the way his chest heaves against hers.

He is nervous.

Even so, when she rolls onto her tiptoes, he lowers his face to hers and something electric occurs. His lips are warm against hers. They are slow and gentle. They hold so much promise, and with them comes the feelings. Every single feeling she has been rejecting in the last few weeks. The glances, the slight touches, the moments alone where they were supposed to be studying, but they were learning about each other instead. All of it melts into a warm glow with his lips on hers.

It is drifting, trembling, and splitting wide open all at once.

This is their secret. This potentially ruinous thing that feels more powerful than the lightning and the Voice of the Gods put together, is something that belongs only to them.

Her father cannot take it from her.

Yet Bryar can give it to her. Again and again. And he does. Her hands knot in his tunic, holding him close, and his palms press steadily against her back. When the tension building begins to feel *truly* ruinous, Bryar pulls away breathlessly, flashing her that beautiful smile, something she sees differently all at once—now that she is more closely acquainted with his lips.

"I like your attempt at honesty...I will see you later at practice." With one last kiss, he turns away.

Something about the idea of swordplay now seems so extremely dangerous.

CHAPTER 10

PRESENT

THE STANDSTILL WHICH FOLLOWS in the wake of tragedy is yet another loss. A loss of both gained ground and time spent trying to win back Caspian's throne. All of it trickles into the periphery of immense, all-consuming grief. While life in Old Falkmere used to bustle with purpose and dignity, a shadow of nothingness hangs over it now.

Three days have passed since Elenore's murder. The Ashborn have returned home, leaving Old Falkmere to its grievous silence, Bryar cannot coax his wife from their room. His heart is shattered, and he has no wish to complete his duties. Indeed, he would be in bed if one of them were not needed to run the palace.

Her armor and crown are discarded on the mannequin, hidden from all light and life by the heavy drapes pulled shut on the world. Buried deep within the large bed, which was once a place of play and passion, she lies with the furs drawn over her face so no one can see her tears.

Another morning dawns over their crumbling dreams, and he closes the door behind him, leaving Elsa to sit quietly with Myla so he can attend to their sons and try to set their armies right. Ethstan greets him at once.

"My lord," the old monk bows quickly before straightening as much as his old frame will allow. "I have the young masters started on their lessons and will take them to practice their riding once—"

"No," Bryar interrupts with a tone harsher than intended. He corrects himself before continuing, offering Ethstan an apologetic look. "They will not leave the palace. Do you hear me?"

Ethstan nods, a sad understanding blanketing his already meek countenance. "I am sorry. Yes, my lord, I will keep them inside."

With an expression caught somewhere between concern and aggravation, Bryar shakes his head and leaves Ethstan with final instructions. "I will be coming to collect them after I meet with the council. Let them know I will be there shortly? And Ethstan, do not worry about their lessons. Let them grieve."

With a bow, Ethstan departs, and Bryar moves through the halls of the palace to the doors separating him from the council members. A room full of men who will no doubt want answers from him. Where to send the troops, if they will finally advance on New Falkmere, and what will be done to ensure an ambush like the one that killed his daughter will never happen again. Bryar's throat tightens as he reaches for the door handle, stopped by the heaviness he carries with him everywhere. Guilt, so much of it threatening to crush him.

Guilt and grief: they make the perfect couple. The vile rot of death rises like sour bile in his throat, and Bryar leans a forehead against the door, his eyes squeezed shut as tears, riding the wave of something worse than sadness, threaten to spill freely, coaxed by an anger which simmers barely beneath the surface of his chest.

Visions of melting bodies do nothing to quench his need for more. More revenge, more answers. He wants this feeling to rage, loud and violent. He wants to kick down the door before him and leave with his wife's army on this very day. He wishes to lead them to whoever is responsible for taking his sunshine and plunging his family and kingdom into this undefeatable darkness.

Instead of satiating his thirst for vengeance, Bryar turns the handle with a trembling hand, pushing the door open and erasing all signs of emotion from his expression just in time to offer those gathered within the room an indifferent nod. The first face he sees is Lord Thurston. "Are your ships and armies ready?"

"They are, Your Grace."

He offers a brief nod before questioning the next council member. "And yours?"

Another answer in the affirmative.

Bryar looks from each and every face until he has gained assurance that his wife's council has not floundered in their absence. "Good. There will be no more waiting. Though delayed, our plan to storm New Falkmere shall stand. I want the troops ready to leave by tomorrow. I will lead the attack myself."

"Will Her Grace accompany us?" Rhyland asks now, a soul-deep sadness etched in the lines on his forehead.

Bryar turns to leave the room, shaking his head in response. "I do not know. Just...make sure everything is in order, alright?" He looks to Rhyland directly for this. Only a lifelong friend could read his expression. Desperation.

"I will," Rhyland says, quieter now as he steps toward his friend. Speaking as family, not a subordinate, Rhyland places a firm hand on Bryar's shoulder. "Go be with your wife."

"I cannot." Bryar's voice cracks and is quickly rectified. "My sons need me."

Elsa sits perched on the edge of the bed. The sobs have subsided into periodic sniffs, but Myla does not move. The blankets entrench her in her sorrow and, in so many ways, Elsa's presence is superfluous.

Nevertheless, she would not dream of leaving her friend in this room alone.

Over a decade earlier, she sat on Myla's bed while she cried. Those were vastly different circumstances and a vastly different type of pain, but pain, nonetheless. In every circumstance, it would seem knowing what to say is often impossible. Just *being* is often the answer.

"Darling," Elsa whispers after a time, coaxing the covers lower. "I do not see how you can properly draw breath under there."

The uncovered Myla is a slip of a ghost compared to who she was a week ago. A mane of dark, tangled hair falls across her crumpled frame, and the only color to her is around her eyes, which are red, swollen, and chafed. The sight is enough to bring tears to Elsa's eyes, and the anguish she witnesses is a grievous reminder of the days that followed Callum's death. Elsa's belly twists as she swallows her own experiences with loss. Myla held her against her chest for hours, stroking her hair and singing a song Elsa cannot recollect. All she remembers is the darkness she was swallowed in, and the gratitude she felt to see her friend there, unwavering, unafraid of the darkness she was joined in.

That is what friends do. They join you in your darkness, and they brave the horrors alongside you, so you do not have to do it alone. So, with a breath, Elsa continues, risking a gentle brush, clearing Myla's face of her tangled hair.

"I can say nothing," Elsa whispers as she moves to take Myla's hand, "but that I love you and you will survive this."

Slowly, one weak motion at a time, Myla sits, lifting her heavy eyes to meet Elsa's. The usually full features of her friend are gaunt now and twist as she breaks with the words into a choke of sobs. "And if I do not want to survive it?"

"Then I would say tough shit," Elsa responds with a tremble in her tone before squeezing Myla's hand a little tighter. "You have two sons who very much need their mother." Her voice is gentle and kind and gives way for all levels of emotion, but her words are firm, nonetheless. "You are to stay in this room for as long as you need, but I beg of you, do not stay any longer than that. For every moment you remain in here, Maverick is out there, believing he has won. And whoever is responsible for Elle's death believes they got away with it."

"He *has* won," Myla answers, hot tears streaking her splotched cheeks. "They *did* get away with it! She is..." Her words stop before *dead* can leave her lips; a reality Myla cannot seem to speak aloud. "They did get away with it," she repeats, her head drooping into her hands.

"No," Elsa responds with sharpness and certainty. "While you are still breathing and giving at least *some* part of yourself to your children, there is no room for you to concede any of those battles. Elenore deserves *much* more. Think, when you give yourself to your children—something he never did for you—you are breaking the cycles that Maverick started. Do not let him be the injury that cripples you into continuing that cycle."

A fresh stream of tears cascades down Myla's cheeks as her breath breaks into a sob and, beneath the surface of her skin, the little specks of starlight twinkle, begging to be released, to rage at the world. Elsa's gaze flickers briefly to the pulsing lights before her eyes meet Myla's again. "Come." She stands, reaching for Myla, though she recoils. "No, my love. You must let it out. Come."

Pulling the broken queen to her feet, Elsa reaches for a simple knit shawl and wraps it around Myla's shoulders. "It will do you no good to keep it all inside."

Together, ignoring the sympathetic gazes of the guards and house-maids alike, Elsa guides Myla outside the palace, where daylight greets her with harsh rays of sun spilling between the breaks in the clouds. Through the overgrowth of the garden, past the row of guards, who stand in a tighter formation than usual, and to the thickening of the dense woods behind the palace. They walk and Myla breathes, though every breath feels like a betrayal.

Pointing to the sky, Elsa directs Myla's attention. "You have been given a power which most do not possess. The Gods have chosen you as their vessel for this gift. When your daughter left this earth, I believe she went to them, and they are up there, holding her close. Now let out your anger and your tears so she might hear you again. Let her hear that her mother will not rest until those who harmed her are brought to justice, Myla. Crying will not bring your daughter's killer to justice."

When he enters, the room is quiet. Although play is certainly not what he expected to find, Aidan and Caspian asleep on the window seat is unforeseen. Yet there they are, curled up together, Aidan asleep on his big brother's shoulder. Ethstan sits in silence, a book in hand, abandoned to the task of watching the boys intently. Bryar doubts he has read much of anything given the way the book lies limp on his lap.

"Thank you," Bryar whispers. "You may go. I would like to be alone with them for a bit." As Ethstan stands, Bryar turns to the old man. "Have they said anything?"

"Not young Aidan," Ethstan says sadly. "He refuses to speak."

"And Cas?"

Ethstan's eyes sag as he averts his gaze. "Master Caspian asked if I would take him to train."

Bryar stiffens. "Did he say why?"

"Yes," Ethstan offers a brief nod. "He says his sister would not have been taken if he had been faster to kill their attackers."

Once Ethstan has removed himself and firmly closed the library door behind him, Bryar sits on the edge of the window seat, careful not to wake the boys as he does. Caspian's arms, bruised from exerting magic his small body should never have channeled, are wrapped tightly around Aidan, holding him so close. Nuzzled behind his knees is Prince Gourdy. Bryar's throat tightens.

"It's not your fault," he whispers, the words barely slipping past his lips before breaking entirely. "You are the *bravest* boys I know," he continues, far too quietly for any to hear him. "You did well, and I am proud of you. But it will never happen again," he says through gritted teeth. "I promise."

While his family finds respite from their grief in copious amounts of sleep, it would seem rest evades Bryar. Every time he closes his eyes, his mind plays tricks on him, convincing him that the natural sounds of the palace are intruders, or that the silence in the dead of night is because his family has been killed. The one time in the last three days he fell into a dream, his arms tingled with the memory of his daughter, unmoving beneath the sickening curse of death in his arms. That was enough alone to keep him from the unreliable jaws of slumber. His wife and sons run from near-constant torture into the safety of sleep, and he drowns in that same torture paired with exhaustion.

Yet here in this library, lulled by the fire and the illusion of peace, he is tempted to lie beside his sons and put his arms over them so he can sleep with them tucked safely there next to him. Nothing could possibly happen to them if he were holding them close, his body a shield from harm. Not a single soul is able break through his own fireproof body to harm them.

The thought lurches his stomach, and he squeezes his eyes shut, trying to unsee the little wrist with the aquamarine bracelet, for it reminds him of the first time he put it on her. Elenore's eyes shone with delight, and she never took it off. Now, it is sitting in a chest at the foot of Aidan's bed, for even he could not bear to look at it when Elsa offered it to him.

Brought back to the present by a heavy, sleepy sigh from Caspian, Bryar leans down to curl his body around the back of the older boy, careful not to disturb the cat, while resting his arm over both of them. They breathe in unison, their small forms heaving up and down peacefully, raising Bryar's arm with the motion. Little by little, the lightest parts of the room grow dark, and it feels like a long-awaited slumber falling over him. But the darkness continues in a pattern he recognizes. The light is being sucked from the atmosphere. Just as the darkness truly begins to take form as an early nightfall, the earth trembles and outside in the forest beyond the palace grounds, the trees whip violently. The unmistakable flash of blinding light leaks into the library accompanied by a startling, deeply mournful wail, which wakes the boys. First Caspian, whose icy-blue eyes fly open in fear, soothed only by a gentle touch from his father, and then Aidan, who sits upright, gripping his brother's shirt.

It is the sort of scream which hails from the open, bleeding wounds of a broken heart. There is nothing otherworldly about it yet. It is hers alone, forcefully thrown into the winds in hopes that the Gods will catch it and give her true release.

"What is that?" Caspian asks, turning in a panic to look out the window, stopped only by Bryar's hands over his eyes.

"Don't look, son." Bryar grimaces against the hot rays. "Cover your ears now."

Both boys obediently cup their hands over their ears just in time for the wailing to turn into a deep, terrible howl, the gift of deep anger from the Gods. The glass windowpanes rattle, and the stones beneath them shift with the trembling.

Everything within him wants to defy the forces of the Gods and stand, to run outside despite his sightlessness and find her, to hold her through the grief, but the tremors and the light and the aching of the cry brings him to his knees as he tucks the boys to his chest. There they stay, their eyes closed, faces pressed against him, and his hands covering their heads in an attempt to buffer the reverberations of the Voice of the Gods.

When it finally subsides and the earth stills and light disperses back into its natural state, Caspian lifts his head, glancing at his little brother who still trembles in his father's arms. "What was that?"

Bryar takes a deep breath and wipes the tears forming in his eyes before he answers the boy. "It was your mother."

"It's alright." To Bryar's surprise, Aidan speaks, lifting his little head cautiously. "She isn't going to hurt anyone. She is just sad."

A sting in his nose threatens more tears, but Bryar pinches his lips together, willing them to retreat. *He is too young to understand this already.* Nodding assuringly, he helps the boys stand. "That's right, she is sad."

Caspian does not let go of Bryar's hand once he is on his feet. Instead, he holds on tighter, looking up at Bryar with glistening eyes. "I am sad too, Father."

Reaching down, Bryar presses a gentle palm to Caspian's cheek. In the past, when faced with frightened children, Bryar would always be sure to seem braver or stronger even than he felt, if only to bring reassurance. For the first time in the boy's life, Bryar does not will himself to seem strong for the sake of comforting him. There is no good in hiding it. They are all hurting, and no amount of comfort or strength will take that away. "I know," his response is simple. "I'm also sad. We are all sad, and that is how it is going to be for a long time."

Aidan pulls his hand free and turns to look back out the window, quick to add, "That is how it is going to be *forever.*"

Yes. Bryar thinks, lifting Aidan into his arms. *I think this will hurt forever.*

They at last find sleep in the library, and Bryar finds relief in the silence. With his sons' warm bodies against him, his subconscious calls to him, lulling him back to the sweetness of memories. Instead of haunting him, his dreams offer him the kindness of a vision, so familiar, so taken for granted. He has just finished renewing their trade deals with Ivan. His family is nowhere in the Valyndor palace, and there is only one other place he can look for them: the library. His wife, nearly invisible thanks to a shroud of pillows and three toddlers on her lap, laughs with bright joy. *She is always smiling*, he thinks. *Why do I feel like I miss that?* Her eyes gleam as she looks up at him, struggling to contain all three of their children *and* the book she reads to them. Whatever story she is telling breaks the silence of the library, filling it with laughter. Elenore slips free of her mother's hold, nearly tripping on her skirt as she barrels into Bryar's arms the second she sees him.

"There you are, Daddy! I missed you!"

Though he is not quite sure why, a tear slips down the bridge of his nose, and Bryar buries his face in the mess of curls, breathing deeply and savoring the sweet smell of his daughter.

CHAPTER 11

PAST: MYLA, FIFTEEN

"YOU WERE GONE *ALL night*, Myla Alerys!" Lavinia hisses, sitting upright from her daughter's bed. "Do you know how worried I have been and—*what* are you wearing?" Lavinia propels herself from the blankets, and Myla immediately notices the puffy swell of her mother's eyelids, red with tears.

Myla flinches, startled by her mother's presence at all, let alone the undone state she is in now.

"I'm sorry," she replies, placing her nice gown on the edge of the bed with caution, as though any sudden movement might implode the room entirely. Nothing about her feels sorry though. *Well. I am sorry she is sad...but...*

Every single part of her vibrates with the residual effects of the kiss.

"'I'm sorry'? Is that all you have to offer me? A pathetic excuse for an apology? I ask again, what are you wearing?"

Myla stops short, glaring at her mother. She has been missing all night after what might be considered the worst revelation of her life. She did not send anyone to search for her daughter because, Gods forbid, Lavinia herself would have to be honest for once, and when Myla does return, all she truly wants to know is where the dress came from.

"I borrowed it from a tenant's daughter because mine got wet on my way back from Druid's Cave," she lies. The only thing worse than lying to her mother is for the one person who truly seems to care about her to be exposed and hurt because of it. She would rather make up a stupid lie than get Bryar into legal trouble for something a boy of a higher station would be merely reprimanded for.

Lavinia scoffs and stands, moving closer to Myla, causing her to shift uncomfortably. Can she see it? Can she tell that something is different? Before this evening, Myla had never even held a boy's hand, let alone kissed one. Nevertheless, she holds her mother's gaze, lest looking away be an admission of guilt. *Fuck. My lips feel swollen. Are they swollen? Maybe more red? Does mother know what kissed lips look like?* Irrational thoughts trail through her mind like a taunting parade, passing only once Lavinia's narrow eyes resume their natural shape.

"You will stay home. You are not to leave this house until Elsa has moved in next week and can accompany you everywhere."

"Mother!" Myla protests, following the angry woman across the room as she is about to leave. "I have lessons today!"

"They can wait until next week."

"They cannot, and you know why." Her voice is desperate now. "Please, Mother, I will go straight from lessons to home, but please don't risk everything because of this!"

Lavinia turns on her heels, gripping Myla's wrists tightly. "*You* are the one risking *everything*! Your anger is going to get the best of you soon enough."

"Please," Myla asks now, her voice level and her cheeks red with imminent tears. "Come with me then. Supervise my lessons and see me home."

Lavinia sighs, and a flicker of guilt and compassion washes over her features. She nods. "Alright. I will take you to your lessons, and we will come home directly."

That is all Myla needs. After a bath, where she refuses to let down her braid, Myla changes into a slim-fitting pair of black trousers and a long black vest, which stops a few inches above the knees. The vest buckles in intervals down the chest, and beneath it, she wears a draping white tunic loose enough for fluid motion. Finally, she slides on tall black boots and checks her reflection. She looks ready to train harder than she ever has. If she is going to stop men from using her, she must be ready to kill them if they won't take 'no' for an answer.

Lavinia's expression is less than approving when she sees Myla's attire, but she says nothing, and their walk to the institute is a quiet one. Perhaps it might be awkward and frustrating for Lavinia, but for Myla, it is a blessing. Each step brings them closer to her mother forgetting everything about last night.

When they finally arrive at the institute's entrance, Elsa walks briskly toward her, grinning vivaciously. "I knew you'd be here—" She takes note of Lavinia and flashes an even warmer smile. "Lady Alerys, what a pleasure! I just came to watch Myla's training. I have heard it is getting intense!"

Lavinia plasters a cordial smile on her face, well versed in the art of pretending to be happy, even when she is not. "Indeed, it is. From what I have been told, Myla is a natural."

As their conversation drags painfully through social niceties, Myla notices Bryar approaching with Callum and Rhyland. From behind Lavinia, she gives Elsa an urgent nod indoors and, like the reliable friend she is, the beautiful blonde girl directs Lavinia inside, without the latter realizing that her daughter does not follow.

With a breath of relief, Myla turns on her heels, nearly smacking into Callum, who seems almost too distracted by whatever is behind her to notice she is there.

"Ouch!" he exclaims, and Myla realizes she is standing on his foot.

"Well, pay more attention," she hisses, too relieved to see all three of them to be cross with him. "Rhyland," Myla takes a few steps closer.

"I am so glad you made it. Thank you...I need you to make her forget everything...the *whole* night. Not just the Druid's Cave."

Concern crosses Bryar's face, and his eyebrows furrow in a question, one which she answers with a slight nod.

"Easy enough," Rhyland responds, obviously perplexed by the desperation in her voice. "Mother isn't too fond of you out at all hours then, is she?"

"To say the least," Myla answers. "Come on, I need to get in there before she flattens the place." Myla turns to go in, and just as Callum and Rhyland pass her, Bryar grabs her hand, holding her back. "I need to go in," she whispers. "She is furious."

Bryar nods quickly. "No, I know. I am just wondering if...well, if it is safe for me to go in or if I should make myself scarce until Rhyland clears it all up?"

Myla's breath catches most inconveniently as she looks up at him. The sun casts a brilliant glow on his hair and shines a golden warmth on the freckles across his cheeks. Practice has just become a lot harder. "No—no," she says haltingly, pulling her hand free of his. "I didn't tell her about you...I would never do that."

He nods, relief flooding his face. "Alright then, you go ahead, and I will follow shortly." He smiles at her, and the stress slips away.

Elsa stands just inside with Lavinia as she admires the magnificence of the institute from indoors. After a moment of easy conversation, rushed slightly by Myla's urgency to get downstairs, the three begin the walk to the blademaster's arena, all the while Lavinia is questioning the need for such steep stairs.

The boys are already in the room when Myla opens the door, making way for her mother and Elsa. Roderick is handing Bryar a heavy steel blade and pointing this way and that, rambling on about angles and core strength when he sees his pupil and visitors.

"I see we have many onlookers today! We shall simply have to make it the most interesting session yet." Roderick bows to Lavinia. "Do I have the pleasure of speaking to Lady Alerys?"

"Indeed." Lavinia curtsies and extends a hand for the blademaster to kiss. "You have worked wonders for my daughter. I thank you."

"It is easy—look at her! She is smart *and* quick."

Lavinia smiles uneasily, nodding in conclusion to the conversation before moving to the side of the room and sitting on the stone bench. Rhyland conveniently stands a few feet away, keeping his face turned, so she does not recognize him.

"Center up!" Roderick commands, handing Myla an equally large blade to the one he gave Bryar. It is heavy, so her muscles engage immediately to hold it upright. "Feet," he commands calmly, watching in satisfaction as their feet align with their hips. "Very good, very good."

Myla shifts her weight from side to side, looking her opponent square in the eyes as she has been taught. Only this time, her opponent has held her by the hips and kissed her. He knows it, she knows it, and their eyes lock in a sort of teasing dance. Who will lunge first? Who will break the barrier of proximity and risk the tension imploding right there for all to see?

Bryar does with a sudden lunge which, in her state of distraction, nearly knocks her off balance. Their swords flash in the candlelight, and she recovers in the span of a breath, parrying his attack with a strong brace of her arm as his blade descends. They stand locked. Should either person shift, the blades would slip, and someone would lose the upper hand. His face is mere inches from hers, and Myla tunes out the boisterous cheers of Callum and Rhyland to hear his whisper.

"Your hair is still braided."

Myla musters her strength and pushes against him, propelling him in the opposite direction. She spins out to brace herself for a second attack. Her braid swings with the momentum, whipping against his shoulder. She smirks at him, careful to keep her features as unreadable as possible with her mother watching.

"You are too slow!" Roderick shouts from the sideline. The critique is aimed at her, and she ducks in time to miss the flat side of Bryar's blade. With his arms extended in full swing, Myla takes advantage of the opening and elbows him, creating a brief moment where she is able to get a full swing in at him. With a heave, she raises the blade above her head, but is quickly blocked by another flash of metal, followed immediately by a taunting smile from the curly-haired blacksmith. The urge to kiss him is replaced quickly with a need to see him sprawled on the ground, defeated and at her mercy. She lunges in one direction, misleading him before cutting through the air toward him, an assault he barely dodges.

Roderick now cheers, throwing his hands in the air. "Beautiful *feint*, beautiful!" Now clapping, he moves to the other side of the room, seeking a different vantage to observe from. His movement draws Myla's attention as he crosses the line of sight past her mother. Rhyland now stands closer, and it is apparent that he is trying to follow through with his promise, but she cannot watch to see its fruition, for Bryar's heel catches behind hers, and she loses her footing. With a slight gasp, she stumbles backwards and flails to catch her balance. She steadies herself just in time for Bryar to swing again. She does not let him get the best of her, and instead matches his advance. The clank of metal is startling as it rings through the circular room, each sharp sound gaining in volume as the parries increase in frequency. Their motions are swift, and neither is a match for the other. The battle could continue for several more minutes, and Myla wishes it would. There is something invigorating in the way they can exchange fierce expressions and prolonged eye-contact without it being questioned. All too soon, however, Roderick calls for a halt, and they both stop, breathless with their swords down.

Panting, Bryar nods down at her. "Well done, Miss Alerys." The tone of his voice is formal now, as Lavinia is watching and listening. When they separate and Roderick takes the blades from them, Myla casts a glance her mother's way. She sits now, dazed on the bench, and a nod from Rhyland sends a shockwave of gratitude through her.

Lavinia has forgotten.

With no reason to remain, and complaining of a headache, Lavinia returns home, leaving Myla and Elsa in the blademaster's arena with the three boys. It is only when the chaos of play-combat and the stress of her mother's suspicions have subsided that Myla notices Elsa. Dressed in a simple night-blue dress, cheeks rosy, and lips turned in the coyest smile a girl can possibly wear, she stands before Callum, both of them entranced in some deep conversation. *Not the suitor her father was hoping she would stumble upon if she kept close to me...*Myla's gaze now crosses the room to where Bryar stands, back to her, diligently sharpening a stack of blades against a whetstone. *Oh, Elsa...what are we doing?*

That thought is interrupted by a timid tap on her shoulder. Myla turns quickly to find Rhyland standing behind her. "It worked," she says with a grateful smile. "How can I ever repay you? I think you've saved me from something horrible."

Rhyland flashes a chivalrous smile, the kind that does not simply possess the lips, but also the eyes, with raw sincerity. He is a kind person. Myla can feel the energy radiating from him.

"You owe me nothing. Many with my gift use it for selfish reasons. I want to use it to help people, and it was obvious you needed help. Your mother will not remember anything about yesterday or this morning." He shrugs lackadaisically before whispering. "She will probably be agitated. I would keep out of her way for a while."

Sir Roderick leaves Bryar with brief instructions on closing the training room, then turns to Myla. "I will be speaking to your father about additional hours. You are doing well, but your methods are still sloppy. I would like to refine that."

"Sloppy?" Myla asks, straightening a bit beneath his inquisitive gaze.

There is a warning therein as he peers at her and takes a few steps closer so he might lean down to whisper. "When a person begins to shed the healthy fear we are all born with and lean into their rebellion, there is a hardness that grows in their eyes. I see that hardness forming in yours. I know all too well that sort of rebellion comes from a place of anger. But do not let your anger make you sloppy."

Is he still talking about swordsmanship? Myla watches, perplexed, as the blademaster exits the room, securing the door behind him and leaving the group of teenagers alone. Not a second passes before Callum stands and paces toward where Bryar diligently sharpens blade after blade. The latter does not look up as his friend approaches, but rather he keeps his head bent low, meticulously watching the grindstone do its job.

"I am meeting with the King's Guard Captain this afternoon. Shall I put in a word for you?"

Bryar shakes his head and remains focused on the task. "Afraid not."

Rhyland's head jerks in Bryar's direction, and a solemn look steals across his usually cheerful features. "That's absurd. Of course, we are putting in a word for you. We do everything together, and this is no different."

At this, the whetstone ceases to spin, and Bryar looks up, resting his forearms against his knees. "It's no good. My father cannot obtain a commission. This is something you will have to do without me."

Callum and Rhyland exchange disappointed glances.

Approaching from behind, Elsa joins the trio, her hands clasped before her with an expression that reads *I can solve this.* "My father has connections at the institute. Apparently, there are opportunities for scholarships. Perhaps there is one for commissions."

Scholarships. Myla wonders why she has not thought of that before and suddenly, an idea comes to her. "Elsa, we must go," she blurts, grabbing her friend's hand and pulling her toward the door, much to the dismay of the three boys who watch as they leave without so much as a 'goodbye'.

"Well, that was rude," Elsa says, glaring as Myla continues to tug her through the institute until they are outside. "What could possibly possess you to leave? We were *alone* with *boys*."

A grin stretches across Myla's rosy cheeks, but she says nothing, continuing home despite Elsa's many protests and some remarks about how she wouldn't mind being entirely alone with Callum. "Will you at least tell me what is so important?" Elsa finally digs her heels into the stone steps beneath her, stopping short and crossing her arms. "I'll not take another step until you tell me."

"*Elsa,*" Myla chides, tugging at her friend's hand. "I have to get home and speak with my father before he leaves for the docks."

"Then speak quickly!" the exasperated blonde insists.

"Fine," Myla responds with a huff. "I have a charitable allowance. I have yet to donate to a cause of my choice, and I am wondering if my father will allow me to petition Sir Roderick to implement a scholarship through his services and into the King's Guard."

What was previously an unimpressed look at the words '*charitable allowance*' turns to a coy smile and flushed cheeks, pushing Elsa's eyes into a satisfied squint. "If I did not know any better, I would say you are taking my advice."

"He isn't charity, Elsa."

"No," Elsa responds, brushing past her to walk toward the door at the top of the stairs. "You just want him for supper."

After last night, Myla begins to think she might know what Elsa means by that. All the way home, through the golden crops of wheat and corn, with a backdrop of the blue autumn sky, Myla cannot help but hope her plan works.

Chapter 12

Present

THIS WAS ELENORE'S FAVORITE type of weather. The entire world transformed with the magic of glistening ice, cold enough for cuddles, and long stories by the fire. It is past midnight, and Myla perches on the window-seat beside her vanity, her fingers resting on the ornate frame while she peeks through the stained glass into the snowy night beyond. An eerie blue glow from the cool moon casts a blanket of light across the fluffy snow, not yet disturbed by the trampling of horses, guards, and woodland dwellers. It is immaculate and deceptively beautiful. No signs of charred earth in the forest are visible beneath all this snow, and the piles of burnt lumber in the village are nothing more than fluffy mounds. Snow is such a beautiful disguise for so many ugly things.

Breathing heavily and one tucked in each crook of Bryar's arms are Aidan and Caspian, asleep. They have slept more in the last few days than in the previous month of bedtimes put together. Myla glances over her shoulder to see her husband's eyes are heavy, but still open. Sleep, a most elusive necessity, evades him still. Whatever he had woken from earlier in the day tormented him well into the evening. He wears the signs of it. Dark circles form beneath his eyes, and his mouth is turned into a near-constant frown.

"It's snowing," she mutters absently while running a strand of hair between her fingers and thinking how the bare branches of the trees look like long, gnarled fingers reaching out to take them all away. There is nothing for him to say, though his eyes flicker in her direction. He thinks it too: *if Elenore were here, she would be sitting on the window seat watching the snow. I would be brushing her hair, and Bryar would be failing to convince her that snow in the morning is better than snow late at night. It would end with everyone bundling up at midnight to go play.*

Beside Myla, on her vanity is the missing hairbrush, which was retrieved from Elenore's things yesterday. Through the many joys of motherhood, Myla has found her favorite to be sharing with her children. Sharing food, sharing her bed, sharing cloaks when they forget to bring their own, and sharing in the sort of lighthearted laughter only children can conjure. The hairbrush taunts her, for it will never again brush Elenore's hair. It will never vanish again from where she leaves it, stolen when a daughter misplaces her own. Myla picks it up with trembling hands and runs it through her hair, wondering if any of the brown strands tangled in its teeth belonged to her daughter. Something irrational convinces her to pluck the hairs from the brush and examine each of them, waiting for some sense of recognition, a revelation which will not come. Mother and daughter share the same hair color.

The tears have become so persistent, so redundant, that Myla does not notice them until Bryar gingerly rises from where he lies, and sits behind her, wiping them away with his thumb. There are no words spoken, for none will help. There is only the gentle kiss on the back of her head before he takes the very hairbrush which prompted the tears into his own hand. Stroke by stroke, he slowly works at the days of tangles dried in tears until moments have passed and the comb glides smoothly through the long tendrils. Bryar replaces the brush on the vanity, and collects her hair in his fists, maneuvering the sections into a loose braid falling down her back. It is only when her crying subsides that she hears the stifled sobs behind her.

Together, they weep, watching the slow and sad snowfall collect on the stone windowsill. A sight which should be peaceful is another dagger in raw flesh, carving out their grief piece by piece.

"I want revenge," Myla whispers, grabbing Bryar's hand. "I know we have no proof, but I believe my father is behind this."

His palm closes around hers. "We have been plotting to overthrow him for years..."

"I do not mean *overthrow* him; we are far beyond simply wanting him off Caspian's throne," Myla sighs. "I want to kill him."

There is a vendetta in her voice, a thirst for blood not easily satisfied. The light in her blue eyes fades black with the declarations, and she turns to face Bryar. The muscles of her jawline are fully engaged, as though she has already sunk her teeth into Maverick's throat and needs only to rip. "I want to watch Maverick Alerys die by my blade, and I do not want to give him the chance to make one more excuse. I have heard enough."

Bryar flinches as his wife transforms before him from grieving mother to malevolent queen. The ruthlessness she was often accused of takes shape before him as she weaves every thread of grief and anger into a cloak fit for the title. The Ruthless Raven Queen.

"I am here," he answers in the only way he knows possible, his voice trembling. Many fears take form: for their sons' safety, for the wellbeing of their people, their army, and most unexpectedly...fear for his wife's soul. Though he too longs to feel the flesh of his daughter's killer split beneath his blade, something about seeing that viciousness in his wife's face is chilling. "What do you need of me?"

Myla stands and moves toward the mannequin where her armor sits, cold and ready to be warmed with revenge. "I need the Raven's Veil."

At Rhyland's command, additional soldiers than are customary have been commanded to patrol the halls and perimeter of the palace. So, despite the late hour, Old Falkmere is far from quiet.

Ten Raven's Veil assassins and six council members enter the war-room with as much civility as can be mustered when woken a mere three hours after they have fallen asleep. Many fumble with the straps of their sheathed swords or the buckles of their cloaks, still righting themselves upon entry. The snowy chill is overwhelming, and the sparse candlelight creates a dim profile of each figure moving about the table.

Yet, none of their eyes droop with sleep when they behold their queen in long-since-retired armor. It wears the scars of the Battle in the Seam when she defeated Vesperian Shayd, the Blood Stealer. Though the breastplate has been reshaped to fit her no-longer-expectant stomach, it is otherwise unchanged. The woman wearing it, however, is changed by the gravity of grief, and is a sight to tremble before. She turns to face them, her long black cloak dusting the floor in a magnificent *whoosh*.

"It was a mistake for my father to underestimate me when I was a girl," she begins, rolling the point of her fox dagger against one long finger. "I was well-tempered then. I was malleable and often did his bidding simply because he was my father and that is what daughters were supposed to do, so I thought."

Rhyland specifically side eyes Bryar, concern furrowing his brow. Myla hones in on him, taking a few steps closer. He knows, yet he of all people questions.

"But I am a woman now. I have been for a long time. And the woman I have become is not to be underestimated." She flashes the rest of her council a chilling expression, colder than the frosty breeze drifting in from the open balcony. "My father *continues* to underestimate me, and I have suffered the consequences of allowing him to believe I am still well-tempered when I am, in fact, *a tempest.*"

The room audibly shifts, and the only eyes not lowered in submission are those of her husband, who instead watches her pace before him. They seem to plead, to ask her: *is this necessary?*

Sacrificing her humanity is a small price to pay for vindication.

"Our armies are to retreat." Bryar looks to Rhyland and Lord Thurston. "Her Grace is no longer interested in waging open war. Not today at least."

"Your Grace—we have this perfectly mapped, surely—" Lord Thurston objects. He seizes a taper-candle from a by-standing guard and hovers its light over the metal miniatures symbolizing their army's locations and mass.

"Surely *what*?" Bryar interjects, seizing Thurston's arm. "Surely you do not question both your queen *and* your captain?" A red-hot glow ripples off Bryar's shoulders, and a flaming ring forms around his irises. His amulet flares with energy, as does Myla's, casting the brightest lights in the room and serving as a warning. Neither the queen nor her captain is to be disobeyed tonight, for broken hearts are the least forgiving.

"We will be infiltrating New Falkmere Palace under the cover of night tomorrow." Bryar continues. "The queen demands the blood of her father as recompense, and that is *exactly* what she will get."

All in the room bow obediently despite the shudder they all attempt to suppress. An entire army waging open war in a carefully planned ambush is one thing. Storming a heavily guarded palace in the dead of night on a whim is an entirely different one.

"What is the plan?" Rhyland asks as he moves toward the map, pointing a finger at the model of New Falkmere Palace.

"We will acquire the armor of two New Falkmere soldiers—"

"Acquire?" It is a member of the Raven's Veil who speaks now.

"Yes," Myla responds, pointing to four of the assassins. "You will all leave immediately. Make for New Falkmere and use discretion in obtaining two sets of armor. Whatever you do, do not be seen. You will meet us at Druid's Cave at dusk tomorrow night with the armor."

"And that will help us how?" Rhyland asks cautiously.

"Not you," Bryar corrects. "You and Thurston both will remain here. You are tasked with keeping our sons safe." Bryar looks to the remaining assassins awaiting further instructions. "Six of you shall accompany Her Grace and me to Druid's Cave. From there we shall journey together to the palace, where two of you will be disguised as guards. You will be escorting a prisoner." Bryar points to one of the assassins. "Once inside the palace, you will make to the servant's entrance, and you will let us in. Now off with you; time is not on our side."

With much still to do, Rhyland and Lord Thurston, excused by Myla, turn to leave the war room in order to make final preparations. Before Myla can turn her attention back to the landscape of war on the table in front of her, her interest is drawn by a continued conversation.

"Captain," a fifth Raven's Veil Assassin steps forward. "My comrade has suffered a twisted ankle in training. Allow me to go in his stead. We will move quicker if all of us are fit."

Myla eyes the volunteer head to toe before dismissing the injured soldier with a wave of her hand. "And you are?"

"Sir Emerson, at your service."

"Remove your veil," Myla demands.

The Raven's Veil garb is intended for discretion. Their sleek, black leather armor befits those in need of stealth, and the cowl hood worn over their heads drapes down their foreheads, stopping just above the eyes. Complete with a fitted mask over their mouth and nose, any distinguishing features are concealed. A dark embossed raven perched on a downward blade is imprinted upon the breast of their black armor, inconspicuous and barely noticeable. Particularly in the cover of darkness, which is where these men tend to dwell.

The assassin does as instructed, revealing a hairless head and a dark, well-groomed beard. A grotesque white scar etches a path beginning at the bottom of his nose, across the ridges of his lips, down the center of his chin and disappearing beneath the high collar of his armor. He's lucky he survived such a wound. However, something about him is familiar, and Myla wonders if he played a part in her failed attempt to weaken Vesperian from inside her palace. It was such a long time ago, there is no way for her to place him, but she is certain he has been in her service for many years.

"Thank you," she tilts her chin in his direction gratefully. "Be quick and do not be seen."

Bryar leaves with the rest of the council and remaining assassins to make final arrangements for their journey. Though the night is not half over, sleep will not find Myla, so she extinguishes the candles and exits the war-room. Slowly, she makes her way toward her chamber with the intention of checking on the boys. The corridor is dark and only lit by a few sparse candles, so the spaces between them are dark. Pillars to her right support the arched ceiling, where stained-glass windows impair her vision of the stars.

Where only her steps should be heard, something else ahead makes itself known with breathless gasps. Myla slows her pace and lightens her feet, gathering her skirts closer to minimize their rustle. A secondary hall juts to the left, and Myla peers around its corner.

The sight is provocative; unlike anything she has ever seen. Not two, but three bodies take advantage of the shadows and the late hour. Tangled in something tender and reverent, they display a swirl of effortless motions, limbs moving around limbs expertly—a practiced task which blurs their subjects. It takes Myla a moment to register just what and *whom* she has stumbled upon. It is not a passionate encounter; it is religious. Two men worshiping one woman: *Elsa.*

Her back arches against the wall with an exposed thigh looped around one man's waist. One of her hands is tangled in the long, blonde hair of Lord Thurston while her other hand, to Myla's shock, desperately grips the back of *Rhyland's* collar, holding him close.

Lord Thurston—or 'Henry', as Elsa so passionately moans—has one hand lost in Rhyland's trousers and the other explores up Elsa's skirt.

"I am so glad you are not leaving," she whispers breathlessly, pressing a soft kiss to Henry's jaw before turning to Rhyland, whose mouth is already pelting her neck gently. *"And you."* The inflection in her voice shifts as Thurston's wandering hand finds its way home.

Myla turns just as both men meet each other in a kiss, which escalates the moment from religious to passionate.

The only question Myla can conjure is: *who started it?*

CHAPTER 13

PAST: MYLA, SIXTEEN

MYLA IGNORES THE JAR tipped across her father's desk. Its contents are strewn, cast aside in anger. Honey drips from the cork lid, and the potent fragrance of freshly scattered dill, thyme, and cinnamon seeps into the room. She had etched his name in a sigil, placed it in the witch's jar with herbs meant for persuasion and receptiveness, and sealed it in blue wax. Apparently, this time, her efforts to soften him have had the opposite effect. Turning away from the broken spell, Myla looks through the window over the colors of autumn which warm the scenery just outside with golden grass, and late summer flowers, trying not to let her father see the red flush in her cheeks, a direct result of a strike from his hand. Again.

Maverick leans back in his overstuffed chair and takes a long draw from his pipe before speaking to her. "I know you did not come in here to argue with me about your responsibilities. Why are you here?"

Responsibilities, meaning the manipulated promenade with the king's advisor. A political strategy. One that interferes with her plans to meet Bryar tomorrow. "I wanted to discuss my charity allowance," Myla answers, steadying her voice. In terms of compartmentalizing, she must master it this time. Bryar's future counts on her ability to disassociate from the burning of her cheeks and the anger tingling at her fingertips.

"What of it?" He asks absently, a slight roll of his dark eyes yet another dismissal. Whatever she has to say is already catalogued as unimportant.

"I have decided how I would like to spend it."

Maverick lets out a faint chuckle. "I am not sure you are fit to make such a decision; leave that to me."

Myla stiffens, gripping the white material of her dress, hoping the uncontrolled strands of light would burn a hole there and not between her father's eyes. "I believe there is no greater cause than ensuring the king's safety."

There it is—the flicker of interest. Maverick sits upright, the pipe drooping limp from his lips. "Go on."

"Well, I overheard Sir Roderick discussing possible funding for soldiers and even King's Guards. He says the institute has granted him no such funds. I should like to donate my allowance to the cause." *A little lie never hurt anyone.* Sir Roderick has said no such thing, but Maverick would never believe she came up with it herself. Therefore, a lie will have to do.

"Your allowance would only afford three, maybe four commissions," Maverick says with a tilt of his bushy eyebrows. "Why the interest in the king's defenses?"

Myla sits in the chair across from him to hide the way her knees now tremble. "Most girls donate to the orphanages and the hospitals. Which, of course, are noble causes," she responds dutifully. "I would like to concern myself with the matters of the king instead."

Maverick's mouth snags with the briefest flicker of a smile, erased quickly by the need to suppress his inhibitions. "I am impressed," he says, probably for the first time in her entire life, and Myla smiles down at the broken spell, wondering if it is working still. "It is a pleasure to see you concerned with the needs of the king. I shall see to it that Sir Roderick receives the funds."

"Thank you, Father," bobbing in a brief curtsey, Myla turns to leave. "I have extra lessons today, so I shall be on my way." *Another lie.* Nonetheless, she needs to tell Sir Roderick of her true plan before Maverick gets to him and her scheme unravels.

The sun casts an unusually warm glow for this late in the year, but it is welcome. Myla hurries across the city, unattended and glad for it. The last year of attending classes at the Institute of Mystic Arts has allowed her to see more of New Falkmere than she might have should her studies have been confined to her father's estate, as most ladies are. She moves through the streets with confidence now, unfazed by the hurried flows of traffic. If anything, blending into them and moving with the current of people creates a sense of wholeness and unity. She loves everything about the city.

Especially when she passes the blacksmith.

Today, she does not simply pass it and continue. She goes in.

"Miss—Alerys—" Caspian greets her between grunts as he drives a hammer into hot metal, shaping it and sending sparks flying. After he plunges the blade into a cold bucket, filling the air with the aroma of pungent metal carried on the drift of steam, he lays the weapon down and leans against the anvil. "How can I help you?"

Caspian has grown accustomed to seeing her in his shop. Though begrudgingly, he welcomes her every time, usually while also chiding both her and Bryar for their recklessness. It has now been a few months since she first met Caspian, but every time she meets him now, she is able to look past the gruff exterior to where that same softness his son carries is found in him as well. The corners of his eyes crease with many years of smiling, and Myla wishes her father were half as kind as Caspian.

"I was looking for—"

"—my foolhardy son, yes." Caspian nods toward the door leading inside their home. "He is studying inside." The stoic cemented features break into a warm smile as hers grows too, and Myla moves toward the door, stopping briefly to press a kiss to the man's soot-covered cheeks.

"Isn't the sunshine so glorious today?" she asks, opening the door.

"The *sunshine*, yes," Caspian agrees, "and young ladies not getting my son strung up. Hurry inside before you are seen."

Myla closes the door quietly behind her, noting how Bryar leans over her notes, scribbling away on his own spread of pages. He looks up briefly, flashes her a smile, then turns back to his work.

"One moment," he insists, his writing growing quicker.

"That's alright," Myla whispers, pulling from her basket a stack of books, which she sets neatly on the shelf.

"What are those?" Bryar asks, standing quickly. "Books—Myla, those look expensive!"

"Yes!" Myla says happily, reaching for one in particular, which she hands directly to him.

"*A Mage's Compendium: Harnessing the Arcane Arts,* Myla, this is...where did you get this volume?"

"I stole it from my governess," Myla answers, her tone far too frank and comfortable to be admitting to thievery. A response they both chuckle at before Bryar hands her the book.

"I cannot take this."

"Of course you can," she insists, pressing it back into his palms. "I have too many books, as does my governess, and frankly, I would rather give them to you than be forced to read them myself. I swear, if she makes me read one more book on the harnessing of my magic, I shall hang her with mine and be done with it."

Bryar places the volume beneath his pillow, no doubt to avoid Caspian's questions, and faces her, arms crossed. "Don't do that. Even noblewomen are punished for murder."

Myla shrugs and perches on the edge of the table. "I am not afraid of what any of those men could do to me."

"Yes," Bryar says with an exasperated sigh, side-eyeing her in a partially playful way, poorly concealing the concern within him. "But I am afraid of what they will do to you, which is why I have to tell you...you cannot come here in broad daylight anymore. They will question you."

The edge of the table shakes as if it might splinter beneath her fingers as she nervously rubs them back and forth. "There is nothing they could say that will keep me from you." The confession: vulnerable, raw, completely intentional.

"Oh, *Myla.*" He steps closer, taking both of her hands inside his. "If they see you here, *unchaperoned,* they will undoubtedly question your virtue. You are not even out yet. And to be ruined before you've had a chance to court men of your station?"

Myla pulls her palms free, crossing them in stubborn defiance. "You think I am worried about what they say of my virtue?" She thinks of how easily Maverick caved to her proposition as soon as it involved the king. Plans for her virtue are already set in motion, and not in the least by her.

"Well...you should." He shrugs, leaning on the flameless hearth behind him. "If they suspect anything untoward between us, you would not be eligible to marry anyone of your station."

"Meanwhile, every man in my station can be found a mile up the road in the whorehouse. Tell me how that is fair," Myla retorts, her palm finding a gentle resting place against his chest. Beneath her touch, each heartbeat pounds as if trying to reach her, and she longs to feel him closer.

A smile creeps across Bryar's face, and his shoulders lift in an effortless shrug while a soot-smudged hand closes around hers. "I suppose men are not as valuable as women." His tone is haughty and playful, and the way his eyes tease her feels like an invitation. One she might accept, if his father was not just outside the room.

"If women were more valuable than men, I think we would have a queen and not a king right now," she replies quietly, not wavering from his intense examination of her. The craving pulls like a tether stretched taut between them, tightening and urging them to close the small distance. In recent weeks, Myla has worked up the courage to ask Elsa some pointed questions which neither her mother, nor any respectable woman, would dare answer. Now enlightened, what Elsa would call a 'natural urge' seems to have buried itself deep within Myla, awaiting discovery.

Discovery that simply cannot occur here, now, with the possibility of interruption. "I have bad news," Myla blurts.

The spell is broken, and Bryar averts his gaze bashfully. "I do not like the sound of that."

"Neither did I." *Nor the slap I received when I protested.* "I am to promenade the palace gardens with Lord Heron, the King's Advisor. Tomorrow."

Bryar nods slowly. "We can study another day. I am ahead now, so there is no risk of me suffering for missing a lesson."

Either he does not see it as the crisis it is, or he does not show it. Regardless, irritation sparks in Myla, and she stands straight now. "Yes, I suppose you are right. Another time."

"Hey." Bryar reads her reaction immediately and takes a few steps closer, grabbing her hand. "I will never make it hard for you to do as your father commands. That is not why I am here."

"Then why *are* you here?" She asks softly. "What if I want you to make it hard?"

He draws her closer, his hands on her hips, and electricity fizzling from his fingertips, deep into her body, coiling with a heat that screams to be indulged. "Then I would say I simply cannot do that."

"Why?" Myla presses her palms into his neck, gently rubbing her thumbs across his sun-tanned skin.

"Because loving someone is not supposed to be hard."

Bryar's lips are a hair's breadth away from hers when the door creaks open and Caspian appears, quickly spinning away as he averts his gaze. "You damned fools." His tone is reproachful with a hint of humor, and the exclamation drives an invisible force between the two, and they release one another in time for Caspian to turn once more. "I know well enough that some things simply cannot be stopped." His palms are suspended helplessly at his sides. "If I am honest, I don't dare try to stop it. But look—" He gestures toward the open window. "Be smart, Gods-damn it." The concerned father moves forward, standing between Myla and his son. "All due respect, Miss Alerys. But it is not you who shall pay the price if this is discovered. You will live with shame, but you will *live* to watch him *hang*."

A moment of silence seizes the trio before Caspian sits on the edge of his bed, running both hands through his graying hair with an exasperated sigh. "I heard enough of your conversation to know there is no sense in asking either of you to stop." He nods toward Bryar. "You're stubborn if not stupid—" then a nod in Myla's direction, "and you are hot-blooded. *Gods* help you both."

Leaving the smithy feels like both bliss and shame. *Loving someone is not supposed to be hard.* The words still ricocheting off every corner of her brain send a course of adrenaline through Myla, while Caspian's intervention shrouds it all in a wet blanket of hopelessness. Despite his warnings, the glow of Bryar's words outweighs the subtle concern pricking at her. The warmth follows her all the way to the institute, where she finds Sir Roderick dismissing two male students with a defeated sigh.

"Some are not so teachable, Miss Alerys." He greets her with a gentle wave of his sword. "Have you come for an extra lesson?"

"No," Myla replies with a polite curtsy. "I have come to ask for both your help and your discretion."

Roderick twirls the blade before sheathing it while wearing an intrigued expression. "I do love secrets," he coos. "Tell me more, Miss Alerys."

"I wish to purchase a commission into the King's Guard for Bryar."

"Ah." Roderick replies simply, unsheathing his blade once more. "You shall fight me first, and then we can discuss this madness."

Although Myla wishes to be quick about the conversation, she knows there is little use in arguing with the blademaster; therefore, she moves to the wall of swords to select one, stopped by the "*Tsk, tsk,*" of Sir Roderick.

"You shall use your magic."

"My magic? Why?" Myla questions, envisioning all at once how her magic could lower the stone ceiling on top of them should she miscalculate.

"Because I cannot trust you to make decisions for your *friend's* future if you cannot control your own."

Myla tenses and finds her fists balling, a surge of anger washing over her. She cannot control it right now, and he knows it. *How does he know it?* "Sir Roderick," Myla appeals. "I cannot tell you how urgent this request is. I have but twenty minutes before I am expected home, and my father plans to visit you tomorrow while I am away, and if I do not explain this to you, all will be lost." Her plea is desperate, and the tone is in no way lost on Sir Roderick. With a sigh, he lowers his blade.

"What have you gotten yourself into?"

"Nothing just yet," Myla answers with a nervous laugh.

"I do not believe you," Roderick retorts. "Nevertheless, tell me what you need from me."

"When my father offers you my charitable allowance, accept it. And he *must* believe it was your idea. Please be sure some of it is used as a scholarship to purchase Bryar's commission into the King's Guard. You know he is good enough."

Sir Roderick bites down on his lower lip, nodding slowly. "Indeed. He *is* good enough. I do not think he would accept charity, though. I have already offered free lessons which he has turned down."

"No," Myla agrees. "He will *not*. Which is why you will not tell him. Promise me?"

Time suspends as Sir Roderick weighs the risks of being Myla's accomplice. After a moment, he nods in agreement. "Alright, Miss Alerys. I shall do as you ask, with one condition."

"Anything," Myla replies with a smile, pleased at her success.

"You will attend extra classes with the mage."

"Why?" Myla asks with a small gasp. No answer is required, for she follows Sir Roderick's gaze to her exposed arms. Unknown to her and in response to her calamitous emotions, little stars of light, like freckles across her skin, begin to bleed from her pores.

CHAPTER 14

PRESENT

IN WAR, TO SEE another day is to praise your God again. Tonight, Maverick Alerys will cease to praise any Gods.

The ground, blanketed in snow, crunches beneath her boots as Myla steps through the woods. *Crunch, crunch, crunch.* Despite their efforts to proceed with stealth, they announce themselves with every footfall. *Not that Bryar wouldn't do that all on his own,* she thinks, watching as the broad man moves with less grace than a three-legged blind cow. Of course, his lack of patience could be attributed to his need for revenge. One rarely moves toward murder with grace, especially when that murder is so very justified.

Tonight, they both crave blood.

Each tree skeleton seems to shudder as she passes on the breath of vengeance. Ahead, Bryar advances, waving his men onward. They travel wordlessly and have done so for over an hour. The woods are no longer theirs. This territory, once hers, now belongs to the Imposter King. *A soon-to-be headless king.*

Carried on the midwinter breeze is an eeriness foreign to these woods. For years, their rocky terrain—moving up the side of the mountain to Druid's Cave—was a comfort. It whispered "welcome home" to her as she meandered, grounding herself in the unwavering embrace of the Spirit Mother. Now, something sinister has taken root in her sacred forest. Where it was once a comforting solitude to the creatures who called it home, it feels barren and devoid of life. Its whispers are no longer welcoming; instead, they bid you to leave. They warn of evil spreading its seed throughout New Falkmere. Like all sacred places marred by the sinister, these woods are angry.

And Myla can feel it.

She can feel it in the way the earth sighs with exasperation as her feet tread upon what little patience it has left. She can feel it in the passing of whispers from the boughs of the trees. They gossip about what they have seen. How Myla wishes trees could talk; perhaps they would tell her what has gone so wrong.

Whatever it is proves itself unnaturally cold. Icy air, which seizes the lungs and tempts one to draw no breath, dries Myla's lips and turns the tips of her fingers blue. They grow numb despite the thick leather gloved bracers she wears. As they ascend the mountain, mist forms in the air, swirling like a diamond breeze in the moonlight. A winter gale moves through the trees, disturbing the mist and snow, creating a flurry, like thousands of needles burying themselves in her face. Wincing, Myla presses palms to her cheeks, shuddering at the sudden and immense discomfort. Given the grunts as her assassins and husband all stop dead in their tracks, it seems they too are at the mercy of the Spirit Mother.

But this is not the Spirit Mother.

Myla straightens despite the quickening wind, which disrupts the snow and impairs her vision. "Something is wrong," she says, turning to look at Bryar.

He nods in grim agreement. His hunter's eyes scan the tree line ahead, processing every detail so he might taste or smell or feel whatever is amiss.

"This is not a natural winter." He gestures to a tree trunk ahead, which is completely entombed in ice. Its sharp, gnarled fingers stretch upward, consuming the branches and curling overhead in sword-like points. As they strain to peer past the blizzard-like conditions and into the forest, more colossal bodies of frozen water appear.

"We must continue," Myla says wearily. "We can't abandon our men to this." She presses onward, ignoring the cold even as it seeps through her thick boots, biting at her toes and sending a tingling up toward her knees.

Obediently nodding, Bryar turns back, instructing the assassins, "Stay alert."

Progress slows as the wind forms beastly snow drifts which they trudge through, all members of this secret mission frozen and miserable. Even Bryar shivers, because he refuses to draw attention to them by using his flames. There is no red glow to him; he is as dark and shadowed as the rest of them.

Frost crystalizes on Myla's eyelashes and the tips of her hair, freezing the locks into matted clumps. With every exhale, a frenzy of frosty breath swirls into the foreground.

The night is unusually quiet, save for the crunch of snow beneath her and Bryar's boots.

Ahead, the mouth of Druid's Cave appears. Its opening is encased completely in ice with some frozen points hanging menacingly like sharp teeth. Myla's eyes strain in the darkness, and she passes over the forest before her once, then twice in an effort to see her men. She strains to listen, but hearing nothing, she moves forward.

Bryar's hand clamps around her arm, jarring her to a halt. His fingers dig into her, a silent warning. His eyes are wide, and his jaw flexes forwards, then backwards. A look she recognizes.

Anger.

Myla follows his gaze, past more villainous blasts of ice, to the bloody contrast of three piked heads stuck in a snowdrift.

They have not the dignity of their cowled hoods, and nothing suggests there was honor in their deaths. Their eyes are wide with terror and rolled to the backs of their heads. Tortured mouths hang agape mid-agonizing-scream and their hair is disheveled from serving as handles. Freezing blood drips from the curled skin of their severed necks, rolling down and saturating the frost-bitten stakes which stand to deliver a message: *killing me will not be so easy.*

In a pile before the pikes lie their bodies, stripped of their uniforms. From the tangle of naked, mutilated flesh flows a river of gore, melting into the snow and trickling down the steady incline.

Three heads, not four.

Myla scans the rest of the clearing, looking for the fourth assassin. "We must take them down," she says, breathing hard as her chest swells with an urge to scream, to flatten the forest, to become a beacon.

The abundance of death taunts her, and she hungers for a response, for this cowardly killer to show themselves and face her.

"Stop—" Bryar's grip tightens, yanking her back in his direction. "It's a trap—"

No sooner have the words left his mouth than powerful spears of ice lunge from behind tall mounds of snow. The unnatural weapons stretch farther and farther and annihilate everything in their paths. Trees crack and splinter as the ice impales their thick trunks. Some ancient evergreens are split in half entirely.

"*Run,*" Bryar commands, pulling Myla away from the cave.

They turn, narrowly missing another volley of frozen spikes. The sharp ice spears hurtle past them, and toward a man of the Raven's Veil directly behind them. He lets out a blood-curdling scream as the icy points bury themselves in his chest, launching him off his feet. He is suspended in the air by the deadly monument, hot blood spewing from the wound and running like a steaming river over its frosted surface.

Chaos follows as the assassins attempt to scatter.

"Formations!" Bryar yells, his booming voice demanding to be obeyed. Reluctantly, they regroup, forming a circle, shoulder to shoulder. "Someone is causing this," he continues. "Watch out for the ice. We must see where it comes from."

"I am not waiting around to be impaled," one young man cries, his voice quivering just as he breaks away. The choice to abandon his comrades is a deadly one. Another blast of ice tears through the branches with a shudder, lodging in the assassin's skull. He falls to the ground, already dead.

"There!" Myla points, and her men turn to face their foe.

This enemy moves over the snow effortlessly, propelled on a wave of ice beneath blue-soled boots, which carries her over the terrain at an otherworldly speed. She wears iridescent glass armor which refracts the moonlight. Volts of blue meander across the armor sporadically, seeming to coil around her limbs in a similar manner to the frosty mist about her being. Her black cloak is rimmed with an equally black fur, which shrouds her face. Despite the drooped hood, Myla detects a glint of white iris. Riding the wave behind her is a bald man wearing a scar down the center of his mouth and chin. Myla gasps. Her man, her assassin. A member of the Raven's Veil. The very man who volunteered to execute her plans. *Sir Emerson.*

The mage raises her palms to send another glowing volley of ice their way.

As the biting and frozen stalactites drive a crevasse in the snow, spiraling violently in their direction, Myla and Bryar raise their palms in unison, their amulets throbbing with the union of magic. No communication is needed; they function as one now, each calling on their own abilities to form a marriage of the supernatural. A blue flame takes life in the space where their palms meet, blasting an unbearable heat as the flames take flight, charging toward the ice with purpose. Myla braces herself against the force of the magic churning at her fingertips,

threatening to propel her backwards. An acute sense of responsibility
for the men behind her banishes what should be fear. Their skill with
the sword is no match for this form of sorcery.

She and Bryar will protect these men, or they will die.

When ice and fire meet, the unimaginable happens. Instead of melting the blast as intended, the fragments of ice split angrily, breaking apart before coming together again, using the current of fire to
close the space between itself and its opponents. The ice consumes
the fire, freezing the current and sending a shock of biting agony up
Myla's arms. Both she and Bryar are launched backward, hitting the
solid snow with painful thuds. Gasping in pain, both her and Bryar's
arms reverberate from the force of the assault, breaking the bond and
leaving their men exposed. Every muscle in her body feels paralyzed,
and a glance in Bryar's direction tells Myla that he suffers the same
impairment. The impact dulled her senses, and a ringing between her
ears muffles the screams as the ice viciously shreds the last of her men.

The traitor brushes past the mage, advancing with his sword drawn
toward her and Bryar. A sick smirk twists his scarred features. "What a
shame that you left your *precious* children unattended in a palace *full*
of traitors."

Panic lurches in her chest, and despite the reverberating pain in her
bones, Myla stumbles toward Bryar, pulling him to his feet. His body
is hot to the touch, and fire ripples from the surface of his skin.

Every instinct begs her to turn and confront Sir Emerson. To plunge
a blade between his eyes, but Bryar tugs her away from the scene. Eyes
alight with the glow of an angry flame, he looks toward the mage, who
thrusts her palms in their direction once more. A ballistic inferno takes
life as Bryar summons his wings in the span of a breath. Bryar's arm
wraps around her middle and with a mighty lunge, he spirals upward
past the canopy of the trees, barely dodging the icy teeth intended

for them. The mage lets out an angry scream, loosing smaller spears toward the sky now.

Bryar lurches to the left, evading a deadly volley before grunting with exertion as his wings beat vigorously, hurtling them out of the mage's reach. Although they are soon out of danger, he does not land. He speeds directly over the mountains which separate them and their sons. Myla's arms are looped around his neck, holding on tightly, and she presses her eyes shut, not daring to look at the craggy cliffsides beneath her. *Far* beneath her. A fall here would be death.

The palace is not asleep.

On the contrary. Where Myla would have expected to find minimal lights and noise, she and Bryar are met with mayhem. Bleeding, screaming mayhem. Every torch leading up the stone stairway through the entrance doors is lit, and within the palace, the main thoroughfare is hemorrhaging guards. It is a panic. The way they dart back and forth as though still in search of an enemy is alarming. Many seem to be hardly awake. Others walk slowly, sticky-red blades limp at their sides.

"What is the meaning of this?" Myla asks, gripping the arm of a dazed guard as he passes, eyes still heavy with sleep.

"Th—there was an ambush, Your Grace," he stumbles in a panic over his words. "I still do not understand." He staggers away without being dismissed. Only when he has turned fully around, does Myla see a seeping, bloody gash in the back of his leg.

"Bryar—" Shocked, and pulse battering within her, Myla turns to find her husband is already running down the busy hall toward the boys' bedroom. She follows.

The chaos thins as they approach their sons' door. Two guards stand with spears crossed, refusing entry to those who might try. At their feet, four men in Raven's Veil regalia lie in a careless pile in a pool of their own blood. From within the room, the audible sound of crying filters through the wooden door.

"Let me *pass*," Bryar growls angrily, shoving past the two guards. Myla trudges over the bodies with a quick glance down, noting how the cowl hood has fallen from the face of the man at the top of the pile. Only he has no face, for it has been cut off entirely. She shudders and pushes into the room.

Elsa sits on the floor. The front of her white nightgown is steeped in a spray of scarlet, causing the thin material to cling to her skin. Blood drenches her hair, and tears streak through the splatter of crimson on her porcelain skin. In her tight embrace, Aidan and Caspian shake, holding on to her as though letting go might be the death of them all. Bryar leans down as though to touch her, but a shaking flinch moves him to retreat away from the terrified woman. Rhyland, to her right, is crouched, a firm hand rubbing her shoulder reassuringly, and to her left is Henry Thurston. His arm is wrapped affectionately around her head, holding her close to his chest.

"What happened?" Myla demands, sinking to the floor where the boys quiver. The moment she is within reach, they clamor into her arms, each gripping her desperately. "Look at me," Myla insists, cupping each boy's face in turn as she assesses their wellbeing. On Caspian's face, a thin red line of a quickly healing wound marks from the corner of his right eye to his mouth. Myla's stomach twists angrily.

Rhyland and Henry straighten, exchanging wary glances before Rhyland answers. "Everyone was asleep when we heard the young princes cry out." His voice wavers. "We rushed as fast as we could to find those—" his features darken with an animosity born from the worst of betrayals as he points a bloodstained finger toward the pile of Raven's Veil assassins. "*Those traitors* were in here about to..."

"In any case." Henry places a comforting hand on Rhyland's shoulder. "We stopped it."

"Stopped it?" Bryar asks, grabbing Henry's hand to take note of a bleeding slice up his arm. "You need to get this cleaned and bandaged."

He looks from both men to where Elsa sits. He clears his throat before saying, "We are indebted to you, all of you. You saved our sons."

"Elsa cut a man's face off," Aidan whispers into Myla's neck, pointing a small finger at a bloodied blade which lies discarded on the floor and catching the glint of the firelight. "And Caspian's face was almost cut off."

"I saw the faceless man," Myla whispers. "Your auntie is very brave. And I am glad Cas still has a face." Though her voice is strong for the boys, Myla's eyes meet Elsa's and through a stream of tears, gratitude gleams.

The trio nods in agreement, and Rhyland helps Elsa to her feet. The motion prompts an unbridled sob from her, and she collapses against his chest, her resolve crumbling as the shock fades.

"Brave, indeed," Henry agrees, closing around Elsa's bare side with a hug which joins the three of them in one warm embrace.

Myla looks from the group to where Bryar stands. He is all astonishment, wide eyes darting from each of them until finally settling on Elsa, sandwiched in the middle of two men, both clearly devoted to her safety and emotional comfort. His eyes grow wide with understanding, and he diverts his gaze to where Myla sits. She shoots him a face which says, *"Ask questions later."* Then she stands, motioning for Bryar to pick up Aidan.

Gathering Caspian into her arms, Myla looks to the guards at the door. "I want every single member of the Raven's Veil taken to the prison cells."

After an hour of bathing her sons and holding them in her arms—something she told Bryar was for their comfort, but really, it was for hers—Myla steps out of her bedchamber and into the cold corridor. Tension chokes the air like thick black smoke. Although the palace is now quiet and the boys are safely asleep with Bryar, as Myla walks the halls, flanked by four guards on each side, betrayal chills her. It screams at her, and it demands that she open her eyes and *see*.

It seems she has missed many details in the last year. Details which led to Elenore's murder. Details which almost killed her sons tonight. She shudders at the thought and crosses her arms over her chest in an effort to ward off a cold which is not truly there.

There is a detail I really missed...

Elsa's door is closed, but from within, Myla can hear there are more than two voices inside the room. Hesitant at first, she knocks and the voices silence, followed shortly by the rhythmic sound of boots approaching. The door creaks open, revealing Rhyland. *Shirtless.*

"Oh—" Myla begins to apologize. "I did not think..."

"It is alright," Elsa says from behind him. "Let her in."

So, the door swings open wider. The trio have shed their bloodied clothes and now wear fresh garments. Rhyland steps aside, allowing Myla to enter. She briefly notices the runes tattooed on his chest, interrupted by several scars running from one side of his broad chest to the other. She makes a note to ask him about them later.

Elsa sits in the center of her bed, cupping a heavy goblet between her hands. Henry sits on a chair beside the bed, but from the drowsy look on his face, Myla assumes she has interrupted the three of them preparing to sleep.

"I can come back tomorrow," Myla says with an uneasy glance in Elsa's direction.

"No," Henry says politely, standing to pour a crystal glass of port before handing it to her. "Perhaps we should leave." He glances at Rhyland and, with a nod from his companion, both men exit the room.

"Are you alright?" Myla asks immediately, crawling up the foot of the bed until she sits beside her friend. "Darling," she adds, pressing a hand to Elsa's cheek. "I am so sorry you had to experience that."

A weak smile curls the corners of the blonde's lips. "I did not realize our eyes were attached by...well, threads."

Myla nearly chokes on a sip of port, the red of it suddenly causing her stomach to twist. "Comforting to know they will not simply fall out?"

"Oh, Myla," Elsa says with a shudder. "It is all going so horribly wrong."

Myla nods slowly, her entire body trembling with the letdown of adrenaline. "So many dreadful things have happened." Visions of a small face framed in unruly curls stop her words. To speak of it now would undo her all over again. "Tonight *was* dreadful." Myla recounts the ice mage they lost their assassins to in the woods, chasing the pink of Elsa's cheeks away until the blonde woman sits pale and horrified.

"She sounds powerful."

"She is," Myla responds with a frustrated sigh. "I just do not understand—who is she? Where did she come from? How have I never heard of her?"

Elsa shrugs. "It sounds like she too wields magic of the Gods?"

"Most certainly," Myla responds with a convinced nod. "So why haven't I heard of her?"

"Not all powerful women aspire to *power*," Elsa reminds. "You would have happily lived a life unacknowledged if you could."

"Yes," Myla agrees. "But she has chosen sides, she is using her powers, she clearly is not indifferent."

"Perhaps she is being paid well." Elsa offers.

Myla replies after a moment of mulling, "That is the only answer that makes sense."

"I am scared," Elsa whispers now. "I fear this is only the start of the horrors."

Myla shakes her head, knowing deep down that she too, shares Elsa's fears, but also knowing that to accept them is to accept defeat. The two boys asleep in her bed deserve more than defeat. "No," she answers firmly. "I am...damn, Elsa, I am so scared too."

They lean against one another, arms entwined.

"Speaking it into existence gives the horrors permission to persist. We cannot do that. This must end, and we will be the end *of* it. I am here," Myla says now, willing herself to reach deep beyond her own grief, to offer her best friend some dose of courage. Whatever is left in Myla, it seems they must both share it. For tonight at least. "You are so very far from alone." She chuckles now, thinking of Elsa's bedmates, now realizing why a lock is so very necessary.

With a determined nod, Elsa laughs nervously, seeming to snap out of her frightened daze as she turns to look at Myla. "Are you disappointed in me?"

Confused, Myla's brows furrow, and she shakes her head. "You saved the boys, how could I be disa—"

"I don't mean that," Elsa interrupts. "I mean *them*." She nods toward the door where Henry and Rhyland disappeared through. It creaks open at that moment, making way for a nimble furball, purring as he makes his way to Myla. Prince Gourdy leaps up, his fluffy body heaving with the exertion, before snuggling onto Myla's lap with a contented sigh. *Reminders of her.* Even the cat brings Myla to thoughts of her daughter.

"Oh, I see." Myla's cheeks flush and a weak smile stretches across her lips. She tugs herself from her own grief, allowing her friend a soft place to fall for the night. "No, never! I am not disappointed. It would not be my place to be regardless, as it is none of my business." She gently runs the fingers not occupied with her glass of port through the cat's ample fur before smiling warmly at Elsa. "Really, if anything, I am impressed. I can only manage one. How on earth do you manage two?"

Elsa giggles slightly. "A man at the tavern in Valyndor asked Henry that not long ago. It was asked quite disrespectfully, though."

"And how did he answer?" Curious, Myla leans in.

Elsa grins. "He said, *'the same way you rely on both your left and your right hand. Consistently.'*"

The women burst into laughter, and Myla imagines the wit between Elsa and Henry must be unmatched.

"Well, I ask it respectfully," Myla continues. "And it seems like a happy arrangement for you, which is *truly* all I am concerned about when it comes to your romantic pursuits."

Elsa's eyes gleam, and she lets out a shaky sigh. "I do not know how to explain it," she admits, setting her empty cup on the end table to run two flat hands over her eyes with a heavy sigh. "You know, ever since Callum died, Rhyland and I have been close."

"Well..." Myla's voice is soft, a safe space for Elsa's fears to unfold and heal. Taking her friend's hand, Myla levels with the seemingly small blonde. "You two loved him the most. I am not surprised you would heal from his loss together."

"No," Elsa agrees, absentmindedly stroking Prince Gourdy's fluffed fur. "But it was not supposed to become this."

"What—with Thurston?"

"Well, no," Elsa corrects. "It was only ever friendship between Rhyland and me...well, and this *one* time about a year after Cal died. We were drunk, and well...It was *me* who was not supposed to happen. Romantically, that is. They have been together for over two years."

All at once, so much makes sense. Where there was one, the other could often be found close behind. Myla nods in realization before looking at Elsa again. "So how did you...well, join?"

A rush of red floods Elsa's pearly cheeks, and her blue eyes flick downward. "Do you remember your birthday celebration at Valyndor last year?"

Myla's eyebrows arch as memories of the evening surface. It was unusually energetic that evening. Any children in attendance had been taken to the other side of the palace to be looked after and put to bed at a reasonable hour. The adults remained in the feast hall, and there was far too much Serpent's wine, one of Imogene's personal favorites. Myla still doubts whether it was just a strongly brewed wine or if it had something extra in it. The music was loud, and the night seemed endless. Myla distinctly recalls her and Bryar sneaking into one of the many shadows. He had given her a memorable birthday gift there that night. She does not remember all the details, but an exhilarating one would be the vision of his pendant glowing against his bare chest and his hand over her mouth so she did not alert the guests to their nearby activities.

"I—*yes*," Myla says simply. "I remember."

"Well," Elsa says with wide eyes. "There was alcohol involved."

"Oh, I was there," Myla chuckles nervously. "I remember. What of it?"

"Well, they were looking for an *addition*," Elsa emphasizes the word 'addition', as though it encapsulates so much more. "I was feeling adventurous."

Myla grins and shakes her head. "And the adventure has simply not come to an end since?"

"Hear me out," Elsa defends, more animated now. "Half the fun is watching."

Myla gasps, a mental image of sweat and muscles and tangled men suddenly flashing in her mind's eye. "Well—I—yes," she concludes. "I can see how that would be exhilarating, but is that all it is? Is it just sex?"

"If I said yes?"

"Then I would ask if you were having fun."

"And if I said no?" Elsa asks more cautiously.

"Then I would say you are loved twice as much as the average person, and that is almost better than watching." Myla observes the way Elsa slumps backwards into the bed with a sigh. "Is it love?"

Elsa is quiet, her jaw flexing back and forth with thought before nodding a silent 'yes'. Then out loud, her bright eyes cautiously meet Myla's. "I love them; *both* of them. They love me. Saying it out loud feels like a terrible betrayal, though."

"Elsa," Myla speaks firmly now. "Callum died for so much, you included. Imagine someone finding him up there, probably making love to the Goddesses, and telling him, '*Elsa is miserable because she wants you to know she still loves you*'. What would he say?"

A sad grin claims Elsa's face as she, no doubt, envisions Callum, draped in the full bodies of multiple Goddesses. "He would tell me to fuck off and go live life."

"Yes," Myla laughs. "He would tell you to fuck so far off, to take *both* of those beautiful men to your bed, to go be in love, to drink lots and eat your favorite foods, and play with your nephews, and *live*. Because he did not die so you could also be *dead*."

The room stills and, for an agonizing moment, Elsa turns tear-filled eyes to the cat, distracting her from her pain, before finally speaking. "You are extremely right," she admits with a tear-filled sigh. "It is agitating."

Myla nods in approval. "Good. Now stop hiding your two boyfriends from Bryar and me. It's making things weird and, frankly, confusing."

Elsa laughs and rolls on her side to face Myla. "What are you going to do about the Raven's Veil?"

"Oh," Myla lets out a long and exasperated sigh. "Elsa, I have no idea. Bryar has put nearly fifteen years into them. I know he feels the betrayal deeply. I would hate to execute them all, but I just do not know how else to ensure this stops." An involuntary sob lurches in her throat as stifled emotions break free at the first sign of reprieve. "To think, one of our own allowed the ambush on the village."

"Are you sure?" Elsa gasps.

"It cannot be a coincidence."

"Then they must all die," Elsa insists. "I think Bryar cares more about his children than his fifteen years."

"Yes," Myla says with a sigh. "There will be blood. There will be an atonement. I just do not know whose yet."

CHAPTER 15

PAST: MYLA, SIXTEEN

ORDINARY. WHAT A STRANGE word to use when discussing a young woman. As far as Myla is concerned, there is absolutely nothing ordinary about being female. Everything in nature has a choice over its mate.

Unless it is a human female.

As she sits in the auditorium, willing her attention not to drift to the ornate etchings in the wooded beams overhead, Myla ponders the word *ordinary*.

Each end of the institute's many beams is crafted to look like the pointed and ever watchful head of a dragon, observing the students below as they study their magic. Thus, despite her best efforts, her attentions drift. They wander to the craftsmanship of the richly funded room. They flit between the faces around her, peering, wondering when she is going to answer their instructor.

You are an ordinary girl, so surely you have no reason to refuse practice. He had hissed the words as though she should be grateful for the chance to demonstrate her raw and unpracticed arcane talents. Of course, he does not know about the magic simmering just beneath her skin's surface, always waiting for its moment to reveal itself.

Clearing her throat and absentmindedly arranging her pile of messy notes into a neater stack, Myla stands with hesitation. Not ten minutes ago, the archmage had finished a lecture on how the most common way to summon one's magic is to correspond your actions with your emotions. As Myla has been constantly reminded during her lessons, magic is a physical manifestation of one's emotional state. It is why summoning your magic when the need is absent is frowned upon, for it takes that much more energy to call upon it.

As it so happens, her emotional state seems to be volatile at best as of late. As she approaches the head of the room, her gaze passes over a boy with absolutely no soul in his eyes. His features droop with boredom and an absence of thought. *Call upon him. He needs some emotion in his life.*

"Hurry up, Miss Alerys," the archmage chides. "There are others who might like to demonstrate." A unanimous groan suggests otherwise, but Myla hastens regardless, squirming uncomfortably as a classroom full of eyes now rests on her.

"Do not be discouraged if you must practice before something truly remarkable happens," the archmage drones on. "Tap into whatever it is you are feeling—girls your age have all sorts of *pressing issues*, and this is an excellent rehabilitation of them. Let them free here and let us see what you can come up with."

Myla resists the urge to scowl at him and ask exactly what he is insinuating with "girls her age". Instead, she tries to think of the least tragic thing she can conjure. Anything other than her smarting cheeks after her father's hand lands with a nasty *smack.* Anything other than the invitation from the palace sitting on Maverick's desk. Anything *but* the secret she carries alone since Rhyland took it from her mother and the Druids. Gods—*anything* but that.

As they so often do now, Myla's thoughts speed by unharnessed, when she hoped to keep them tucked safely inside the coldest places of her heart. Her fingertips tingle and ache with the buildup of unused magic.

"Yes!" the archmage exclaims as Myla squeezes her eyes shut, begging the Gods to cork her magic. "That's it, now tap into it!"

Panic pulses within her, pumping fresh waves through her body quicker than her heart beats. The tingles grow, as does the awe-struck volume of her onlooking classmates. Exclamations of amazement, some in fear, others in admiration, only fuels the accumulation of emotions, thus feeding the light. Myla does not dare open her eyes, for even through her closed lids, the glow of the light is unmistakable.

"Ouch!" a young woman's voice complains. "Alright, we get it."

"*How* does she do that?" another asks, a question which prompts unwelcome anger. How she wishes magic were hard for her. But it is not. It pulses through her, freer than the blood from her heart, primal and angry like the extraordinary females of nature who demand to be seen and heard. Wild animals have more right to snarl ferociously and scream at the sky. And here, the wild animal within claws at its cage, ready to show its teeth.

Throughout her entire life, she wished her father would listen. Or that he might see her for *her*. Now she stands, seen. And she hates it. It unravels her. With a deep breath, she forces her eyes open. Expressions of deep admiration and even jealousy look upon her from the benches.

"Well done, Miss Alerys." The archmage claps vigorously, though his expression is a wince as he leans away from the tendrils of light threatening to brush his skin and illuminating the blackness around him. "You may take your sea—"

It is like a horse with no reins. No way to force it to a halt. The light brightens, and the shaking in her body grows violent as the silence flows through her veins, screaming in the only way it can: in a blinding light. It is no longer tolerable. Those who were watching with marvel let out shrieks of pain as they turn their backs, throwing arms and hands over their eyes.

"Miss *Alerys*." The archmage's voice is stern now, insisting she stop. His hand reaches out to grab her, but he recoils, yelping in pain as the lights from her body sear his skin. "You must stop, Miss Alerys!"

There is thundering and screeching as her classmates stumble from their chairs, abandoning the room in a stampede, leaving behind a circulating energy which grows from her body, rustling the papers and drapes in the room, and rattling fixtures. Somewhere in the chaos, Myla hears the archmage announce that he is going for help. Even his departure does not rein in the flow of light. It seizes her body, tensing every muscle, and constricting around her chest. Breathing becomes nearly impossible, and with that inability comes panic, a sentiment amplifying her unbridled magic.

Magic matches her emotions. Scared and chaotic.

The fear grows heavy until Myla is certain her limbs will snap if she stands upright any longer. Blindly, she fumbles for the podium before her, gripping its rim as she lowers herself to the floor. What feels like an hour passes. Although in reality, it is only the time taken for the archmage to rush downstairs, bringing Sir Roderick back with him.

"How long has she been like this?" he shouts. Though Myla cannot see him, she can almost hear the wince as he recoils from her light.

"Five or ten minutes!"

"Myla." The voice of her blademaster is closer now and soft. It's the kind tone she has become accustomed to from him. The voice he uses when he wants her to do something hard. He does not yell or demand or scare her into performing. He does not strike her to show direction, and he does not belittle her to fit his image of perfection. He makes her believe she can.

"Your magic does not own you, Myla. You can let go whenever you're ready. It is like a blade, you see. You can pick it up and let it serve *you*. When you are done, you simply *set it down*."

Something in the way his voice coos is a balm to the exposed and vulnerable parts of her. With every gentle word, the violent reckoning of her magic slows to a vibration once more. When the room stills, she allows her eyes to fall open and behold the mayhem. Before her, the archmage and the blademaster are crouched, one wearing a hungry sort of pride and the other, concern. It is the second face she watches. He smiles finally, nodding in approval. "Like I said, you wield it. It does not wield you."

The background comes into focus. Papers are scattered across the room. A vial of ink has tipped and spilled down the sides of a desk. And at the door, nervously chewing his bottom lip, is Bryar. He is sweating from exertion, and his eyes scan the room, taking in the wreckage.

"Bryar." Sir Roderick looks over his shoulder casually. "Miss Alerys and I have lessons together in fifteen minutes. Please escort her downstairs and see to it she is given something to drink. I will be but a moment longer." Sir Roderick extends a hand, his eyes slanting in a comforting smile as he pulls Myla to her feet, guiding her past the frowning archmage and immediately across the room to where Bryar waits.

The slamming of the door behind her, closing them into Sir Roderick's arena, is a comforting sound. Bryar closes the door, shutting out the last twenty minutes, and extinguishing the buzz of gossip. His eyes lock with hers and ask a hundred questions at once, though all he can manage is, "Wow."

"I know." A rogue laugh slips out in spite of the more prominent urge to throw something, and Myla presses the flats of her palms against her eyes before slumping into an exhausted heap on a chair.

"*Wow,*" Bryar reiterates, a grin spreading across his face. Pulling up a chair, he sits opposite her. "Truly, Myla. I am in awe of you."

"You should not be," Myla insists, leaning on her elbows toward him. "This is not an ability I am proud of."

"Well, you have no reason to be ashamed of it..."

"I am not ashamed of it either," Myla retorts, albeit softly.

"Then what is wrong?"

"I am *scared* of it," she whispers, focusing her gaze on the flexing of his arms rather than his understanding gaze. "More than scared, really. I am horrified."

His brow furrows. "I do not understand."

The energy between them shifts as shock fades into terrible realization, and Myla finds her body weak and trembling. While they are so intimately attached now, she has not exposed the truth. He is none the wiser about her secrets and the real danger she dances with every time she calls upon her magic. Or any time she is with him. Any time she leaves her home, really. "I want to tell you," Myla says finally, her words a mere whisper.

Bryar reaches out, his warm hand closing around hers. "I know you have a secret," he offers gently. "If you want to tell me now, you are safe to do so. If you'd rather wait, I will wait too."

"You say that, but once I tell you, there is no taking it back. You will wish I hadn't said anything."

"Why would I want you to take it back?" he asks, sincere and alive with the need to reassure her.

Sighing, Myla allows her fingers to mingle with his, holding them tightly, afraid that if she loosens her grip, the truth will cause them to break apart right when they are just beginning to come together. "I never told you why I came to you that night."

He shakes his head. "I did not want you to feel pressured to tell me, either."

"Yes, and I was grateful." Myla offers a weak smile.

"But you are going to tell me now?"

"Rhyland has not already?" Myla asks warily, searching his face for any sign of dishonesty. As he shakes his head, she is unsurprised to find there is none. Of course, he tells the truth. He is honest about who he is; meanwhile, she has dragged him into her life and her heart without giving him all of the information. Shakily, she speaks. "I have this thing—this *curse.*"

"Curse?"

"—A curse to me—" Myla sniffles over the following words, lowering her eyes as tears slip down her cheeks. "The woman Caius is looking for, the one who will supposedly help him end the reign of the Blood Stealer...I believe I am that woman. I have the magic prophesied by the seer."

Her words land with a sharp sting, visibly stunning the young blacksmith. His hands recoil, and his brows press inward, realization washing over him like a late spring storm, unwelcome, and ruinous. "The—*King* Caius? *Wait.*" Bryar stands, his head violently shaking in disbelief. "You cannot mean the magic Sir Roderick spoke of when he told us the seer's prophecy to King Caius?"

"The very same," Myla responds, slumping back into her chair. She does not watch as he paces; something inside her chest aches as he moves further and further away. Of course, anyone in their right mind would. She swindled him into sharing a piece of his heart with her when she knew she could not accept it. "I am sorry for not telling you that very night. I could have saved you wasted time." With a dignified breath, Myla stands and smooths her skirt against her thighs, anything to occupy her before she works up the courage to walk out of the room.

"Wasted time?" Bryar blurts and his pacing stops. "Whatever do you mean by that?"

Uncomfortable, Myla senses heat flush her cheeks, and she gestures weakly his way. "I only mean that...Well, that *we, I mean.* It is already very complicated, and I find it unlikely that you would have pursued me if you knew this."

"*It?*" Bryar clarifies, but something about the way he speaks, paired with his eyes searching hers, willing her to speak further, tells her he knows exactly what she is saying.

Stubbornness, stuck deep in her like a thorn, urges her to dig her heels in and force him to work it all out on his own, but those soft eyes seem to melt away at her tension, warming a safe space for honesty. So, she speaks. "Let's play a game," she whispers, daring a step closer to him. "Where we both say *honestly* what we are thinking."

A smile teases at the stoic corners of his mouth, but he remains composed, nodding in agreement. "Alright, you first."

"Yes," Myla agrees breathlessly, willing the pulse in her chest to slow so she might hear her own thoughts loud enough to speak them. "I think I am so afraid that you will not find time with me worth it now that you have discovered my secret. In fact, I am almost more afraid of that than of the secret itself. Because I *know* that I love you."

His eyes flicker, a spark of happiness perhaps? Or maybe satisfaction. Whatever it is, she loves it. "You are getting very good at this game, Miss Alerys," Bryar whispers, stepping closer so their toes nearly touch, and she swears she can hear the pounding in his chest above her own. "My turn," he continues, leaning down to press a kiss to her forehead, his hands gently cupping her shoulders. "I think it was never a matter of pursuing you," he says, leaning back now to study her. "It was a matter of resisting you, something I failed at immediately because I knew that if it were the will of the Gods that I should love someone, that someone was undoubtedly you."

Unchecked, a smile passes over Myla's otherwise somber features, and she rolls onto her tiptoes, arching to reach his face, eager and hungry for his touch. "Before now, I did not think being loved ever felt safe."

"I do not have much experience in the matter," Bryar admits, kissing the tip of her nose. "But I have to assume you should always feel safe with someone who loves you."

His lips are a hairsbreadth away from hers when the door opens, framing a startled Sir Roderick. "Gods be damned," he nearly growls, rushing further into the room to shut the door behind himself. "Bar the fucking door or something," he chides, glaring especially hard at Bryar. "I have had my fill of cleaning up your messes, Miss Alerys. Let me have no more of it today. Imagine how the headmaster will treat my *neck* if he finds I have fostered improper relations between a common boy and a noble woman." He hands a heavy blade to Myla and dismisses Bryar with an agitated wave. "Off with you. Go sharpen my blade. I want it at its finest when they behead us both with it."

CHAPTER 16

PRESENT

A DAUGHTER FOR A daughter.

Rhyland holds the unfolded, wrinkled note still. This small inscription is the only evidence the Raven's Veil traitors left behind after the assassins were thrown into the damp prison cells below ground. A guard discovered it tucked carefully within a pillow's stuffing while assisting in the barracks-wide search. While reading their minds might have made the task of uncovering the betrayal so much easier, it seems their traitor prepared for this complication and wiped the memories of over half the Raven's Veil.

"You have put too much money into these men for them to be so fucking stupid," Elsa blurts while glaring over Rhyland's shoulder. Her eyes flicker to Bryar, who paces angrily, gnawing his nail dangerously low. "You would think they would have had the wherewithal to burn it at least."

"They'd have to remember that they had it hidden to burn it," Rhyland says with an exasperated sigh. "Whoever erased their memories, left the note intentionally. They wanted us to find it."

"Yes, but what does it *mean*—" Henry asks, taking the note from Rhyland for closer examination. "A daughter for a daughter?"

"*Stop*," Bryar snaps, slamming a hand down on the war table. "Stop *saying* that."

The trio exchanges weary glances before Elsa delicately retrieves the note from Henry, slipping it in the cuff of her sleeve. "Has Myla seen this?"

For a moment, his eyes close, envisioning the look of horror on his wife's face when she first read the message. Bryar nods, gripping the end of the table as if crushing it might stop him from crushing *someone*. "She has."

"And?" Rhyland clarifies.

"And I believe the Raven's Veil will be lucky to see dusk." He straightens and breathes deeply, summoning every drop of composure he can. "Her Grace has been challenged now, and we all know she is not going to sit back and let it continue like this."

"Myla? Sit back? It would be easier for you to set fire to an ocean than for Myla to sit back," Elsa snorts. "One of us should go down there and get her before she starts a war among her own people."

"Her own people have brought war to her," Henry corrects, pressing two flat palms to his face with a stressed sigh. "Anything she does will merely be to stop it."

Bryar nods in agreement. "Nevertheless, I do not see how any good can come of her staying down there with them. They cannot give her answers, and I need to go tell her." He moves toward the door, but Rhyland intercepts, placing a gloved hand over the handle.

"Allow me to go," he says in a low tone. "I believe I may be able to help her this time."

Hesitantly at first, Bryar steps back with a nod, allowing it. "Last time I went down there, she nearly blasted a hole in the floor when I suggested she come back up. Watch your head."

"Perhaps I should go?" Elsa interjects nervously.

"No," Rhyland answers. His voice is firm, and he looks first at Elsa, then Henry. "Myla and I understand each other in moments like these. I will go."

Although very few lanterns glow, there is little need for their illumination as the queen hurls bolts of light against the prison cell bars. She could easily be mistaken for a feral animal. Her hair, previously tied into a neat braid, is loose and stringy, swinging back and forth with the motion of her body as she heaves another wave of blinding magic. It catches on the metal bars, warming them and lighting the space behind them. Rhyland could almost laugh were it not for his friend's visible agony, or for the men behind the bars huddled in a tight cluster in the furthest corner possible, trying to avoid the violence of their queen's wrath. Unbeknownst to her, it is obvious many wear an expression of confused guilt. They know they aided in the wrongdoings against their queen's family, but they have no recollection of it.

It is obvious Myla isn't hurting the assassins, nor is she trying to. She is scaring them, but more concerning, she is running herself ragged.

"Your Grace," Rhyland calls as he descends the final steps and approaches her. His attempt at getting her attention is either not heard or ignored. Two guards stand at the base of the stairs, watching as he passes with expressions that seem to warn him to leave. It is evident they do not want to be there anymore than her prisoners do.

"Myla," Rhyland says, firmer now. At the sound of her name, she spins to face him.

Her blue eyes glow with an otherworldly intensity, fueled by the exertion of her magic.

He meets her gaze. "Save your energy."

"For what?" she pants, straightening slightly. "Why should I save my magic for the enemies out there?" She points toward the stairs leading upstairs and, inevitably, outside. "When they are nothing compared to the traitors who have pretended to safeguard my family, only to kill and destroy those they *swore* to protect! *I* see now my enemies have slept under my roof and eaten at my tables for years."

"Indeed, they have," Rhyland flashes a betrayed glance at the prisoners who were once friends, now cowering behind the bars opposite him. "And you will bring none of them to justice with your rage."

Defiantly, Myla tucks loose strands of hair behind her ears, then plants her hands firmly on her hips. "Perhaps not. But then again, maybe I have been too trusting—too willing to see the good." The latter is hissed as her eyes travel back toward her prisoners.

Rhyland shifts his stance, mulling over his words before daring to speak.

"Why are you here?" she asks, raising her fingers to toy with a thread of fizzling light.

"We need to figure out what that note means, and we would all prefer you to join the discussion."

Myla growls, releasing the filament of light. Its stinging white travels tactfully between two bars, ensnaring one of the Raven's Veil soldiers. He is jarred violently from where he sits, and with a grunt, she yanks her hand backwards, urging her magic to propel the likely traitor forward until he is wedged uncomfortably against the rails. "*That* is precisely what I am doing," she answers as she paces closer to the sniffling man. "Perhaps the note was yours?"

"N—no, You—your Grace!" He stumbles over his words; the very tremble in them is a cry for mercy. "I swear it. I think...I'm sure I have been loyal to only you!"

Myla tugs harder on the magical tether, and the man's face bangs against his metal confines. She ignores his wince.

"You think? How *fucking* comforting, you idiot! Well, I *think* I may just kill you! You see how that feels?"

The man's trembling increases. Rhyland sees the whites of his eyes, wide with unbridled terror of his queen. Myla leans toward the miserable ex-assassin.

"You are either loyal, or you are not, and unfortunately for all of you, your declarations of loyalty are no longer trustworthy! At least one of you, if not all of you, in this very cell has grossly betrayed me. You were responsible for many lives I care about. One of them being *my daughter!*"

Rhyland steps forward, cautiously placing a hand on Myla's shoulder. "I must insist you come with me before you make enemies out of your subjects. Myla," he whispers now. "Their memories are gone. Nobody here can provide the answers you seek. Not anymore."

An expression of horrified fury claims Myla's body, running a rigid chill over her entire being, and with glassy eyes, she scans the blank faces of men she no longer trusts for reasons they do not remember. As she turns begrudgingly to follow him, Rhyland cannot help but feel a tinge of accomplishment at convincing her to leave.

"Wow," he says with a weak smile her way. "I did not actually think that would work."

"It didn't," Myla sneers, and it is only when the flickering glow of the guard's torches touches her face that Rhyland observes her eyes are red from hours of tears. "I just need someone new to yell at."

"That is comforting," Rhyland chuckles sarcastically, following her up the stairs, and oddly grateful for the light the windows allow as they make it to the main corridor. "So, shall I brace for your wrath?"

Myla turns to face him, crossing her arms over a heaving chest. "I do not know what to do. I thought I was so close to ending this war. A month ago, I was a mother to three children, and I hoped we would spend the summer in New Falkmere..."

The raw vulnerability catches Rhyland off guard, and so he allows a slow breath before answering with a fact that feels more important than any discussion of war. "You are *still* a mother of three. Death cannot change that."

The queen's chin wobbles in a way that reminds him of the girl she was before ruling robbed her of her childlike sense of justice.

Rhyland sinks onto a bench cluttered with the children's cloaks and boots. "This is not the first time I have braved darkness with you, and I doubt it will be the last. Let me help. What can I do?"

The ghost of a smile passes briefly over Myla's face before vanishing entirely. It seems they are all braving the darkness together. "I suspect I know exactly who wrote that note. I need you to investigate something for me. Something that will validate my suspicion."

Rhyland's body runs with chills, but he dutifully nods, noting the way her eyes pool with darkness—memories, perhaps—something she does not wish to recall but must. "Anything. What is it?"

"I need you to look into my mother's death."

The war room is eerily empty when Myla enters, her fit of rage still swarming with a heady wave of emotions. Rhyland follows close behind.

A sense of betrayal is what Myla notes most heavily when she is greeted by her husband's creased face. His features are heavy, from the droop of his eyebrows to the way his shoulders slump over a stack of papers needing signatures. Everything about his persona oozes defeat. Everything in his demeanor calls for a gentle touch, yet gentle is the opposite of what she feels.

Without thinking, her feet carry her swiftly around the table to where he is bent, and as though possessed by some evil force, she pushes flat palms into his side, catching him entirely off guard. He stumbles backward before straightening and flashing a shocked glare her way.

"What the—" He does not finish his sentence.

Myla lands another blow to his chest as an angry shriek lurches from her lungs. "How could you let this happen?" Her words are a blend of screaming and tears as she pounds her palms against his armored chest, one blow after another.

He does not fight back; instead, his arms brace against the wall behind him, steadying himself with every strike. Though she does not care to see it, the grief on his face is unmistakable.

Regardless, the words fall from her lips. "Those were *your* men! How could you not see them conspiring? How could you not notice them whispering and plotting? Our daughter is dead, our sons are a target, and innocent men are *beheaded*—and it is *your* oversight!"

At this, his hands grasp her wrists, stopping another attack, and his blurring green gaze finds hers, saying so much in his silence. Eyes that beg for mercy, compassion, or acquittal. Anything to staunch the bleeding of his own grief. But it is a mercy she is not ready to extend.

"What was more important than commanding my army and keeping control of the Raven's Veil? What kind of captain trains and equips the most lethal force in Myrnith and then neglects to *control* them?"

The final words are declared with enough conviction to evoke a stunned gasp from Rhyland. "Myla!" He steps closer to separate them. "That is uncalled for."

Myla swats his hand away and pushes against Bryar's chest again, unaware of the hot tears pouring down her cheeks. "You allowed our daughter to *die*!"

"Stop!" Wearing a look of horror, Rhyland advances to pull Myla away. He loops strong arms around her middle, pulling her off of Bryar who is otherwise unmoving, and willingly accepting the brunt of her anger. "This is not fixing anything!"

At last, Bryar speaks, straightening. "No." His voice is level as he swallows hard, and his hands rise to the clasp of his captain's cloak. "She is right," he rasps, yanking the cloak from his shoulders. "I shall serve as captain no longer." Spitting the words angrily now, he tosses the garment to Rhyland. "You can lead her army. I do not have the stomach for it anymore."

The room tenses as he turns and walks away. Stunned, Rhyland looks at the heap of responsibility in his arms and then to Myla who lets out an angry shriek, reaching for the stack of papers on the table to scatter them across the floor.

As her husband disappears through the open door, she trails behind him. "Yes, Bryar! Run away! If only it were as easy for me to take off the crown as it is for you to take off the cloak!"

He turns on his heels, a foreign rage in his eyes as he utters treason, "You don't have a crown, *wife.*"

CHAPTER 17

PAST: MYLA, SIXTEEN

SUMMER FEELS EUPHORIC IN a way it never has. In previous years, Myla had spent the hottest days in her mother's sitting room, fanned by their servants while stitching some tedious needlepoint pattern. Thanks to her studies at the institute now, and with Elsa's "chaperoning", it is far easier to be unaccounted for by her governess or her parents.

Today, she thanks her father for enrolling her in the Institute of Mystic Arts, for she finds herself lying in tall grass by a trickling creek, listening to the banter of her friends while the hot glow from above brings a flush into her cheeks. A satisfied smile steals across her face as rhythmic footsteps approach, followed by Callum and Rhyland letting out victorious *whoops*. She keeps one eye open and watches as Bryar approaches, grinning from ear to ear. Overhead, he holds a scroll, verification of his scholarship, she can only assume.

"You got in?" Callum asks.

Bryar nods, and his confirmation is followed by more cheering.

The sound is glorious. With her secret involvement well hidden, she stands, feeling a swell of pride and joy and so many emotions she does not even know how to name. Whatever they are, they encourage her to abandon all propriety.

His gaze meets hers as he offers the scroll for inspection. "I got in!" he repeats, watching eagerly as she scans over the conditions of his scholarship. It is all as it should be. *Thank you, Sir Roderick!*

"I am so proud of you," Myla speaks softly, with little care to the three pairs of eyes on them as she links her arms around his neck. "You deserve this."

Instead of freeing her, Bryar leans back enough to see her face, flashing her that beautiful, innocent, boyish smile, before pressing sun-warmed lips to hers. She melts against his kiss, his warmth, sharing in his joy and his success. It is the most satisfying feeling she has ever experienced.

"*I knew it!*" Elsa lets out a triumphant shriek, and the sound of clapping is unmistakable. "Dinner is served!"

"*What! Excuse the—*" Rhyland cackles somewhere behind them. "How did I *miss* that?" With a confused glance at Elsa, his brows furrow. "Dinner?"

"Because you mind your own business," Elsa replies, still laughing. "It's commendable, really. I could *never*. And don't worry about dinner, Myla gets it."

"Gods, man," Callum chimes in. "Get it out of your system—I can *smell it* from here."

Smiling, Myla leans back, looking up into Bryar's green eyes. "I suppose we could have given them a warning before that."

"Nah." Shaking his tousled head, Bryar steps backward, flashing their friends a playful glower. "The element of surprise is always more satisfying."

Soon, shoulder to shoulder, the five sit on a fallen log across the widest part of the creek with their bare feet dangling in the water. The way the sunlight catches on the ripples below them somehow reminds Myla of her life now. The darkest shadows of the stream hide in the dips and shallows of the current and cannot reach the golden rays, and *dark* they are. But every now and then, the water rises, propelled by the harshest aspects of darkness, and its face finds the sun. And it is *so* beautiful. She wonders how life can be so contrary. Perhaps it is the act of living two lives at once. An existence of duty, reform, and scheming under her oppressive father's roof, and a life of fresh air in her lungs, dirt between her toes, and the kindest of hands holding hers, here beneath the shelter of the Gods. Myla looks up, lulled into a deep tranquility by the warm breeze loosening the curls in her hair.

"Hey," Rhyland breaks the silence. "Remember when we watched the older boys get outfitted, and we thought *we should all do that together?*"

Bryar and Callum, both smiling, nod eagerly. "Yeah, and we all said it thinking there was no way it might *actually* happen," Callum adds, with an undertone of nostalgic pride unmistakable.

"Well, it has," Rhyland says with a broad grin. "I think we are going to do some pretty incredible things together."

Leaning forward to catch a glimpse of each other, Elsa and Myla exchange content smiles before Bryar speaks up. "Yeah," he says with a chuckle, "or some pretty stupid stuff."

Unanimously, the group laughs, and Myla imagines the incredible things they might do. Deep down, she wonders if she will get to see any of it. With her father carefully paving her path in a direction completely opposite any that might parallel that of her friends, she doubts it. The thought is a lonely one, and she takes a deep breath, urging herself to live in the moment. Something in the back of her head screams, *enjoy it while it lasts.*

"So, what are the chances of you ladies remaining unaccounted for the rest of the evening?" Callum asks, flashing a particular coy smile Elsa's way.

Myla watches as Elsa holds his gaze, unabashed, unwavering, bold. Myla is certain that when Elsa's father anticipated the Alerys family throwing his daughter into the paths of eligible men, this is entirely *not* what he meant. Nonetheless, Myla watches as Callum leans toward Elsa, whispering something which makes the blonde girl beside him snort in laughter.

"I may or may not have told Maverick that we would stay at the institute late so Myla could study the contortion of other people's energy into magic. He looked confused, but I assured him it was possible. As we know, it is not." Elsa laughs as she recounts the details, to the delight of all. "He was about to go reference his own library to search for proof of those methods, which I expect will keep him occupied all night. Just in case, I informed him the blademaster also wanted his daughter to get some extra hours of training in."

"I suspect Sir Roderick would absolutely corroborate that story if questioned," Callum responds, tossing a rock into the creek with a plop. The spray of the water is cooling, a kindness in the heat.

"He would," Bryar answers matter-of-factly, and Myla nods in agreement, stretching her legs to fully submerge her feet.

"He shows us favor," Myla admits. "I am not sure why. But I know he is trustworthy."

"How does that feel?" Rhyland asks, his brows furrowing. "To trust your blademaster more than your own father?"

Bryar elbows him. "Shut up, man."

Myla shrugs and finds that the comment, though oddly insulting, leaves no sting. "No," she says with a resolute nod. "He is right. I do trust Roderick more than my father, and it feels like the Gods knew I needed help I would not find at home."

"*Hey,*" Elsa interjects. "What about me?"

"*You* need help, too." Myla answers with a grin. "Maybe more than me. *Other people's energy,* Elsa. He is going to ask me why I can't summon every time he gets angry now." Myla snorts, the realization of just how ridiculous Elsa's ploy was suddenly hitting her.

"Oh, stop," Elsa responds with a laugh. "Also, we did agree that both of our fathers are assholes." She leans forward to catch Bryar's attention. "I hear your father is nice. I propose we shall share yours and pretend ours do not exist."

Bryar merely chuckles and shrugs slightly. "I can only imagine how he'd respond if I showed up with not one, but two noblewomen."

Callum lets out a boisterous cackle before splashing water at his friend, the droplets landing mostly on Mya instead. "He would say, '*Well done, son!*'"

"We were given two hands for a reason," Rhyland adds, making obscene gestures with his.

"Gross," Myla says finally, trying not to laugh at the vulgar conversation, though her eyes catch with Elsa's and her friend twitches her eyebrows suggestively, sending her into a fit of laughter.

"Alright, alright," Myla interjects. "Since it seems we do not have to go home for several more hours, what exactly will we be doing?"

"Hopefully, things that would piss my father off," Elsa answers, her voice full of innuendo as she looks once more at Callum.

"I think we can deliver." Rhyland stands on the log and pulls his tunic over his head, leaving his dark skin to glisten in the heat of the sun. "Who wants to swim?"

The response is thunderous as the five friends wobble to their feet in a row, one by one attempting to balance their way off the log. Unashamed, the boys strip half naked while Elsa and Mya stand side by side, watching.

"I don't think they should stop with their shirts," Elsa whispers, her fingers eagerly grabbing Myla's arm. Her eyes fix on Callum, and a look of ownership passes over her.

"Elsa," Myla warns. "Maybe we should wait here."

"And continue to bake?" Rhyland chimes in, overhearing their exchange. "The water is incredible this time of year, and we didn't go through all the effort of teaching Bryar to swim for nothing!" And with rowdy shouts, the three boys throw themselves into the stream, splashing one another repeatedly until Callum dives for Rhyland, submerging him completely.

"Come on!" Bryar insists, and something about the way he stands and holds his hands out to her dries her throat. Water droplets run down his bare abdomen, and his curls cling to his forehead.

"I have decided something," Elsa whispers, leaning close to Myla so only they can hear. "Men in tight, wet trousers is my new favorite thing."

"I thought it was just *men* in general," Myla murmurs back, her eyes still locked with Bryar's.

"No," Elsa replies decidedly. "It is men in tight, wet trousers now."

Giggling, and willing herself to ignore the tension coiling in her middle, Myla reaches to the nape of her neck, pulling at the ribbons of her collar. "Help me."

Satisfied, Bryar nods in approval, then turns to offer them privacy as both girls strip down to their shifts.

They spend the next hour cooling off in the water. While Callum and Elsa play wrestle and laugh at each other while whispering amongst themselves, Myla is acutely aware of how Bryar does not touch her. After a while, he exits the creek entirely, lying in the sun to dry. Myla is about to follow him when Rhyland swims nearer.

"How have things been with your family?" It is a genuine question, and she can see there is care in his eyes.

"Tense," Myla admits with a deflated sigh. "Although that is nothing new."

After a moment of silence, Rhyland tips a chin toward Bryar. "He has been my friend since before we could walk—all three of us, actually. Our parents worked the same harvest one year."

Myla smiles, dipping lower into the water and shivering as the cold inches its way up her neck. "How fortunate you all are to have such a bond."

"Yes," Rhyland agrees. "I have never seen him so protective of anyone before he met you." The words warm her despite the chills the cool creek brings on. "I think being loved by him is the best gift any person could receive."

Myla looks at Rhyland now and sees the ache in his eyes as he glances at the young man lounging in the grass.

"You are one of his best friends," Myla says, testing the context of his statement. "I am certain he loves you."

Rhyland grins and pulls the black corkscrew curls at his shoulders into a tight bun at the nape of his neck, revealing freshly shaved sides. "Not the way I wish he could. Not the way he loves *you*."

Myla's belly flutters and falls at the same time. "You love him?"

Rhyland nods, then flashes a charismatic smile as though to dismiss the sentiment entirely. "Who wouldn't?" He flings a spray of water in her direction playfully before speaking again. "I'll have to wipe that from your memory someday."

"Or," Myla challenges with raised eyebrows. "You could trust me with it and know it is safe with me. Sometimes sharing a burden makes it less painful."

"I do trust you," Rhyland says with a genuine smile. "That's why I told you."

"Have you told anyone else?"

"That I am in love with my best friend? Or that I like boys more than I like girls?" Rhyland clarifies.

"Well, both are good questions, I suppose." Myla answers, drifting closer to Rhyland to keep their conversation as private as possible.

"Callum and my parents know, and now you."

Myla watches Rhyland for a moment, wondering how it must feel to be him, to love someone who cannot love him back, and her heart aches. "Thank you," she says, smiling at her friend.

"For what?"

"For sharing that part of yourself with me," Myla answers before dunking beneath the water, submerging herself in the glorious cold before returning to the smoldering shore.

They dry themselves on the edge of the creek bed as the sun sinks behind the mountains which shadow New Falkmere, passing Rhyland's flask back and forth. The sharp heat of the liquor warms Myla's throat as it travels into her belly.

Elsa mentions the rapid chill growing with the loss of the sun, no sooner do Bryar and Callum stack dried sticks and with extended palms, work together to start a campfire before them. Myla watches in awe as their sputtering flames grow, curling from their skin into an inferno on the kindling and wood.

"I wish I had useful magic like that," Elsa says after a while. "I can only heal scratches." She takes a long swallow from the flask, then hands it across the still-growing fire to Bryar.

"That is useful," Callum insists, sitting beside her. "Show me." And to the shock of all, he pulls a dagger from his boot and cuts a deep line of red across his palm.

Wide-eyed, Myla takes the flask from Bryar and draws another long sip, never looking away from the bleeding wound.

"You idiot!" Elsa croaks, shoving a hand into his shoulder in chastisement. "Why would you do that?"

"So you can heal me," Callum says sheepishly. "And then I will have an excuse to kiss you in thanks."

For the first time, possibly ever, Myla watches her friend glow bashfully, her blue irises suddenly hidden behind her eyelashes.

"Smooth," Bryar chuckles under his breath, nudging Rhyland as they both silently applaud their friend's candor.

Myla observes the exchange differently now, noticing the way Rhyland's gaze lingers a few seconds after Bryar's. As their eyes meet across the fire, she smiles at him, then turns her attention to Elsa.

A violet glow curls from Elsa's palms as she levitates her hand above Callum's bleeding one. After a moment, she pulls away and he drags a bloodied palm over his pants, shocked when he reveals unmarred flesh. "Wow," he says finally, showing off his undamaged skin as though it is a trophy. "You actually made it disappear...entirely." He looks at her, and she visibly shudders with anticipation, but instead of caving to his conquest, she stands, dusting the back of her dress off, and claims the flask once more. After a long drink, she hands it to Rhyland who shakes it, eyeing it in disbelief. It is no doubt half empty already.

"Of course I did. And you should not need an excuse to kiss me." Though her words seem chiding, her eyes flicker playfully in his direction before her tone softens entirely. "I wish that *this* could be our every day."

A unanimous chorus of agreement sounds, followed by Callum taking a deep breath. "Something tells me this is very temporary." He gestures to their surroundings as if referring to the summer day, but deep down, they all know he actually means three common boys sneaking around with noble girls.

"In that case," Elsa says, turning to look Callum square in the eyes. "We should make the most of it, shouldn't we?"

Callum leans back, tipping his chin upwards to examine her standing over him. "What did you have in mind?"

The moment transforms into something Myla feels very deeply as though they should not witness. She watches with lips parted in disbelief as Elsa extends a hand to Callum, pulling him to his feet before leading him into the shadows of the forest behind them. They vanish

from sight entirely, and the three remaining pairs of eyes watch the
woods in shock until, one-by-one, they bashfully return their attention to the blaze before them.

"Is she always like that?" Rhyland asks with a laugh, sipping the
remains of his flask slowly. He offers a final sip to both Bryar and Myla,
but they both refuse, the latter due to the way her head spins.

"Always," Myla enunciates the word, making firm eye contact with
Rhyland as though her squinting eyes will convince him further.

"Well," Rhyland answers jokingly, "I want to know why that never
happens to me."

At this, Bryar chuckles and nods toward the woods. "Don't feel too
left out. I'm pretty sure that's never happened to Callum, either. Until
now."

Myla cannot help but giggle. Maybe it's the warmth of the alcohol
in her veins which loosens her tongue, but she speaks anyway. "Then
for our sake, I hope they kept walking for a while. Callum is in for an
education."

Two pairs of shocked eyes land on her, silent at first, before both
boys belt out in laughter and Rhyland, clearly wobbling from the
effect of his drink, leans back on his elbows and lifts his face to the
sky to shout, "Don't cry, Callum! Trust your instincts—or at least, the
process!"

Bryar laughs now, shaking his head in visible disapproval, although
the dimples in his cheeks deepen as he inadvertently starts laughing
with Rhyland. "Leave him be. This might be a once in a lifetime
experience for him."

Suddenly, the fire feels too hot as Myla's cheeks flush, and she finds
there is only one question she wants to ask. For all of her inexperience,
of which she is fully aware thanks to Elsa's vast explanations, she
cannot help but wonder what sort of experiences Bryar has had. *Well,
I am obviously* not *asking that question.* Instead of humiliating herself

completely, Myla gives way to the weight of the drink pulling her head in every direction and allows herself to fall onto the soft ground beneath her. The stars spin overhead, or perhaps they are dancing. Surely, stars dance. If she were a star in the sky, Myla is certain she would not be still. There could be nothing more beautiful than existing purely to bring light and beauty and movement.

The fire sways, its flames bounding in jubilee toward the sky, and with a slow sigh, Bryar lays down next to her, grabbing her hand and holding it to his chest. She glances sideways at him, noting how he watches the stars, and she hopes they are dancing for him too.

CHAPTER 18

PRESENT

MYLA ORDERED RAVENS TO be sent two days ago, requesting the aid of Titonfall, Elspire, and the Riverlands. When Myla wakes to Elsa shaking her shoulder, holding a handful of responses, her grim face bares the news without words.

"They will not come," she whispers, sitting on the edge of the bed. "Only the Ashborn have responded, and they are on their way."

Myla slumps back into the pillows, running hands across her flushed, sleepless face in defeat. "Did anyone say why?"

Elsa cringes before handing the small scroll to Myla. It is crumbled slightly with travel. Elsa hands her a magnifying glass from the end table and, with a disheartened sigh, she processes the message before her. Titonfall specifically recounts her performance during the Blood Stealer's occupation in her palace, referencing specifically how she fled, abandoning the throne entirely.

"I am seen as weak. They blame me for abandoning my rule...to save *them*. Have they forgotten that I defeated him *while* pregnant? What a sorry bunch of assholes."

"Apparently," Elsa smirks at her insults, noting the empty space in the bed beside her. "Not that I am displeased by it or anything, but where is your husband?"

Myla crushes the tiny papers in her fist before discarding them on the floor, the question only adding to her defeat. "He did not come to bed last night. I have no idea where he is."

"I can answer that." It is Fern who speaks now, entering the room encumbered by an armload of clean clothes, which she puts away. "I checked on Caspian and Aidan in the night. He was asleep with them, though he was not there this morning when I dressed them."

Elsa's sharp eyes probe for answers. "What happened?"

"Rhyland did not tell you?"

She shakes her head. "Rhyland? The epitome of discretion?"

Sliding off the bed, Myla walks to her wardrobe. "Well, ask him. I do not have the energy to recount it. For once, he will have to abandon discretion."

Elsa nods understandingly and helps Myla dress in silence. Her outfit is simple today, as it seems she will not host any visiting dignitaries. She wears leather trainers; the trousers fit her tightly. She tucks her clad legs into knee-high black boots. Next, Fern pulls a loose forest-green tunic over her head, and the hem falls just past her hips, flowing around her comfortably. Myla rolls the sleeve to her elbows and glances at her reflection, noting the amulet resting on her chest. It strobes gently, which indicates he's not in danger. But perhaps his body feels as though it is. Guilt seeps from her pores.

"I need to go find Bryar," Myla says, finding the fox dagger on her bedside table and sheathing it to her thigh.

"But your hair—" Fern objects, waving the brush, only to remind Myla of her sweet daughter.

Myla glances at her hair. It tumbles in loose curls over her shoulders. "Never mind it," she says finally. "I will be back. Do not let the boys out of your sight."

"Where are you going?" Elsa demands. "You cannot leave the palace alone."

Myla sighs, glancing over her shoulder. "My husband would not let anything happen to me." She gestures again to the amulet. "He is nearby."

In the hall, she meets a somber Ethstan, who holds a cup of steaming tea. "Myla," his old voice wobbles as he extends the drink to her. "I thought you might need something to warm you this morning."

Myla smiles warmly at her old friend. "Thank you, Ethstan. I have no time for tea. Have you seen Bryar?"

His wise eyes, framed in wrinkles, narrow. "I have not. Is something amiss?"

She nods. "I am afraid I said things I regret. Unforgivable things." An ache creeps through the muscles of her back, wrapping around her abdomen and deep within her chest, finally sinking its hot talons into her heart. *Is this what guilt feels like when it is trying to break free?*

Ethstan urges her to take the tea regardless, and they sit together on a cold stone bench beside one of the arched outcroppings overlooking the forest. His brown habit appears warmer than usual in the glow of the morning light. "I told you once to listen."

"Not with your words," Myla counters slightly, offering a weak smile.

"Nonetheless," he answers, returning the smile. "You have so much passion. Sometimes I wonder how a single body can carry as much zeal as yours does. But with that comes impulsiveness. If you regret what you said, maybe it is because you should listen now, instead of speaking."

Myla brings the cup to her lips and sips before responding, noting the way she feels, as though she could completely unravel. Every morning in the last week, she has woken up and tied off the emotional loose ends which seem to brush painfully, like nerves, on every little inconvenience and setback. This morning though, with the combination of

Bryar's absence and the rejections for aid, Ethstan's kindness seems to offer permission to break.

"I am afraid he will have nothing to say to me."

"I seriously doubt that," Ethstan says with a nudge as he takes the empty cup from her. "But there is only one way to find out."

Snow crunches beneath her boots as she ventures into the woods behind the ancient and partially dilapidated palace. The overnight guards had informed Myla they had spotted Bryar walking north into the forest early in the morning. Now, with his tracks to guide her, she follows his longer strides for about ten minutes to the base of an impressively tall tree. Its branches grow upward, reaching for the sky, and its height towers over most other trees surrounding it.

"Bryar." She glances upwards, awed at the maze of tightly braided rope pathways connecting the branches higher overhead. It looks like a perch. Unfortunately, it appears as though one must climb, or even fly, to reach the start of the corded bridges. Further up, she can make out what appears to be someone sitting nearly at the top of the tree.

"Do not make me come all the way up there," she pleads, surveying the branches staggered barely within arm's reach of each other. "Bryar?"

Still, she is met with silence.

"Alright," Myla says finally with a sigh. "I'm coming up." With one last stubborn glance upward, noting his rigid silence, she lets out a slow breath and reaches up to grab the first branch. *Thank the Gods I wore trousers. No need to scandalize the forest beneath me.* Branch after branch, aware of her palms growing sticky with sap, Myla hoists herself up the tree, silently cursing herself and her quick tongue. This is clearly a direct consequence of her temper. Gently, she pats a tree branch. *Not that I do not love this bonding experience...*

At last, the ropes are within reach, and she notes how they sturdily wrap from branch to branch, and coil tightly about the wide trunk, creating a winding path up the remainder of the tree. Myla grips the ropes and with a grunt, she pulls herself onto them. She allows herself a moment to recline against the trunk with the slightly swaying platform beneath her as a seat before beginning the far easier ascent for the remainder of the way. She appreciates the craftsmanship of the twisted twine path, observing how it works with the tree, not against it. Iron clamps secure the tough knots, stabilizing the handmade bridge. The trunk narrows as she reaches the top, and the rope splays carefully in all directions with the branches, woven tight underfoot to create a sturdy platform. The perfect place to recline and watch the sun's movement.

Bryar sits with the trunk at his back and his forearms propped on his raised knees. His eyes are fixed on a cleared spot between the branches. He focuses on a view of the craggy mountain range which separates them from New Falkmere. His jaw rolls forwards and back again, over and over, as though he is gnawing on his emotions.

Breathless, and humbled by the shame coiling in her stomach, Myla sits beside him, their heads nearly touching as she slouches against the trunk. "Did you make this?"

She gestures to the rope fixtures, and he nods in response.

"It is beautiful," she says, risking a glance his way.

He is expressionless. It is as though he is not even there. But his chest rises and falls quicker than usual.

"What is it for?" She hopes he will answer, but knows it would be better to begin with *I'm sorry.* Somehow, those words stay lodged in her throat, stuck between the shame and the grief.

"Caspian and Elenore will never have wings like Aidan. I wanted them to see the world from his perspective." He stops short, still fixated on the view ahead, then reaches overhead for a pine needle to roll between his fingers. Anything to avoid looking at her. "Now Elenore will never see any of it, anyway." Somehow, he manages the words despite the pursing of his lips and the furrow of his brow. His face mourns, but his voice remains steady.

Grief dislodges itself from her throat in a miserable sob, forcing the shame to vanish. Myla reaches to grab his hand, aware of how very small hers is around it. "You are a good father," is all she can manage in a feeble whisper to stay the tears.

Once more his face is cold and unreadable, and he still gazes forward, refusing to look at her. In all the years she has known him, silence is something new. His unwillingness to speak openly, as though he is trying not to say something he shouldn't, feels foreign.

"I said hurtful things," Myla admits, holding fast to his hand despite the indifference radiating off his body. "*Untrue* things," she continues, "and I regret them deeply. I am *so* sorry."

His eyes flicker in acknowledgement now, and the brief glance her way exposes the red, puffy skin on his eyelids. She can see her own undoing in his gaze; perhaps if he looks at her a little longer, she too will cry again.

"Losing Elenore and almost losing the boys...I'm frantic, Bryar. There's nowhere to turn, and I feel sad and *angry*. So very angry. And all of those feelings are boiling and sputtering, and I do not know *how* to exist right now when all I can think of is our daughter, lying alone in a crypt." Myla's voice breaks, so she leans against him, grateful to find warmth as he draws a strong arm around her shoulders.

His voice is rough yet soft when he speaks. "All I think of is Elenore down there, too, when I do not hear her laughing. And again when I *do,* and I realize it is nothing more than my mind tricking me. I think about her absence when I tuck only two children into bed and not three. When I stare at the ceiling and recall in the darkest hours of the night that she is not awake, asking us to sleep next to her, because she is gone. And I think of her most of all when I remember I am supposed to be waging a war, and none of it seems worth it anymore."

Myla sobs now, pressing her face into his chest, holding on to him tightly with both arms, hoping he will hug her and hold her and forgive her. "I am so, *so* sorry for what I said," she chokes. "I needed someone to blame, but the truth is that I do not blame you at all. It was no more your fault than it was mine, and if we carry the blame, then we will carry it together."

His arms tighten, both wrapped around her to hold her as close as possible, and with a shaking sigh, he presses his lips to her forehead. Nothing can be heard beyond the wind in the trees, the creaking of the ropes beneath their weight, and the intermittent disruption of their cries. In time, their tears pause, and his grip loosens enough so he can look down at her.

"I am sorry you are hurting, but I hurt too. *We* lost *our* daughter. I wish I could take that pain from you, but do not think I carry none of my own." He kisses her forehead again. "I will never forgive myself for what happened to Elle. You might have blamed me with your words, but I already felt guilt and responsibility long before you said it." He looks now at the masterpiece around him. "For years, my focus was being a good captain— not just a good one. A great one. Then Caspian came, and the twins after him and...well," he admits. "Being a great captain was no longer the priority. I wanted to be a great father—"

"And you are!" Myla insists as she draws her knees to her chest and leans her head into his shoulder.

"Yes," he continues, "but I cannot be both at once and somehow, trying to be a great father took my attention off my men and...Elenore paid the ultimate price. It is better for me to give the position away. I will never be able to pay more attention to leading your army than I will to our children. So, Rhyland must take over. He is capable."

"Is he?" Myla nearly laughs in spite of her tears. "I do not think I can do any of this without you."

"You won't have to," he promises. "It will just be different." Myla sits upright now, crossing her legs to face him. He reaches out and tenderly brushes her loose hair from her face, tucking it behind her ears. "You look like a girl today." Soft familiarity washes over him, and his hand lingers gently on her face. "You always look like a queen now, so stoic and strong. But I remember you like this. Just a girl."

"I feel like one," she admits. "And like a girl, I do not know what to do. I do not know what happens now."

His hand lingers, cupping her face while his eyes study her until she feels he may expose every vulnerability she is feeling. "We do not worry about tomorrow," he says finally. "We worry about surviving today."

"I think today feels like too much."

"Then we will just focus on one hour at a time. Eventually, all of the days and hours will see us through until we do not hurt as deeply as we do at this moment." His hand slips to her neck now and is hidden by a curtain of her hair. His fingertips press into her skin, rubbing gently and urging her closer. Wobbling awkwardly on the rope netting, she moves to seat herself on his lap, where she slumps into his arms. There they sit, held together by nothing more than the promise of living to see one more hour together. After a time, Myla leans back and cups her hands around his rough face, the stubble of his cheeks scratching her skin.

"I love you."

"And I love you."

Another evening descends on Old Falkmere, and it is cold in the still-ness of grief, without Elenore's laughter to keep the family warm.

"Silence is our biggest betrayal," they had agreed before leaving the healing confines of the tree. And so, with the cloak of darkness hanging over the boys' bedchamber, Myla and Bryar sit on either side of their sons, swallowing their own need to rot in the agony of loss, for the sake of the boys.

"I do not know how to feel," Caspian whispers, once again articu-lating himself with a wisdom beyond his age. "I keep wanting to call to her, and then I remember she won't answer."

A lump catches in Myla's throat, and her hand tightens around her son's. "I believe if we listen hard enough, she will answer in other ways."

A slight smile tugs at the corners of Aidan's mouth. "She talks to me."

Both parents straighten now, exchanging glances before zeroing in on the younger boy. "What does she say?" Bryar asks.

Aidan shrugs. "Silly things, as usual. It's all in my head, like she is sharing her thoughts with me still."

Myla trembles and works to steady her voice before probing for more. "I would love to hear those silly things, if you don't mind telling us?"

"Well," Aidan says, distracted as he watches Prince Gourdy race into the room with kitchen scraps hanging from his mouth. "I was sleeping, and I heard her voice. She told me that the seer spoke to her as she was going to the Gods."

Resisting the urge to stand, and with shock pulsing through her body, Myla looks to Bryar. He offers her a calm nod, though she can see the tension in his forearms as he holds Aidan to his chest. "What did the seer tell her?" He asks calmly.

"It was silly," Aidan repeats, clearly abashed. "'You will taste atonement when the oldest raven eats the fox.'"

The oldest raven. Myla's brow furrows, but she does not have time to ask further questions before Aidan speaks again.

"She also reminded me that Prince Gourdy likes to be let into the kitchens before bed..."

"*Aidan!*" Caspian nudges his brother. "You aren't supposed to tell!"

Unexpectedly, a laugh seizes Myla, an impulse she feels immediately guilty for. But she laughs anyway, noting the smile lines at Bryar's eyes as he responds. "So that is why he is so stout."

CHAPTER 19

PAST: MYLA, EIGHTEEN

"HAPPY BIRTHDAY." BRYAR'S BREATH is ragged against hers. He drops his cloak and sword before hungrily claiming her mouth with his. He has been on duty at the palace for the last two days, and his relentless training on top of that has claimed almost all his free hours. The exhaustion seems permanently etched on his face, his shoulders, and even in his voice. In the two years since joining the king's army, his time has been almost constantly accounted for. As a result, seeing one another has been increasingly difficult. In addition to that, his name now holds weight amongst his fellow soldiers, and his face is more recognizable, as is hers, given her involvement at the institute. Interacting together anywhere within Falkmere has become a risk. For those reasons, they decided to spend her eighteenth birthday at Druid's Cave.

"You made it," she coos after catching her breath. Satisfied by the way he embraces her, she curls her fingers in the wavy hair at the nape of his neck to hold him and study his breathing pattern for just a second longer, despite Elsa's pretend gagging in her periphery.

Like I do not have to keep a lookout while you and Callum tongue-wrestle on a regular basis.

"I would not miss it," he answers, kissing her again before looking past her to where Rhyland and Callum are already filling mugs from a larger pitcher. "Is that my father's?" he asks while pressing a flat hand to the small of her back to guide her deeper into the cave.

"Ay!" Rhyland salutes. "It is only fitting to celebrate our lady-rebel with a stolen pitcher and the same *disgusting* ale we endured when we first met her!"

Elsa flops into the dirt and extends a lazy hand to Callum. "Join me," she says wistfully, pretending not to see the playful frown on Bryar's face before adding, "I helped Rhyland steal the pitcher, you know. He distracted Caspian, and I made off with the loot."

Silent now and exchanging grins with Myla, the two young women watch as Bryar sheds layer after layer of protective wear until he stands in a tunic and training leathers.

"You're aware you did not have to steal it? It's not like my father possesses the only pitcher in New Falkmere."

Rhyland chuckles, nodding in agreement. "Yeah, but it was much more fun this way!"

As the men work on starting a fire and filling mugs for everyone, Myla sits beside Elsa, their backs to the wide opening of the cave. "Was today any easier?" Elsa whispers, noting the way Myla massages her fingers together anxiously.

Myla shakes her head, flashing a weak smile. "No," she admits. "I think I am at risk of betraying myself just because I am thinking about it so much. I know the headmaster is anxious for my aptitude test—I am not supposed to take it for another year. He keeps saying he believes I have 'untapped potential'."

Tension between herself and Maverick builds as he pressures her to excel magically *and* socially. All the while she is straining to hold her power back and hide from as many of the king's events as possible. The conflicting impulses for such an extended time have caused her magic to become sporadic and unpredictable. If she can only keep her magic hidden until after the evaluations, she might be able to slip by unnoticed.

Elsa leans forward, watching as flames come to life, bringing light to the darkness of the cave and illuminating the uneven surfaces of stone. "So, stop thinking about it." She pauses before adding, "It's only because the Blood Stealer is on a rampage. They want a solution quickly. Just...don't think about it."

Myla nearly laughs and accepts a mug of ale from Bryar with a soft smile in thanks. "Once you figure out the art of *not thinking*, let me know."

"Oh darling," Elsa says with a proud grin. "How do you think I manage to get myself into half the tangles I do?"

Myla snorts into her mug, wiping a dribble of ale from her chin before answering. "Yes, I heard about your and Callum's near miss last week—you know women are not allowed in the barracks."

"Yes," Elsa admits with a sly flicker of her eyes in Callum's direction. "Turns out, pretending to be a working lady and rushing out really fast is the best way to avoid questioning."

"Elsa!" Myla laughs. "Did you really?"

"She did," Callum confirms with something akin to pride passing over his face before a bashful shade of red takes its place.

"Anyway," Myla continues, louder now so the rest can hear. "I need to figure something out before assessments. Or I am as good as queen."

At this, Bryar's expression grows grim, and he averts his gaze, watching the light of the fire ripple off the surface of his ale instead. Myla rises, steps around the flames, and sits beside him, leaning a head on his shoulder. "That is not what we will worry about tonight though, is it?"

Tilting his head, he looks down at her, and the frown is replaced with a half-smile. While still soft, his eyes seem heavy with concern, and she worries he has spent too long thinking about the "what ifs".

"It certainly is not," Rhyland answers for him. "In fact, I think the best way to celebrate Myla tonight is with very, *very* strict rules: only fun. Nothing depressing tonight."

"If staying hidden is the goal, I fear you all have failed miserably," an older voice breaks outside the cave, and Caspian appears, bearing a small bundle wrapped in muslin.

"Father?" Bryar asks with a confused grin before the salt and pepper beard bobs in response.

"I should be offended, not being invited to Miss Alerys' birthday." He casts a glance at the humble party before settling on the stolen pottery between the group. "Is that my pitcher?"

Laughter erupts, and Myla stands, moving to hug the old man. "You came to celebrate *me?*"

Caspian's eyes gleam with a smile that reminds her of his son. "I wouldn't miss another entertaining night with you."

He, no doubt, is envisioning an evening several months ago when Elsa suggested they all show up at Caspian's house for supper, an uninvited experience he was quick to welcome. The old man ended up hosting four of his son's friends into the early hours of the morning, where they learned that before being a blacksmith, Caspian was a soldier. He would not divulge more information than that, which surprised all, Bryar included.

"Well," Myla says with a smile, accepting a small, wrapped bundle which Caspian offers her. "I am glad you are here!" As she pulls the ribbons loose, the muslin unwraps from around an ivory hairbrush. "This is lovely." Myla examines the delicate design with etchings of peonies on the handle.

"It was my wife's. Alice loved peonies, and I hear you do as well." Caspian flashes a smile at Bryar, who wears a look of sad approval.

"Thank you," Myla answers with a hug, noting the tinge of sadness forming in her chest.

His thoughtful gift became even more precious when she realized her own father neglected to even wish her a happy birthday.

While the long stretch of forest separating them from New Falkmere is quiet, the safe capsule of space within the cave is full of merriment, and something more: anticipation. Sometime between the ear-aching made-up songs Rhyland belts, and the far-too-large fire that forces them to the cooler safety of the open forest air, Callum and Elsa disappear for the night, no doubt savoring their alone time before Callum is on duty again.

The hour is late when Rhyland takes his leave, admitting that he is far too drunk to tackle tomorrow night's watch without a solid twelve hours of sleep. Bryar offers to "walk his drunk ass home", but Rhyland insists that the silence will do him good. A discreet wink in Myla's direction and she realizes removing himself is very intentional. Caspian, whether to keep an eye on Rhyland or give his son and Myla alone time, follows the young man. As they watch the sturdy frames walk away, eventually becoming one with the dark shadows of the forest, the hushed stillness says so much.

For the first time in months, they are alone. When they first met, being alone was something they experienced often, but they didn't covet it. Now, she finds herself grasping at every spare moment they have, hoping one of them will end up alone so she can fall into his softness and find sanctuary in that space that has become so sacred to her.

After several moments of listening to the crickets chirping deep within the woods, a choir of nature's voices telling her to trust herself, Myla rises from her snuggled perch against Bryar's chest where she'd been warmed by his legs on either side of her.

Silently, he observes as she moves away from the flickering light of the dying fire and deeper into the cold, dark woods. As she has done every year for as long as she can remember, she lets her hair fall free from its fastening at the back of her head, and she plucks a few strands, offering them to the wind, to the Gods. With her back to Bryar, she slowly unfastens the laces of her bodice, aware of how he stares. The thought of him watching her undress is exhilarating, and as she sheds the layers, never once looking back at him, she wonders if his eyes travel down the curve of her hips, past her backside, if he imagines his hands tracing those curves. Her skin pebbles at the idea, but she does not look. Instead, she kneels naked in the dirt, as her mother taught her, allowing the earth to chill her body, and her flesh to warm the earth, to seek harmony with nature and prepare for the new year.

After several moments of silent worship, she senses the beat of her heart, the pounding of desire, and still facing away from Bryar, she gathers the courage to say what has been on her mind for months now. "I know what I want for my birthday."

Steps approach from behind. "Oh? What is that?" His response is warm but calculated.

His fingertips brush a strand of hair from her bare shoulder before trailing down the length of her arm. Everything about him is familiar. From his voice to the way his footsteps sound as they come and go. His comforting embrace, his laugh, his eyes. Myla feels as though she knows every part of him, but she does not. There is an intimacy she longs to share, a part of herself she can choose to give him, that no others have had.

"I want *you*." Myla closes her eyes, allowing herself to feel the way her pulse drums nervously. She turns now to face him, finding his eyes closed and his jaw tight as he breathes deeply, hungrily. There is a writhing in her middle, something starved and needy, something only *he* can satisfy. "This is a piece of myself that I want you to have."

"Myla..." Bryar hesitates now, his eyes opening but not daring to venture beneath her collarbone. Instead, he presses a kiss to her forehead, his breath traveling hot across her skin and chilling her all at once. He is hungry too. "I want to," he admits. "You *know* I want you like that. But it would ruin you." Despite his words, his mouth travels as he kisses from her cheek to her neck again and again, as though tasting her skin like this is all he will ever get, and in that, he must find contentment. His hands curl at the small of her back, gripping her with desperation, as though he must hold on to something lest he lose control altogether.

Desperate to finally feel his warm and possessive hands roam across her body after so many years of longing, she presses her body flush against him, savoring the strength of his arms against her bare skin. "I should be allowed to choose who I give my body to," she argues. "Anything less *would* ruin me."

Bryar's eyes fall closed, and he takes a deep, trembling breath. "Yes, but if your father finds out..."

Determined, Myla presses her hands around his neck, centering his attention on her. His eyes are not soft now; they are tortured. "My father does not get to decide if I lay with the man I love. I will not let fear of his wrath stop me from living while I am free to do so."

"Gods," he pants, holding her close as his lips move lower to pelt kisses along her collarbone. Each warm contact sends shivers through her body, and she leans into him, aching for him to concede. Of course, there are innumerable reasons why they should leave this boundary uncrossed, but every reason seems like it belongs to someone else, a rule mandating them to deny what is so natural. As his fingers grip the soft skin of her hips, pulling her closer to him, Myla wonders why something that feels like the Gods fated it should be denied at all.

Weightlessness takes hold as his lips on her neck grow more intentional, lingering and savoring. He breathes deeply, inhaling her scent, sensing her desire, and his hands relinquish their hold on her hips to hesitantly travel upwards. First to the middle of her back where one remains, holding her steady. The other meanders with uncertainty toward her heart, grazing the roundness beneath her breast before pressing a flat palm to her pounding chest.

Myla's breath hitches. She wants nothing more than to feel his warm hands caressing every inch of her. Gripping his collar, she slowly lowers herself to the ground, pulling him with her. His energy shifts as duty and resistance shed, and the muscles in his trained body relax with the hillside behind as support to them both. Her eyes fall closed as his hands feather across her throat, resting momentarily on the fluttering pulse beneath his fingers before exploring lower. Myla breathes deeply, ecstatic at his touch and urging herself to bask in every sensation.

"Are you sure this is okay?" he asks, pulling himself from her long enough to perceive the sincerity in her ocean-blue eyes.

"I have never been more certain of anything in my life," she breathes before pulling him down to kiss her.

There is nothing more to say. It has all been said. For years, they have whispered "I love you" when no one could hear. They have shared their darkest thoughts and their most unattainable hopes. Through it all, they have loved with every strand of consciousness and passion, and all along, their hands and bodies have been unsatisfied beneath the craving born from such love. At once, they give permission to the hunger and the yearning, and it snaps, tense like an arrow loosed from an archer's bow.

The soft touches turn to fire, and their mouths compete for a greater hold on one another, desperate to taste and feel and be felt. Where restraint in the past may have been exercised, it is now abandoned entirely, and Myla relinquishes any thoughts of modesty and temperance. Something about the tenderness at his fingertips feels like a contradiction to the path in life he has chosen, and yet, being the subject of his tenderness is a gift. Leaning deeper into him, her fingers digging into his back, a soft susurrus of air skips from between his teeth as he breathes into the kiss. Myla vibrates with excitement as his hands trail down her sides, past her hips to the thickest part of her thighs where he reverently holds fast, urging her as close as possible. A tingling of anxiety flashes through her being, and she grips his arm, holding him in place firmly and stopping his pursuit.

"I have absolutely no idea how this works," she whispers with a nervous laugh, searching his eyes for expectation and finding none there.

Bryar joins her in laughter, kissing her gently. "Neither do I. We can figure it out together." With a slow nod of agreement, they fall into the unknown. Bryar sits upright, perched on his knees as he straddles her, and with cautious fingers, he moves his attention to her bare breasts, where a trembling hand inches before Myla playfully swats at it.

"It isn't fair that I am naked, and you are not," she whispers against his lips, nipping gently at him before shoving him onto his back. He surrenders, watching as she now moves on top of him, working nimbly to undo the laces of his tunic first. Undressing him is a slow and methodical process, and layer by layer, the clothing is removed until nothing but skin shines in the moonlight. Myla tingles as the earth beneath her bare body seems to heave with a need to touch and taste the miraculous body before her.

"You," Bryar whispers, sitting naked across from her. "You are beautiful."

Slower now, breathing nervously, they meet in an uncertain kiss, and Myla can feel his body tremble beneath her touch. And touch she does, with timid strokes across his chest, meandering curiously to his back where her fingers brush the dips of his body.

"Lie back," he suggests, watching as she does, his eyes devouring every inch of her. His touch is magnetic, and heat radiates from his body as a soft glow forms beneath his skin.

"Are you alright?" Myla asks, eyeing the display with concern.

Bashfully, Bryar grins, nudging her knees apart and settling on top of her. "Yes," he confesses. "I'm excited."

Myla curses her timing as she bursts out giggling before flinching in surprise when their bodies meet and something firm presses against the inside of her thigh. "I can tell."

It is Bryar who laughs now briefly, before swallowing hard. Propped on one elbow, his free hand presses a gentle thumb against her bottom lip, parting them. Surrendering to his touch is the simplest thing she has ever done. Myla has spent her life fighting against the system of ownership, but here, beneath an open sky and an honest man, being possessed is the easiest surrender she's ever experienced. As his hand grazes her jawline, then her throat, she inwardly thanks him for helping her find her voice. And when his fingertips travel past her heart, she is thankful for having someone who fits there so effortlessly. At last, his hands brush the hardness of her nipples before massaging her breasts reverently with a satisfied moan. Myla arches her back, pressing herself against him, delighted by the tingling pleasure evoked as he lowers his mouth to her breasts, attentively tasting each one. As he rolls her nipples against his tongue, his hand instinctively continues its exploration, first gracing the ripples of her ribcage, leaving behind a trail of fire as his skin gently warms hers, until they cautiously linger on the inside of her thigh.

"I want to touch you," he whispers, bringing his lips to hers. "Is that alright?"

With a shaky breath, Myla nods before curling her fingers in the black tendrils of hair at his neck. Her body thrives and awakens in a foreign way as his fingers brush the sensitive skin between her thighs, and together they shudder. Hesitantly, Myla reaches down, cupping her hand over his to guide his fingers to their target.

"Here," she whispers against his mouth. "It feels good here."

With purpose, Bryar moves his fingers in a circular motion, exploring until they are wet and glistening and Myla writhing beneath him. "Like this?" he chuckles, kissing her collarbone as she whimpers a soft "yes".

"Can I—" Myla's eyes dart downward as her hands eagerly inch closer and closer to where he is pressed hard against her.

"Please." He releases a satisfied breath as Myla's fingers close around his hard length. Together, they explore and touch, testing sensations and kissing until Bryar readjusts directly on top of her. Her body is relaxed, and the wet space between her thighs throbs with readiness. Hesitant at first, she watches as he moves his hips toward her.

"Are you sure this is how it's done?" she asks, knowing full well this is exactly how *it's* done, given Elsa's detailed explanations.

Laughing nervously, Bryar nods. "I hate to admit it, but the tavern has been an excellent accidental education."

Myla joins him in laughter, briefly remembering visions of couplings in corners from time to time. "Just go slow, okay?"

With a reassuring nod, Bryar returns to attentively kissing her, and his hips move upward slowly. Myla wills the muscles in her body to relax as the pressure of him entering her feels shocking at first. With a wince, her fingers dig into his shoulder, and Bryar immediately withdraws. "Am I hurting you?"

"No," she assures him. "It's just a little sore. Try again."

Connecting is awkward and beautiful and painful and perfectly imperfect. Together, they fumble their way through learning how they fit, and after some time of gently coaxing, Myla lets out an ecstatic moan. Bryar finally moves within her fully, and the rhythmic motion brushes the nerves inside, countering the pain. Practice turns into worship.

And as her mother taught her, there is no better place to worship than the woods. Oh, how the Gods would approve.

Dawn finds Elsa and Myla sprawled leisurely on Myla's bed, whispering and recounting events of the prior evening.

"Surely there's something we can get for it?" Myla argues as Elsa insists she can simply heal the itching welts.

"This would be so much quicker," Elsa insists with a sigh, followed quickly by a giggle. "Is your ass *actually* covered in bug bites?"

Myla glowers at Elsa while resisting the urge to violently scratch her backside. "Unfortunately, yes."

"At least that's the worst you got from your first time," Elsa offers, rolling on her back and sparking a wave of purple between her fingers. "I got emotional damage from mine."

"Elsa," Myla responds with a sigh. "You should not joke about such things!"

"Why not? That's exactly how I learn. I suffer, and then I laugh because how could past me be so stupid?" Elsa sits upright now. "Come on, let me see it."

With a groan of embarrassment, Myla stands and pulls her shift above her hips.

Elsa is quick to spiral into a fit of laughter, cackling as she observes the red-hot, raised bites which cover Myla from the back of her knees to her hips. "Well," she says between unbecoming snorts. "At least you have a nice ass."

"*Elsa!*"

"Alright, alright. I'll fix it. Lie down and show me your butt again."

CHAPTER 20

PRESENT

A BIRD OF PREY can shriek, and its cry might be considered majestic. But the cry scraping against Myla's ears is not majestic. It is chilling. But she compares the horrific sound to a bird of prey as the closest approximation when she is violently torn from sleep by its grating call, reverberating through the palace.

"Get up!" Bryar shouts, a hand clamping around her shoulder and shaking roughly to wake her.

Myla's legs fly over the edge of the bed before her eyes are completely open. The screech of unsheathing metal rakes a chill down her spine as she watches Bryar, dressed only in trousers, swing their chamber doors open to step into the hallway.

"Go—get the children!" he commands before disappearing further into the hall with a swarm of guards flurrying in every direction.

Shriek after murderous shriek echoes from outside. The vengeful sound is met quickly with the cries of mortal men. Agonizing screams, bloody, and tortured. Despite the flashes of magic sputtering chaotically in every direction as men outside fight for their lives, the battles seem to be short-lived against the assault of an enemy invisible to her from her current location. Deep in the recesses of the forest outside her window, a sickening *rip* reaches Myla's ears, followed by a thud on the pillars below. A body, she can only assume.

Heart pounding, and entirely confused, Myla pulls on her discarded trousers and boots and runs across their room into the hall, pushing against the flow of traffic toward the boy's room. She hears their muffled cries before she sees them, and upon stepping into their room, relief floods her to find the commotion nothing more than a response to fear. Caspian has crawled protectively into Aidan's bed, where they hide beneath the covers.

Myla pulls the bedding away. "It's mama," she reassures softly and holds out a hand to them, brushing their heated, damp cheeks as their horrified sobs lessen. "Quickly now!" Myla urges.

Both boys stifle their tears to stand obediently, and as quickly as she can manage, Myla gathers their cloaks and boots. "Hurry," she murmurs, watching as Ethstan and Elsa enter the room. "Put these on and let's go."

"Not outside!" Elsa whispers, her voice wobbling with terror. "There is nowhere to go."

"Hush," Ethstan chides. "Do not worry the children." Though his voice is steady, his hands quiver at the fastenings of the boy's cloak. He, too, is terrified, yet with a calm demeanor, he picks Aidan up. The child buries his head in his caretaker's shoulder.

Myla scoops Caspian into her arms and moves toward the door, all the while her mind races in concern, wondering what foe now descends upon her home. "What is it?" she asks with a glance toward Elsa as she guides the group back toward her chamber.

Elsa whispers one horrifying word, "Dryads."

The blood drains from Myla's face.

"Oh," Aidan chirps, lifting his head from Ethstan's shoulder and now clearly less concerned than his brother, though the remnants of tears stain his cheeks. "We read about those!"

"Yes, my love," Myla chuckles nervously, trying to mask the beast of fear raging inside her. "Do you remember anything that could be useful to us right now?"

Caspian lets out a dramatic sigh. "Other than 'keep away, there are no wild beings so violent as dryads'?"

The name conjures vile images. They are beasts made of the very fibers of nature itself and often attached to forests. Dryads never leave their homes unless displaced and seeking retribution. So why have they come to hers?

In a matter of minutes, the entire palace is a frenzy of bodies darting to and fro. Any semblance of strategy is abandoned, and Myla hears Rhyland, Bryar, and Henry attempting to stay the mayhem, but their voices echo in every direction. It is to no avail, and her husband soon emerges from the dark shadows of the palace, which remains unlit in the darkness. Sprays of blood cover his bare chest. He gasps for air as he motions for them to move in the opposite direction.

"They are in the palace!"

No sooner have the words left his mouth before the sickening, high-pitched cry of a dryad reverberates inside the walls.

"*Move*!" he insists, and Myla notices the impossible horror plastered on his face.

"Wait!" Aidan shrieks, wriggling in Ethstan's grip and pointing back toward their bedroom. "Prince Gourdy!"

Conflict passes over Bryar's features as he calculates the risk of turning back for the cat compared to the devastation the boys would feel should he be left behind, or worse. He mutters a breathless *"shit"* before sucking in a deep breath and barreling past them, toward the direction of the dryad's screaming. All in the name of Prince Gourdy. When he emerges only a half-minute later, followed closely by Rhyland, and holding a fluffy cat against his bare chest, the boys let out a grateful squeal.

"If I knew I would be carrying you to safety," he says to the purring feline, "I would have insisted we feed you a little less." Bryar passes Prince Gourdy, who droops like a weighted sack, to Elsa, and turns to lead the group.

"Did you just risk your life to save our children's pet?" Myla hisses, following closely at Bryar's heels.

"They don't need any more loss." He breathes heavily as he responds, already exerted, and an untimely smile passes over Myla's face.

"Remind me once we survive this to decide if I need to yell at you or *reward* you."

Despite the stampede of chaos, he flashes a brief smile over his shoulder.

As the fleeing party navigates the pandemonium of blood and shadows, bumping into one another for the lack of light, an eerie figure emerges from a balcony window. First slender, gnarled fingers claw over the windowsill, then a twisted, unnaturally shaped body hoists itself inside the hall. The tall creature looms, its knotty head nearly scraping the ceiling stones as it sways. Branches fork from the brow of its head, like a nature's crown, and a chilling green hue ripples off its body. Bright green sparks fizzle here and there with its every step, leaving a trail of glowing green in its wake. Two slanted emerald eyes roll and blink, fixing on the huddled group, and with the speed of lightning, its mouth gapes in a Gods-awful, deafening cry.

Prince Gourdy's fur rises along his back, and he lets out a feral hiss in the creature's direction.

Myla reaches within, looking to conjure her own powers, when a blast of leaves exits its mouth, carried on a gust of magic which releases a sickening fragrance into the air, and she becomes lightheaded.

Poison.

"Go!" Rhyland nearly chokes as he stumbles backwards, being the closest to the beast. "The other way—" He turns, ushering them backwards.

"Not this way!" Ethstan commands.

Myla's body ripples with shock as the old man breaks every oath he has ever held dear, releasing a powerful gust of wind from his palms to dispel the poison from the air around them.

A monk using magic.

Ethstan gasps now, holding Aidan close as his old eyes flare in panic. Directly in front of him stands another dryad with inquisitive eyes. Its elongated hands made of spindly branches twist menacingly, outstretching toward them.

Those same sharp ends pierce Ethstan's chest.

"*No!*" Myla chokes on a scream as the dryad's poisonous fumes seep back into their proximity and fill her lungs.

The beast lunges to strike the child in the old man's arms when Henry yanks Aidan free, nearly tripping over Ethstan's falling body.

A second dryad reaches out with angry, prying limbs and wrenches Caspian from Myla's arms. Her physical strength is nothing compared to the evil brute. Screams of horror erupt like a wave through the group, but especially from the boy, and Bryar lunges forward with flames ignited in both hands, ready to lose volleys. With a sickening crunch, the wicked creature's twiglike fingers sink into Caspian's fragile flesh. Myla's heart shatters as her gaze meets her son's, his eyes wide with shock. Blood instantly bursts and oozes from the child's impaled wounds. Before Myla can react with her own furious magic, flames engulf the being. Rhyland, with Henry's help, seizes the boy before the blaze can injure him further.

"Caspian!" Myla collapses on the floor beside her little boy, who writhes in pain no young one should ever experience. Little chokes and cries slip from his crimson-stained mouth, but his big blue eyes glow.

They glow.

"Bryar," Myla cries, yanking at her husband's pants. He collapses beside her, brushing the child's hair from his face with a tender hand as Elsa moves to heal him.

But he does not need her healing. An ethereal aqua-blue light rises like a healing mist from his wounds, and a relieved grin passes over Bryar's face.

"Myla," he chokes on tears as lifting the boy's shirt to reveal nearly healed entry wounds. "I could kiss Caius right now."

Instead, Myla gathers her rapidly healing child into her arms and kisses his sweaty forehead. "My sweet Caspian." She looks up to Bryar now. "The prophecy," she cries. "His immortality—"

The brief moment of peace is disrupted by the dryads from behind gliding their way with lethal precision.

"Run!" Bryar demands, grabbing Caspian from her. "*Myla*—" He grabs her arm with a free hand, pulling her upright as she is about to bend down to help Ethstan. The motion jerks her out of the way of the dryad behind them. Myla looks again at the monk, limp on the ground, wearing the hollow expression of death. "You can't help him," Bryar whispers, pulling her behind him.

The group is separated in the chaotic rush, each darting whichever way they can find a clear path. Rhyland leans down to pull Elsa to her feet while she insists through angry shrieks that she can heal Ethstan. Something in her eyes is far away, as though the body before her does not truly belong to Ethstan, but to someone else, and the wound is not that of a deadly dryad puncture, but a dagger to the throat. Without a moment to spare, Rhyland sucks in a panicked breath and kneels beside her, taking her trembling wrist and watching the magic extinguish.

"I need you," he whispers into the golden tendrils hanging limp around her ears. "Do not make me suffer a world without you for someone who is already gone." Though her eyes swell, Elsa nods and allows Rhyland to bring her to her feet and together, they dart downward toward the dungeons.

Henry carries Aidan over his shoulder as the child wails in fear, and Bryar holds on to both Caspian and Myla as he follows Lord Thurston toward the war-room balcony.

"How does this help us?" Bryar growls angrily as Thurston shuts the doors behind them, the barring making a loud thud.

"You have wings," Henry insists. "Carry your sons to safety and I will see to your wife."

"No!" Bryar hisses, his eyes flickering toward Myla in a panic.

"Yes," Myla answers, determined. "You can carry them away from here! *Go.*"

Amidst the pleading of the boys not to leave their mother, and Henry insisting it is the only way to ensure the boys see dawn, Bryar steps closer to Myla, his eyes searching hers. "I will not leave you!"

Myla collects Aidan from Henry, pressing a kiss to his forehead. "Yes, you will," she answers with as cool a tone as she can manage despite her inner voice crying not to let him go. "You will take them to Valyndor—flying, it will only take you a few hours, and then you can come back for me."

"Mama!" Caspian says with a cry. "Come with us."

"I will," she answers reassuringly. "I just have to help Lord Thurston get out of here first." She kisses the dark tangle of curls before pressing a gentle hand to her husband's face, sure he is listening. "I will be alright. Take them. *Now.*"

There is no more time for arguing. A rhythmic pounding rattles the door on its hinges, and a shriek from the other side is determined to enter. Bryar, wearing a look of conflict, glances once more at his sons, then nods.

With a quick kiss, he whispers, "I love you, be safe," before getting a better hold on the boys. His wings expand in a flash of angry heat from his back, and in a fluid motion, he leaps out of the balcony, taking flight toward the black night sky where the faintest hints of dawn begin to peek from behind the mountains.

Myla's stomach twists in fear as green sparks burst through cracks in the door with every *thud,* and Henry looks toward her with a devilish grin.

"I suppose it is just you and me, Your Grace."

"I do not find that at all comforting," Myla admits with a weak smile as she braces her feet on the tile beneath her, calling upon the Gods to grace her with their powers.

"Well," he says with a roll of his shoulders as he draws two blades from sheaths on his back. "I guess it is a good thing you are the Queen Who Bleeds Stars. I hope you can call every star down and burn these motherfuckers to a crisp so I can keep my blades clean."

As the doors violently fly open, a grin passes over Myla's face as the all-too-familiar tingle in her fingers travels upward until it seizes her entire body. The room is aglow, illuminating the hoard of dryads before them. Nothing will be more satisfying than watching the living, breathing trees be incinerated in the name of Ethstan.

As it so happens, Myla has never battled dryads. Her first volley of light clashes with the fog of green venom, refracting and disappearing entirely. Shock stills her body. A creature seems to laugh as its long arm reaches toward her and, at an inhuman speed, elongates.

"Shit!" Thurston curses, watching in shock as Myla's body quickly reacts. She lunges his way, barely missing the dryad's thrust, to push Henry out of the way, just barely dodging the sharp hand as it lodges itself into the stone wall behind them. The stones crumble and the wall caves entirely, an action which causes the dryads to temporarily retreat. Myla stumbles forward and pulls Lord Thurston up behind her. Together they exit the war room before it completely crumbles.

The scene sparks an idea, and with quick eyes, she scans for the location of the dryads' retreat. A trail of luminescent green gives the creatures away, and Myla focuses on the wall ahead of them.

"Your Grace!" A cluster of exhausted soldiers rally to stand behind her, weapons drawn, though it becomes increasingly obvious their metal is useless against the vile creatures.

With a quick flick of her wrists, a trail of powerful light flashes from her fingers like a viper, embedding the force into the stone hallway where the dryads approach. The structure moans momentarily, and Myla determines another volley is needed. Her muscles strain beneath the pull of her magic, and somewhere beyond the buzzing energy building up within her body, Henry shouts behind her.

"For the love of the Gods, please do something!" His swords are worthless against the dryads, making his survival reliant on her and her alone.

They all are. Myla allows a flickered glance at the men flanking her, and she whispers a quiet "thank you" for their noble solidarity as their useless blades waver where they tremble, hoping she can save them. Swallowing her fear, Myla digs her heels in, willing her aching muscles to give more than they have.

The force of strength is palpable as the strands of light blast from her palms, the second round doing more damage to the walls. Carved stones over the dryads break loose and with unmistakable *crunches,* collapse on the beings. Sparks of green, not unlike a spray of embers on a disturbed fire, burst in every direction beneath the deadly stones, and with the crushing weight, a sick whine of air is pressed from the lungs of the defeated dryads. They let out a final, angry wails and are then silenced more quickly than they sounded.

"Well done," Henry blurts as he moves past her, his loose blonde hair flowing in tangles around his shoulders.

"There are more," Myla says with a shiver as they listen to the continued mayhem. At her feet, Myla slips in blood and cringes as she notices a soldier entirely delimbed.

"You don't say," Henry responds with a cheeky grin while holding up a sinewy branch broken off the dryad corpse. "Maybe if we wave around their fallen brothers' limbs, it will deter them."

"That is ridiculous," Myla seethes as she stumbles over the rubble of her destruction. Every step forward, followed closely by her swash-buckling companion with far too many smiles, feels utterly dysfunctional, and all Myla can focus on is if Bryar and the boys are safe. Or where Elsa and Rhyland have gone.

It seems they follow closely in their footsteps. As Myla struggles over the craggy pile of rocks, she finds her escape cut off and turns back.

"We will have to go through the dungeon," Myla pants as she leaps from a tall split stone back onto the floor. "Hopefully, Elsa and Rhyland made it out," she adds absently before noting the look of true, tedious concern on Henry's face. "Those two are survivors. Has Elsa told you about The Blood Stealer? Or when Rhyland survived the Seer's Mountain?"

Henry grins again, nodding quickly and offering her a hand. "I have heard both of those tales. I am sure they are alright."

The dungeon is a mess of limbs, impaled bodies, and splatters of blood, rendering the floor slippery. To Myla's horror, the worst of the carnage lies inside the cells, where not a single Raven's Veil prisoner breaths. Myla gasps, and a wave of guilt washes over her.

"Gods," she whispers, wrapping a shaking hand around the cold metal of the bars, noting how her hand sticks with scarlet residue.

"They deserved it," a soldier mutters to his comrades. Though a chorus of voices concur, Myla looks over her shoulder at the men behind.

"That may be true for some, but there were those among them who were also victims." *Victims of association.*

"They have moved on to different adventures," Henry hums, though his eyes are sad as he takes in the brutality before him. "I pray the Gods have great things in store for them."

"What of Rhyland and Elsa?" Myla peers through the indistinct shadows of shrubbery and trees, trying to catch a glimpse of blonde beneath the sparse glow of daylight which continues to wake the world.

"I don't hear Elsa cursing the dryads to a shriveled life without rain nor sun, so I presume Rhyland is alive. And I don't hear Rhyland sobbing uncontrollably, so I must conclude that Elsa also lives."

With a furrowed brow, Myla casts a glance at Henry, whose face seems frozen in a half-grin.

"Do you always joke at the absolute worst times?"

"I don't believe there is ever a bad time to try to feel better about shitty situations," Henry retorts, still smiling.

With a sigh and a subtle shake of her head, Myla proceeds out the small door, which exits at the backside of Old Falkmere. The forest is abuzz now, vibrating with energy, and heavy with the scent of dryad venom.

"Try not to breathe deeply," Henry says, drawing an arm over his mouth and nose before pointing ahead of them with a wavering blade.

Directly into the woods toward Valyndor.

"We cannot go into the forest like this," Myla whispers as she shreds the hem of her tunic to tie around her face. "We need to find Rhyland and Elsa, and wait for Bryar."

"That will be hours away—and what more will he do that we cannot?"

Myla side-eyes the strangely calm man, assessing with skepticism the relaxed way he examines their surroundings before she offers him an answer. "He will bring help."

"You mean Ashborn to carry us out like children?"

Sighing, Myla turns to look back at the door, wondering if waiting inside the dungeon is their safest choice. Shrieking continues as dryads lay waste to the palace. Everything inside her wants to reenter the fray and see who else she can rescue from the wreckage.

"Only fools are still in there," Henry says softly, as though reading her mind. He follows her gaze only to flinch into a ducked position as a pillar overhead shatters free, tumbling violently onto the ground before them with a *thud*. Someone overhead whimpers, and the sound of a blade hacking at something hollow grates through the air.

Myla steps out from the protection of the wall to catch a glimpse of the fray.

"—Your Grace!" Henry reaches for Myla's arm.

Myla evades Henry's grasp and gathers light within herself, which she is about to launch at the dryad attacking her men in the struggle above, when a sharp *twang* followed by the whiz of an arrow stays her hand. It passes in a blur before her, landing with a *thunk* in the tree behind her. Instinctively, Myla sinks backward, leaning into the wall for protection.

"There you are," Henry whispers with a relieved grin as Elsa, now carrying Prince Gourdy in a makeshift sling across her chest and followed by Rhyland, moves from around the far side of the palace, running to join them.

Rhyland, holding a hunter's bow in his fist, seems horrified. His eyes pass between Henry and Myla, noting their lack in numbers. "Where is Bryar? The boys?" His voice nearly cracks as he asks the question, and Elsa's face grows ashen with distress.

"He flew with the boys to Valyndor and will be back shortly," Myla reassures them, watching as their faces relax a fraction.

"Shortly won't be soon enough," Rhyland answers, glancing over his shoulder. "They are everywhere; the forest is teeming with them."

"They are hard to kill." Myla lets out a frustrated breath, realizing the prospect of these ancient foes being here at all is preposterous. "Why are they even here?"

Rhyland hunkers in the door's archway leading back inside the palace, beckoning the rest of them to join him to keep out of sight. "I have no idea why they are here, but I know they are supposedly peaceful if left to their own devices."

"So why attack us?"

"Someone must have attacked them first," Elsa chimes in, ripping a clump of grass at her feet to wipe her bloodied hands in. "Someone incredibly stupid, I should add."

"Regardless," Henry continues. "I think I would rather be killed as a moving target than a still one."

"So, we what, make a run for it?" Myla asks, focusing her attention on the forest speckled in luminous green as the beings of the trees now bob to and fro, seeming to look for a place to rest. "What about everyone inside?"

"I think most everyone has run away," Rhyland responds. "Elsa and I were nearly trampled on our way out."

Myla's attention travels deeper into the forest, wondering if her soldiers and household were cut down in the woods. "Has anyone seen Fern?" she asks finally, with a defeated sigh.

A unanimous shake of heads is the answer she needs. "Alright. We go into the forest, head toward Valyndor, and stay close together until

Bryar finds us. We need to get to the main road, because he will look for us there."

"That is the quickest way," Henry points with his sword toward the densest portion of the woods. "My advice? Leave the trees alone. Go quickly and quietly."

CHAPTER 21

PAST: MYLA, EIGHTEEN

"WIPE MY MEMORY," MYLA whispers, looking sidelong at Rhyland, who stands with his back to one of the massive pillars of Caius's throne room. He gleams in his Falkmere armor, and his eyes are set ahead with false focus.

"You are making no sense right now," he whispers, nudging a boot her way as though to dismiss her.

"It makes perfect sense. You just don't like it. Make me forget how to use my magic. It will delay my evaluations."

Rhyland lets out a sigh. "That is an extremely specific line of memories you want me to erase. What if I erase everything associated with magic—such as *learning* at the institute? You might forget Sir Roderick or Bryar or *me*."

"Oh, Rhyland," Myla says with a smile, stepping behind the pillar as her father passes to avoid his probing questions. "I could never forget you."

Rhyland makes something akin to a growl or a grumble before glancing briefly over his shoulder. "I am off duty in an hour. Meet me in the gardens, and we will do it. But if you turn into a mindless idiot, that is on you."

Myla moves discreetly away from the pillar, trying to hide her beaming, victorious expression as she allows a deep breath to expand in her lungs.

I cannot perform for them if I do not know how.

"Daughter." Maverick's voice is soft and uplifting as his fingers dig like claws into her elbow, guiding her toward the edge of the dance floor. "I have yet to see you dance with the king."

"That is because he has not asked me," Myla answers sweetly, shaking her head in mock distress. "I cannot begin to understand why."

Maverick's eyes narrow in reprimand, though his smile remains. "Perhaps because you hide in the back of the room rather than showing off your beauty before him." Naturally, Maverick refers to the captivating and expensive dress he had ordered the very day he received the invitation from Caius.

If it were not ordered by Maverick for the sole purpose of parading her through court like a sellable trophy, Myla would love the dress. A tulle neckline, covered in flecks of golden petals and diamond beading, hugs her neck tightly, delicately depicting floral designs over her collarbone and shoulders, where at last, ivory satin rests against her skin in a sweetheart neckline. The bodice is form-fitting until it cascades off her hips, gliding ethereally to the floor, shimmering with every step as more golden petals trail down her skirt, as though set aflight by a breeze. The nearly translucent sleeves billow loosely around her arms, shimmering over her skin until they cuff at her wrists. From the hem of the sleeves is a delicate string of gold, which slips around her middle finger like a ring. Everything about her ensemble is breathtaking. If only it were not intended to catch the king's eyes.

From across the room, mingling with a nobleman and appearing entirely disinterested, Elsa catches a glimpse of Myla on the move and joins her.

"This entire night," Elsa seethes. "I could murder someone. Whose idea was it to come here—*look* at these men? They have—*all of them*—seen better days, and they have the nerve to ask me to dance. I might vomit on their shoes and force them to say thank you."

"Hush," Myla nearly laughs.

She links arms with Elsa as they join a harem of other young women mingling at the forefront of the crowd. They watch the king lounging on his throne with demure expressions, which Myla can only assume they hope will earn them his gaze.

"What are we looking at?" Myla asks sarcastically with a slight roll of her eyes. Elsa slips an unbecoming snort before placing a hand to her lips and correcting her expression.

Under her breath, she whispers, *"If men compare cock sizes, what do women do? That is what they are doing. Showing the king who has the biggest tits to smother him with."* At this, both girls erupt in giggles, quickly hushed by the judgmental gazes of the ladies beside them. Several painted faces turn, examining her with utter confusion.

"The king, of course," one young woman with deep brown skin and a beautiful crown of brown ringlets answers Myla's previous question. The lady's eyebrows rise in disbelief as Myla still fails to stifle her laughter.

"But he is sitting. I do not see what is so captivating," Myla goads.

"Miss Alerys," another young woman Myla recognizes from the institute speaks, her voice calculated and every word carefully chosen. "He is the king, and we are privileged to consider him *captivating* regardless of what he is doing."

"Imagine," Elsa says loud enough for those in their immediate vicinity to overhear. "Owing a man our deepest respects simply because he was born with a crown." She lowers her voice now, leaning closer as her eyes scan the room to find where Bryar stands, also dutifully on guard. "He looks well-rested. Callum said he didn't come back to the barracks last night."

A discreet smile faintly passes over Myla's face, and she intentionally avoids looking his way at all. She could not ensure her eyes would keep her secret. "He was occupied elsewhere."

Elsa's brows rise briefly as her eyes flicker to Myla's skirts. "Occupied between your legs?"

"Hush," Myla responds with a nervous laugh, before guiding Elsa to the far end of the cluster so she can stand and be examined with as little disturbance as possible. To her horror, as Caius's eyes travel across the crowd beside her, his eyes do not merely pass over her. They fixate on her, and she is made uncomfortably aware of just how blue his gaze is. His silver hair and icy eyes are accentuated against his inky black, richly embroidered tunic. Myla attempts to stifle the urge to wiggle anxiously beneath his chilling, disturbing gaze. As the regal man pushes himself to his feet, the crowd silences and the dancing at the center of the room ceases.

"Oh, Gods," Elsa whispers, gripping Myla's arm. "Look anywhere but his direction, maybe he won't notice you."

It is too late. He takes slow, methodical steps down from his perch at the throne, then *four, five, six* footfalls later, he stands directly before her.

"Miss Alerys." His voice is confident, and though the room is hushed now, all hang on his every word. "I have a mind to dance, and you look like a most captivating partner. Join me."

He does not ask, and Myla is nearly ready to refuse him for his lack of courtesy when Maverick's searing gaze across the dance floor catches her attention. His expression is clear. Defiance will be punished severely. Instead, she curtsies, offering the king as much of a smile as she can muster before responding, "I am honored, Your Grace."

The music resumes and couples move to the sides of the dance floor, leaving most of the remaining space empty for the king. Caius extends a hand and with trembling fingers, Myla accepts, allowing him to guide her to the center of the room. Standing at the back of the room, assigned to guard the door, is Bryar. Though he is expressionless and unmoving, his eyes meet hers, watching intently as the king slides a gentle hand around her waist, barely touching the ivory satin of her bodice.

"You do not care to dance," Caius says casually as they move in synchronicity with the bard's music. "Why?"

Nervously, Myla stumbles over a laugh, which deep down, she wished to release as a snarl. *Not every girl wants to dance with the king.* "I am a terrible dancer," she lies instead. One which the powerful man sees through quickly as he leans into her steps, propelling her into a twirl. Her shimmering gown is on display now beneath the candle-light, and onlookers gasp in awe. She can only imagine the spectacle is beautiful. If only she could simply be beautiful for the soldier standing behind her.

"You attend the Institute of Mystic Arts?" Caius asks, although Myla is certain he knows already. Surely, a king in his position would know the happenings of every lady in his kingdom.

"I do," Myla responds, avoiding his eyes as they bore into her.

They seem to dissect her, to peel back her layers and look for what she hides beneath.

Unfortunately for him, her biggest secret will be a secret, even to her, very shortly.

"The headmaster informed me that you show promising abilities."

"Promising to what end?" Myla goads, regretting it immediately as his eyes narrow, seeming to search her further to discover the source of her defiance. He needs only to glance behind himself to where Bryar stands guard, and he may better understand her resistance.

"I am told you may be awakening some remarkable abilities," he clarifies with a diplomatic air. "I look forward to seeing them on dis-play."

As the music crescendos and then fades, the king loosens his hold on her, allowing Myla to stand opposite him.

Offering him a parting curtsy, she wearily gazes into his god-like eyes. "I can only hope I do not disappoint you, Your Grace," she responds, remaining stooped until he turns away. At which point Myla straightens, making an immediate turn for the door, hoping to collect Rhyland and escape before Maverick demands detailed recounts of her brief conversation.

Passing Rhyland, Myla circles her fingers around his wrist long enough to hiss, "We must go now," before passing him entirely.

Once outside, Rhyland lets out a dramatic sigh before collapsing on a stone bench behind a hedge where they can be entirely out of view of the palace. "This is the stupidest thing you have ever talked me into doing."

"Worse than the drunk man at the tavern?" Myla asks with a brief chuckle before sitting beside him.

"No," Rhyland corrects. "That was stupider. He followed me back to the barracks, so I had to get the captain to forbid him entry to the palace, and it was a terrible discussion. Explaining it was miserable."

Myla grins and leans against Rhyland, splaying her legs before her as the propriety of the king's ballroom sheds. "Please," she says finally. "I really do not see how else I am going to keep this hidden."

Rhyland wraps a friendly arm around her, matching her slouched position. Together they lean against the hedge, watching the stars—he in his full suit of armor and she in a dress far too beautiful for someone so hopeless and distressed. "I will do it," he agrees softly. "But it is essential for you to remain focused on your magic until it vanishes entirely. If you think of anything else, I am pretty certain it will erase that too."

Before Rhyland can fulfil his promise, Elsa and Callum turn the hedge quickly, bearing golden chalices which drop and slosh with red wine. Elsa lets out a satisfied giggle and looks to Callum with an "*I told you so*" expression.

"I knew they would be out here."

Callum's eyes fix instantly on Rhyland, and something instinctual triggers in him. "We are interrupting something."

Elsa snorts, handing Myla a chalice of wine. "Interrupting *what*? I don't think I have ever seen Rhyland look at a woman."

Callum lets out an exasperated sigh and places gentle hands on Elsa's shoulders. "Gravity cannot handle your disruptive wobbling. Sit, before you hurt someone." He looks at Rhyland and Myla, who both sit sheepishly, avoiding eye contact. "What were you two cooking up before we arrived?"

Rhyland clearly has half a mind to lie, but Myla is quick to respond candidly. "Rhyland is erasing my memory of magic."

Unanimously, their friends gasp, and the statement sobers Elsa quickly. "You cannot be serious!"

"I am," Myla says, squaring her shoulders.

"You both are fucking idiots," Callum scoffs, slumping against a hedge where he props a hand against his head in frustration.

"Yes," Elsa agrees, nodding vigorously. "Imagine the *audacity* to erase a gift from the Gods. This is not common magic, Rhyland. You will attempt to strip the Gods' energy from her soul. Do you realize how dangerous that is?"

Rhyland groans and takes the drink from Myla, swallowing long and hard before tossing the empty vessel to the ground. "And if I do not help her, she will be married to the king within the year, and we will all wonder what would have happened if we had simply *tried* to help her. Can you live with that?"

The bickering ceases, and Elsa looks from Rhyland to Callum before finally settling on Myla. A wave of emotion flickers across her features.

Finally, they both shake their heads in unison. "No," Elsa whispers. "I suppose I cannot live with that either."

"Then it is settled," Rhyland says now, his voice trembling. "Let's get on with it."

Straightening in her seat, Myla nods, meeting Rhyland's gaze as an ethereal purple rims his deep brown irises. Ignoring the apprehension radiating from friends as they stand and watch, gripping each other's hands, Myla reaches out to touch Rhyland's shoulder.

"Thank you," she whispers as her mind drifts to that spot of tension. Images of her magic, its source spilling from the Gods and infusing her in its purifying energy, fill her mind. Impressions of the stars falling from the sky and landing on her skin to shine for eternity, their light bleeding through her and blazing beyond her fingertips...all of it centers itself in her mind's eye as a heady fragrance bombards her senses. Something within her resists, whispering that the sacred bond between her and the Gods cannot be severed.

Then, it relinquishes its hold. A fog of nausea rolls from her head to her belly. It confuses her and dulls her senses, seeming to chip away at her cognizance and leave her lightheaded and all at once, her eyes fall open. Rhyland's eyes pulse in a swirling lavender, and Myla's brow furrows.

"Oh, Gods, what did you just do to me?" Myla asks, pressing shaking palms to her drumming temples.

Rhyland's eyes churn still, the purple irises swirling like a whirlpool around his pupils as golden flecks absorb at a sickening rate into the deep violet. He braces his body against the hedge with a violent *grunt.*

Myla stands, dazed, watching as Elsa and Callum rush to either side of Rhyland, grabbing his arms to slow his fall as he collapses on the ground. His body writhes and twitches, seizing as it struggles to stabilize beneath the weight of whatever has just occurred.

"I fucking told you!" Elsa blurts, falling into the grass beside him, pressing a palm to his forehead and diffusing a healing light.

"What happened?" Myla demands, moving to kneel beside her friend with a sour taste in her mouth, something telling her this is her fault.

"The moron took your memory of magic," Callum hisses beneath his breath, moving behind Rhyland to hold his body steady. "Grab his legs, try to hold him still!" Callum insists. "He is going to hurt himself more—can you help him?"

Elsa shakes her head in a panic, responding in broken words. "I—he is shaking!" A sputter of magic bursts from her palms, channeling with the uneven thud of her pulse. Panic is the enemy of magic.

"Calm yourself." Callum's tone is gentle as he nods reassuringly. "You can do this."

Rhyland continues to convulse in place, his eyes rolling to the back of his head and sweat running down his brow. Elsa leans over him again, both of her hands pressed now to his head where her magic collects calmly at her palms before absorbing into his being. There, she continues to deliver doses of healing magic for what feels like an eternity until his body stills and his eyes droop open, heavy with exhaustion.

"Rhyland," Myla whispers, reaching for his hand. Her voice wobbles as tears of guilt intercept. "Can you hear me?" Though he does not respond in words, Rhyland's fingers tighten around hers. "Oh," she exclaims gratefully. "Thank the Gods, you are alive."

A cheeky grin crosses his face, and his eyes fall open slowly as he glances overhead to where Callum cradles him, before looking in Myla's direction. "Summon your magic."

"I do not care about that," she whispers, leaning closer to her friend, searching for signs of injury.

"I care," Rhyland coughs as he tries to sit, an action Elsa denies as she gently nudges him back into a reclined position. "It almost killed me, I think. So, I want to see if it worked."

"You *think*?" Elsa corrects. "Gods, you two are so fucking dumb. I will never forgive either of you for this," then she nods toward Myla. "Go on, make sure it wasn't for nothing."

Fear pricks her senses as Myla looks down at her hands, watching the pads of her fingertips, waiting. She thinks to call forth some vital energy, but nothing happens. Nothing in her mind feels prepared to spark that life of energy. "I do not think I can." She stares blankly at her palms a moment longer before returning her attention to Rhyland, who, despite the fatigue, appears pleased with himself now. "You made me forget it?"

"Do you remember all of our names?"

"Of course I do."

More hesitantly, he asks, "And what about Bryar?"

Myla's cheeks flush, and she nods. "How could I forget him?"

"I could make you."

"You would not dream of it."

"What of Sir Roderick, do you remember him?" Rhyland questions, examining her for any signs of significant memory loss.

"Who?" Myla's cheeky grin gives her away.

"Oh, fuck off," Callum blurts with a nervous laugh which the others join in momentarily.

"Excellent," Rhyland says. "At least this throbbing headache is worth it."

Myla, on far lighter feet though encumbered by a monstrous headache, followed by Rhyland, Callum and Elsa, reenter the gathering. And the spectacle is shocking.

A previously cheerful scene has transformed into chaos. King Caius is now surrounded by a wall of guards, their shields linked and rippling with magic. The guests have huddled into corners like sheep in a pen, quivering as two figures slash violently at one another at the center of the room. Myla's heart catches in her throat when she makes out the face of the man nearest her. *Bryar.*

Opposite him, and moving with blows intended to kill, is his captain.

"What happened?" Rhyland asks the nearest soldier in alarm.

"The captain attacked the king," the young man replies quickly, twisting the hilt of his blade nervously in his hand.

Myla swallows her concern, willing herself to stand still as the opponents swing at one another with every intention of severing limbs.

The captain, an older man with close-cut black hair and a shaven face, wrinkled with years of frowns, barrels across the floor, sliding on his feet as his momentum lurches him toward Bryar. The blade swings in his hand like an extension of himself and threatens to cut Bryar from behind, but he is too quick. Bryar sidesteps the man and, holding his blade with two hands, he parries the attack with a screaming *clank* of metal on metal. Something in Bryar's demeanor shifts, perhaps frustration? As the moments pass and the tension in the room mounts, several soldiers move forward to help their comrade, a motion which is halted when Caius holds up a hand.

"Let him prove himself."

With a frustrated growl, Bryar throws his blade to the ground, an action which is met with a ripple of horror across the room, shortly replaced with gasps of awe as he extends his hands at his side and a flash of hot flames pool in his palms. A mixture of horror and pride swells in Myla's chest as she watches, gripping her skirts with anxiety. He wears the Falkmere-crested armor, and the room seems to darken around him as his flames glint off the metal and illuminate green eyes beneath the focused furrow of his brows.

The dazed assailant picks up Bryar's abandoned blade, now gripping one in each hand. He shows no sign of fear for the inferno dancing between Bryar's fingers, nor does he seem to recoil when, with the might of a god, Bryar braces his feet a pace apart and extends his palms, launching the flames at the captain with fatal precision. It is only then that the supernatural hold on the man is released, and he lets out an agonizing cry as the flames engulf his body. He writhes on the floor, rolling in the flames until his wails turn to inaudible cries, silenced only when Bryar lowers a merciful blade into the man's heart.

The room is silent.

For a moment, it seems to stand perfectly still, each person glancing at the individual beside them, wondering how to process the masquerade-turned-murderous evening.

At last, Caius stands. His stone-cold gaze assesses the damage, first with a pitiful look to the scorched corpse on his dance floor, and then to the panting soldier standing over him with smoldering hands.

"What is your name?" Caius asks, pacing the floor before Bryar.

"Bryar Monroe, Your Grace." Bryar dips into a kneel before the king, resting weary arms on his retrieved sword. Myla watches as his shoulder rise and fall with deep breaths.

"You intercepted a victim of the Blood Stealer, Sir Monroe. You stayed an attempt on my life."

Bryar nods, remaining silent as his eyes scan the tile flooring beneath him.

"You displayed remarkable valor, you were quick to action, and you were loyal to me, your king. Your bravery and dedication to the crown will be rewarded."

The room is hushed as every eye watches the soldier kneeling before the king. To so many, he is just a name, a face in a crowd of thousands of Falkmere blades. To Myla, he is the reason the sun rises. And the way the king promises a reward feels as though it will not bode well for them. An inclination Caius is quick to affirm.

"It seems I am sorely lacking a Captain of the Guard now." He stops his pacing, urging Bryar to stand. "Are you up for the task?"

A wave of gasps passes through the onlookers and Myla is quick to note the ravenous eyes of many in the room who seem to devour him, his looks, the sweaty curls clinging to his forehead, the fire from his palms, the sharp green of his eyes, and his quick claim to valor. His new *title*. Everything about him becomes tangibly desirable, and Myla detests the curiosity which sparks in the eyes of the girls who had just an hour ago vied for the king. In a matter of minutes, the nameless soldier becomes a worthy suitor to the gentry women in the room.

With a single glance at Maverick, Myla observes the way he scrutinizes the king's new protector, his eyes moving from Bryar to Myla as though assessing the new threat. A sickened feeling settles in Myla's belly. New title or not, her father would never allow it.

After a moment, visibly stunned and exhausted, Bryar nods, his head falling reverently in thanks. "I am, Your Grace."

CHAPTER 22

PRESENT

"FUCKING HELL," RHYLAND LETS out a whispered shriek as a dryad emerges from the heart of a tree trunk mere inches from his face.

As they have dozens of times in the last two hours, the group falls motionless. Rhyland furrows his brow and squints his eyelids tightly together, visibly holding his breath as the gnarled woodland beast drifts across his path with a skeptical look his way.

It was Elsa's idea to pass through the forest peacefully, rather than in a stampede of escapees. As has been so often true in the past, it turns out she is right. The group now inches their way through Old Falkmere woods on the main road, headed for Valyndor. Every several minutes, a new dryad with twisting branches and mangled roots for limbs will appear. Some watch the party curiously; others pass unaware. Much like a bear, it seems calmly keeping one's distance between the creatures is the easiest way to not become impaled, which, by the scatter of bodies they pass here and there, seems to be the fate of so many of her soldiers and court.

"This is tedious," Henry blurts once they are momentarily alone again. "I would rather make a run for it and hope for the best."

"Stop talking like you only have one testicle." Elsa hisses, dragging a finger absently over Prince Gourdy's twitching tail while flashing Henry a severe look, which sparks confusion on the faces of everyone not aware of the reference.

"What a weird thing to say," Myla adds absently, passing through a thick bundle of ferns with delicate steps so she does not crush their bouncy leaves.

Elsa grins over her shoulder. "We met a man in Falkmere a few months ago. He was blubbering drunk, cried, had zero patience, and had only one testicle. It's an inside joke now, I suppose."

Rhyland shakes his head, flashing Elsa a knowing grin. "I learned my lesson about asking questions."

"If he had a full set of testicles, it might have been just fine," Henry adds sarcastically.

"Can we stop staying testi—"

All at once, the three whisper 'testicle', and Myla stops in her tracks, exchanging severe glances with every one of her comrades. "This is a life-or-death situation. We do realize that, right?"

Henry shrugs, nimbly tugs his long blonde tendrils into a knot at the back of his head and continues walking. "Die having fun, Your Grace. Life is too short to go out any other way."

"If I didn't know any better, I would say you look forward to death."

At once, Rhyland and Elsa quip, "He does."

"Bury me by the sea and tell my many loves that it was worth it."

"Worth what?" Rhyland asks, glancing at Henry with confusion as they scan the forest ahead for movement.

"The random itching."

Elsa lets out a gasp, her face contorting with disgust. *"Excuse me?"*

"Kidding!" Henry holds up two hands in surrender before turning on his heels.

"Can we just keep walking?" Myla asks finally, moving to the head of the group now. "How you three manage to stay sane as a...unit...is beyond me."

Behind her, Myla overhears Elsa vying for reassurance that the *itching* was just a joke.

The group has spent hours silently moving through the woods and avoiding the trees that seem to glow with life. At last, a *whooshing* overhead draws their attention up beyond the canopy of the forest. Flying shadows circle above the trees before, one-by-one, a large group of Ashborn navigates the foliage for a smooth landing. To Myla's relief, Bryar lands several feet before her.

"Oh, thank the Gods." He lets out a strong puff of air as she runs several steps, falling against his chest.

"The boys are alright?" Myla asks, frantic to hear that her sons are safe.

"I got them inside the ward. Lenore is with them now at the palace."

Hearing mention of her favorite person, Elsa rolls on her tiptoes with a chipper squeal, entirely unfitting for the circumstances, and flashes her two boyfriends a satisfied grin. "Oh, how I miss Lenore—I am so glad the boys are safe with her." She glances at Henry specifically. "Promise you won't offer to watch her fledglings this time though? That was a nightmare..."

Flashing Elsa a silent "*not now*", Myla takes a steadying breath, her fingers nearly buried in the golden tattoos on Bryar's forearms as she looks back up at him. "What are we going to do? Our home is demolished."

It is Pierre who answers now, clearly conveying the message on behalf of his parents. "You will have a home in Valyndor, as you once did. Our families are to be joined in marriage someday, and there is no harm in allowing the fledglings to connect while you sort out this war." His expression is kinder than the last time they spoke, and his words carry an underlying commitment of allegiance, no doubt urged by the Ashborn king and queen.

She only wishes the kindness and the warmth could be enough to wash away the layers of emotional soot which seem to cover every single surface of her being, inside and out. It is a heavy sentiment she carries, wondering if her husband can feel the added burden as he links a strong arm behind her knees, pulling her from the ground with a mighty leap toward the Gods. As the sky grows closer and the ground beneath fades from the details of death to an aerial view of loss, Myla spares a thought for her precious old friend, Ethstan.

Another dear life is lost, carnage on her path back to New Falkmere.

Oh, how these scars will be etched in the very iron of the Raven Throne when this is all finished.

On foot, the journey to Valyndor would have taken two or so days from Old Falkmere. By wing, it is a mere three or four hours. Two hours of flight have passed when the Ashborn decide to take a break from carrying full-grown adults through the windy skies. The descent is cold as Bryar plummets toward the ground, passing through the breeze like a dart. Despite the heat shared between Bryar and herself, Myla's cheeks are freezing and the tip of her nose feels like ice by the time they land.

"Fifteen minutes to rest and then we shall be in Valyndor by supper," Pierre announces absently as he places a soldier on the ground.

"Thank the Gods," Rhyland mutters as he stumbles away from the strong Ashborn man who had served as his ride thus far. "I have to take a piss so bad I thought I was going to water the trees from overhead." The statement is met with a mildly horrified expression from the Ashborn, inducing a brief chuckle before Rhyland disappears into the thicket of trees which separates them from the River to the Sea.

"He is disgusting sometimes," Elsa says with a soft smile while meandering over the uneven rock bed beside the river to where Henry scoops a palmful of water, splashing it against his face.

Henry stands and opens his mouth to respond when a dark shadow passes over the sun, briefly interrupting the golden glow of midday. It is barely noticeable, and Myla dismisses it as a fast-moving cloud until it happens again. Peering overhead, she scans the skyline beyond the mountains and trees, hoping to see what the cause is.

"Is anyone unaccounted for?" she asks Bryar.

Equally confused and watching the sky, Bryar simply replies with an absent "Hmm?" His trained gaze scours the horizon, darting to and fro with every sense.

"Of the Ashborn—is everyone here?"

Bryar redirects his attention to the Ashborn who accompanied him on the rescue mission. After a moment of counting, he nods. "Everyone is here."

"Then what is that?" Myla's mouth dries with the question as her eyes water from watching the direction of the sun. The disruption is at first fleeting in her periphery, a large shadow rising from behind the mountains. Yet, the heaving of the airborne beast's great wings pulls it higher into the sky until it is directly overhead, hiding them from the face of the sun entirely.

Questions are entirely unnecessary as every person on the ground stands paralyzed in utter disbelief.

Dragons are supposed to be extinct.

Yet circling above, raining gusts of wind toward them thanks to massive beating wings, is indeed a dragon.

"Flames!" Pierre's wings extend from their place tucked at his back, and he stretches muscular arms at his side to call upon his fire. The Ashborn, Bryar included, follow suit until Myla finds herself surrounded by flames, and soldiers holding wobbling blades, nothing more than pine needles to the scaled beast circling overhead.

"It is rare to stumble upon men in the woods with their cocks out."

A voice from behind startles Myla, and she spins on her heels, greeted immediately by more faces than she can count. Faces grim and severe, most covered in tattooed runes and other symbolic markings, others appearing smug, as though they have accomplished something great. These are large people, tall and trained and hard. Their armor is made of leather with iron fittings, while their cloaks are sewn from animal furs. Many wear ermines or foxes around their necks, and almost all of them have long, braided hair. Some of the men wear their hair in knots and braids down the center of their heads with the sides shaved and often covered in more tattoos.

A woman stands behind Rhyland, holding a curved blade to his neck as she inches closer and closer. Her hands are wrapped in strips of leather, which continue up her forearms. She wears a long blue tunic, which is fastened at the waist by a leather belted corset. Her trousers are also leather, adorned with many fastenings and a garter on her thigh with compartments containing blades and throwing stars. She has long blonde hair which is twisted and braided intricately into a high ponytail, clanking loudly with every turn of her head thanks to the metal beading within the tendrils colliding with one another. Beneath her eyes are black tattoos in a language Myla cannot read, the symbols traveling vertically down her cheeks and beyond, disappearing in the collar of her tunic.

Familiarity glints in the eyes of several Ashborn, and something ancient churns between them. Before Myla can comprehend exactly what occurs, they summon wings of fire. Flashes of heat exude from them as the Ashborn move to attack, shouting something about the "traitorous bastards".

Pierre leads the charge, moving nimbly toward the newcomers with fists of flames, rage pulsing in his eyes. "How dare you come here!"

The fierce warriors unsheathe their weapons, and Myla's head spins as the clamor around her threatens to end in bloodshed. "Stop!" she demands, boldly raising her hands and putting on display the stinging light which she is ready to launch at whoever moves next to fight. "Who are you?" Myla continues with a wary glance up toward the dragon, who continues to circle, before flickering her gaze back to the gleaming blade hovering over her friend's bobbing throat.

The woman's silver eyes narrow, and the blade nudges Rhyland's throat in a more threatening manner. "Who are *you*?"

"You speak to the rightful Queen of New Falkmere," Elsa answers with a fierce expression, no doubt fueled by anger at the sight of her lover held captive. "I suggest you address her as such."

"And *you* speak to Skaldra Thyra," says a man from behind the woman he names. He is massive, not in height alone, but also in sheer body mass. He looks as though he may very well be a God from above.

"Thank you, Forseti," Thyra hums with an upward glance at the colossal man. "We did not anticipate finding anyone in these parts," she says hesitantly before slowly lowering her blade. "We have no intention of fighting right now, if our encounter can be settled peaceably." She eyes the Ashborn with skepticism, and Myla notes the tension between them curiously. Finally, Thyra's hands move away from Rhyland entirely, allowing him to shrug away from her with a disgusted scowl over his shoulder.

"I still have to piss," he hisses angrily. "That was rude."

"Shut up," Henry urges under his breath as Rhyland joins him and Elsa behind the safety of the wall of Ashborn, which now separates the newcomers.

"Where have you come from, and what is your business here?" Bryar speaks now, calling his flames back within him. "And where did you acquire a dragon?"

"Our kind never lost their bond with dragons," Thyra answers, a statement which evokes proud nods and grunts from those around her. "We have been dwelling in the Aetherwing Territory for centuries, but with the dryads removed from the forest bordering our lands, we have been able to pass unharmed into Myrnith."

Memories of tables spread with ancient maps on her father's desk bombard Myla's mind, and she can almost smell the old parchment. "Aetherwing, you say? So, further west than the Seam?"

"So far west, traitors can live unnoticed for centuries," Pierre hisses, a remark which prompts angry curses from the Skaldra's people.

"What does a winged wimp know, anyway?" a faceless voice from the shadows of the crowd taunts, and Myla shoots Pierre a discouraging glance, allowing time for the Skaldra to answer instead.

Thyra dips her chin in affirmation. "Yes. Much further beyond the Seam. We have journeyed for days. We were, at first, following the trail of the dryads, but they led us too close to civilization for our dragons' comfort."

"*Dragons?*" Myla confirms, watching as the great winged creature spirals from its place overhead, plummeting closer to the ground until it lands finally across the river, its massive proportions taking up almost all of the free space between the trees and the river. Its wingspan alone is likely broader than the palace at New Falkmere. The creature's head could not be hidden behind the estate she grew up in. Its black scales catch the sun's gleam, casting an iridescent blue ripple across its heaving skin. As the dragon turns its attention to the gathering, its monstrous claws bury deep into the earth, churning dust beneath its feet. "More than one dragon?" Myla asks finally, willing herself to look away from the mesmerizing creature.

"We are fortunate to have three riding dragons and several hatchlings," Thyra remarks, nodding toward the woman dismounting. "My wife, Skaldra Vigdis, is a skilled rider." Vigdis is more severe in appearance than Thyra. Her hair is black as night and falls in long waves past her shoulders. Feathers, iron runes, and other baubles adorn her loose tendrils, catching the light of the sun. At first, Myla mistakes the full blackness covering her eyes and cheeks for war paint, but she realizes quickly that the black streaks trailing from around Vigdis' eyes are tattoos. Another black line marks the very center of her lips and continues downwards to her chin where it tapers off in the shape of a blade at her neck. Myla realizes that no one, not even their children, is painted. Rather, they are all marked with distinct tattoos, rendering each individual fierce and terrifying in their own right.

"I suppose a lack of dead enemies means Jorvath must continue to hunt for his supper?" Vigdis nods toward her dragon. Her voice is scratchy, like unrefined wool snagging on rough skin, and her eyes observe everything in a matter of seconds, passing over Myla's small company with annoyance before turning to press a calming palm to her dragon's flared nostrils. "We are told this realm is stained with war. Is this true?"

"It is about to be," Myla promises, crossing her arms with a sigh as she loses patience for the pleasantries. "Am I looking at another foe?"

"Yes, a foe that deserves death." another Ashborn asserts, silenced only when Henry lodges an elbow in his side.

"Shut the fuck up, man."

The question remains, accompanied by nothing but silence, something that irks Myla as the two Skaldras converse in silence. It is an exchange Myla is familiar with. Spouses communicating without saying a word. She and Bryar have made unanimous decisions without speaking once many times. It seems that is what Thyra and Vigdis do.

When at last, Thyra speaks, she straightens diplomatically and gestures to a child standing close behind her. "Brynja," she whispers affectionately. "Call your dragon, child."

What occurs next is chilling, haunting even, and Myla finds herself seeking the safety of her husband's side.

Brynja, a girl no more than eleven or twelve, strides past her Skaldra, wearing a confidence most grown women would envy. Even in youth, she is covered in scars and tattoos in equal proportion, the most notable scar being a deep, gnarled twist of skin traveling from her right temple down her face until disappearing beneath the collar of her black fur cloak. Her black hair is intricately braided at the sides, falling in loose curls to her waist, and silver beads adorn her braids at even intervals. Her tattoos are similar to Vigdis's, shadowing the entire circumference of both eyes and streaking down her cheeks like tears, but Myla notes that the girl's neck is also almost entirely covered in tattoos—runes, it would appear. A row of bone earrings pierces her ears, and a full suit of black leather armor clearly communicates exactly what she is: *a child warrior.*

A warrior Myla finds herself wary of.

As the girl, two heads shorter than Myla, walks past, her eyes flicker to meet Myla's gaze, and something about the exchange feels like a warning.

A mighty presence in such a small person sends a wave of awe through Myla's middle, and she wonders what is so special about the girl that would call her comrades to silence as she passes. A question soon answered.

From her small lungs comes a mighty call, something more akin to the roar of a wild beast than the shriek of a child. With each exhalation comes a violent summons into the sky, one wave after another until the earth rumbles. It is not supernatural; there is no magic to be found in the moment, but whatever it is, it calls into sight a black-scaled beast large enough to bring night upon the day.

Brynja's dragon darts into view, claiming the entire horizon with its immeasurable frame. If Myla had to give a size estimate to the deadly creature, she might venture to say it is as large as the Institute of Mystic Arts, if not larger. Its skull alone could serve as a sleeping chamber if one wished to go through the trouble of renovating.

As it curls in the sky, churning the clouds with every pass of its massive wingspan, it lowers, falling closer and closer to the ground, which does not render enough of a clearing for the dragon to land. Wings thrumming, the gust of wind propelled downward bends the trees causing a few of the younger ones to snap and the insignificant humans below to double over as well, shielding their eyes from the upturned dust and pebbles which now flurry as though a windstorm is thundering past.

Meeting the ground with a shuddering *thud,* the inky black dragon crushes the forest beneath it, settling into the carnage as though it is nothing more than a bed of hay. It swings its massive head toward Brynja, and the child rolls onto her tiptoes to barely graze the chin of the beast whose exhale nearly blows her off her feet.

"How do you think she even rides it?" Myla whispers, casting a sidelong glance at her friends who, equally stunned, silently watch the spectacle.

"Surely, she has wings, too," Henry says finally. "I could not mount the beast if I tried."

"I never thought I would hear those words come out of your mouth," Rhyland mutters back, met quickly with an elbow in the ribs, courtesy of Elsa.

"I think we are about to find out," Bryar chimes in, nodding a sharp jaw toward Brynja.

Horrified, Myla watches as the mouth of the dragon opens, and Brynja steps into it. Inside the splayed jaw of the beast, she stands perched on the sharp round of a bottom tooth while holding on to another, which juts from above. Slowly, the dragon raises its head, bringing her with it, and turns its long, muscular neck until it hovers her over its back, at which point she leaps from the dragon's jaws, landing lightly on the back of the mountainous creature.

Eyes wide with disbelief, Myla looks first at Bryar, then at the Skaldras, who both wear equally smug expressions.

Vigdis gestures with a splayed palm toward the girl and the dragon. "Tell me, Queen of Falkmere, are we friends or are we foes?" Her eyes travel slowly to where a cluster of horrified Ashborn stands, appearing small with the backdrop of a supposedly extinct beast.

"I must first know," Myla says—her lack of compliance clearly a disapproved approach in the eyes of her comrades. "Why have you come? What are your intentions?"

Thyra interjects before Vigdis can speak, stepping closer until the two queens stand toe-to-toe. "There was an especially dark night a few weeks ago, and the Gods told us something grievous had occurred." Myla glances sideways toward Bryar, noting the flex of his jaw as they both picture said grievous event. "Would you believe me if I told you the Gods sent us to fight on your behalf?"

Myla stiffens, willing her gaze to remain fixed on the Skaldras before her and not drift to her comrades in search of opinions. "I would admit that I am skeptical," she says at last, a response which brings both fierce women before her to laugh.

"If it is easier to believe then, I shall simply say we want vaster skies for our dragons to fly and warmer places to hunt. Winters in Aetherwing have become unforgiving, and as you can see, our dragons are too large to be jailed by a dryad forest."

Her words strike Myla as odd. "Dryad forest, you say?"

"Yes," Brynja speaks now, her dark eyes turned downward as she runs her hands absentmindedly across the spikes of her dragon's back. "Skuggi and I were flying when we noticed the putrid green fog no longer trapped us behind the forest." She shrugs lightly. "For whatever reason, the dryads relocated, and it gave us a way to pass through the forest."

Myla takes a closer look at the dragon. Its scales, like black glass, long, pointed teeth larger in circumference than a large man, observant blue eyes, and a tail so long it would take twenty tall men lying head to foot to equal the length. The beast is magnificent and deadline. *Skuggi. What a friendly name for such an intimidating dragon.*

"Is that why our woods are now teeming with dryads?" Bryar asks, his jaw set angrily as he glares now at the Skaldras, no doubt wondering if they did something to displace the dryads. "We were ambushed in the night, and many of our loved ones and soldiers were killed."

Thyra and Vigdis immediately wear somber expressions, exchanging pitiful glances before Vigdis nods solemnly. "I am sorry to hear about your troubles. We have been plagued for many years by the dryads." She glances warily at Pierre, who visibly restrains himself on Myla's request, then continues. "The Aetherwing and the Ashborn have a history of chaos. I wonder if, with centuries of peace behind us, there is any use in laying old quarrels to rest?"

Pierre's eyes, seeming older now as he stares at the ancient lineage across from him, scan the war party. "What would the Ashborn stand to gain in an alliance?"

Thyra does not miss a beat. She steps closer to Pierre, seeming less and less impressive the closer to the tall Ashborn prince she strides. "It looks to me as though you have aligned yourself with the Falkmere Queen?"

"Our families are fated," Pierre confidently answers. "Of course, the Ashborn are aligned with the Queen Who Bleeds Stars."

Inwardly, Myla wonders what has occurred since the betrothal dinner that has changed Pierre's tune so drastically, but at the moment, she can't bring herself to care deeply.

"Intriguing," Vigdis says with a slight smile, eyeing Myla before turning her attention to where her wife paces. "Then your alliance would be strengthened by our support. Should you allow our dragons to hunt freely in these territories, and perhaps offer my people refuge as we seek new places to settle, then we shall aid you in your war."

Unimpressed, Brynja lets out a sigh from atop her enormous dragon. "We will aid them in their war, regardless." Her sharp eyes flicker to where Elsa stands, cradling a cat, and Myla can't help but giggle at the contrast. A child navigating war and politics from the back of a deadly dragon, and a grown woman, aiding in the endeavor of saving a cat's life. "Who are we to defy the instructions of the Gods?"

Ignoring the girl, Pierre fixes his attention on the Skaldras. "And should we refuse?" He tests the waters of possibility, casting a wary gaze at the black dragon who rolls his head back and forth through the earth, carving easily a divot large enough to bury many bodies.

"Then," clearly the one quick to fight, Vigdis answers. "Skuggi and Jorvath will not have to hunt for their supper any longer—what is the command, Brynja?"

A wicked smile crosses over the girl's face and her lips purse to speak, but Thyra raises a hand to halt her. "Do not breathe a word, Brynja!" The command is obeyed, and Brynja's face sobers as her and Vigdis's little game is quickly stopped.

Pierre looks slowly from each of his warriors, perhaps weighing the potential loss of the fight before he returns his attention to the Skaldras. "We have much to lose in this war, and I have no interest in adding to our ever-growing list of enemies. You shall dine with us in Valyndor tonight."

Myla lets out a sigh of relief. *Thank the Gods we don't have the hot-headed version of Pierre here today.*

Chapter 23

Past: Myla,
Twenty-One

"What do you *mean* she is no longer summoning?" Maverick's words sizzle in the thick heat of the summer air, but hotter than the anger in his question are his reddened cheeks as his displeasure rises visibly to the surface.

Promenading a few feet ahead with Elsa on her arm, Myla is keenly aware of King Caius watching her pass from his tent, shading him from the unforgiving sun.

The headmaster speaks, his words a mere whisper. Myla wonders if he is afraid of other people overhearing, or if he is simply afraid of her father's wrath. "It has been three years since she summoned anything spectacular."

"Yes," Maverick dismisses the comment with exasperation. "I know; you keep telling me that. But what does it *mean*?"

Myla can hear the irritation in the headmaster's voice as he proceeds, spelling it out as though he speaks to a child. "It means that in three years, your daughter has gone from the top of the Institute of Mystic Art's roster to the very bottom, and despite our best efforts to revive her magic, we rarely get more than a few sputters out of her."

Myla cannot help but grin. Although she has felt her magic reviving in recent months, her carefree days spent learning at the institute, making social calls with Elsa and her mother, practicing swordplay with Bryar, and then disappearing into the woods with him has seemed to be the cure for magical outbursts. It has been three years since Rhyland wiped her memory clean of the magic which threatened to throw her right into the arms of the king. Since then, despite her father's frequent tantrums, she has managed to maintain a low profile.

"So, what is to be done?" Maverick asks now, audibly at the end of his rope.

"There are but two choices," the headmaster says timidly. "You commission a spellweaver or we must expel her from the institute."

In one breath, the headmaster both terrifies Myla with the worst of threats and brings her a wave of relief with the next. Spellweavers are nefarious people trained in the dark arcane arts to coax the strongest of magics from an individual. They are hard to find and, even then, generally frowned upon. Their methods are said to be painful and often poisonous to the minds of their subjects. There is a reason the king has not employed one within his vast team of magic users. No, the best option would be for Maverick to concede the fight and accept Myla's expulsion.

Of course, that would be shockingly out of character.

"And these...spellweavers. You know how to contact one?"

Hesitant to respond, the headmaster is silent for too long before answering, "I do."

"He cannot truly mean to use a spellweaver on you?" Bryar visibly seethes with anger. Flames ripple off his body, illuminating the space around them in the black of the night.

"Calm yourself," Myla huffs gently. "You are calling attention to us." Sequestered away in the forests behind her father's estate, a fire gleaming in the trees would no doubt cause an investigation. Thus, she places a hand on his, rubbing her thumb gently over the ridge of his knuckles until she watches the flames flicker out, relinquishing their hold on his skin and retreating inward. "I believe spellweavers are incredibly expensive to hire. I cannot imagine my father will waste funds on such an endeavor."

Bryar is quick to flash her a skeptical frown before dropping his gaze to the stream trickling past. Its babbling is soothing considering their high nerves, and Myla leans against him, still holding his hand.

"Perhaps if I relinquish the reins on my magic and make him believe my talents are returning, he won't feel the need to send for someone so...heavy-handed."

Bryar nods slowly, but his response is simple. *"Perhaps."* There is defeat in his tone. Or maybe it is resignation.

"Do not lose hope," Myla whispers against his neck, pressing a kiss beneath his ear. He shudders, responding easily to her warm breath on his exposed skin. "Think," she continues, wrapping her arms around his middle. "We have managed to navigate the turmoil for years now. The Gods smile on us."

He turns to her, wrapping his arm around her waist to hold her near. "I believe Maverick Alerys would laugh in the face of a smiling God and ask how much coin they would take for the rights to his daughter's fate."

Shivers travel down her body, pricking even the skin of her legs, and dread follows the wave closely until her determination to raise his spirits fades and she is left only with the desperate need to fix herself. "Look." She stands now, comforted by the warm earth and grass against her bare feet. "I have been ignoring the call for months. I know it is coming back."

"Myla," Bryar grunts in frustration as he stands beside her. "Stop, someone might see."

She smiles over her shoulder at him, and in the moonlight, she is a vision. Her gown is far too simple for a noble woman, but perfect for meeting a lover in the woods when the rest of Falkmere sleeps. Her hair, unbound from a day up, now curls around her shoulders and back while her smile is the aching kind, the sort that wills him to be alright even though deep within, she feels herself losing her grasp on control. Everything about her exudes quiet desperation, and he feels it.

"It is alright," she whispers, leaning back against him, reveling in the warmth of his hands as they travel up and down her arms, drawing heat to the surface of her skin.

"I know," he agrees calmly, nuzzling his face into the crook of her neck. His curls brush her jawline, tickling the sensitive skin and coaxing a relaxed smile. "We won't let Caius find out."

No sooner do the words leave his mouth than twigs snapping in the brush behind them alerts them to a voyeur. Before Myla can process the very real danger of them being observed, Bryar has released his hold on her and darts deep into the woods, following the clamoring sound of someone running. He chases swiftly, his shadow disappearing into the woods, and Myla trailing after him in a panic. With every step, her feet plunge into the tough overgrowth and her skirts snag on the groping fingers of branches, hungrily reaching out to ensnare her. The soles of her feet burn as thorns and rocks scrape away at the soft skin, but the pain does not deter her from keeping up, stopping only when Bryar's body pummels into the back of whoever it is he follows. They fly to the ground in a tangled, resistant pile, their limbs entwined, each grappling for a stronger hold on the other. Despite Myla's best efforts, she cannot see who Bryar wrestles with. Her heart thuds in her chest, the pounding drumming out any semblance of sound until finally, Bryar stands, his fists securely holding fast to the collar of the man's tunic. Only he is not *just* a man.

He is a Falkmere soldier.

"What business do you have out here?" Bryar demands, and Myla is grateful he is not wearing his uniform. In the dark, he might be unrecognizable. Wearing the king's crest, however, would be a dead giveaway.

"I saw a fire," the soldier spits confidently. "I was doing my job, so I *investigated.*"

"And what did you find?" Bryar asks, but it is not a question.

It is a threat.

A threat that saturates the air like poisonous fumes. The soldier glares boldly at Bryar in spite of it. He must think his uniform protects him. Myla is willing to wager that he does not know enough of what is at stake to bite his tongue; an error he is quick to confirm.

"I heard enough to know that your lady friend is worth a lot to the king."

Bryar growls in anger, his motions quick as he slams the soldier flat against the tree behind him.

Bile forms in Myla's mouth, and the very same panic she felt moments ago returns, more potent now. "Bryar," she whispers, her voice wobbling with fear. He looks over his shoulder at her briefly before turning his gaze back to his captive. She can barely speak. "He will tell Caius. He will—I'll be—"

"I know." Such insignificant words, yet spoken in a somber way. A final way. Myla realizes there is only one answer, an answer which will compromise everything about who they are, or who they *think* they are.

"I should go get Rhy—"

"There's no time." Bryar looks past the stoic soldier to where a gleam of sunrise begins to tease the horizon. "What is your name?"

The soldier spits again in Bryar's face before answering, "Does it truly matter? I shall be nameless come morning, won't I?"

He does not sound scared; in fact, Myla feels as though the soldier is tempting Bryar to do his worst. It is in this moment of distraction and deliberation that the soldier's leg flies up, landing a blow to Bryar, causing him to momentarily double over. His fists lose their hold, and the soldier bolts. In one fluid motion, he lunges away from the tree, only to fall flat on his face as Bryar's hand grabs the man's ankle.

"The king deserves to know!" the soldier spews, flashing a glance at Myla. "Surely you can both see that our people cannot withstand the Blood Stealer much longer!"

His pleading falls on deaf ears as Bryar's heavy body thuds against the man, flattening him further into the ground. Of course, Myla can understand the sentiment. Small settlements all over Myrnith are falling to the vices of the Blood Stealer, and people go missing regularly now, no doubt joining the Fae God's army of the unwilling. Selfishly, Myla finds she would rather Bryar kill this man right here before her than be dragged to the palace to fulfil a prophecy she is certain is not true.

And kill, he does.

It is no longer a struggle to restrain. The soldier's hands find a grip around Bryar's throat, and the stakes flip. Unfortunately for the poor soul, Bryar has the upper hand, no matter what the nonmagical soldier might attempt. Choking for air as the gloved hands tighten and restrict his airflow, Bryar's own fingers find a hold on the man's neck, and he pushes his bodyweight entirely into his forearms. At once, a red-hot glow forms at his fingertips, traveling until his palms are entirely engulfed in flames. The soldier lets out a gurgling screech as he struggles beneath Bryar's fiery grip. His hands loosen from Bryar's neck, reaching to grapple at the fingers around his own, but it is to no avail.

Myla watches in horror as fire and fists together suck the life from the soldier and the forest falls silent once more.

Bryar is slow to move, his eyes locked on the lifeless man limp beneath him. First, his fingers uncurl and in a jerking motion, he leans back, his expression one of shock and sickness. Myla watches as something changes in him. Perhaps it is shame. Or perhaps it is his very last shred of innocence slipping away, trickling from his fingertips, into the body of the man he has killed.

The man he has killed to save her.

A lump rises in Myla's throat, and she presses her hands to her mouth to silence what feels like a misplaced sob.

At last, Bryar stands, stepping away from the body gingerly, as though disturbing the dead is a mark against him which the Gods simply will not forgive.

"I need you to go home," he says finally, looking at her firmly. "You can be nowhere near this."

"Bryar—"

"*No!*" He is stern, leaving no room for arguing. "I need to deal with this, and you cannot be a part of it any longer. The less you know, the better."

When morning spills into her bedroom and Elsa arrives, carrying a cheerful gown and a smile equally so, Myla leans back against her pillows, unable to pretend all is well. She has sat in her bed, upright, staring at the wall for the last two hours, willing the image of the dying man to be banished from her brain. Alas, her efforts are in vain, and when Elsa slumps to the edge of the bed, clearly tired as well, Myla finds she has nothing to say.

The silence appears to startle Elsa, and the blonde girl leans forward curiously, propping herself up on her elbows. "You look like someone died."

Though the statement is jarring, Myla finds peace in knowing that Elsa is none the wiser. "That is why I have you," Myla answers. "To make me look *alive.*"

"The job becomes more and more exhausting by the day," Elsa teases, pushing herself from the bed with an *oomph.* "You know, I really need you to keep this whole magic of the Gods thing hidden because I cannot fathom tending to a queen. I do not think the long hours would suit me."

Myla snorts, sitting upright with the weight of dread urging her to lie back down immediately. "Your timing, Elsa dear, is simply impeccable."

"What is that supposed to mean?" Elsa asks absently as she holds two satin ribbons to the sunlight, not giving Myla time to clarify before asking, "Which one?"

She offers Myla a deep blue ribbon and an off-white one. Ribbons feel far too cheerful and innocent for having just witnessed a murder, so Myla simply shakes her head, dismissing the accessories entirely, opting for a modest twist at the nape of her neck instead.

"I have lessons all day," she lies.

"No, you do not," Elsa retorts, pushing Myla to sit at her vanity with a *thud.* "I know your schedule like it is my own...because *it is.*"

"Well, that is what my father needs to think," Myla says with a sigh, pressing her fingers to her brows.

"That is what he shall be told then," Elsa replies with a stoic nod. "What will you actually be doing?"

Before Myla can truly contemplate whether sharing her secret with Elsa is wise or not, she finds the need to confide in her friend overwhelming. "I need to check on Bryar," she whispers.

"What an odd way to say you are going to suck his dick."

Myla glares at Elsa through the mirror, shaking her head. It is only now that Elsa seems to note the severity in Myla's voice.

"*Oh,*" she whispers now, leaning closer. "Whatever is the matter?"

"Elsa," Myla says with a tremor in her voice. "It is just terrible."

"What?" Losing patience now, Elsa crouches beside Myla's chair, her eyes searching her friend's for any sign of a joke. "Tell me, or I will go find him and ask him myself—oh Gods, are you expecting?"

"What? No! Elsa—he *killed* someone last night."

"Oh." With an oddly calm tone, Elsa stands and begins brushing Myla's hair. "Is that all? Myla, he is in the King's Guard. He probably kills people more than you think."

"*Elsa.*"

"Okay, I am sorry, but truly, I do not see why this is such a crisis. Who did he kill?"

"A soldier who was going to tell the king about my magic."

Silence befalls the room when Elsa's brushstrokes cease entirely, and she gazes at Myla through the mirror. Her lips twist with thought before she speaks again, this time with a more serious tone. "Leave him be today. I will go to Callum and see what is to be done. I am certain Bryar would not deal with the aftermath of it without Callum's help."

"No," Myla agreed. "He would not, and that is what worries me. I am certain by the end of this, everyone will be tangled up in my mess. I do not think it is worth it anymore, asking all of you to keep my secrets."

Elsa's grip is firm and threatening as she turns Myla to face her, her usually soft features equally firm as they find Myla's face. "I would rather die keeping your secret than live knowing I aided in helping one more man control a woman. I know that goes for them too. You have not asked this of us; we have chosen it ourselves."

CHAPTER 24

PRESENT

VALYNDOR FEELS LIKE HOME. In so many ways, it is where her most vulnerable pieces lie tucked away, safely within the ward of the Ashborn.

Coming home to Valyndor, carrying with them broken hearts and an abundance of fears, feels only right. Pierre has flown ahead to warn his parents of their new alliance and make ready more space for the Aetherwing, who have agreed to surrender their weapons in exchange for admittance into the ward. When Bryar sets Myla safely on the stone path leading to the palace, a bittersweet sense of comfort creeps into her soul.

Her sons, followed closely by Lenore, come running down the steps toward her, their arms open already and welcoming her with relieved hugs. She melts into their little bodies, grateful to feel their curls brush her cheeks and hear them pant with exertion. The pink in their cheeks, calling attention to their constellations of freckles, is the color of life. And this evening, she is all the more grateful to find them breathing.

Myla stands at last, still holding their small hands tightly, and smiles warmly at her friend. "I want nothing more than to sit in your home and slowly sip tea until you talk me out of my troubles."

Lenore's full lips curl in a weak smile, her eyes burdened with grief. "Some sadnesses are not meant to be wished away, dear friend. But I shall hug you for as long as you need and I will listen for as long as you would like to talk."

"I am not sure I have the words," Myla whispers, watching Lenore's pinched expression twist into a restrained sob as she pulls Myla in for a long, warm hug.

"Then we shall sit in silence. It is never good to grieve alone."

Silence is the exact opposite of what Myla finds as the night progresses. Welcomed into the ward, the Aetherwing are quick to descend on the feast hall where their gracious hosts have prepared a spread fit for all the monarchs of the realm, excluding of course, the Imposter King.

Congregating at one table, sit the members of House Alerys. A sad relief settles over the company, though the presiding emotion is raw sadness.

"Ethstan should be here," Henry says under his breath, a comment which raises the alarm for Aidan and Caspian.

"Fucking hell," Elsa growls, visibly kicking Henry under the table. Anxiously, Rhyland casts a glance in the young boys' way as their little eyes scan the table.

"Father," Aidan tugs at his father's sleeve, peering with trepidation into Bryar's eyes. "Where is Ethstan?"

Myla lets out a long, shallow breath before sliding a hand around Caspian's shoulder. The stoic boy slouches, hiding his face in the fluff of Prince Gourdy's back, no explanation needed, but Aidan's eyes widen and a look of horror passes over his face.

"We didn't go back for him?" The idea of death, though a grim reality to the child, has not yet sunk in. "*Mother!*" He raises his voice now, drawing the attention of Aisling, who sits perched beside her parents at the base of their thrones. Her inquisitive eyes pierce him as he shouts. "Why did you not go back for Ethstan? You are supposed to save people!"

His little voice wobbles, and Myla struggles to keep her own steady as she answers him, though a rim of tears blurs her vision. "I am sorry, my love." Before Myla can offer an explanation he might comprehend, Aisling glides down the steps where her parents sit and cautiously walks to Aidan.

At first, his expression is callous when meeting her gaze. But for the first time in their young lives, Aisling looks upon her betrothed with kindness—or sympathy at least. Myla watches, speechless as the girl reaches to the crown of feathers sprouting from her full head of hair and plucks one. It is a beautiful white feather tipped with a faint hint of orange. Her eyes lower, her lips purse with uncertainty, then she extends her hand, offering the feather to Aidan.

"I am sorry about Elenore."

Shocked, Myla looks from Aisling to her parents, who sit watching the exchange, obviously surprised. Myla determines they had nothing to do with the act of kindness. It is all Aisling.

Slowly at first, Aidan nods, a silent acceptance of her kindness, a breach in their feud, an offering of camaraderie. It will do for now. He reaches to accept her gift, his small hands closing around the feather before he looks up at Aisling. "She thought your feathers were pretty."

Aisling smiles. Aidan smiles. Then, the moment ends as Aisling turns to leave, rejoining her parents. Although Myla knows her son grieves the loss of his tutor, she knows that the *people* he wanted her to protect better was his twin.

"Tomorrow," she whispers, leaning close to her husband so only they might hear her words. "I want Rhyland to erase their memories of how Elenore and Ethstan died. I want the boys to remember them, and I know they need to know Elenore and Ethstan are gone...but I do not want them to close their eyes at night and see it in their memories. It is too much for children."

She does not expect her request to be met with resistance, but when Bryar nods in agreement, Myla is relieved.

Once supper concludes, Imogene insists that the fledglings be put to bed. In a flurry, governesses guide the young ones, Caspian and Aidan included, out of the room. Myla watches across the room as an Aetherwing woman collects a few children, the girl named Brynja among them, and leaves. The hall grows quieter with the chaos of small voices no longer sending shrill sounds sporadically through the room, and Myla allows herself a moment to gaze at the opening in the ceiling where she views the stars. She finds peace in it, watching the skies, wondering if her mother rocks her granddaughter to sleep. Perhaps the Gods tell her stories of valor.

"Do you suppose she misses us?" Myla asks, a little louder than intended, and it is Rhyland who answers first.

"No." His tone is gentle, intended to reassure, and his face stretches in a soft smile. Myla wonders how he, having been the one to discover the child, can smile so, but his response is exactly what she needs to hear. "She is experiencing something we can only dream of. Something most of us crave. She was a brave little girl with the blood of the valiant in her, and the Gods are no doubt celebrating her arrival."

Bryar grows tense beside her, and she turns to look at him, met only with a stone-cold expression. Though Rhyland's words strike a chord of comfort in Myla, they seem to do the opposite for her husband. He stands, swinging a leg over the bench to leave when she takes his hand.

"Are you going to bed?"

"No," he grumbles without looking her way. "I am going to tuck our sons in. A stranger being the last face they see before sleep does not sit well with me." That is not at all what he means, though, and

Myla feels a proverbial dagger piercing her heart. Elenore may be with
the Gods now, but the last face she saw was a stranger's.

In Bryar's absence, Elsa is quick to move from Rhyland's side. She
settles beside Myla, promptly sliding a full mug into Myla's empty
palm. "Drink."

"No," Myla responds, pushing the mug away to allow room for her
elbows. With a shaky sigh, her head falls limp into her palms, and she
closes her eyes. *You are supposed to save people.* Her son's brutal honesty
echoes in her mind. *What a fine fucking job I am doing.*

A body shifts on the other side of Myla where Caspian had been
seated, and a familiar voice breaks the silence where Myla's friends
appear to be short on helpful words. "Nothing is going to make any
of you feel better, and nothing should." It is Lenore, candidly slapping
her palms against the table as if to bolster the energy around her. "Now,
who is getting drunk with me and my husband?"

"Me," Henry is the first to respond, and Myla lifts her head slightly
to peer at the man across from her. Usually a cheerful-looking man, he
wears the exhaustion of travel and death. His hair, normally flowing
around his shoulders, is tied at the back of his head in a topknot, and
something about the severity of it ages him.

"Fuck it," Elsa says with a weak smile Lenore's way as she disperses
mugs to her boyfriends.

"No, no," Lenore says suddenly, reaching out to claim the mugs.
"The queen has a special drink for us. Why do you think the fledglings
were dismissed?"

"Serpent's wine?" Elsa asks almost hopefully, her eyes following
Lenore's every move as the beautiful Ashborn woman glances around
the room expectantly.

"The very one." Lenore confirms, and Myla lets out a small grumble
in protest.

Serpent's wine was the drink in attendance at Myla's birthday last year. It has an uncanny way of loosening tongues and *legs*. Perhaps it is the most effective way to erase the feelings of agonizing grief, if only for the night, but the idea of losing herself to its oblivion feels wrong, so when maids distribute pitchers to each table, Myla simply stares at the mug in front of her. While her companions are quick to partake, guzzling down one mug, then another, she simply stares.

She watches as the room grows lighter, no doubt Imogene's attempt at bringing euphoric relief to what feels like incessant agony. The Aetherwing people seem to mingle more comfortably with their once sworn enemies, who now demonstrate a more welcoming environment. Vigdis and Thyra lounge on a cushioned chaise at the opposite end of the room. They look out of place amidst the colorful refinement of the Ashborn. They are dark and cantankerous looking, but something in the way they lean against each other, their eyes lulled with drink, seems warm and welcoming. In fact, as the minutes pass and Myla scans the room, she notes the effortless shedding of weight. Any tension, grief, exhaustion, or other impairments seem to be replaced with the relaxing numbing of the Serpent's wine. Back across the table, Elsa now sits with a man on either side of her, like two great pillars framing her petite figure. Their hands are occupied on her body, meandering up and down her torso, across her thighs, brushing the ridges of her collarbone, and her eyes droop closed as she submits to their attentions. Attentions which still leave room for each other. Henry, now tenderly running a hand through Elsa's long hair, leans behind her, a motion Rhyland mirrors, before their mouths gently collide. It is a harmonious dance as touches are traded from one body to the next, none neglected.

Myla averts her gaze as Rhyland's mouth falls open wide enough to accept Henry's exploring tongue. Something about the exchange makes her crave her husband, a response she is immediately ashamed of. *You are supposed to save people.* How does life go on? How does one eat? Or sleep or smile at her remaining children? How does she laugh with her friends? Where does sex fit in with grief? How does her marriage survive this? It has been weeks since she touched her husband, held him, felt him inside her, and now somewhere in the palace, he sits grieving alone and she sits grieving without him, surrounded by people who love her but simply cannot staunch her pain.

Nobody can staunch her pain. Nobody can steal her guilt.

Myla longs to stand, to find her way to where her husband is, to tell him she is hurting, and she needs his help, but she knows he won't be able to help her any more than she could help him. Instead, she watches the room. She watches through blurred vision as Imogene laughs into Ivan's neck, now straddling him on his throne, her hips rolling against his. She watches as small couplings and much larger ones move to darker corners of the room, some shedding clothing as they go, others waiting until the shadows shield them more. Elsa stands now, leaning back against the wobbling frame of Rhyland as she downs a third mug of Serpent's wine before reaching down to grab Henry by his collar, pulling him to his feet, then turning to face Rhyland.

"I want *you* to make me forget how sad I am," she tangles her slender fingers with his before eyeing his hand suggestively. "With these."

Myla gasps slightly and lowers her eyes once more to her still untouched mug, though looking away does nothing to silence their voices as the trio converses.

"I have better ways of making you forget," Rhyland growls, and in her periphery, Myla observes their bodies moving away from the table to a window seat set behind a slightly parted curtain. Only a few tables away, Lenore has laid claim to a bench and leans backwards against the table as support. At first, Myla is confused, trying to make out what exactly is occurring until she realizes a large pair of wings fanning in front of Lenore, nearly curling around her entirely, acts as a modesty shield of sorts. Lenore reaches down, grasping at something, and Myla can only assume it is her husband's head, given the way she writhes and pants.

"I leave for half an hour..." His voice cracks with exhaustion, and Myla jumps at Bryar's voice so close behind her. Turning, she smiles weakly. His eyes look tired, and she wonders if he fell asleep with their sons for a time.

"Serpent's wine," Myla explains.

"Ah." He reaches to glance inside Myla's mug before smiling side-long at her. "None for you?"

Henry lets out a loud, satisfied gasp from behind the curtains.

Bryar's eyebrows furrow. "What the...?"

"They are making Elsa forget how sad she is."

From behind the sturdy drapes, Elsa shrieks an exuberant "*yes!*"

"Effectively, it sounds," Bryar says before taking Myla's mug. To her surprise, he takes several long swallows before handing her the remaining half. "The boys are asleep. We are safe. *Drink.*"

Obediently, Myla allows the sweet wine to pass between her lips in one slow swallow followed by many more until it dribbles down her cheeks and she empties the mug. Lowering the tankard with a clumsy *thud*, she meets her husband's gaze, and her earlier desire for him is only amplified by the weightlessness of the alcohol and the gasps of pleasure and rhythmic motions of bodies surrounding them.

He wears only his tunic and trousers now, the rest of his uniform undoubtedly discarded in the boys' room. His sleeves are rolled just above the elbows, revealing the flaming tattoos rippling over his toned forearms, and he reaches out to brush the wine from her mouth with a thumb before licking it clean, his eyes never wavering from hers.

They lose themselves in the Serpent's wine, and with every sip, every downed mug, the room grows fuzzier. Somewhere behind the veil of curtains, Elsa demands that she wants to watch.

Her request is answered with an, "As you wish," from Henry.

Rhyland barely eeks out, *"May I?"* before one of them begins moaning and demands that Elsa touch herself if she is to only be observing.

"Can't let us do all the work, darling."

It is arousing, and Myla longs for the freedom they so easily fall into. Everywhere she looks, couples and groups of lovers give in to their vices, yet she sits here, watching her husband drink, unable to shrug the feelings of guilt despite her severe inebriation.

Bryar seems to read her thoughts, and in one fluid motion, he takes the drink from her hand. His green eyes reflect something they seem to have lost years ago, something she glimpses breathlessly: *they are soft.* He looks at her with softness. He looks at her as though they have fallen back in time and she is just a girl, sitting on a barrel behind his home, convincing herself they are only there to learn.

"I am sad." She leans into the small voice in the back of her head which begs her to keep talking to him, no matter how long the pain continues. She knows she must talk, even if it is to only ever say the same three words: *I am sad.* Perhaps if they keep talking, they will survive this.

"Yes," Bryar agrees before sinking his finger into her hips, sliding her across the bench closer to him. "We will never again *not* feel sad. But we can forget it for tonight." His hand snakes around her neck possessively, pulling her face to his before laying claim to her mouth. He tastes of wine, sweet and intoxicating. His beard scratches the soft surface of her cheeks, and the pain of it only makes her want him more. Myla pulls away from him and slides off the bench to her knees, completely oblivious to the ecstasy seeming to bleed from every corner of the room. The gasps, the beating of wings as lovers become airborne, firelight reflecting off bare skin, and the blur of bodies in motion.

The only ecstasy she is concerned about is his.

"Wife," he growls in satisfaction, tangling a fist in the hair at the nape of her neck. "What are you doing?"

"Stop talking and find out," Myla responds with a lazy smile as she fumbles with his belt, frantic to loosen it and free him of his trousers.

"Here?" he questions, glancing around the room.

"Look at *me*," Myla demands, sliding her hand into his pants. Her fingers wrap around his hard length, her touch silencing his concerns, and his eyes lock with hers. Touching him brings her to life. It reminds her of their bond, and even if temporary, it feels healing.

His eyebrow twitches, and a spark of coyness flickers in his eyes as though he doubts she will follow through. Behind them, the trio, unconcerned with who can hear or see what, seems to move in unison, their cries and moans fueling Myla's determination to partake. Accepting the bait, she frees him from his trousers, and he throbs in anticipation as her fingers glide up and down his hard shaft. She is met with resistance when his fist clamps around her wrist and at first, Myla thinks he is ready to put a stop to their tryst, when he pulls her hand to his mouth and licks her palm, lubricating her. A sly smile creeps across Myla's face, and without breaking his gaze, she wraps her fingers around him once more, teasing him slowly from base to tip before she lowers her mouth around him in a brief tease before pulling away again. The motion evokes an anticipating shudder from him. Myla parts her lips to lick him, dragging her tongue tantalizingly across his shaft while watching from between his thighs as his head falls back and the muscles in his jaw tense. Drawing her splayed palms up his thighs, Myla digs her fingers into his skin, moaning as she parts her lips to allow entry, and with a slight thrust of his hips, she takes him deep within her mouth, moving up and down his shaft as her tongue glides across his sensitive nerves, tasting him.

"Gods," Bryar gasps as Myla allows her teeth to gently graze his tip before dropping her jaw again to feel him against the back of her throat. The repeated motion evokes a trembling in his legs, and he arches his back, surrendering to her control entirely. Though his hand remains balled in her hair, encouraging her to move up and down him, his hold is loose, allowing her to control the pace and rhythm.

The stones beneath her knees are cold and send an aching fire up her thighs as she curls over her husband, but the pain pales in comparison to the pleasure she feels in her core as she swirls her tongue around the tip of his cock, sucking him into her mouth once more, a motion which forces him to relinquish his hold on her and grip the edge of the bench. His body tenses, and Myla feels him harden further before, with a final thrust deeper into her mouth, he throbs in release. Myla swallows and replaces her mouth with her hands, massaging slowly as he trembles, recovering from the sensation before sitting upright and gripping her waist. His tongue delves into her mouth, his lips moving violently against hers, hungry to return the favor.

"How do you want me, my love? Mouth or hands?"

Myla grins as he pulls her upright, seating her on the bench so he can better worship her. "I want you to watch," she whispers as she allows her thighs to relax and separate, her hands grappling at the fabric of her skirt until she has found her target, already wet and ready for her fingers. Bryar, on his knees before her, visibly melts, sucking his lower lip between his teeth as his eyes, trained to never miss a detail, watch her hand slide in and out of her own body.

"This is cruel," he says, trembling. "Let me *have* you, Gods damn it."

Myla giggles as, in unison with his complaint.

Rhyland lets out a relieved, "*Fuck, yes,*" from behind the curtains.

"Come and claim me, then," she taunts, spreading her thighs further for his inspection.

Like a wild animal, starved and teased with fresh meat, Bryar lunges toward her, his strong fingers burying themselves deep inside her. Myla's hand remains in place, but not for long as he nips at her wet fingers.

"Do not make me compete with you," he says, looking up at her. "We settled this a long time ago. I will always do a better job of it than you."

Playfully, Myla lets out a satisfied sigh as she presses a flat palm into the back of his head. "I think I need a reminder then, prove yourself." The words have hardly left her lips before he loses himself between her thighs, his tongue plunging deep inside her while he frees his grip on a thigh to show her extra attention with his fingers.

A relaxed smile passes over Myla's face as she leans back against the table, her body quivering from an overload of ecstasy as her husband attends to every sensitive inch of her.

Somewhere in the curtained oasis next to her, three voices at once let out cries of pleasure before Elsa joyfully announces, "There is nothing better than two dicks at once!"

CHAPTER 25

PAST: MYLA,
TWENTY-ONE

A GLOOMY-LOOKING HORSE TROTS up the path, its hooves causing disturbing little splashes on the cobblestones as it sends rainwater spraying. It is an absolutely terrible day for the aptitude tests, and walking now behind the horse who carries her undoing, Myla cannot help but wonder what life will hold for her by the time the sun sets on New Falkmere.

"He will make this all well," Maverick announces to Myla and Lavinia with a swell of pride in his voice, as if subjecting Myla to the grueling manipulations of this spellweaver is something she should relish.

"Make way for the king!" From behind, a familiar voice urges civilians to move to the sides of the road so Caius can pass. Myla turns on her heel at the sound of Bryar's command. He walks a few paces ahead of Caius, his axe held over his shoulder casually, but his eyes quick and observant, taking in every movement in the king's direction. Until they meet hers and linger a little too long.

They are not soft today; they are stoic; they are concerned; they are angry, but they are not soft. And it breaks Myla's heart. The moment as he passes seems to move in slow motion as her very heartbeat staggers, aching in her chest, watching as he moves ahead and out of sight, into the institute. When she turns to meet her father's gaze, Myla finds him still fixated on the back of the procession, no doubt devouring the sight and imagining himself there someday soon.

Replacing any feelings of begrudged duty, hatred takes seed, and she follows Maverick inside. Lavinia's trembling hand slips inside Myla's, coiling her fingers tightly as if to offer the last bit of strength she has.

"The Gods have already decided how this will end," she whispers to her daughter. "Lean into your intuition and trust that the Spirit Mother will guide you."

Her words feel hollow. They lack conviction. She says them, but she does not *feel* them. Myla stares blankly at Lavinia, a stinging pinch at her nose threatening weakness where she has room for none. Wordlessly, Myla turns away from her mother. Regardless of how she feels, this is not the moment to accuse the woman of enabling her abuser. Something in Lavinia's expression feels like an admission of guilt, anyway.

For the last seven years, Myla has walked the halls of this institute. It has been the living symbol of contradictions in her life. It has housed some of her happiest moments, and it has seen some of her most frightened. Today, in the gardens behind the Institute of Mystic Arts, it may very well be the voyeur of her unraveling.

It has been months now since Bryar silenced the guard behind her estate. Even trying to coax her magic into existence has not satisfied her father. Despite her best efforts to show him that a spellweaver is unnecessary, Maverick has felt otherwise. As a result, she and Elsa have spent their free time trying to discover any text in the libraries that might suggest she could resist the magic of the spellweaver. No such text seems to exist.

The institute is bustling with excitement. Many of her classmates have long since taken their tests and been placed in roles of service to the king according to their performances, so today, Myla will be assessed with a much younger group of wielders. The line seems to be fifty pupils deep, and most of those around her seem unconcerned, excited even.

"We shall be watching for you," Maverick grumbles, his words sounding more like a threat than a bode of confidence, before he follows the path of the spellweaver into the gardens.

Lavinia's breath hitches as she opens her mouth to speak, but Myla interrupts, turning her body away from her mother. "There is nothing to say, Mother. I shall see you afterwards."

When the name Myla Alerys is called, she barely hears it, as the thrumming of her heart drowns out any natural sounds.

"That's you," the girl behind her whispers, offering a slight nudge, which propels Myla out into the garden in a daze. The sun shines now, despite the rain, and so the contradictions of this place continue. Like the smiles on the faces of those spectating, despite the way she wants to scream. Like the way Maverick wears a look of pride as he leans in to speak to Elsa's father, despite the face of anger he normally wears for her. And it is the way Bryar watches her from the king's side, his expression like stone. There is nothing in his demeanor that would betray his feelings to those in company.

Caius sits on an elevated platform with guards and courtiers alike surrounding him. He is well-groomed and dressed in a deep green that complements the colors of the garden.

As she comes into view, his eyes dart to where she is, and a look of curiosity flickers across his regal features before he rights his expression.

"Our next demonstration will be of Miss Myla Alerys," the headmaster speaks, his voice booming as he addresses the king specifically.

"We have employed a spellweaver for this particular student, Your Grace, as we believe there is great potential beneath this young lady's resistance."

Curious, Caius leans forward now, resting his elbows pensively against his knees. "Am I correct in understanding that most people consider a spellweaver's work a barbaric practice?" he asks skeptically.

The headmaster nods, offering a reassuring smile. "In cases such as these, Your Grace, I believe the benefits outweigh the very *temporary* consequences."

"So it must be," the king answers. "Proceed."

A single word sends sickness through Myla's belly, and her knees tremble as the spellweaver emerges from the crowd. Expressions from onlookers vary; some appear eager to witness the spectacle while others seem disgusted. Such is the common response to employing a spell-weaver. Many believe it to be just another use of magic, while others, Myla included, feel it is a violation.

"I shall simply ask the lady to be seated." His voice is like a snake, slithering and cold and undoubtedly suspicious. The man gestures gracefully to a chair behind her, which Myla looks at before tilting her chin rebelliously, unmoving, prompting the spellweaver to speak again. "Pulling one's magic beyond those blocks which we so often, subconsciously construct, can be painful," he says with a glance toward the ground as though he is a demonstrating teacher. "Sitting would be most wise, but if you prefer to stand, I shall begin."

Myla remains wordless, knowing that anything she has to say would be considered exactly as she intends it: disrespectfully. All note her silence, and many in the crowd watch her through squinted eyes, as though peering harder at her might explain the indignant response.

With a final glance in the king's direction, the spellweaver nods, assuming her silence gives him permission to proceed. Bony fingers reach out to brush her forehead, and angrily, Myla's hand flies upward to meet his, gripping him by the wrist.

"Do not touch me." Anger simmers beneath her skin. Myla can feel it waking up; the slumbering beast inside her. The crowd gasps, and Maverick is at once on his feet, moving between rows of chairs to come to the front nearest Myla. Lavinia trails behind, and in the commotion, Myla finally glimpses Elsa, Callum, and Rhyland watching from behind a hedge, their faces each wrought with concern.

"Your father has employed me to help you, Miss. I implore you to allow me to do my job." The spellweaver, however, does not look at her while he speaks. Instead, his attention is on the king. Caius nods and once more, the vile man before her reaches out to touch her brow.

Myla slaps his hand. "Do. Not. Touch. Me," she declares, louder this time.

Gasps ripple across the crowd of onlookers.

"Myla Alerys," Maverick growls, and to her humiliation, he strides toward her until he stands toe to toe. He seizes her wrist, and she suppresses a wince. "You behave as though you have something to hide. Enough of this nonsense!"

Maverick turns to face the king, composing himself now and with a bow, he speaks, "My daughter is spirited, Your Grace. I beg your forgiveness."

Caius stands, and behind him, Bryar shifts uncomfortably, his eyes finally finding Myla's. His expression sends chills through her body. It feels like a promise of protection, but she knows it is nothing of the sort. It is just love, and this love cannot save her.

"You must be nervous, dear," the king says, his voice kind but laced with impatience. "I must insist you sit, as the spellweaver asked."

Defying the king is an entirely different form of rebellion that Myla is unwilling to explore. She lowers her eyes and offers him a curtsy before turning on trembling legs to sit. When she does, she is shocked to watch as Caius quietly whispers to two guards who then proceed to her side, each taking hold of her arms to keep her still. Myla's eyes dart to Caius and find him watching intently, his hand stroking the fine hairs of his beard, and his eyes devouring her hungrily, as though he can already sense that she conceals the weapon he needs to win. Another silent exchange passes between the king and the spellweaver, and with a final nod to proceed, Caius settles deeper into his chair.

The spellweaver's fingertips descend like ice onto her flushed skin, or perhaps this is the worst headache Myla has ever felt. He moves his skin against hers, drawing some sort of design across her brow while muttering an incantation over and over.

"Alorya i'thune de'ruva. Alorya i'thune gund'ra."

Awaken the power. Awaken the Gods.

Myla trembles as his words seem to thicken the very air around them, and darkness shrouds her being. There is nothing beyond herself and the spellweaver. The gardens, the spectators, the king, even Bryar: they all vanish. Dizzy from spinning, all Myla can see is the wicked, slight man before her. His eyes glow yellow, and the incantation grows distant, though his mouth moves quickly, violently, like he is screaming them. The headache turns nefarious. The fingers on her forehead seem to push beyond her flesh, past her skull, and deep within the most sacred parts of her consciousness until his invasive touch grapples with the nerves connecting her spine and her brain. As he twists the fabric of her being between his stabbing, burning fingers, he summons that which she has tried to conceal for years.

It begins with the lights. Although darkness surrounds her already, her vision impaired by the grappling of the spellweaver, Myla watches as particles of sunlight drift into her being like millions of stars collecting at her core. They sear her skin, sending pulses of lightning stabbing through her body and mind, hundreds at a time.

Not like this.

She resists, her body convulsing and tightening around the urge to surrender and release her magic to the skies, and the act of rebellion is punished by that twisting hand. Blinded, Myla tries to stand, but the guards restrain her firmly, unafraid to bruise if needed. Muffled from behind her, they command her to be still.

"Let her go!" a woman's voice from the crowd shrieks in distress.

Mother.

Myla longs for the rough hands of her assailants to be replaced by the gentle embrace of her mother, but the grip on her mind tightens more, urging her to focus on the source of her magic. Her anger. Her love. Her passion. Feelings thrum through her body, torn from her mind thread by thread, spinning into the spellweaver's palm until a void remains, and the emptiness calls to be filled with revenge. Retribution that might acknowledge her emptiness and bite the hand stealing from her. Justice that will tremble, that will quake the earth beneath their very feet and perhaps consume them as punishment. It coils like a cornered predator, desperate to be freed, desperate to draw blood.

"There it is," Caius says in the distance, and she can hear the intrigue. "Explore that more."

The spellweaver's hand wriggles within her head, jerking her forward and back as if groping for something more tangible, and the air around her putrefies with defeat. She longs to crush him.

If rage can kill, injustice can annihilate.

Logic fails Myla as she relinquishes her hold on the will of the Gods, and predatory magic leaps forth in a thunderous, quaking form. Agony rivets through her body. Her head snaps back with her magic's tension, dislodging the spellweaver from her mind. It is too late, however, to halt the fury which burns through her veins, and as Myla's vision restores, she is stunned to see it is black as night still while she absorbs all natural and unnatural light across the expanse of New Falkmere. The clouds, black and rolling in anger, gather overhead, crowning her in the Gods' rage, and that dreadful constricting inside her throat builds until release is the only option. Desperate to speak, to protest and punish in the same breath, Myla surrenders herself as a vessel of the Gods' wrath.

Her lips part, and a cracking from above sounds as though the Gods are breaking through the sky to deliver vengeance. From her mouth pours deafening, distorted rage.

And the earth trembles in grief.

With it, Myla allows her own natural wail to mingle with the Voice of the Gods, carrying her disputes on their mighty breath, so when the light is restored and her voice settles into nothing more than her own, relief mingles with natural sobs. Her tear-filled eyes focus on Bryar's face.

No one doubts that this is not a moment of victory, but a moment of death.

Caius sits unmoving, reclined in his chair and wearing a look of bewildered awe. It is not until his eyes flick to her feet that Myla realizes the spellweaver lies dead before her. A mangled stump reveals his cause of death; his eviscerated hand is a bloody spray of flesh and splintered bone.

He touched the light...

The realization that she killed him washes over the crowd at once, and the guards' grips tighten further, bruising deeper when they yank her to her feet, not as a student any longer, but as a prisoner. Voices shout from every direction demanding either her arrest or her release, but Caius sits still, visibly deliberating. His gaze dissects her, and Myla wonders if he can tell that she has been hiding from him all along.

"Let me go!" Myla snarls as she tries to jerk free from their iron grasp.

Although the attempt is futile, the visceral reaction evokes a grimace from Bryar. His eyes redden with suppressed tears as he stares ahead, bound to his posting.

"Unhand her!" Rhyland speaks with a raised voice, pushing through the crowd until he stands before Caius. "I implore you, Your Grace, do not allow them to treat her so. This woman *bleeds stars*. Can you not see she is a gift from the Gods?"

Stunned, Caius turns his attention to Rhyland, his mouth twisting in a frown. "You address me without permission, soldier."

Rhyland drops his head, and Myla feels a twinge of fear surge through her chest. *Do not get yourself killed on my account. It is already done; you cannot save me anymore.*

"Forgive me, Your Grace. I only thought their handling of this woman to be unjust given her remarkable demonstration."

The words *remarkable demonstration* triggers his regal diplomacy, and Caius stands, stepping past his guards toward Myla. He reaches out, brushing tears from her cheeks with a gloved hand before tipping her chin upwards to look at him. "Will you run, dear?"

A whimper escapes her lips, and Myla shakes her head in defeat. "No, Your Grace."

With a nod, Caius dismisses the guards before standing beside her to face the crowd. For the first time, Myla finds her father's face.

He is beaming.

Further behind him, still partially hidden behind the hedges, Callum holds Elsa against his chest as she cries, his own face twisted in a suppressed sob.

"The Gods speak through this woman," Caius announces, projecting his speech so all might hear. He reaches down to take her hand. He holds it in his own reverently, pressing it to his chest. Myla's arm hangs limp, suspended between her body and his like a tether. Every part of her is empty, and her presence is ornamental at best. She feels nothing, not even the rage which ruined her only moments ago. Her being is flat, hollow, and inanimate. Like a garden spade or a wooden mixing spoon, she is a tool, an instrument for man's design.

Myla does not scan the crowd further. She does not seek the face of her beloved. She does not open her eyes.

She does not exist.

Standing now is only the girl who bleeds stars. Or, as she hears from the proud voice beside her, the *queen* who bleeds stars.

CHAPTER 26

PRESENT

LENORE AND ELSA LIE on the cushioned windowsill, slumped against one another, groggily complaining of headaches while fumbling with the heavy drapery, unsuccessfully trying to block out the sun.

"I have memories from last night." Lenore winces as she tries to sit up. "And I would rather *not* remember them." Her expression, softly glowing with a satisfied smile, says otherwise.

Elsa slumps against the cushion as Lenore's body is removed as support. "That is where we are different, darling. I am replaying it. Over and over, and *over.*"

Playfully mocking, Lenore grins at Elsa. "Over, and over, you mean *oh, oh, oh*!" Her breathy gasps scandalize the room, and Myla stifles a laugh as Lenore reenacts. "Yes, don't think we did not all hear your vocalizing last night."

Unashamed, Elsa straightens. "My men like validation. They perform best that way."

"As I recall," Myla groans, wincing at the sunlight to catch Lenore's attention. "You once told me you would kill for an uninterrupted night like last night."

Lenore's brows arch, her expression completely satisfied. "That I did...and you, friend? Are you reveling or remorseful?"

Myla lets out a bashful laugh before shaking her head in confusion. "Perhaps both?" It is hard to focus on anything. A sharp pain in her head and the knowledge that she is to meet with Rhyland soon to erase the boys' memories feel like a nasty concoction.

"I'll drink to that," Lenore answers cautiously, her gaze lingering a second longer on Myla. Suspicious.

"Tea, right?" Myla forces a smile, reaching up to the table beside her, careful not to spill as she lowers the teacup to her mouth.

"Yes," Lenore agrees. "*Tea.*"

"What do we think of the Aetherwing?" Elsa diverts the conversation, and inwardly, Myla digests all that occurred the day before.

What do we think of the Aetherwing? Did the Gods truly send them to help? Regardless of whether they are friend, foe, or nothing at all, they seem like fierce people with dragons large enough to erase Myrnith from the map entirely.

"There is much history between the Aetherwing and the Ashborn," Lenore adds, and something in the way she says *history* feels questionable.

"Do elaborate," Myla insists curiously.

"There were centuries when our people were at war for the land. The Ashborn won only on account of a half-breed."

Myla cringes, hating the word for reminders of how Bryar had to prove himself to be acknowledged as Ashborn. "Half-breed?" She asks, nearly spitting the nasty words out, a response which does not go unnoticed by both women across from Myla.

"Yes. An Aetherwing and an Ashborn had a child. It was scandalous. Aetherwing do not have magic, but they have the blood of dragons in them, which is why a dragon will bond with them at all. They sense their own kind. Give an Ashborn the blood of a dragon and their fire burns hotter than any known to this natural world, or any unnatural world for that matter. Ashborn cannot withstand it, and dragons cannot withstand it. So, when the half-breed, Degyn Waev, finally sided with the Ashborn, on account of Valyndor land being ours from the start, she killed many of their dragons before the Aetherwing surrendered. We did not realize they had any remaining dragons. It seems they have spent centuries allowing the beasts to reach maturity. The largest dragon, ridden by that child—what is her name?"

"Brynja," Elsa and Myla answer in unison.

"Yes, Brynja. She rides Dagyn Waev's dragon. That beast must be several hundred years old now."

"So why did they stay hidden?" Myla asks, thinking of how she never saw nor heard mention of their territory beyond Dryad Forest.

Elsa sits now, pushing her hair behind her ears as she groans into the motion. "I imagine so when they did finally reveal themselves, it could be as they have done now, with formidable, *mature* dragons on their side."

Myla's brow furrows, and she presses palms to the sides of her head, focusing in on the concern which raises alarm. "If they come here, strong enough to flatten us, why align themselves with us?"

Lenore purses her lips, and her wings twitch with anxiety. "I have my suspicions, but I believe you best ask Imogene that question."

Before Myla can probe further, a knock disrupts their conversation, and Rhyland enters.

He is early.

"Why, hello," Elsa says, flashing him a flirtatious grin.

"I cannot even *look* at you, woman," he blurts with a sheepish grin while holding a hand up to shield his gaze from her, which evokes laughter from all. Ignoring the presence of the lusty blonde across the room, Rhyland focuses on Myla, briefly furrowing his brow upon finding her on the floor. "Uh...Your Grace? I have more information regarding the task you gave me. May we speak?"

Information—he is not here for the boys.

Myla straightens slightly, noting how his usually lighthearted disposition has shifted to something sinister.

"Of course," she answers timidly, accepting his hand and allowing him to pull her upright. Rhyland's drooping gaze does not go unnoticed, and Myla flashes a dismissive look to her friends, one which both women read quickly. They stand, Elsa wobbling, and leave.

"You are scaring me," Myla says as the door closes behind Lenore and Elsa. "What is it?"

Rhyland runs a palm across his flushed brow before shaking his head anxiously, his dark curls bouncing. "When you tasked me with finding out more about your mother's death, I had this feeling that if I were to find answers anywhere, it would be with your father's personal guard during the time."

Myla's skin prickles, and she rubs her hands rapidly across her arms, trying to chase the cold away. "And?"

"I sent one guard to search Maverick's old estate in case we missed anything the first time...and I sent a few discreet and trusted soldiers to uncover the whereabouts of the man. He is retired now and is living off a soldier's pension in New Falkmere. My men delivered him to me this morning," he admits with a sigh. "I interrogated him in the prison."

"Go on," Myla insists, her eyes wide with fear for what Rhyland might say next. "Tell me what he says."

"He did not say anything," Rhyland answers with an exasperated sigh. "He seemed clueless as to what I was asking about. So, I had to invade his memories."

Myla cringes, watching as shame washes visibly over Rhyland.

"The thing about my gift is that if a novice wielder wiped someone's memories, they're likely just smudged for the person, like a really fuzzy dream, so I can see the memories even if they cannot. If a previous wielder wiped his memory, I can find those memories still. It is difficult to untangle the threads of the subconscious to get a clear vision, but that is what I did and—"

"Rhyland—what did you find?"

Having no room to soften the blow, Rhyland spirals into an explanation. "This man stood guard outside of the brewmage's chambers as he gave Maverick a vial of something that would supposedly make a person feel as though they were drifting to sleep. A sleep they 'would not wake from'. It would appear to any physician that she had died of some underlying health defect, and not poison."

A sob catches in Myla's throat; one she swallows before biting down on her many questions to simply ask one: "And you are certain this vial was given to my mother and not some other poor soul?"

At this, Rhyland sits, his kind eyes zoned in on Myla, watching her as he chooses his words carefully. "This soldier poured the tea himself during a conversation between your father and mother where he chastised her for trying to undermine his plans for you. The memory clearly showed Lavinia taking a drink of tea before...falling *asleep* in her chair. Maverick then carried Lavinia to the bed, and they both left the room."

The very bed Myla found her mother dead in. It is incriminating. "I..." she stumbles over her words, watching through blurred eyes as Rhyland shifts uncomfortably before her. "And what of the search? Was anything found in his estate?"

"Only a few notes, some ledgers. But the guard had the wherewithal to bring a few samples so we could compare his handwriting to that of the note."

A daughter for a daughter. "And?"

"It was identical."

Myla stiffens, her jaw growing tense as she bites down on the sudden urge to scream. Feeling lightheaded with the news, she steps forward, curling her fingers around the back of a chair to steady herself before speaking. *He killed my mother, and he killed my daughter.* "What have you done with the prisoner?"

"Nothing yet. What would you have me do?"

"I will leave that up to Bryar," Myla whispers, loosening her grip and noting the perspiration on her palms. "Your business for the day is not done. We must take care of the boys' memories."

Hesitantly, Rhyland nods. "I can be discreet about it. They will not even know anything has happened."

Myla nods, wondering if taking their memories, traumatic as they are, is wrong. "I must speak with Bryar before we do anything. Send him to me."

Bryar's fingers glide gently over the tendrils of hair which cascade over her shoulders. Lying against his chest, Myla cries, her arms wrapped around his middle.

"It is like they have both died all over again," Myla sobs, her tears soaking his black tunic. "There is a God of Mischief above that is laughing at his own cruelty, to give this world a man like Maverick Alerys."

"I know," Bryar whispers, his own voice quivering as he presses a warm palm to her bare shoulder. "It is needless and unforgivable, and I curse the God that has allowed it."

Myla trembles to hear the words spoken and feel the curl of his hand around her arm, holding her tight against him, each drowning in an anger that could ignite a lifetime of wars. "My own father. Capable of killing my mother and daughter. And for what?" Myla spits the words, tasting their venom.

"He is angry," Bryar answers between his teeth, sucking in a breath which seems to nearly suffocate him. "At least...I know now that Elenore's death was his way of punishing me. He believes I took you from him." He pauses, and Myla feels the muscles of his body tense with a sob. "So, he took my daughter from me."

Myla flinches, sitting upright and pulling her knees to her chest. "That feels like a stretch, even for him. He has the throne. Why does he still want *me*?"

"He spent twenty-seven years controlling you, trying to fashion you into his *tool*. A man like him does not surrender control simply because he is powerful. He will fight to keep the control, and as a result, the power too."

Bryar's body feels limp, and for the first time ever, Myla does not feel the strength she is so accustomed to when she leans on him. Broken and defeated at the hands of her merciless father, her husband lies beside her now, as cracked open as she is.

His eyes are red with tears, and his jaw grinds relentlessly. "I am so angry," he confesses, his eyes daring to meet hers briefly before fixing stoically on the ceiling above them. "When your father meets his end, he will wish that it was at the hands of anyone but me."

Myla swings her legs over the side of the bed to stand and shakes her head, wiping her eyes dry. "No. When Maverick Alerys meets his end, he will wish it was anyone but *me*." The words are chilling, and Myla means them with everything inside her.

"Where are you going?" Bryar asks.

"I am going to speak with Ivan and Imogene. I need you to speak with Rhyland. He is waiting for our instructions on exactly what parts of Cas and Aidan's memories should be wiped."

Bryar nods slowly before clarifying. "And we are in agreement? They should have visions of the *actual* deaths taken away, but they should still remember that Elenore and Ethstan are gone?"

Myla lets out a somber sigh. "I believe it is best. I don't want them envisioning death. It is too much for children so young. Do you agree?"

"I do."

Bryar turns to leave, but Myla stops him. "Rhyland also needs guidance on what to do with the prisoner. I say kill him for his part in my mother's death, but that I will leave to you." Myla moves toward her husband, pressing palms to his chest before rolling on to her toes to kiss him. "Tell everyone of what Maverick has done and send word of it to his allies. I cannot think the Riverlands, Titonfall, nor Elspire will stand by someone who murders innocent women and children."

When Myla finds the King and Queen of Valyndor, they appear light-hearted and unconcerned. As Imogene links her arm with her husband's, smiling up at him, Myla feels a tinge of envy. She and her husband have been burdened with war and strategy during their entire marriage. She longs to live in peace as Imogene and Ivan do.

"Your Graces," Myla offers formally, before falling in stride with them to walk the scenic route up the mountain framing Valyndor's west side.

"I would offer some pleasantries, but I can see you mean business," Imogene says frankly, examining Myla through her brows. The plume of feathers crowning her head is extravagant and beautiful, even fiery, in the morning light.

"I believe we must discuss this alliance with the Aetherwing. I learned of their history with the Ashborn, and I cannot help but wonder why you are so comfortable forming an alliance with them, knowing their dragons could incinerate all of Valyndor with a breath..."

Myla winces, thinking of the child and her mighty dragon. "Especially Brynja's. I am told that dragon is almost as old as Valyndor."

Ivan gazes ahead, his eyes fixed on the sharp peak they gradually climb upwards to. "Our secrets betray us, darling." He speaks to Imogene, who responds with a *thunk* to the back of his head with one of her wings.

"Hush."

"Come now," Myla says impatiently. "Have we not known each other long enough to do away with the mysteries?"

Imogene sighs, and her attention falls to the city beneath them, whose rooftops glint now beneath the sun and whose citizens bustle about their day. "What do you know of your husband's father?"

"Less than you, or so you have said." Myla answers shortly, wondering what Caspian has to do with the Aetherwing. "I only know what I witnessed myself. He was a good father, a quiet man. He kept to himself."

Ivan chuckles, glancing between the two women. "You two are so alike, it amazes me that our alliance has lasted. Darling, just tell Myla and let her do with it what she will."

Imogene's eyes narrow at her husband and with a huff, she looks past him to where Myla walks. "I told you once that I knew of Bryar's parentage. I should have disclosed what I knew then, but...I needed to know that our alliance was strong. In the early days of knowing one another, I was not sure I could trust you not to run off with our most powerful asset and use him against us...It seems I have no choice but to tell you now."

"For the love of the Gods," Myla says, heart thrumming in anticipation. "Our children will rule Valyndor together one day! It is in both of our interests to maintain this alliance. Your secrets are safe. But why would my husband be your strongest asset?"

"Well," the queen says with a sigh, halting their ascension up the mountain to face Myla squarely. "Your husband's father was Aetherwing."

Her words reverberate off Myla's body, sending shock pulsing through her.

The queen continues, "If I am honest, Bryar's magic was almost unbearable for me when I fought with him those many years ago. It was a poorly hidden secret in Valyndor that his mother fell in love with a wanderer from the west and had a child with him."

"Did you know Bryar's mother?"

Imogene pauses, glancing wearily at Ivan before nodding. "She was my sister."

At once, horror freezes Myla's veins, followed quickly by rage. "Imogene!" she hisses. "That makes our children related! You *knew* this and allowed us to betroth them?"

"Oh!" A comical expression passes over Ivan's face before both he and Imogene burst into laughter, something that immediately grates on Myla. "No, no," Imogene clarifies. "I should say she was my *adopted* sister. There was no blood relation. Both of her parents, close friends of my own dear parents, died in a battle between the Aetherwing and the Ashborn, so we took her in and became her family."

Myla lets out a sigh of relief, leaning momentarily on the rocky outcropping behind her. "Gods, Imogene. I thought I was going to have to walk off this mountain and tell Bryar not only is he part Aetherwing, but our son is betrothed to marry his cousin!"

CHAPTER 27

PAST: MYLA,
TWENTY-ONE

TONIGHT, THE HIGH-BACK GREEN chair is not welcoming. It does not feel like she has curled up in it hundreds of times to read by the fire. Its arms do not support her; they suffocate. And the fire laughs at her in all of its blazing fury, each jester's flame a reminder of the heat that used to exhilarate her but will now taunt her. A window in the parlor is open, billowing the linen curtains, and the wind brushes her skin intimately.

The way Caius will.

The way Bryar will never again.

The thought sends a panicked sob through Myla, and her hands fly to her mouth, muffling the sound seconds too late. A heavy set of footsteps followed by quicker, lighter ones announce Maverick and Lavinia before they enter the parlor. Myla briefly glances up at her parents, noting the stark contrast of their expressions. With a backdrop of the darkened room, Maverick's pale face stretched in a victorious grin seems eerie and out of place, while Lavinia's, gaunt and concerned, at least feels appropriate.

"Wipe the tears, girl." Maverick lets out a longsuffering sigh, perching on the sofa across from her, his eyebrows arched as he observes her, curled on the armchair as if to hide. "You will be queen. Imagine all you will do with that power."

"You mean what you will *make* me do with that power?" Myla snaps with no care for how he punishes her. The back of his hand will feel like silk compared to the headache still left by the grappling hands of a now-dead spellweaver.

Death seems a kindness. Perhaps his temper will take him too far this time. *What a fucking shame to break the final rung on your ladder of power.*

"Watch it, Myla. Should you speak to the king, who will subsequently be your husband, in such a manner, a slap on the face will be the least of your concerns. Now tell us why you cry so that we may hear of it and be done with the ordeal. We have important decisions to make."

"*Maverick,*" Lavinia pleads, seating herself hesitantly beside her husband. "Give her a moment to catch her breath! This is all new and terrifying for her."

"We do not have moments, Lavinia!" Maverick runs a hand through his beard, moving the hairs in a disheveled pattern while his eyes scan the room in a panic as though he is missing something. "What is the problem, Myla? Every girl in New Falkmere weeps tonight because they *want* to be you."

"Married to a man as old as you are? I think not," Myla hisses angrily, pulling the sleeves of her nightgown over her hands to resist punching her father square between the eyes. "It is disgusting and unthinkable. You saw how he ordered his guards to hold me down!"

"*Yes!*" Maverick bellows. "Imagine someone finally having the fucking power to put you in your gods-damned place, girl! A dose of that is exactly what you need."

Myla grips the arms of the chair, wondering why, though she is so far beyond working her way out of this, a small voice inside her still screams, *no man will ever have inescapable power over me.*

Maverick growls angrily and looks at his wife. "She is impertinent and ungrateful! I have found—*historically* the most notoriously sought after match for her, and she speaks of it like this!" He looks back to Myla now, his face contorted in the harsh light of the fire against the dark of the shadows which draw his cheeks long and hollow. "You have sought no suitors, daughter. You cannot live in this house forever, and it is obvious your interests lie anywhere but in becoming a wife."

At this, Myla's flesh grows clammy and tingles with the fury of her magic. She imagines releasing its wrath in Maverick's direction and leaving his fate to the Gods. "I have thought very much about being a wife, father. Just not to *him*," she corrects; her voice so low she hopes he does not hear her.

But he does.

He exchanges a confused look with Lavinia, and his silent question is answered with the confused shake of his wife's head. "Then *who*?"

Myla swallows the name. *His* name. She closes her eyes and wishes the vision of his soft eyes and boyish curls out of her mind. Anything that might betray him to her father must be banished. "No one." Her lie is feeble and turns to dust before them.

"Myla Alerys!" Maverick's voice makes no attempt at kindness. It is cold and harsh and threatening. She can feel the ice in his words; in the way he says her name as though he intended on crushing it next. "Is there something I need to know?"

Lavinia's hand skirts to her husband's knee, intended as a softening effect, but he slaps it aside as he looks at her. "Did you know about this?"

Lavinia trips over her words, shaking her head violently. "I do not think there is anything to know of!" Lavinia looks at Myla hopefully, her eyes darkening with fear when she finds Myla's eyes fixed ahead, unwavering and full of the secrets of her youth, but her lips stretched in a thin, unspeaking line.

"*You will speak, Gods damn it*!" Maverick bellows now, slamming his fist on the couch before standing, pointing a threatening finger at Myla. "Everything—everything we have ever done for you has truly come to this?"

"Father, I had no idea this is what you wanted of me!" Myla lurches to her feet, allowing his finger to dig into her chest, stepping into it so he might feel the way her heart threatens to beat its way out of her chest and strangle him.

"You knew!" Maverick snarls in return.

"Would knowing have changed anything?" Lavinia interjects, her voice gentle despite the way Myla and Maverick's voices thunder through the estate, no doubt waking Elsa upstairs.

Her question is too tender, breaking Myla's resolve. Immediate tears spring to her eyes as she looks from Maverick to Lavinia, finding them so contrary to one another. Regardless of any factor in her life, Bryar included, Myla does not want the king. She would not want him in this lifetime, nor any lifetime to follow. There is a darkness in him that terrifies her.

"It would have changed nothing," she confesses softly. "But I *love* another, and I am *begging* you, do not make me do this." Her words are staggering. Myla steps forward, grabbing Maverick's hands, pleading with him, hoping he might find it within his heart to see her as a daughter.

Maverick sinks into the couch behind him, and Lavinia follows suit, both gazes fixed on Myla and each concerned for different reasons. Maverick breathes deeply, wringing his hands before him anxiously before speaking. Though it is obvious he is angry, Myla is shocked to find his voice level.

"Your mother and I married for love, child. I am no stranger to its fickle and unyielding power. But this lover of yours is likely not a suitor the king would stand down for, so there is nothing to be done. You will marry him."

"Father! You say the king is a good man. You can make him see!" Myla wraps her arms around her middle to cradle herself; to hold on to her shaking body so it does not rattle into broken pieces at her father's unforgiving feet. "You must hear me! I love another, and I shall not marry the king!"

"Myla! I cannot look at the king and tell him my daughter is to snub her nose at his proposal—*and* the prophesy—in favor of a—a what? You will not even tell me who he is!"

"Maverick." Lavinia looks to her husband, her eyes cunning now. "Perhaps this conversation will be more productive woman to woman. Find yourself something to drink, and I will meet you in your study later."

As soon as the door closes behind Maverick, Lavinia slouches, her composure fading and her elbows now resting on her knees so she can hold her face in her hands. Myla watches for several moments while the weary woman breathes slowly, calming herself before asking a question Myla hoped she would not. "Have you lain with this man?"

Face red with anger, Myla glares at the lapping flames within the hearth, imagining those gentle flames to be Bryar's fingertips on her body. Lain with him. Loved him. Worshiped and *been* worshiped. Dreamt of a future away from New Falkmere. There is no inch of his body that she does not know well, and there is no dream nor fear in her mind that he has not borne witness to. *Laying* with him should be the least of Lavinia's fears.

Myla's silence undoubtedly confirms Lavinia's question, and the woman lets out a long sigh. "You must tell me who it is, Myla. I will protect him and you, but I cannot help if I do not know who."

Myla straightens before looking across the room to where her mother sits. "How will you help? You cannot even protect yourself, let alone me. Why would I trust your promise to protect him?" Myla visualizes a carriage in the night, whisking them both away to somewhere across the Thalinir Sea. If that is the help Lavinia is offering, Myla would gladly accept, but she is no fool.

Lavinia's form of help is a far cry from that. "I will take you both to someone who will make you forget. Heartbreak is the cruelest pain there is to endure. It will crush the human body beneath its weight."

The anger and betrayal simmering within her, a beast that has fed on years of contempt and abuse, bursts forth as tears first, then screams. Myla's quick motion to stand and approach her mother tips the end table beside her over, and a vase of flowers atop it shatters.

"I will have none of your so-called help!" she says in a vicious whisper, turning to face the open window. Even from here, the lights of the palace are visible between the trees, flickering, teasing her, threatening her with something she does not want to imagine.

"Fine," Lavinia murmurs, rubbing her brow as if to rid herself of the burden. "It is customary to examine a woman before marriage to a king. They will want to confirm you are a virgin. I will ensure the exam is not in the contract. Fortunately for you, Caius needs you. I doubt he will press the issue."

Myla wishes they would check. She wishes Caius himself would peer inside her body and find her tainted and unworthy. Oh, to be an unvirtuous woman, to scare the sanctimonious men away.

Perhaps then, they would leave her the fuck alone.

Myla's lips twitch in a snarl, threatening to share the thought out loud, but instead, she finds she is only capable of saying, "Thank you, Mother."

Many hours later, when the house is asleep, Myla slips from the tension of her father's estate and runs barefoot through the fields and forests separating her home from the smithy. It is no surprise to find the forge still hot and the lights inside glowing. Caspian has been working late into the evenings. Supplying a sizeable army with swords enough to withstand the Blood Stealer's forces has kept him in business, but exhausted. On his nights off, Bryar comes home to help his father. Which is where she finds him now. Side by side, the two men lean over the forge, both covered in sweat and soot.

Bryar looks distressed.

Myla pulls her shawl tighter around her shoulders and runs across the dusty street, catching their attention.

"You cannot be here," Bryar says, abandoning the forge. Though his words chastise her, she can see it in his face. He needed to see her as much as she needed to see him.

Wordlessly, Myla collapses against him, letting out a shuddered breath as his arms engulf her, shielding her from the world around them. They linger here, frozen in a moment that may very well be their last, until Caspian clears his throat.

"Perhaps it is best to go inside."

Myla remembers the first time she stepped inside Bryar and Caspian's home. It was very shortly after the death of his stepmother, Alice, and traces of her remain. Even now, her chest of belongings still resides faithfully at the foot of their shared bunk bed, a place Bryar rarely sleeps now. And behind the back door is still that little garden and barrels, though more weather-worn. The broken fence is overgrown with hanging ivy, for Bryar has not had to sneak out in many years. The shelf on the wall, courtesy of Myla, is stacked with far too many books, and the soft boy has grown into a good man, and he is still the warmest thing in the room. With his still soft eyes, he looks at her now in a way he never has before: as though she is already lost. As though he cannot say what he is thinking or feeling, for she is not his.

"I stood beside the king today," he whispers, twisting his fists together angrily. "I thought about how easily I could kill him. One swipe of my blade and our problems would be solved."

"With an audience such as we both had today?" Myla manages a weak smile, sitting carefully in one of the chairs. "Unlikely."

Bryar sits across from her, expressionless. He appears almost as hollow as she feels, and that thing in the silence between them—*dread*—feels loud. So loud, it is impossible to hear one another over it. It might even create confusion, miscommunication, tension, angst, anything but the safety of reprieve they wish to find in the chaos of this nightmare. When at last Bryar speaks, there is little to no conviction in his tone.

"This is not what we wanted, but I foresee the great queen you will become, and when I picture that, I know you will be alright."

"And you?" Myla whispers, reaching across the table to take his hand. Hers is dwarfed within the safety of his, held there like something sacred. She imagines him holding it through the years, from youthful and soft, to old and wrinkled, something she will never see in this lifetime, but everything she yearns for. She has heard the druids talk of how hands tell stories, and Myla wonders now, as she looks at theirs, what stories their hands might tell on the day they die.

"I will be tasked with the safety of the king and queen of New Falkmere," he mutters. His eyes are locked on their joined hands, and Myla knows if he were to meet her gaze, she would find tears in his eyes. "Even if I am not alright, *you* will be."

"Imagine," Myla whispers, allowing a sorrowful expression to cross her face. "We run away."

Indulging her, Bryar looks up now, blinking away the glisten in his eyes until there is only a false expression of excitement. "We take a boat," he agrees, whispering so only they can hear. "We sail until there is no sea left."

"We settle somewhere too far to be found, and we have many babies," Myla adds, her voice cracking at the realization that her babies won't look a thing like him.

Bryar's thoughts must be similar, for his face twists into a grimace of pain, his heart breaking there before her. "And I will spend every day worshiping the ground you walk on as you carry my children."

"Yes," Myla whispers, smiling through tears at him. "What a wonderful life it will be."

Before either of them can speak again, the door to the smithy creaks open and Caspian enters, his expression apologetic as he interrupts their moment of refuge from reality. "I wish this moment could last longer. For both of you," his voice is kind as he draws their conversation to an end. "I fear it is far less safe for you to be seen together than it was last night." He nods toward the door. "Someone is outside asking after you."

Myla nods and stands slowly, feeling pieces of herself bleed into him as their hands separate. "Bryar," she draws his attention upward with a gentle touch of her fingers to his jawline, which is speckled with stubble. "I love you."

"I love you too, Myla."

Myla moves toward the door, and as she passes Caspian, he stops her with a gentle touch of the hand. "I will always think fondly of the little noble girl who couldn't keep away from my smithy. I hope you do great things, Miss Alerys. That is how we make our misfortunes worth it." He nods toward his son. "Believe it or not, I know all too well how you both feel right now. May the Gods be with you."

Stepping outside with a heavy heart, Myla expects to find Elsa followed her to the smithy. Instead, to her horror, Lavinia stands wearing a dark cloak pulled over her brow.

"Mother—"

"Come," the woman hisses, taking Myla's hand and pulling her from the smithy at a quick pace. "I may be nothing more than your mother, but I was a girl once. Did you think no one would imagine you might sneak out to meet your lover? *Myla!*" Lavinia stops short, grasping her daughter's hands in her own. "The blacksmith boy? He is the one you've trained with, is he not? My God, child! You've been sneaking around with him for *years*?"

Despite the urge to fight back, to rip her hands away, or to say something biting, the strongest urge of all is the one Myla listens to. As a sob bursts through her dam of composure and the final feelings of Bryar's touch fades from the skin of her fingers, Myla falls against the body of her mother, grateful to find the warm comfort of her embrace, holding her, and running a hand through the tangled brown mess.

"I know," she coos. "If I could carry this for you, I would."

CHAPTER 28

PRESENT

"TROOPS AMASS IN THE thousands outside of New Falkmere," Rhyland says as he stands over the map, pressing a gloved finger into Maverick's location. The weeks have worn heavily on him. His new responsibility manifests its weight in the corners of his eyes, the crease of his brow, the depth of his breath. He wobbles over his words, the role as her new Captain of the Raven's Veil seeming to knock him from his steady confidence as a soldier. He continues, "Lord Thurston has joined a scouting party to ascertain a headcount and from there, he will rejoin Maverick's council to collect information on his plans. He intends to meet us ten miles outside of New Falkmere in five days."

Myla's breath hitches as realization of the impending battle hits her, and as committed to *trying* as Rhyland is, she would find more assurance in their cause if it were Bryar wearing the captain's cloak. Shaking off her doubt, Myla steps up to stand beside her friend, gauging the distance between Valyndor and New Falkmere. "We shall keep the dragons concealed until the last moment," she says resolutely. "Everyone else must march as one. Our army is not small, and we should not be seen as such. With the dragons, we stand a chance."

Rhyland clears his throat. "I think it is better to be underestimated and take them by surprise."

"Meaning?"

"*Meaning*," Rhyland elaborates. "We conceal the aid of the dragons and the Ashborn."

Myla's brow furrows, and she tries to imagine walking into battle with half her army at her back. "And this helps us how?"

"They will be less concerned and therefore, in theory, less on guard should we make camp with an army smaller than they anticipated. The dragons and Ashborn can wait near the monks until we send a signal for them to descend. On wing, it will take mere moments for them to arrive. We can take Maverick's army by surprise and crush them from behind."

With a hesitant nod, Myla pats Rhyland on the shoulder. "I like it," she lies. "Please discuss it with the other generals. I must speak to Bryar on a number of topics. I shall return later."

"We must ready the troops, Myla."

Chilled, she turns with a stoic nod. "Ready them."

Bryar sits on the highest bench in the training arena. It is chaotic and reminiscent of their time spent here many years ago. Myla can almost picture Bryar, younger of course, in the arena himself, training alongside the fledglings.

Now, she finds him watching with pride as their son trains.

"How is he doing?" She asks, rubbing her palms vigorously to ward off the chill.

"His very best," Bryar says with a grin. "Look, he is summoning his gauntlets."

Myla lets out a gasp as she catches sight of Aidan, arms crossed before him, shielding himself from the creatures as they burst forth from the runes. Elora paces back and forth, unfazed as ever, watching attentively as each fledgling performs. He is shorter than most of his peers and, by all appearances, struggles more than they do. Nonetheless, Myla's heart swells as his small forearms are engulfed in a lapping blue flame, deflecting the assaults from every direction.

"No other Ashborn has a blue flame," Myla begins hesitantly, risking a suspicious sidelong glance at Bryar. "Only you and Aidan."

His lips purse and he shrugs, causing the curls around his ears to bunch at the nape of his neck. He then stretches tall, extending his arms overhead as he moves free of the focused slouch. "Gods, I feel old today."

Noting the way Myla is still focused on Aidan's blue flames, he lightly chuckles. "Not everyone can be as interesting as me, my love. Our son was lucky enough to inherit it."

For the first time in a while, Myla feels a light laugh ring from her lungs, and she grins sidelong at her husband. "You feel old because you have been bent over in *many* uncomfortable positions lately. *And.*" Her tone grows more serious as she reaches out to brush a strand of hair from his eyes, noting the gleam of a few sparse silver hairs. "Really. Have you asked yourself why the flame is blue?"

"Well," Bryar says with a shrug, his attention still mostly fixed on the boy as he exerts himself in the arena. "I have not. Why?" He turns to look at her now, a sudden wash of curiosity passing over his face. "Has something happened?"

Myla sighs, nodding and turning her body to face him head-on. "Alright," she takes his hands and steadies her breath. "Imogene and I had a discussion."

He lets out a puff of air paired with a weary smile. "I do hope our alliance is still intact."

"Oh," Myla offers a nervous shrug. "More than ever, actually."

"What does that mean?"

"It means she told me who your mother was," Myla offers hesitantly.

Bryar flashes a halfhearted smile, nodding almost dismissively. "We already know that my mother was Ashborn."

"Yes." Myla emphasizes the *s*, delaying the inevitable confession, continuing only when Bryar's eyebrows droop inquisitively. "But we did not know she was an Ashborn *princess*—adoptive perhaps, but that status is there, nonetheless."

His expression sobers, and Bryar's head tilts in confusion, or perhaps, denial. His lips part to speak, but Myla is quick to continue. "That is not all. Apparently, they tried very hard to bury exactly why her relationship with your father was so forbidden. Bryar...how did you feel...standing beside the dragons? Because I, *frankly*, felt horrified."

The frown lines on his forehead are more prominent now, and his green eyes sparkle with a hundred questions. "What do the dragons have to do with this?"

"How did you *feel*?" She probes, reaching out to touch the side of his face, pulling his attention to her entirely. "My love. They tried to bury it because there is an ancient feud between the Aetherwing and the Ashborn, settled only when a half-breed between the two annihilated the Aetherwing's dragons. That is when the Ashborn forbade external marriages. So, when your mother fell in love with your father, resulting in you, they broke every rule."

"Rules? What are you saying?" Face wrought with denial, Bryar stands now, running a hand through his hair. "What does this have to do with the history of the Aetherwing and Ashborn?"

Letting slip an exasperated laugh, Myla stands. "Because your mother was an Ashborn and your father, an Aetherwing."

Bryar belts out laughing, the response taking Myla by surprise. It is a hearty laugh. *Ignorance makes good company for denial.* She hears his own words repeating in the back of her mind as she watches him wrestle with a longing for one and a battle with the other. "Myla. My father did not ride dragons."

"Not all Aetherwing ride dragons." Myla gently urges him to sit, and reluctantly, he does. "This is why they were so quick to give you a place in Valyndor. It is better for you to be on their side than the Aetherwing's. This is why your father insisted you work the forge, to cover up any inadvertent disasters due to your fire magic. *This* is why he was so hellbent on pushing you *away* from your magic and just about as far from the Aetherwing territory as you could have gotten without crossing the sea."

Silence. Bryar sits, staring at her blankly, until finally, he blinks and casts his attention downward again to where their son wages a mighty battle against another fledgling. "When I stood near the dragons," he says finally "I felt weightless."

They will not see another night in Valyndor. The feast hall is packed yet another evening in a row, but this time, its occupants are sober. On the eve of their departure, the air is heavy with anticipation. Save, Myla realizes gratefully, that of her sons. This night, they sit beside their parents, laughing and eating and recounting their days' events lightheartedly. Myla looks to where Rhyland sits, discussing something of a serious nature, it appears, with Elsa. *He has taken the painful images from their minds.* Myla is grateful for it and finds healing in their smiles. She finds hope in the light of their eyes.

"How was your day?" Myla looks down at Caspian, urging him to take another bite of his supper. Though he obliges, he only takes tiny nibbles because he hates the taste of fish.

"Boring," he answers. "Except when I got to climb the mountain with Brynja to watch her call her dragon."

Myla smiles slightly, looking across the room to where the fierce child sits now, surrounded by many warriors, all older than her. "Can you believe how big he is?" Myla asks, taking a slow sip of cider.

"I think Skuggi would need an entire lake if he got thirsty—did you know they call her 'The Menace'?"

"Skuggi?"

"Skuggi is a *he,* mother. I mean *Brynja.* I keep hearing her called '*Brynja the Menace*.'" Caspian pushes his plate to the center of the table, as far from him as possible. "This is disgusting. I do not want another bite."

Myla grins, enjoying the rambling of the boy. "Finish your potatoes at least. Tomorrow shall be a long day."

"Will I fight?" Caspian asks, pointing to his abdomen. "They cannot kill me, Mother."

Myla shudders, the image of the dryad impaling her son a vivid memory which plagues her. "No." She answers, gently tousling his hair.

"Why?" Caspian argues, ready to turn and ask Bryar in hopes of a more satisfactory response. "Brynja will be fighting!"

"*Because.* They might not be able to kill you, son," her voice softens. "But they can kill other people, and that is not something I want you to see."

Caspian shrugs, letting out an exasperated sigh. "I have seen many people die..." his voice trails off as though chasing the remaining figment of a memory before confusion crawls across his little face, soon shaken off. "Though I cannot remember when."

"Then you have seen too much," Myla says with a gentle kiss to the top of his head, relieved that the memories seem to evade him. *And you will see no more.*

From beneath thick brows, Caspian glares before shooting a be-grudged look across the room to where the child warrior sits. He mutters something about her being unfair, then stands to leave the dining hall. Within seconds of him standing, Elsa does the same, only her departure is less inconspicuous.

Her hair falls onto flushed cheeks and puffy eyes as she lowers her palms with a flat *smack* against the table. She and Rhyland meet in what feels like an old argument, their eyes competing with one another for more ground to hold in the battle.

"I am *sick* of it, Rhyland!" She hisses the words, leaning to be eye level with him. "You and Henry both! I am sick of it!"

Rhyland's head slumps and his shoulders lift in a slight shrug before a hand aims to cup hers, a comforting gesture she is quick to recoil from. He whispers something Myla cannot make out, then flinches as Elsa turns away.

"I am *done,*" she adds with unforgiving finality in her voice before turning and exiting the room, leaving in her wake a deflated Rhyland. Myla glances from Rhyland to Bryar before focusing her attention on her meal. As much as she wants to chase after Elsa, something in the way Rhyland's eyes follow Elsa's exit makes Myla think it is none of her business.

When at last, the evening wanes and meals are finished, the boys are tucked soundly in their beds, Prince Gourdy in company and Elsa asleep on a cot at their feet, Myla finds her way to the chamber she gave birth to Caspian in so many years ago. Bryar sprawls on the bed, hands linked behind his head, and his eyes fixed on the ceiling above. The room is warm with the glow of a raging fire, which wards off the spring air flowing in through the open balcony doors, and the gleam of light dancing across the floor should be comforting. It is anything but. The warmth feels stuffy, and the light leaves far too many shadows, places for her ghosts to hide.

The silence is the worst. As Myla closes the door behind her, she notes the way her husband's eyes remain fixed above, unwavering. He is deep in thought.

Sideswiping one's husband with identity-altering information. Added to the bottom of the list of ways to get laid. Myla sarcastically makes a mental note before disrobing beside the fire, thankful to take a deep breath as her tight corset falls to the ground. Cleaning up shall wait until the morning. Leaving the garments in a pile, Myla moves to the bed, her weary body thankful for its cushioning as she falls onto it.

"Your thoughts are far away," she whispers, rolling to her side and placing a palm on Bryar's bare chest. "Tell me where they are."

With a slow swallow, he turns to meet her gaze, and the stoicism Myla finds in his features terrifies her, but the gravity of his words shakes her more. "I hope when our children are in their thirties, they do not look back at all the secrets we keep to protect them, and hate us."

On the day Rhyland has erased memories from their children's minds, and he has uncovered his own father's secrets, Myla wishes he would say anything but this. She swallows the stinging in her throat and forces a weak smile. "Hating your father will not bring him back to answer your questions any faster."

Bryar chuckles lightly, but his face is anything but humorous. "Forgiving him won't either."

"No," Myla agrees. In her mind's eye, the man appears. He is a distant memory, but the smile lines and the laugh are as vivid as when she last experienced them so many years ago before his passing. "I think you can sympathize with your father more than you may wish to admit right now."

"How so?" Bryar questions, lazily rolling to face her.

"There is nothing you would not do to keep your children safe. Even if it means withholding vital parts of the truth from them."

"Allowing the boys to forget the gruesome details of their sister's murder is not the same as my father concealing my lineage."

"No," Myla whispers, reaching to trace the gold tattoos up his forearms until her finger meanders to his collarbone, brushing the chain of his amulet. There, she presses a palm to his chest, reveling in the way she can feel his heartbeat just beneath the surface of his hot skin. On anyone else, it would be feverish, but on him, it is just hot anger begging for release. "You would conceal anything from your children to keep them alive, and I cannot help but believe everything Caspian did was to keep *you* alive. How can I hate him for that?"

"There seems to be hate in abundance tonight," he says with a sigh, clearly not ready to admit that perhaps his parentage has been concealed out of love. "I wonder what Elsa and Rhyland were bickering about."

"Oh," Myla lets out a long sigh before slumping back into the feathered pillow behind her. "Seeing them, of all people, angry...it feels foreign."

"This war will break many happy people before it is over," Bryar whispers, his eyes closing though his big hand wraps warmly around hers.

"Has it broken us?" Myla chokes on the question, wondering if after all these years, everything they did to find their way back to one another would end in a grievous pile of defeat. She fears the answer, scared to hear him admit she was not worth it. Scared that one day he might look at her and the soft eyes will be hardened.

That is not tonight, however. He opens his eyes once more and looks sidelong at her. Faint freckles still kiss his cheeks, and though mostly camouflaged behind day-old stubble, his smile lines still crease for her, however gently it may be. "The world could break into a million pieces beneath our feet, and we would still be whole. We would still be *one*. I would rather have a broken world with you beside me than a whole one separate from you." He reaches to brush her cheek, his thumb lingering at the corner of her mouth, where he tenderly strokes as his eyes scan her features as if consuming them. "I will love you until breaking kills me."

Myla smiles, pressing her face deeper into his hands, savoring the warmth of his tender touch against her skin, hungry for his comfort. Not to be touched, but to be *held*. "I have broken countless times," she whispers, nuzzling closer until her face is pressed against his chest and his strong arms have secured her in a cradled hold against him. "And yet you kept your promise, and here I am. Alright."

There, she falls asleep, certain that she shall not break before dawn. He wouldn't allow it.

"It's so big..." Elsa, wide-eyed and mouth agape, looks upon the great stretch of open field where bannered tents housing soldiers clutter the earth, with nothing more than a maze of narrow paths between to separate them.

"That is exactly what I want to hear when you are referring to my *army*," Myla answers with a snicker, noting soldiers moving back and forth. All the fighters wear new helmets, or carry them beneath their arms. Myla wishes to ask Bryar about them.

"I like it when she says it about other things," a voice breaks from behind them, and Elsa's face stretches into a grin. She turns on her heels, followed swiftly by Myla, and they both find Henry has returned.

"I could never say that about you," Elsa teases coyly. "But I am glad you are back."

Henry rolls his eyes, scanning the expanse of men and women ready to die for the Raven Throne before turning his attention to his queen. She is clad head to toe in her raven armor, the black shining like an abysmal beacon beneath the sun overhead. "There is much to discuss, otherwise I would punish you for that comment. Where is Rhyland?"

Elsa's brow furrows and her red lips purse with contempt. "Probably off getting himself killed."

Myla matches her friend's expression, confusion trying to make sense of the statement. "Whatever does that mean?"

At this, Elsa glares at Myla. "Ask your captain."

"About that—" Henry interjects. "Is there any sense in asking Bryar to lead the army for this?"

"I won't tell Rhyland you asked that," Elsa grumbles, turning to walk away. "Enjoy plotting your own death." And with that, she departs, leaving Myla and Henry to deliberate.

"Rhyland is very capable," Myla insists, unwilling to meet Henry's gaze, lest he see her doubt. Rhyland has many priceless talents. Myla fears leading an army may not be one of them.

"Riders!" a soldier shouts from below the hill which serves as Myla's vantage point of the encampment.

Turning on her heels, Myla focuses her attention on the armored man as he points toward the distant silhouette of New Falkmere against the skyline. Riders do, in fact, approach. And unless Rhyland sent a scouting party without her knowledge, these riders do not belong to her. Myla looks at Henry, noting the immediate tremble of her palms despite the confidence of her voice.

"Find Rhyland and Bryar. Tell them enemies approach."

"Yes, Your Grace." Any hint of familiarity is dropped, and Henry steps into formality, bowing quickly before turning to make down the hill. Inhaling deeply, Myla turns to face the approaching riders, quickly counting heads. Six. It is not an attack. Regardless, Myla's fingers curl around the hilt of the blade at her waist, subtly glancing at her flank, ensuring her guards stand near. Maverick would stop at nothing to kill her and be done with all contestants to the throne. Casting her eyes upwards, Myla spares a moment for the Gods.

"I have spent years waiting for this moment," she whispers, drawing on the magic of the divine beings above and shuddering as she feels their magic pool within her. "I am terrified, for my losses are great already."

As the thundering of hooves approach, Myla raises her hands to her side, aware of the buzz behind her where her troops amass, ready to draw swords at her command. "Throne or no throne," she whispers finally. "Let me not know the bitter failure of more loss."

The face coming into view is vaguely familiar to her, a lady Myla once saw regularly when she ruled New Falkmere. The Lady of Elspire.

"Lady Alerys," she greets, and her address is not lost on Myla. Not Your Grace—*Lady*. Her allegiance shows already.

"It is a risky business," Myla replies cooly, flexing her fingers around the glow of her magic. "Riding so undefended into my encampment after rejecting my call for aid." Her icy blue eyes sear into the unwavering glare of Lady Elspire's. She is a magnificent woman, sizeable in both height and demeanor. Her jaw is strong, and her shoulders are broad. She dominates attention simply by walking into the room. Now, sitting on a white mare and dressed in finely made armor, she looks formidable.

"Risky indeed," she answers, glancing to her flanks where five soldiers wait protectively. "I have heard a troublesome rumor in the last few weeks, and I have been mulling it over," Lady Elspire continues. Though Bryar and Rhyland take Myla's side, leading soldiers in the dozens behind them, she does not waver in composure, and never does her gaze break from Myla's. "Word of Maverick's corrupt behavior spreads like wildfire."

Myla scoffs, and behind her, a ripple of chuckles sounds from her soldiers and husband alike. "Only now?" Myla asks with an indignant tone of humor. "It is a wonder he has kept allies at all. If he is so comfortable killing family who gets in his way." Myla's eyes narrow and she lowers her hands, a sign of peace. "Imagine what he would do to you if he even knew you were here."

Lady Elspire runs her tongue across her teeth, eyeing Myla skeptically. "How do I know these rumors to be true?"

"You do not," Myla answers. "But tell me this? What nefarious rumors does the realm say of me?"

At this, the shrewd lady grins slightly and shakes her head, an act which disturbs a black curl tucked beneath her helmet. "Haven't you heard? You are known as the queen who condemned herself to a life farming in Old Falkmere." At this, Lady Elspire's eyes flicker briefly in Bryar's direction. "They say your bodyguard has made a broodmare of you and nothing resembling a queen remains any longer."

Myla tilts her chin in defiance, not allowing the scathing words to scratch the surface of her resolve. "And is that what you see, Lady Elspire? A *broodmare* who hides in the woods?" Again, her statement is met with laughter as Rhyland looks back at the encampment, turning Lady Elspire's gaze to the men amassed behind the hill. "Which is worse, Lady Elspire? A murderer or a mother? Who would you prefer on the Raven Throne? Someone who will kill your child out of spite, or someone who will protect your child at all costs?"

Lady Elspire shrugs. "I do not have a child."

"Nonetheless," Myla answers, turning her back to the woman, "make of the rumors, mine and Maverick's, what you will. A week from now, we shall all answer to the Gods for the side we picked. I would rather brave the wrath of Maverick Alerys than the wrath of the Gods."

"Lady Myla," the proud woman speaks once more. "Surely you can see your cause is doomed. This may feel like a large army. But it is nothing compared to what King Maverick has built."

"You mean *bought*?" Bryar interjects finally, crossing his arms with an angry glare at Lady Elspire. "No fortune is worth the loss of your soul."

"Perhaps not," she agrees, "but would the Gods forgive me for committing my soldiers to a doomed cause? We must all weigh the sacrifices." She looks to Myla now with a respectful nod. "May the breath of the Gods blow luck your way tomorrow, Lady Myla."

At this, Bryar straightens. "I assure you, Lady Elspire. The Gods do not breathe in my wife's direction. They bow." A smug expression crosses his chiseled features. "When picking sides, keep in mind: Her Grace wields the magic of the Gods. You don't want to know what it looks like when my wife drains the sun from the sky. You've never known true darkness until the light belongs to her alone, and you are left screaming into a pitch-black void."

In a chilling silence, wearing a sickened expression, Lady Elspire turns, pale-faced, back toward New Falkmere.

War brews outside the tent, and wind whips against the canvas walls, adding a sense of dread to the eerily still night. Though soldiers stand guard at the perimeter of the encampment, Rhyland can hardly breathe around the swell of anxiety lodged in his throat.

Elsa tosses restlessly on the bed set in the center of the large tent, meanwhile he sits in the still darkness, leaning into the stiff wooden chair, his eyes studying the fair-haired man across from him.

Henry appears deep in thought, his lip caught between gnawing teeth, and his brows furrowed with concern. Only a few nights ago, Elsa refused to come to bed, her fair cheeks fuming and red as she demanded they both stand out of the war.

A demand neither would concede to.

Now, here they are on the eve of a battle which has brewed for over half a decade now; torn between their queen and their love.

"She has every right to be angry," Henry whispers, breaking the silence at last. His arm falls limp against those of the chair, and he leans back, drawing a sharp jaw upwards as his eyes fall closed.

Rhyland leans forward earnestly, resting his forearms against his knees. "She's not angry," he counters. "She's scared."

At this, Henry centers his attention on Rhyland, his bright eyes piercing the darkness as he focuses. "We could lose our position, our titles if we abandon Myla now."

Rhyland shakes his head, determined. "Myla wouldn't punish us like that...however, abandoning her is not an option. Regardless of the love I feel for Elsa, I must have my part in this fight." His arms feel heavy with a phantom body, a memory of lifelessness, and at once, an image he is sick with a need to forget sears his mind. "I long for the blood of Maverick's men to stain my sword. I shall lay my blade on Elenore's grave and tell her I *did* something."

Henry stands, a look of realization dawning across his drained features, softening for Rhyland.

"Rhy," Henry whispers, kneeling at Ryland's feet to hold his hands. "You are surrounded by ghosts."

Rhyland leans forward, pressing his brow to Henry's, breathing deep his earthy scent, and finding comfort in his closeness. "When Callum died, I was nearly sick with sleeplessness, wondering why it was him, and not me."

Henry's hands tighten at the words.

Rhyland continues, though his voice wavers, "I wondered if we had moved a few inches over, or if he had seen Elsa a moment sooner, if he wouldn't have been standing in the path of Vesperian's blade. So many variables played in my mind." Rhyland glances at Elsa's sleeping form, and guilt washes over him. "Then I spent months dwelling on when we were children, thinking of how he and Elsa seemed to be written in the stars, and I wondered if I were committing a crime against my best friend, falling in love with the woman he left behind."

Henry watches as Rhyland speaks, his eyes following the movement of Rhyland's lips, soaking in every syllable of pain until he speaks no more. Then he waits in silence, knowing nothing he could say will heal the deep scar Rhyland hides beneath his cavalier personality. When words at last find him, Henry shudders to think this kind man, this *good* man, tortures himself.

"I think the crime would have been to deny Elsa love," Henry whispers finally. "For nobody in Myrnith loved Callum as much as you and her. It is only right that you share your life and grief with one another, in honor of Callum's sacrifice."

Rhyland chuckles slightly, shaking his head in disbelief. "I could never hope to be loved by her the way Callum was."

"—And ought never to dishonor him by hoping that she might," Henry interjects, compelling Rhyland to meet his gaze with a brush of a hand to his jaw. "Thankfully, I have more than enough love—love I want to give *you*—to offset the imbalance."

Henry's touch softens as his fingers trace the sharp line drawn from Rhyland's chin to his cheekbone, dipping past the collar of his shirt, to cradle the back of his neck. "We must fight tomorrow. And she will be scared, but each of us has lost too much to Maverick Alerys' ambition to *not* sanctify our blades with his blood. We can make it up to her once the battle is fought."

Their whispers are hushed and barely brush Elsa's subconscious. Lazily, Elsa forces one eye open, and an immediate warmth coils in her middle. Henry kneels before Rhyland, reverently kissing his neck, an attention Rhyland melts for, seeming to become one with the chair he finds support in. It is not passionate. Elsa observes, it is healing.

Henry's hands move with intention, down Rhyland's shoulders with a gentle, comforting stroke, and lower to the belt fastened tight around his hips, and the anticipation calls to something primal in Elsa.

"Relax," she hears Henry coo, placing his hands on either side of Rhyland's face, bringing the tense man's attention to his lover. "Let me unburden you."

Rhyland lets out a sigh, then nods obediently before slumping into the chair once more, ready to receive.

She has watched them make love many times, but something about tonight feels different. It is not lighthearted or playful; it's not even lustful or passionate. It is tender. They're caring for one another in a way so sacred, even she feels out of place. As she moves to roll over, to close her eyes and leave them to their privacy, a thick voice breaks the sound of heavy breathing.

"Watch us, darling," Henry says, catching her in the act of voyeurism. "Better yet, come help me."

Needing no further invitation, Elsa slides off the bed, chilled instantly by the brisk cold air, which peaks her nipples through her shift.

Henry fumbles gently with the laces of Rhyland's trousers until, with a satisfied groan, he pulls them past his knees, exposing Rhyland's hard length, throbbing already. Elsa's lips twist up in a coy smile as she comes behind, burying her face in his neck, tickled by the curls which have sprung free of the bun at the back of his head. Her hands travel across Rhyland's chest, working nimbly to unbuckle the fastenings of his vest while her eyes remain fixed on Henry's hands. Strong, but tender, they move up and down, pumping around Rhyland's hard shaft, each motion drawing deeper, satisfied breaths from the man at their mercy.

"Where do you need me?" Elsa whispers in Rhyland's ear, allowing her tongue to lap gently at his neck. "Tell me what you want."

Rhyland reaches behind, taking her hand to draw her before him. "There." His hungry eyes find the bulge of Henry's trousers, and with a gentle nod, he assigns Elsa.

How they move so harmoniously, Elsa is unsure. But memory serves their bodies well, and as Rhyland slides slowly from the chair onto the fur rug beneath them, he shudders with anticipation, his hungry eyes watching the shift fall from Elsa's body before she sinks to her knees and takes Henry's hard cock into her mouth. For a moment, he watches, and Elsa wonders if he feels the hot fire burning in his belly as she does. There is no jealousy, no possessiveness, only love.

Henry moans as her tongue slides intently over his tip, then swirls down his shaft until he brushes the back of her throat.

Hands find her hips, and Elsa shivers with delight as something warm and hard teases the wet and ready space between her thighs.

"I want to be inside you," Rhyland whispers from his place behind her, and a little moan from around Henry's cock, her wordless plea, is all the permission needed before he drives himself deep inside her, a motion which evokes raspy breaths from all.

Henry grins from his kneeling position, one hand buried in Elsa's hair, and the other breaching the gap between him and Rhyland, pulling his lover in, their lips entwining and tongues moving harmoniously. Breathlessly, be it from the mouth of the man across from him, or the exertion of his thrusts into the woman below him, Rhyland pulls away, pressing a free hand to Henry's cheek.

"I love you," he whispers, his words met with a satisfied grin as Henry succumbs to Elsa's efforts. His body grows tense, and he stills momentarily as the trance of ecstasy recedes.

As his gasps still, he meets Rhyland's gaze. "I love *you*." Henry then looks down as Elsa runs a palm against her wet mouth, wiping the remnants of his release from her lips, before readjusting her body to lean against his strong chest. Henry's arms wrap around her waist, supporting her weight entirely, and Rhyland's hands grapple at her hips, nudging her ass further back into him. Her back arches and her hips tremble with the pleasure of Rhyland's movements inside her.

Rhyland's pace quickens, and Elsa's body bounces against his. He presses a flat palm to the small of her back, causing her to arch further, and she smiles as he plunges deeper, sending sparks of pain through her core.

"Breathe, darling," Henry whispers before pressing kisses along her neck. He relinquishes the hold of one hand from her waist to first cup her breast, then slowly move lower until his fingers find her warm and wet. "That's it," he coos as she buries her teeth in his chest. "Come for us." Together, he and Rhyland move within and outside of her until Elsa's body cranes and throbs with ecstasy, and the whimpers of delight are sure to wake those in neighboring tents.

A while later, from the comfort of their bed, snuggled warm between Rhyland and Henry, Elsa watches the shadows of tree branches swaying overhead against the canvas ceiling of their tent. None sleep yet, but the stillness and silence lull them each into tranquility.

"I should not have yelled," Elsa offers a whispered apology which is met with a kiss to her temple and a warm hand curling around her naked waist. Wordlessly, she knows she is forgiven. "I need to know that this is the last one," she adds, glancing first at Henry, then at Rhyland. She finds both watching her, their eyes heavy with a need for sleep.

It is Henry who speaks first. "I have no desire to fight. After tomorrow, I promise. No more."

Rhyland nods in agreement, his fingers digging softly into her abdomen. "I do not need revenge as much as I need you. If you simply cannot handle it, I will tell Myla in the morning, and we can be gone before the fight."

His words, like salve to a wound, soften the stinging of her sore and frightened heart. Hot tears build beneath her eyelids, and Elsa blinks them away. With a shaky breath, she looks at him with as much of a smile as she can muster. "I love you for that. But friends do not abandon each other in their time of need. We will all show up, not only for Myla, but for *Callum*. He would've fought this battle. If he cannot be here to do it, we will do it for him."

CHAPTER 29

PAST: MYLA,
TWENTY-ONE

"AND THIS, MY DEAR?" Pinched between strong fingers, Caius holds up a white peony. "It is beautiful, do you agree?" Beneath his elbows, a pile of papers, their marriage contract, sits. And standing a short distance away, just within earshot, are Maverick and the king's council members, quietly muttering about the recently signed contract.

Absentmindedly, Myla turns her attention to the man sitting beside her, eagerly making wedding arrangements. She forces a smile and nods, equally eager to be done with the bullshit of planning her forced wedding. "Mmm," she agrees quietly, her attention shifting cautiously to where Bryar stands, his eyes fixed ahead at nothing in particular, but she swears the room warms around him.

"It has been arranged," Caius continues. "That we shall honeymoon in the isles, if that suits you?"

Honeymoon. It sounds like such a pleasant word to describe a week where she shall be at the mercy of the king's appetite in a marriage which makes her long for death. "Simply delightful." Myla drums her fingers on the table's edge, noting the curl of Bryar's hands at his side. *Do it. Punch him. Knock him senseless and let us run away together.*

Of course, he does not. His fingers relax, and he takes a slow, calming breath, his eyes never meeting hers.

They are sitting at a small round table in a sunny corner of the throne room. All around, servants bustle back and forth, bringing in or taking out, preparing the magnificent room for the dreaded event, which will occur in less than a week. Myla's stomach twists as Caius places a hand over hers. "Do not be nervous, darling. I assure you, I will spare no trouble in making you feel comfortable. Does that sound good?"

Pushing you out of your chamber window on our wedding night sounds good. "I thank you for your consideration," Myla says with a smile instead, pinching her lips together lest she say what she is actually thinking. Even imagining the king's death is treason. Elsa enters the room wearing a smug expression. It is moments like these when Myla wonders if her best friend can read her mind, for surely that is the face of a woman who also imagined the king falling to his death.

Clearing her throat, Myla stands. "I must leave, Your Grace. I have...additional dress fittings I must see to."

Caius stands now, taking her hand in his and pressing his lips to it. There they linger too long. The scruff of his full beard scratches the soft skin on her hand, and Myla forces herself not to recoil. "I look forward to seeing you this evening. And please let me know if your chambers are to your liking."

Maverick had moved Myla into the queen's chambers at Caius's request, both men agreeing it was best to get her settled before the wedding. Tonight, for the first time, Myla will sleep in a room that is not hers, near a man who she will soon belong to, in a castle that does not feel like home.

Myla nods thankfully, quick to turn away and move across the room to where Elsa waits, hands crossed before her impatiently. "What are you thinking?" Myla asks, linking arms with her friend and finding comfort in knowing that Elsa will sleep in her chambers as well.

"That the captain is off duty shortly. You are to be under the willow tree in ten minutes." Elsa whispers, guiding Myla to the back of the throne room. "I shall make your excuses to the seamstress. You will have an hour before your absence is noticed."

Myla feels a rush in her belly, something which confuses excitement with fear. "Thank you," she whispers, tightening her hold on Elsa's arm. "I owe you."

The garden is calm with autumn ending. As the warm hues fade to gray and winter seems mere minutes away, Myla senses peace in closure. At least, in nature's closure. Her own feels combative. As she ducks beneath the draping boughs of the willow tree, eyes set upon Bryar, her heart sinks.

This will be 'goodbye'.

He swallows. His hands flex at his sides. He is unmoving, though visibly restraining himself from her. "I see you standing there and all I want to do is hold you." Bryar's voice trembles though his tone is stoic. "How am I supposed to watch you for the rest of my life, move through this castle and *not* hold you?"

Myla clenches her jaw, biting down on the ache lurching into her throat. "You shall hold my memory," she whispers. Any louder, and she would give way to tears. Instead, she closes the space between him, pressing her hands to his neck and drawing his forehead against hers. "There is going to come a day when you do not recognize me." Her voice breaks, even in the mere slip of a whisper. "For I do believe this will change me. Promise me you will remember *me*. So, when you do not recognize the woman I become, you can recall the girl I was when you loved me."

"I will never *not* love you," he argues, his hands gripping the bodice of her dress, pulling her hips against him. "You may warp as you must to fit into the world of kings and queens, but to me, you will always be that girl, sitting across from me on that barrel, thinking *she* was the broken link." Bryar grabs her chin, tilting her face upwards so he can press a desperate kiss to her lips. They are wet as tears fall from his eyes freely now, rolling down his cheeks and onto hers. Their tears mingle, a final union.

"Thank you." Myla pulls away from him, tracing his jawline with her fingers, committing the details of his face to her memory, for this is the last time she can safely look upon them, study them, admire them. "Thank you for teaching me what love feels like."

Bryar kisses her again, fervently, his lips moving against hers like a prayer or a promise, an offering to the Gods. Should they allow him to keep her.

While she is his prayer, he is her undoing. He worships, and she unravels, sobbing into his embrace as his arms tighten around her body, which seems so slight beside his soldier's build. Hands touching for comfort curl around the need for passion. A final tryst to staunch starvation for a little longer. Though the earth is cold, shivering with the promise of an early winter, Bryar's body moving against Myla's is warm and safe. His lips move from her mouth, pelting kisses along her jawline and leading a trail of fire to her collarbone. Myla's fingers tangle in his hair, pressing him closer to her breast, holding him against her heart, and savoring his breath on her tingling skin.

"This," he says, smiling despite the grief as he looks up at her. "This is how I shall remember you. Trembling at my touch. How I will miss worshiping you."

Myla smiles at him, balling a fist of his collar in her hand to pull him upright. "Worship me once more. So everything else might pale in comparison to what we share here."

Helping the captain shed his layers of protection so she might touch and savor him one last time feels both torturous and merciful. That the Gods would allow her a final moment with him feels like a whisper from above, promising her that it was all worthwhile, and that their love will remain etched in the stones of fate, and bleeding into the earth as something magnificent.

There is urgency in the way Myla tears at the skirt of her dress, willing it out of the way, needing him closer. Although they move quickly to avoid being caught, Myla longs to whisper *'slowly'* so they might savor their final touches. The conflict of needing him quickly, but wanting him to last forever, stings.

Lowering themselves onto the ground, Bryar's arm cradles the back of her head, supporting her body from the roots of the ancient tree which serves as their shield.

With a satisfying groan of pleasure, as Myla's skirts are moved aside, Bryar pushes his hips forward, burying himself inside her body, which aches with warmth and desire, a need only he can satisfy. Myla feels her body sigh with relief as the tip of his hard length presses against the sensitive nerves inside her, and she melts into him, her eyes falling closed as the sensation of ecstasy builds with every slow and intentional thrust.

"No," he whispers, pressing his lips to her mouth. "Open your eyes. I want you to look at me."

Her lips quiver, and though she longs to obey, to will her eyes open, they feel glued shut by the fear of seeing him. Fear that if she opens her eyes and looks into the soft green that has been her refuge, she will break.

"Open your eyes, my love," Bryar whispers, stilling his body.

With a trembling sigh, Myla allows her gaze to focus on him and the way a halo of light formed by the sun illuminates the thick curls of his head, and as expected, her sacred girlhood, belonging to him, cracks open. Tears spring to her eyes as he tenderly moves within her once more, his attention never wavering as he studies her eyes. It *is* worship. An act that has, so many times before, been gleefully fueled by desire for one another, feels like a sacrament now. There is nothing of lust here. It is a promise. It is etching their names on each other's hearts. It is a wish for loyalty where there can be none. It is both life and death in one ultimate moment as their bodies, so harmoniously trained as one, move with intention, drawing gasps from parted lips. Their bodies, with knowledge only for each other, release in unison, and at once, grieve together.

Lying side by side, gasping for air as the final moments of pleasure become a memory, one that will not last nearly long enough, Myla's hand seeks out Bryar's, closing around it with trembling fingers.

"This must be the last time," she whispers, closing her eyes and blinking tears free as Bryar leans over her, kissing her neck tenderly.

"I know," he says mournfully. "In this life, at least." He adds, smiling weakly and pulling her to her feet so she can help him don his armor once more.

She works in silence, her trembling fingers making a mess of his fastenings. She has dressed and undressed him more times than she can count, but today, everything about her seems to be slow and failing. "In the next life, I shall try to be born a regular woman."

"Gods forbid," Bryar laughs weakly, looking over his shoulder at her. "I hope you are born exactly the same, only I shall enter this world with more to offer."

Myla is about to respond when a gasp causes them both to turn.

Mouth agape, and red with shock, Lavinia stands. Slowly, the shocked woman presses a hand to her forehead. "Myla," she barely manages before stepping further into the covering of the tree, and with the chastising tone of her mother comes a rumble of thunder overhead.

Droplets of rain from the sky break through the foliage of the willow tree, and Myla blinks, uncertain if the drops are tears or rain.

"Mother," Myla pleads. "Oh, Mother, you cannot tell Father. *Please*."

Bryar and Lavinia watch each other, perhaps measuring the moment, calculating the risks. Finally, Bryar speaks. "My lady." He drops his chin respectfully, bowing before the feet of the stunned mother.

Lavinia, shocked and trembling with cold and concern, looks from her daughter to the captain. "I did not think it needed to be said, Myla. You cannot see this man anymore."

"Please," Myla trembles, pleading again. "Father cannot know."

Lavinia's features soften and she sighs before gently saying, "My sweet child, I would never hurt you like that. It is why *I* insisted on seeking you out when your father found you were not at your fittings...somehow, I *knew*."

Clink, clank. Droplets of rain grow heavier, and they beat against Bryar's armor, running over his polished crucible steel and refracting the fading light of the evening. "It is done," Bryar speaks finally, acknowledging Lavinia's true concern with a solemn nod, looking at Myla with a faraway expression. It is empty now, the emptiness she has feared to see, and its desolation cuts her in half. His willingness to protect her somehow feels like a betrayal. The rain is no match for her tears, and with a sob, Myla lunges for him, curling her arms around his neck.

"It will *never* be done," she vows, casting a sidelong glance at her mother. Myla is surprised to see tears in Lavinia's eyes as she steps closer to gently grapple at Myla's wrist.

"Perhaps not," she says softly. "But in body, it must be. I can say nothing for the heart, but I must implore you both..." Lavinia watches with a satisfied nod as Myla removes herself from Bryar before continuing, "If you truly love this man, you will walk away now and never look at him again."

Bryar stiffens, and his head slumps ever so slightly, turning his attention to the rain as it forms trails of water in the earth, leading into the gardens.

"If you love him," Lavinia emphasizes, touching Myla's chin to brush a tear away. "You *must* forget him. You are too priceless, and King Caius will not punish you for this indiscretion. He has turned a blind eye already. He *will* see this man killed, and if he does not, your father would show no such mercy."

The words sting, and Myla tenses beneath Lavinia's gaze as she looks sympathetically from her to Bryar.

"If you love my daughter." She studies Bryar now, seeming to size him up. "You will go to that friend of yours and have your memories wiped. It will do her no good to see you pining after her from afar."

Bryar straightens now, and noting the way Myla's eyes widen with fear, he is quick to ease her worries. "I will honor your daughter's marriage. But I will not dishonor her love by forgetting it. The pain of loving her from a distance is worth having loved her at all."

Lavinia sucks in a deep breath before pressing her lips into a thin line, seeming to stop whatever words of conflict beg to spill forth. Instead, after a moment of silently nodding, she extends a hand to Myla. "Cherish your love," she says in conclusion as she leads Myla out from beneath the tree. "Things that can kill us ought to be cherished, lest we underestimate them."

CHAPTER 30

PRESENT

"You shall taste atonement when the raven eats the fox."

Standing in the shadows of the tent is a being who is almost not there at all. While her golden eyes churn angrily beneath a furrowed black brow, the rest of her body seems nonexistent, merely shadows of limbs, pulsing with the weight of war and angry memories to make up her figure. The flesh of her face and shoulders, caught in a strand of moonlight, is a deep bronze with an ethereal glow, and golden spirals across her billowing shadows seem to travel in the same direction, meeting at her brow. She is dressed in translucent layers of ivory and inky black, and somewhere in Myla's subconscious, she interprets the contrasting materials as good and evil.

Though her mouth does not move, her voice echoes jarringly. *"You shall taste atonement when the raven eats the fox."* Repeatedly, the apparition speaks, her words filling the tent until its canvas walls whip violently.

"What does it mean?" Myla asks, sliding her feet over the edge of the bed, startled by how very cold the earth is beneath her. Every step closer to the Goddess feels burdened. "Please tell me what this means."

"You have been here before, Myla Alerys, and the Gods will tell you only what you need to hear. *This* is what you need to hear," the apparition says softly, seeming to dissolve into the heavy material of the tent behind her. Myla fears that if she were to reach out and touch the entity, the being would simply vanish. Scrawled across the Goddess's entire body are visions of the past: the back of a large hand to a small face, a spilled jar, violent swirling of magic in a schoolroom, the impudent hand of a spellweaver inside her brain. But something across the apparition's breast in specific is painfully familiar, and if Myla inclines her head to listen, she can hear the sobs. She can see the drape of blonde hair covering the impaled, bloody neck of their fallen friend. Myla wonders if she dove into the Goddess's body, would she fall back in time and change the outcome somehow? Then she speaks again.

"Only the fallen can satisfy the jaws of the fallen."

Wordlessly, the Goddess is gone. Myla's eyes fly open with the startling touch of a warm hand on her shoulder.

"Are you alright?" Bryar stands behind her, and Myla realizes the Goddess visited her in her dreams. "You should be resting," Bryar adds, his voice thick with sleep.

"Only the fallen can satisfy the jaws of the fallen..."

At this, and with a confused, "Huh?" Bryar turns her body to face his. "Speak plainly, woman." His lips curl in a half smile, one that drops quickly with Myla's response.

"I have been visited by the Goddess of Vengeance."

"Vengeance?" He toys with the word, slightly confused as he moves her back toward the bed. "How do you know she was the Goddess of Vengeance?" Myla lies down, nuzzling alongside him, a response he is quick to accept with warm arms around her middle.

"She did not have a body; it was consumed by revenge and war and justice. Every part of her was a different piece of another's battles," Myla whispers, willing her eyes to close. When they do, her memory most unwelcomely fixates on the image of Callum's lifeless body, dead on a battlefield, lost to his love, *for her.* "I saw my own grievances replayed like magic across her heart."

"Well," Bryar says with a shiver. "Did she bring clarity?"

Myla shakes her head. "I suppose I will know it when I see it. As she said, I have been here before. I must simply continue to listen to the Gods."

"The Gods will not forsake us, nor Caspian. We fight for him," Bryar whispers, running a hand across the curve of her hips. "We will claim the throne for the rightful king, and these scars will be worth it."

"These scars will never *feel* worth it," Myla says, pressing a finger to his lips. "But they will serve as a reminder that we had something to fight for."

Bryar kisses her finger, then presses her hand to his chest, holding her against him. "That we *still* have something worth fighting for."

"Tell me why the things most worth fighting for hurt so badly, even when they should feel healed."

"Just because a wound no longer bleeds, does not mean it hurts any less," he answers gently. "Wounds heal a lot faster than broken hearts, and you must allow time to do its work."

Myla's thoughts drift to the soldiers, each precious life so vulnerably exposed in her name. "The army has new helmets, why?"

Bryar's arms tighten around her. "You will see tomorrow."

They whisper into the darkness, praying together for the soul of their daughter, and praying that, nestled within the darkest ravines of the Seer's mountain, their army of Aetherwing and Ashborn lay in wait for the signal of the queen.

Elsa has established a warfront hospital. She expects a great number of injuries, and she hopes to minimize casualties by having several healers both on the battlefield and off, ready to aid wounded soldiers. Myla has left her in charge of organizing who will remain behind to receive the injured as they arrive, and who will tend the most urgent hurts on the battlefield. As she exits her tent, she is hit by the sickening air of impending war. She tastes and smells nothing but tension. There is no time left for deliberating and strategizing. It is time to lead her army and pray that the Gods will grant her a victory.

It seems I have at least the Goddess of Vengeance on my side, she thinks. *That must count for something.*

Rhyland greets dawn standing before Myla's army, draped in the Queen's Blue. At his side is Bryar, dutifully resting a hand on the hilt of his axe. Myla watches from several paces back as they speak in hushed voices to one another. It seems lighthearted in nature, and she wonders how soldiers who have also been lifelong friends say goodbye. Perhaps this is how.

Hesitantly, she approaches as she fastens the final strap on her gauntlet. Elsa dressed her for battle and pulled her hair into a braid at the back of her head. Minimal fuss, out of the way, ready to kill.

"It is nearly time." She interrupts the quiet exchange, and both men turn to look at her.

"Are you ready?" Bryar steps forward to check that her fastenings are all secure, tightening her breastplate slightly more, then tugs the end of her braid gently. "I recall you being a vicious thing the last time you wore your hair like this."

Myla chuckles. "I promise not to whip you with it today." She turns to face him now. "And...this day is built on the effort of so many years," she admits with a nervous laugh. "I am not sure 'ready' is a suitable word."

Rhyland nods toward her army with a proud grin. "Well, *they* are ready. For you, Your Grace."

Myla takes a trembling breath in, thinking back to the night in the forest when the ice mage destroyed her assassins with a flick of her wrist. There is no doubt that mage will be here today, and all she can hope for is that the dragons will make easy work of her. At least, that is what Bryar and Rhyland discussed this very morning.

They stand in uniform rows, new helmets gleaming beneath the rising sun. They are black crucible steel, and something on each side of the helmets is engraved, runes of sorts, and Myla notes the circulating thread of purple which travels across the metal, following the etchings of the runes. The helmets glow with magic, and Myla turns to look at Bryar. "You have had thousands of helmets enchanted? Whatever for?"

Again, Bryar grins and simply answers her with a kiss. "Really, Henry and I are quite proud of those. Just wait, darling. I think you will be pleased."

"And the ice mage, should we find her on the battlefield? She was incredibly powerful..." Myla voices her fears, unable to shake the nagging feeling in the back of her head.

Bryar nods slowly. "She was. But that was before we had dragons on our side."

With the backdrop of New Falkmere and its mountains to frame her view of her loyal soldiers, Myla's belly soars with pride and concern at once. Not far in the distance, dust clouds the horizon, churned by Maverick's massive army. At least three times greater than her own. Somewhere in the masses of approaching enemies is Maverick Alerys, a face whom she has not set eyes upon in years, and one she longs to see for a final time. Myla sucks in a deep breath, with a sudden thought for her sons, who remain in Valyndor with Lenore, then slowly releases the air from her lungs, imagining the Spirit Mother to her left, and the

Goddess of Vengeance to her right, breathing hope and revenge into her very bloodstream. Steadying her voice, Myla steps past Bryar and Rhyland, falling into view of her army.

They still at the sight of their Ruthless Raven Queen.

"I find myself before you again, humbled by your immeasurable loyalty," she begins. Invisible to her army is the way her hand searches for her husband's, closing iron fist around iron fist. They stand together in this. In war, in life, and quite possibly, in death.

It *was* this lifetime after all. But for how long?

"Most of us seek our honor in death, but for each of you, I can say in all confidence that your honor has been found in life already, and if no one has said it to you, we stand before you, proud. We do not march against the Imposter King for my benefit. We march for our children. Though I seek to claim the Raven Throne today, I do not mean to claim it for myself. I claim it in the name of the rightful heir to New Falkmere, King of all Myrnith: *Caspian Alerys!*"

It is chilling how the name of a child can unite so many. How before her, trembling the earth beneath their valiant shouts, are thousands of men ready to die for her little black-haired boy.

"When you raise your sword on this battlefield today," she shouts over the rush of energy which exudes from the soldiers. "Let it be in the name of justice. Justice for your brothers-in-arms who have been murdered by the Imposter King, justice for those who have been fooled by his empty promises, and if you have any justice to spare, let it be for my daughter, Elenore."

Silence washes over the army as her daughter's name brings reality to the loss. Many of these soldiers have stood guard in their now ruined palace, watching the children as they played. There is not a man or woman on the battlefield who does not know Elenore's face. In her mind's eye, Myla pictures the round cheeks, full with a grin, and her silly thoughts invading serious moments. Steadying her breath, Myla reaches for the sword at her side and curls her fingers around the hilt, gripping it in all its glory, ready to lower justice on the head of her father. Unsheathing the mighty weapon, she recalls wise words belonging to Ethstan shortly before his death and repeats them now for the heaving body of revenge and honor before her.

"We are born confused and sometimes in pain. We often die confused and in pain as well. It is what we make of everything in between that matters."

Raising the blade skyward, Myla lowers the point, guiding her troops to turn and face their foe. She hopes that the in between has been enough to make death worth it, if today is the day they should meet.

War is as fragile as love. You step into it, unknowing, but devoted to your cause, hoping the outcome justifies your actions. Visions of carnage plague her as she sits atop her black mare. She leads her army across the grassy plain with Rhyland and Bryar flanking her sides. They march to meet in the middle, head-to-head with Maverick.

Rhyland's plan, according to Bryar, seems a solid one, so Myla leans into the hope that arriving first with much smaller numbers than the Imposter King will fool him into a false sense of impending victory. As he comes into view, grayer now, but no less smug, Myla swallows years of anxiety at the hand of her father. He seems pleased with what appears to be an insignificant military force.

A silence falls in the space between them. A few strides from either horse and they would meet. His eyes are darkened with years of wicked plots, and they look on his adult daughter no differently than when she was a child, subject to his will. Each rule in their own way now, the conflict churning between them feels like a monster, feasting on the finality of the moment.

Father and daughter. Imposter and queen. Tonight, only one will walk away. They are both certain of this.

"Daughter." The word drips from his lips with antagonistic reverence while his demonic gaze sizes her up. "The years have hardened you, I see."

Myla licks her lips slowly, tasting the venomous words she longs to spew at him, but swallowing them instead. "A hard woman in a cruel world is a good thing to be, *father*."

In her periphery, Myla can see Bryar shifting in his saddle, a ripple of melting heat blazing off his body.

"A hard woman with too few at her back," Maverick taunts, nodding with a sharp beard toward her seemingly small army.

"It does not appear your army is complete either," Myla retorts, noting the absence of the Elspire banners.

With a sickening laugh, he glances sidelong to where a familiar, violent mage stands. Her glass armor is blinding in the sunlight, and the sight of her brings Myla's blood to a boil. "Have you met my captain?" He cackles before waving a dismissive hand. "How foolish of me, of course you have. Joisvell *executed* my plans beautifully, did she not?"

Bryar leans forward in his saddle, the flames now curling from his shoulder blades where his wings beg to be set free. If this war could be won with emotions, Myla would give the command that frees her husband to the skies so he might rain terror and fire upon the monster of a man before her.

Instead she asks, "How much do you pay annually for her loyalty?" Myla passes a subtle glance Bryar's way, hoping his simmering rage will be held back for a moment longer. To her left, Rhyland shifts, moving the blue cloak back as his hand finds the hilt of his sword.

He is just as ready to lop heads as Bryar is.

"Loyalty is always bought, daughter. Surely you know that by now. The price is only a matter of how much that loyalty means to you." Maverick mirrors Rhyland's motions, his hands closing around the blade at his waist. "It seems your price for loyalty is placed between your legs."

Bryar growls as heat ripples from him.

Maverick flashes his icy gaze in Bryar's direction. "Tell me," he taunts. "You have lost your daughter so mine can take her throne back. Will losing your *wife* feel worth it if you get the chance to kill for revenge?"

Bryar sits, stoic and unflinching, though the lines of his jaw straighten as he clenches. Red rings his irises now as fire bleeds from every pore where his skin glows hot. His poor horse whinnies from the oppressive warmth. Steam wafts in violent tendrils from his body, a response Maverick notices, and smirks in satisfaction.

At last, Bryar speaks, "If my wife is harmed in any way, it will be *your* life in question. Consider that loss, *sir*. Ask yourself if this fight is worth risking *my wrath*."

Maverick chuckles now and twists the reins of his horse, turning her head to rejoin the army awaiting his command. "As you well know, *Captain*, your wrath has never really concerned me."

Anger jolts hot through Myla's veins. The Gods grant her their righteous vengeance, and the sky fades to black as its light collects in her body.

It is time.

No sooner has the sky blackened with her use of magic, does an ear-curdling screech, beastly and ravenous for blood, erupt from the peak of the Seer's Mountain. Shuddering beneath the shrill alarm, Maverick turns in time to watch in horror as what might have previously been mistaken as part of the mountain range twists and contorts.

Skuggi's clawed wing curls around the peak, hoisting himself upward with a second violent cry before he takes flight. His wings, spanning most of the horizon, thrum deafeningly as his black body hides the sky from view. Beside him, Thyra and Vigdis's dragons take flight, and an innumerable wave of flaming Ashborn follow suit until the sky blazes with blue flames from the lungs of the dragons, and red from the hands of the Ashborn, raining hell upon the heads of Maverick's army.

"Regroup!" Joisvell commands, urging Maverick to follow her, but Brynja propels Skuggi downward as a massive volley of flames erupts from the dragon, cutting Maverick off from the rest of his army. On all sides, fire fences his soldiers, save a small gap left by Skuggi where a few fighters at a time are able to slip through, falling into Myla's trap. From overhead, Ashborn launch deadly blows of flame, and on foot, Myla and her army stand ready.

"Surround them!" Rhyland commands, directing infantry to either side of the battlefield where they begin enclosing Maverick's forces further, an additional barrier beyond the flames. A dozen soldiers, screaming in pain as the heat of dragon flame melts the earth, stumble through the opening seeking relief. There, they are outnumbered by Myla's army and easily cut down.

"You," Maverick lets out a sickening laugh as he stumbles from his horse, coughing on the fumes of smoke as it devours the grass beneath them. "You have grossly overestimated your position, Myla." As he speaks, a sound, like sharp glass shattering, rings in her ears and Myla watches as Joisvell guides a volley of ice through the barrier of fire, breaching Myla's stronghold, and stretching her icy reach several deadly feet into the row of shields held by anticipating soldiers who await Myla's command. They shriek in shock and agony as the sharp, glacial fingers impale them, easily freezing and shattering their iron breastplates.

In a second, men who were nowhere near the melee now lay dead, sloppy messes of dismembered corpses, piled in, on, and around the ice formation, which drips red with blood. Joisvell laughs gleefully, demented in her victory as she scans for another opening where she can lay waste to more soldiers. As she moves, an ambient snowstorm swirls at her heels, and Myla watches as Joisvell's hand extends, as if summoning the energy beneath her. A shard of ice responds to the call, emerging from the flurry and replenishing the frost at her palms, becoming another weapon ready to loose.

"Stop her!" Rhyland commands as he moves toward the mage, urging a row of archers to join him, but Bryar is quick to interject.

"She will kill you all," he growls, and in an instant, sparks of red-hot embers burst from his back as he conjures his wings of fire, and rises from his sweating horse. "Figure out how she calls upon her magic. That is our best weapon against her!"

A light at her breast is blinding, and Myla watches as the amulet pulses, her husband spiraling headfirst into the battle, and disappearing amongst the mayhem where he no doubt confronts Joisvell, seeking clues to the source of her magic. A thought which brings a knot to her stomach.

Across from her, Maverick paces, holding the blade of his sword and swinging it from side to side, taunting her. "Shall we cross blades now, daughter?"

"It depends."

"On what?"

Myla slices the air between them, a threat to stay back. "On if you are ready to die," she says finally before lunging toward him.

Maverick swings his blade upward, parrying her attack with a jarring *clank*. There is anger in the way their blades meet. It is not the common sort of rage which a warrior finds on the battlefield, something instinctual triggered by a need to survive.

No, this is hatred. It is a disease of injustice which has festered for decades and has been left to rot by the grave of her daughter. Though Myla is vaguely aware of the battle raging violently on all sides of her, she realizes that the only victory she cares to win for herself is justice for her mother and vengeance for Elenore. Should she watch Maverick's head roll from his body, she could walk away from the Raven Throne without a care for who or what fights over it.

Maverick grunts with exertion as Myla lunges, thrusting her blade at an opening left at his abdomen, his own blade deflecting hers. "Are you not sick of raging at your destiny?" he growls through gritted teeth. Gracefully, he sidesteps another attack, and Myla buries her forefoot in the dirt beneath her, halting her body from propelling forward so she can twist and intercept the blade arcing toward her back.

"I shall rage until my destiny is my own," Myla responds, forced to duck as a dragon overhead screeches and nosedives toward them, course correcting only once it has seared the earth only ten feet from them in boiling-hot flames.

Maverick straightens, sidestepping a stray trail of fire as it follows the path of grass between himself and his daughter. "Nobody owns their destiny, girl," he argues, glaring at her from beneath his graying brows.

"You and I meeting here today proves you wrong," Myla replies. She prepares her grip for another violent swing of the blade, when the earth between them splits with a shrieking grind of ice against ice. Joisvell stands at the delivering end of the barrage, grinning down the line of white where it leads to Myla. Panic rises in Myla's chest as she searches her surroundings for Bryar. Nowhere in sight, Myla takes comfort in seeing the amulet thrumming with warm light.

He is not dead.

The last time Myla faced Joisvell, she and Bryar joined their magic, and it was nearly devastating. Now, Myla knows not to come in contact with the mage's frigid magic. Much like her strands of light, the consequences are deadly. If only Myla could identify just *how* Joisvell replenished her energy so quickly. If Myla called upon the voice of the Gods as quickly as Joisvell rained deadly hail, she would meet her end abruptly. *Magic does not come from nowhere.* "I just need to figure hers out."

Myla steps several paces back, thankful for the frozen divide between herself and her father as she summons the Voice of the Gods. It is just as her skin begins to tingle with the awakening of magic that Joisvell turns on her heels, gliding on a burst of ice beneath her feet, into the tangle of mayhem within the flames.

"Go!" Myla glances back at the final reserve of infantry who still await command, urging them to enter the battlefield. With no sign of Maverick, she turns her attention to the barrage of soldiers clashing against one another in violent sprays of red. Angrily, Myla stabs her blade into the monument of jagged ice, using it to grapple onto the slippery terrain and hoist herself over the other side. She is greeted by a Titonfall coward as he runs, undoubtedly trying to escape the prison of flames. Unprepared to meet with an angry queen, he tries ducking to the side to avoid her reach but is too slow. Myla follows him. He slips on a bloody patch of ice, and Myla takes advantage of his stumble, cutting fiercely at his back as he runs, and watching as he falls to the ground, bleeding in the earth between fire and ice.

Myla advances, sweat forming on her brow as she passes through an opening in the flames, into the space where soldiers are mercilessly slaughtered. It is something found only in nightmares. Peaks of dagger-sharp ice pierce from nothingness, jutting from the ground and toward the sky. Atop many are the impaled bodies of her men. Ashborn lay in lifeless heaps on the ground, their wings frozen and shattered by the impact when they fell. Myla's breath catches in her throat, and she watches with disgust as, from the center of the battle, Joisvell raises her palms, as though birthing ice from the earth, and with them, obedient spirals of deadly glacial daggers strike the bodies of those in its wake. One volley after another, too quick to account for, too sporadic to predict, spears of frozen water launch at her command, felling Ashborn from the sky and cutting soldiers in half from the ground.

Another strange contradiction.

From the earth, ice grapples at the sky, cutting, freezing.

From the sky, fire rains down to melt flesh from bone.

From a safe distance, Myla pauses to watch the mage as she continues to grasp at the swell of magic, which seems grounded in the earth beneath her. Time and again, Joisvell calls upon the energy, and every single time, nature's magic seems to answer.

The agonizing cries of soldiers from both sides echo in the night sky, and Myla is certain New Falkmere citizens must be listening to the death at their doorstep. With each addition of freezing ice, the air chills further.

Myla works to navigate the field, dodging each gouge of the icy spears while deflecting the attacks of Maverick's soldiers. They seem hungry to claim the head of their king's daughter. One after another, swordmen after fighter after warrior underestimates her, then falls dead at her feet. Be it from a lasso of eviscerating light, or her blade flaying them in half, Sir Roderick's training warms her muscles and leaves her ready for more. All the while, her eyes scan for Bryar.

Where could he be?

Soon, Myla's breath forms frozen puffs, and she notes the slowed movements of the battle. It is no longer an open field ablaze. The dragons struggle to sustain their flames. The blazes expelled from the beasts' great lungs barely lick the earth before extinguishing.

Joisvell stands, tactfully orchestrating a furious blizzard from the center of the battlefield until the flurry impairs Myla's vision and the cold stunts her movements. Even the dragons overhead suffer, their wings flapping lazily despite their effort.

Shivering, Myla turns to assess her standing, noting the scarcity of her soldiers. Most are frozen in place, standing corpses, eerily akin to a statue garden. Any view of the mountains she had earlier is impaired by the peaks of ice which Joisvell has conjured, and moving between the maze of glaciers is hazardous. Myla sucks in an icy cold breath, realizing she struggles to even speak or blink or...*Come on*...as her body turns to shivers, Myla tries to summon the Voice of the Gods, and finds her efforts hollow. Somewhere behind her, free of the maze of ice, is her husband's voice, calling for a retreat.

Above, Thyra flies on the shuddering back of her dragon, Hrymir, and Myla watches in horror as the beast swoops too low, unable to propel itself higher because of the cold. Concealed somewhere in an icy cavern of her own making, Joisvell sends a mighty blast of ice skyward, jagged spear after jagged spear building one on top of the other, so fast if Myla could blink any faster, she might have missed it. The points lodge themselves into the belly of the unsuspecting dragon, and the poor beast lets out an agonizing screech as it collides heavily onto the wide ice spear. With a crack, the weight of the dragon snaps the burst, sending shards of ice spraying in every direction, and Hrymir falls from the sky, crashing with a mighty, destructive *thud* into the desolate blizzard. Trembling, Myla moves toward the heaving body, hoping to find the Skaldra still alive on its back. As she takes in the devastation this mage wages on her army, Myla is struck with the sinking feeling that her fight might be over.

CHAPTER 31

PAST: MYLA, TWENTY-TWO

"CHEERS, DARLING." ELSA GIGGLES into her tankard of spiced wine. Her blue eyes flicker to where Myla lies, head drooping over the foot of her bed, eyes dizzy with wine. "On the bright side," she continues, her words slurred. "Once you give the bastard an heir, you can probably fuck whoever you want."

Myla snorts, moving upright to face her friend. "Something tells me after I experience his royal, *ancient* cock...I shall not have a taste for fucking ever again."

Elsa stumbles forward, refilling Myla's glass, attempting to lumber stoically about the room, imitating Caius. "This royal cock shall be more memorable than..." she snickers, choking on her wine before resuming in a deeper tone of voice, "than any blue-ribbon rooster you could find in all of New Falkmere."

Myla squeals, finding the wine to be an excellent diversion. Thanks to Elsa, she shall not spend the eve of her miserable wedding moping. "If a position in the king's court is all my father wanted, perhaps he should have taken his smooth-talking right into the king's bedroom and marry him instead." Myla stands, wobbling as she attempts to follow Elsa's aimless path through the room.

"What a lovely couple they would make," Elsa chimes in, raising her eyebrows in agreement. "Just picture the two of them, side by side, ruling the kingdom with their royal cocks."

"That is the problem," Myla says, aiming to set her drink on the table's edge, but missing entirely and watching as the glass falls to the floor in a spray of red. "*Oops*—yes, that's the problem. Men think with *it*."

"I do not think your father thinks with it," Elsa counters. "In fact, I do not think he *thinks* at all."

"Yes," Myla agrees with a groan. "Visionaries, they're either remarkable or ruinous."

"We are visionaries," Elsa says, somberly this time. "We envisioned our lives turning out very differently."

"Yours still might," Myla offers softly, wobbling to the window where Elsa stands, watching soldiers beneath them patrol the grounds, their armor barely visible beneath the dark night sky.

"A soldier's salary is nothing my father will accept," Elsa says wistfully, eyeing the bottom of her cup as though glaring might magically refill it. "Even if he would, I heard Callum and Rhyland discussing some secret force Bryar is building to stop the Blood Stealer. Assassins, he called them. My father will never permit me to wed an assassin." With a forced grin, she looks at Myla. "We are both doomed to a life of unrequited love, it would seem."

Myla, already noting the absence of her wine, reaches now for the decanter, foregoing a glass entirely. "When I am queen," she replies after a long sip. "I shall forbid your father from marrying you off. Loyal ladies are valuable, after all," she says with a weak smile. "Fathers can control daughters," she giggles. "I hear it is hard for them to control queens."

A look of sorrow washes over Elsa's face, and her bright eyes rim with tears, though a steadfast smile remains. "See," she whispers. "You shall make something of this after all. You, darling, shall be one of the remarkable visionaries of our time. I believe it with everything inside me."

"Do you?" Myla asks with a weak scoff before noting the sincerity on her friend's face.

"I do," Elsa continues. "So, tomorrow, when you put on your wedding gown, do not walk as though it is toward your death. Walk as though you are a girl stepping into a power we all wish we could have, for you are."

Myla's skin prickles with chills and together, the girls sit on the cushioned seat beside the window. "It feels like death."

"Somehow," Elsa wills, "you must make something else out of it, for those of us who do not have the means to." Nimbly, Elsa takes the decanter from Myla. "Showing up drunk to your wedding would be iconic, but I think they would half expect it. Showing up sober, now that would really surprise them. Starting now, you must never give the king, nor your father, nor that council of cronies any weapons to use against you."

"Showing up drunk would not be a weapon," Myla says, laughing slightly though her head begins to spin.

"Of course it would be," Elsa corrects, moving to the vanity where her hairbrush—Caspian's gift to her—sits. "They would say you are not of sound mind, or that you are not to be taken seriously. Walk in there tomorrow, sober, and do not let them see you cry. They are not worthy of witnessing your tears."

Myla turns with a gentle nudge from Elsa and watches the stars through the window as her friend runs the comb through her long hair over and over. "I think my father would find satisfaction in watching me cry my way down the aisle."

"Maverick Alerys would find satisfaction in watching you beaten and raped if it meant more power for him." Elsa leans forward, and her eyes lock with Myla's. "Do not forget that, Myla. He is undoubtedly the very last person you can trust here."

"What a lonely thing to hear," Myla whispers, pulling her knees to her chest as Elsa continues to work tangles from her hair.

"You will still have me. And somehow, the Gods saw fit to make sure the men would be here too. Don't you wonder if it was their plan all along? To bring us all together in order to see you through this?" Elsa's voice is light with hope as she continues speaking, and her words bring comfort in a way Myla could not anticipate. "You know, although things must change between you and Bryar, he will keep this palace safe. *For you.* And at every turn, should you need a friend, you have all four of yours within reach, always. You will not be lonely."

"It is curious," Myla agrees, steadying her voice though tears drip freely down her cheeks, leaving dark spots on her white chemise. "I wonder what the Gods mean by it all."

"Perhaps it is intended as nothing more than a gift. Not all good things last forever," Elsa answers hesitantly. The brushstrokes slow to a stop, and Elsa sits beside Myla, her own eyes downcast. "We have not talked about the spellweaver."

"We shouldn't either." Myla grimaces, picturing the shards of bone and sprays of blood from the man's mutilated arm.

"Well," Elsa says bluntly, "I am ever so glad you killed the mother-fucker. He had no right, laying a hand on you."

"I did not mean to kill him," Myla admits, chilled at the thought that she has been the cause of an ended life.

"Mean to or not, I am glad it happened, and I am glad Caius's entire court witnessed it. Now they know what becomes of those who cross you."

"And tomorrow night?" Myla asks, looking sidelong at Elsa with a resolute sigh. "I cannot very well shatter the king."

"No," Elsa agrees, "but you can make him hate it as much as you do."

CHAPTER 32

PRESENT

THE WARFRONT HOSPITAL REEKS of spilled blood and drowns in the screams of the suffering. Bryar's boot slides against the scarlet-slicked mud as he and Henry haul an unconscious Rhyland toward the tent where Elsa works. Already, they can see flashes of healing light as she works tirelessly to save lives. Her hair is matted red and clings to her face, and her sleeves, rolled above her elbows, are drenched as well, the ivory skin of her forearms no longer visible. A white apron covers the front of her dress and has sporadic sprays of crimson across it. Wordlessly, she points to a stretcher, instructing another healer to see to its occupant.

"Quickly," Henry says, his voice laced with concern as he casts a glance down at Rhyland's abdomen where an ice spear protrudes. His brow furrows with what can only be described as agony, to see his heart, outside his body, hurting so. Bryar aches with sympathy, yet notes the way the amulet at his chest pulses.

Gods, let her have retreated. Do not let her still be in there. The violent destruction of their army spins in and out of focus, and it is all Bryar can do not to allow the fear to cripple him. Instead, he quickens his pace until they step under the tent's canopy, pulling Rhyland's limp body inside. Elsa's back is now turned, but her weariness is evident. Her body trembles with every motion, even as her hands exude a healing light, and levitate over the wounded soldier before her.

Bryar is sickened to see Elsa's palms dripping with her patients' blood. Every cot in the room bears a soldier. Piles of scarlet-stained rags are discarded in every direction, and lifeless bodies are carried from various tents to make room for those who might still survive.

"Elsa," Henry says, his voice quivering with panic as he and Bryar lower Rhyland's body across a boarded table near the hospital's entrance.

She turns, brushing a clump of bloodied hair from her face with the back of her hand, and her eyes grow wide. "Gods, no," Elsa pleads, motioning to another healer to take over with the soldier before her so she can attend Rhyland. "What is going on out there?" she asks, gingerly pressing on Rhyland's abdomen around the space where the ice has impaled him.

Before either man can answer her question, a soldier bursts into the tent, panting and dripping in sweat and blood. "Captain!" He looks at Bryar, not bothering to correct the mis-address. "A dragon has fallen!"

Bryar shivers and he casts a final look Elsa's way. "Do you need anything?"

Wordlessly, she shakes her head, and Bryar leaves the tent. The scene outside is grotesque. Retreating soldiers collapse in exhausted heaps, slumping shoulder to shoulder with their backs to the tents. Others stumble, disoriented and undone with fear for what they have seen. Bryar searches every face, hoping to see Myla's, and every time it is not hers, his heart sinks further into the hollowness of his chest. "Did you see the dragon fall?" Bryar asks the soldier.

The man pulls his helmet from his head, and panting, he nods. "I watched the mage spear it from the sky."

"And its rider?"

"No telling."

Skuggi passes swiftly overhead, landing just outside the encampment, Brynja atop his mighty back, and just behind, is Vigdis on her great beast. "It is Thyra," Bryar puffs, glancing over his shoulder to where soldiers continue to teem in.

The battlefield is covered in ice, and even dragon flame seems weak against it. Bryar curses the oversight. He was so certain the ice mage would be no match for their dragons. His certainty has been a fatal error. Although Maverick's army appears no stronger than theirs, the work of the mage alone is whittling away at their defenses. The majority of their warfront healers are dead, and the healers that remain are oversaturated and under-skilled. Bryar lets out a frustrated growl, turning in time to see Imogene and Ivan fly into the fray from overhead.

"It is too cold to fly," Ivan curses, ruffling ice from the feathers of his wings. "What is your plan now?"

They all look to him. Everyone. Even the soldiers who stand like they're nothing more than wilting plants, drooping against the ground, turn their eyes to him, hoping he can fix it.

Bryar grits his teeth, his hand finding the amulet at his chest. The light throbs violently, causing his breath to hitch and then come in unsteady waves as he grapples between the urge to run back and find her, or stay and man her war, which is exactly where she would want him. But she is in danger. He can feel the drain of his own energy. Wherever she is, whatever she is experiencing, she will die without him.

Fuck it. He pulls the battle axe from his side, looking back toward the flurrying blizzard that supposedly houses his wife and the Skaldra, Gods willing, if she is still alive.

"Wait!" A young voice halts his steps, and Bryar turns to find Vigdis and Brynja maneuvering through the mayhem toward him. "You cannot go back in there alone," Brynja says. She is wild. Her armor is covered in cuts, and her body bleeds, yet she is composed. Her black, braided hair is tangled and falls around her face, sticking to her skin with blood. Of every warrior within view, she is the fiercest, and Bryar shivers to see the child before him brush past him without fear.

"Skaldra Thyra is in there," Vigdis hisses between clenched teeth, her eyes wide with a need for vengeance. "I am coming with you."

Bryar's body ripples with flames, and where he would normally feel the warmth of his magic, he is freezing cold. "I need someone to tell me... *Where* is my wife?" Despite the question, he already knows the answer, and he hates himself for not being there with her. So, when Brynja confirms it with a stoic nod toward the wasteland of ice, he fears he may implode. Rage washes through his being, and at once, the fury fans the flame of the Ashborn and heat simmers at his back where his wings are conjured, bursting forth in a spray of embers.

"Stop!" Imogene insists, brushing past her husband to stand before Bryar. Her eyes are rimmed with flame, ready for a fight as well. "There is only one fire that can stop this mage." Impatient, Bryar nearly disregards her, but she pushes a finger into his broad chest. "*Yours,*" Imogene continues. "You have the flame of the dragons *and* the Ashborn inside you. They must simply find one another. You need to ride a dragon."

With an angry roll of his shoulders, Bryar pushes past Imogene, ignoring the probing gaze of all who surround him. The eyes of his soldiers, hoping, praying that he can help them. "Do you see the death around us, Imogene? I do not have time to summon some deeply concealed magic. This is not the moment for an awakening. I need to go find my wife." At this, Bryar takes several determined strides through the encampment, stepping over severed limbs and limp bodies, men who have died before receiving aid. "There must be another way to defeat her," he growls mostly to himself.

"There always is," Imogene argues. "Her ability to replenish her magic so quickly is uncanny, and I am sure if you found the source, then you could cut her off. Do you really want to waste time investigating?"

"That seems like it would take less time than finding a willing dragon to ride," Bryar barks over his shoulder.

Then, Brynja calls after him, "Use Skuggi."

Bryar scoffs, though the hair on the back of his neck prickles. "You say '*use Skuggi*' like you're not asking me to trust a beast larger than a castle not to eat me."

Brynja offers him a smug grin. "You would not be the first rider of your kind to sit on my dragon's back. She is used to half-breeds. You can't tell me you have a better plan."

"No," Bryar agrees with a contemplative sigh, looking past the terrifying child to the backdrop of heaving black scales. "Both our plans look like they lead to untimely deaths for me." The latter is spoken under his breath as he decides a dragon is the quickest way to reach his wife.

"Gods, that took long enough," Brynja grumbles before turning on her heels. "Come on."

Bryar follows her to the beastly claws at the foot of her dragon. The magnificent creature heaves heavy breaths in and out, and its wings pulse gently as if saying *hurry up, let's get this over with*. Brynja rolls onto her tiptoes, lifting a hand which Skuggi responds to with a nudge of his enormous snout, nearly knocking her off balance.

"Skuggi says you may ride him," Brynja says matter-of-factly, turning to face Bryar.

"What?" Bryar's brow furrows as he looks between the girl and her dragon. "He talks to you?"

At this, she snorts. "Do you really think I ever would have gotten into his mouth without the assurance that I was not his next snack?" She taps her temple twice before rolling her eyes. "We share thoughts.

Have you never heard of that? I'm beginning to wonder which of us is the child."

Bryar presses his lips together, eyeing the girl skeptically before choosing to ignore her antagonistic remarks. "How is it done?"

"Offer him your hand."

Under his breath, Bryar whispers a prayer to whichever God can spare him a moment in the chaos, hoping Skuggi does not decide his hand looks tasty. The dragon's head lowers now, like a puppy laying down to rest, until its eyes level with Bryar's and they watch one another. The serpent-like pupils narrow, and the dragon lets out an immense puff of smoldering-hot air. Everything in him wants to turn back and navigate the ice maze on foot. But something about Imogene's words makes him scared of *not* trying. His fire, the dragon's fire, deep inside, he knows that is what this battle needs. More importantly, if his sons wish to see their mother again, this is what must be done. Palm trembling, Bryar raises his hand, acutely aware of the many sets of eyes watching him.

I'd prefer to die in private, damn it. The things I do for this woman.

The scales feel like hot metal, even through his gauntlets, when Skuggi's snout butts against his palm, a tremble of hot ripples between them, and Skuggi lets out a contented sigh. "Now," Brynja whispers, "you must open your heart, and share with Skuggi the most painful parts, and he will share the same with you. There can be no trust in the sky if there is not also trust on land."

Something subconscious occurs. Even the purest of hearts carry darkness, and in recent months, how his heart has darkened, and when Bryar's eyes close, he feels an inferno claim his entire body, hotter than any flame he has ever conjured, as though Skuggi has stepped inside of him, or he, inside of Skuggi. The dragon presses his snout deeper into Bryar's hand, seeming to lean into Bryar's pain, absorbing the dark visions of death and revenge that live inside him. And when

Bryar feels as though he has been cracked open and bared before this mountainous beast, causing the creature to tremble in grief, it does the same for him. His mind's eye, trapped on that agonizing forest road where his daughter was returned to him, is replaced with the dragon's vision. It is an aerial view of a land torn by flames and bloodied feathers. It is a wasteland of dead Ashborn and fallen Aetherwing. Below is the city of Old Falkmere, crumbling into ruin as its destroyer calls the earth to devour itself.

A sapphire-blue dragon flies to Skuggi's right, and then, in a mist of blood, caught in the vortex of hot air swallowed into the earth, the dragon is no longer there. And the pain Bryar feels is unimaginable.

His mate. Skuggi lost his mate.

Bryar's eyes open, and he looks up at the great dragon, not surprised to see pain in the beast's eyes. "I need to go save my mate," he whispers, gingerly pulling his hand back from Skuggi. "Will you help me?"

In answer, Skuggi's mouth cracks open wide, revealing teeth larger than Bryar's body. But he is not afraid and now realizes how effortlessly Brynja could step into the dragon's jaws. He pulls himself into Skuggi's mouth, startled at first by the puffs of hot breath as he finds a hold on a massive fang.

And in one great motion, Skuggi twists his neck, transferring Bryar to his back. As Bryar settles into the large saddle, feeling every muscle of the dragon moving beneath him, he realizes he has never felt so at home.

CHAPTER 33

PAST: MYLA, TWENTY-TWO

IT IS WELL INTO the evening when Myla reaches the gates of the Institute of Mystic Arts. The first time she walked into this place of learning, she felt small and insignificant and *so* frightened. Now, beneath the cloak of night, she looks upon it and feels a sense of gratitude.

As is common on the last evening of the month, the front door is unlocked. She slips in and follows the all-too-familiar path down the hall, through the doorways leading downstairs, and into the windowless, circular room now aglow with candlelight.

Sir Roderick is bent over a pile of blades, polishing them in preparation for a new month. Without Bryar here to do his sharpening and polishing, in recent years he has worked out a new system. When she enters, he looks up, alarmed at first, and then warms with a smile.

"My favorite pupil." He stands, moving across the room to greet her with a polite bow. "And the one who has made me proudest. And to think—tomorrow, I will be able to look at all of New Falkmere and say: *I, Sir Roderick*, had the immense pleasure of teaching our queen how to *kick everyone's ass*."

Despite the lump in her throat, Myla laughs, pushing the hood of her cloak from her head. "I am not so sure my husband-to-be will approve of that sentiment."

Sir Roderick shrugs, leading her deeper into the room, where they sit side-by-side on a stone bench. The very same bench her mother had sat on when Rhyland wiped her memories. "Any good husband would simply be grateful his wife was not frail. Frail women make the finest targets, which is why I was so very pleased to have the honor of unearthing the ferocity behind your frailty. *You*, Miss Alerys, are no target. Remember that tomorrow, yes?"

Myla nods, looking down at the engagement ring on her hand, heavy and hideous, and all too blue. Rows of sapphires adorn her finger, and it has taken everything within her not to rip the damn thing off and watch it fall between her fingers and disappear into the waterfalls before the palace. "Elsa says I should show up strong and proud to my wedding."

"Elsa is right."

"Why does doing the right thing feel so extremely terrible?"

"Because the wrong thing is being done to you," Sir Roderick replies curtly. "And doing the right thing *when* the wrong thing is being done to you must feel incredibly unjust."

"Yes," Myla hums, finding she does not have the energy, nor the tears left to cry. Resolve settles over her, and now the only contestant left in her mental war is logic. "I am afraid the king does not come across as a just man when his cause is at stake."

"That is the difference between a man of honor and a man of power. The man of honor will do the right thing, even when it does not benefit them. Men of power will make you think they are doing the right thing so that when they get their way, nobody can tell them they were wrong." He risks a sidelong glance at her. "Bryar is a man of honor, and Caius is a man of power. Know the difference, Myla. For you will need as many honorable friends as you can manage as queen. Do not allow the men of power to chip away at and erase your own honor, for it will be difficult to not lose yourself to their ambitions."

Myla's fingers trace the botanical designs on her blue cloak, contemplating for a moment before answering. "My only ambition would be to escape."

Roderick chuckles lightly now. "And what good could you do for your friends, for your mother, if you were a runaway? The Gods have chosen you. Imagine being a woman of power *and* honor. What a way to shock every man on your council."

Myla stands, unclasping the cloak from around her shoulders to reveal her training leathers. "Woman of power, woman of honor, woman who can kick ass, right? Train with me, Sir Roderick." She smiles sadly at her instructor. "One last time."

A protesting metallic screech rings through the air as two guards heave the large double doors of the throne room open. Beside her, Maverick Alerys stands, beaming. His gray speckled beard bobs as he says words she cannot make out above the thudding of her heart.

This dreaded moment has loomed, taunting her, yet seeming like a reality she would somehow escape. Now that it has arrived, decorated with crowds of smiling people, her mother included, and a man at the end of the aisle she does not wish to marry, a sickness seizes her, freezing her limbs in place.

Surely, this is not real.

She has not escaped it, and no one will help her now.

"Father, I—"

Maverick interrupts her, his words of encouragement a far cry from the warning within his eyes. "I am so proud of you, Myla. Everything we have worked so hard for has led to this moment. You will change the face of the kingdom. The Alerys name will be written in history."

His lips twist in the ghost of a smile, and something lurks beneath the surface. Unspoken words that say, 'do not make this difficult; we have come too far for you to falter now'.

So, instead of speaking up in one last plea for help, Myla forces the swelling tears back, smiles understandingly, and steps through the doors with the crescendo of the string quartet.

CHAPTER 34

PRESENT

FREEZING FROST IS BORN from every exhale. Overhead, ice forms a jagged jawline of teeth, cutting Myla and Thyra's escape off entirely. The Skaldra stands shrouded in furs, yet shivering. Her eyes are red with tears, shed for the loss of her bonded dragon. Beyond that, the Aetherwing queen shows no outward signs of distress. For several hopeless moments, Myla grips the hilt of her fox dagger, digging the tip into the ice, hoping she can grapple her way over the sizeable walls, before she trades it for her sword instead, hacking violently.

"You are hot," Thyra says absently to Myla, watching as she swings her blade at the ice, failing to make even a dent.

"So I have been told, a few times actually," Myla smirks, hoping humor can raise their spirits.

Thyra chuckles. "Although it may be true, I was not saying it in context to your appearance." Thyra moves closer and presses a leather hand to Myla's cheek, recoiling immediately. "I mean to the touch—you are radiating heat."

Myla nods slowly, grateful for the warmth she pulls from her husband. "Yes," she confirms, examining their surroundings for any avenue of escape. She then touches her amulet. "My husband is Ashborn. We can share magic as needed."

Thyra flashes a half smile before turning the corner of a large pillar of ice, cautiously looking for Joisvell, then shudders as the cold creeps through her layers of fur and leather. "Then I suppose you must be grateful right now that his magic is of fire, and not of frost."

Myla laughs at the irony, nodding slowly as she raises her palms to her side, trying to feel the tingling of her magic beyond the chill in her fingertips, which Bryar's heat has not yet remedied. "Just let me know if you need a hug."

"Is that how he warms you in emergencies?" Thyra retorts, her voice hoarse with the cold.

Together, the two women laugh, both anxious beneath their stoicism. At any minute, Joisvell could appear, skewering them with her magic. Though Thyra, without her dragon, and not blessed with magic, is at a greater disadvantage than Myla, the queen questions just how useful she can be against the ice mage.

"Joisvell," Myla says, glancing at Thyra. "Pay attention to her boots. I believe they are blue kyanite."

The Skaldra frowns and offers Myla a shrug. "What of it?"

"Blue kyanite is said to embody the qualities of ice. But it is also used in grounding—tapping into one's higher consciousness. I believe Joisvell may be using those blue kyanite boots and some sort of enchantment to draw unlimited sources of energy from the earth. If I am right, we have to get those boots off her."

Though she laughs, Thyra's brow furrows in concern. "How exactly do you propose we rid the mage of her boots? I don't imagine asking nicely will do the trick."

Myla grins. "I will blast her legs off if I have to."

What feels like an hour passes as the two women navigate the entrapment of ice. Myla grows increasingly certain as the minutes pass that she and Thyra are the only living beings still on the battlefield. After a time, the frozen formations grow slight and less frequent, providing ample opportunities to climb free. With a sigh of relief, though skeptical of their unguarded escape, Myla moves toward the nearest opening, a jagged breakage in the ice wall.

"For a queen, you are far too easy to catch." Joisvell's words snake along the slick glacial ground, carried on the cold like the nasty threat they are. Myla and Thyra spin to find themselves face-to-face with the mage. "Now that I have you alone..." She flicks an annoyed glance in Thyra's direction. "...Mostly, that is...I shall finish what your father hired me for and be done with this miserable place for good."

Myla tenses as the mage toys with a sliver of ice between her fingers, growing it with every pass of her hands until it is a large enough shard to cause true damage. A quick glance at Joisvell's boots is all Myla needs. The soles of the boots are blue kyanite, and as Myla looks closer, she can see a ripple of energy between the boots and the ground. As Joisvell summons yet another cut of ice, the energy field tightens around her feet before expanding to deliver the shards. Calculating her foe's every move, Myla is slow to respond, intentionally focusing on the source of her own magic. A few slow paces bring her between the Skaldra and Joisvell, and Myla lets out a slow breath of relief as she feels the tingle of magic in her fingertips. She may not be able to intercept the mage's magic with her own, but perhaps a direct hit to Joisvell's legs will be enough to remove the mage from her unlimited energy supply.

"I am not easy to catch," Myla says finally, raising her own hand, putting the shimmer of light on display. "I am simply not afraid of *you*."

"Out of curiosity," Joisvell asks with a slight laugh. "*Why?*"

"Because I wield the favor of the Gods. You simply manipulate them. In my experience, the will of the Gods outweighs evil and trickery every time." A blast of light catapults from Myla's palms. She wastes no further time on verbal jousts. Let it be done, one way or the other.

The mage's expression is stunned at first, then she summons a slope of ice beneath her feet, rapidly propelling herself out of the line of fire. Her magic is quick to respond, and Myla ducks as splinters of ice by the thousands launch at her face. It is a nefarious winter storm, bursting jagged shards repeatedly in violent volleys aimed to kill with each strike. Between breathless dodges of projectiles, Myla tries to locate the mage in her spontaneous patterns to retaliate with luminous cascades in every direction. No doubt from overhead, the melee must be nothing more than a blur of colliding magic. It is a mystical, faint blue, sparkling with spears of ice, dancing around the charged strands of deadly white light, barely whispering against one another.

Aching from the drain on her energy, Myla grits her teeth, falling into a crouch as she dodges a spear of ice the size of her entire body. With a sharp breath inward, she counts. *One, two, three, four...*Another volley jolts her way. Then, *one, two, three, four, five.* After a few moments of calculating, Myla realizes she has only seconds to catch Joisvell off guard before her energy has summoned more from the earth and she is able to attack again.

Shakily, and with a concerned glance at Thyra, who attempts a lunge in Joisvell's direction before thinking better of it, Myla rises from her ducked position, emerging out from behind a slab of ice. "I wasn't ready for the warmth that spring usually brings," she coos into the echoing chamber of ice, hoping to ease her own nerves. "I really should thank you for prolonging winter." Joisvell offers a brief *tsk* before sending a frenzy spiraling toward Myla. She rolls, and as her body curls into an ascent, the light at her fingers, sizzling and ready, looses on the count of four, landing with a deafening shatter just inches from the mage's ankles.

Fuck, Myla curses, bitter that her blow landed a few inches off. Her target does not go unnoticed by Joisvell, and the mage appears momentarily stunned before something similar to a smile takes hold of her. "Your father said your mother used to call you cunning. I see now why she might say that."

Again, Myla aims for Joisvell's feet, nearly striking her before the mage jets on a slope of ice out of the way. "The power of observation goes a long way," Myla hisses.

Time passes as the deadly, magical dance continues, trading energy, which only causes more damage to the earth beneath and around them. Peaks of ice build with every launch from the mage's palm, encapsulating them in a frozen tomb, and the ground beneath them cracks as Myla fires pelts of light repeatedly, eroding the earth's surface. Although Thyra tries to help, swinging at the mage when she nears, her lack of magic renders her incapacitated, huddling behind a jagged wall of ice to stay free of the crossfire. Every nerve within Myla's body vibrates. From exhaustion, from pain, from a need to be warmed.

As the ice builds, and Joisvell's anger does so as well, furious by Myla's ability to withstand her attacks, it becomes clear that they are evenly matched. Magic against magic, which does little but scratch the surface of its opponent's. The seconds pass faster and faster, seeming to claim the very air in her lungs, and Myla finds herself sucking in feeble gasps between every launch of her magic, never tasting the relief of a full breath. Despite the brutal cold turning her skin blue, sweat drips down her brow and into her eyes. Another volley of magic loosed, another stumble out of Joisvell's path, another unsatisfying gasp for air. It feels like suffocating, dying, losing the battle in the most agonizingly slow way possible.

At last, when Myla's body feels unable to continue and her magic is drained, the Gods answer her prayers. As her golden strands reach out to grapple at Joisvell's feet, a thread takes hold and with a violent jerk of her arm, Myla yanks the raging woman off balance, quick to send a volley of searing light at her legs. Joisvell's scream could shatter her own palace of ice as blood stains the snow beneath her. Nevertheless, she is quick to rise and unleash a fierce array of sharp points.

As Myla ducks, wheezing for air, something comforting tingles within her. Unfurling from above, like a thunderous clap piercing the freezing winds, is the ear-splitting screech of a dragon. Its cry shudders and reverberates, cracking the glacial formations. The thrum of massive wings overhead snuffs Myla's magic as it is propelled into the cold, solid ground beneath her. The three warriors, momentarily stunned, turn their eyes to the sky where, just overhead the one-hundred-foot-tall walls of ice, Skuggi spirals toward the ground.

The warrior child does not sit in the dragon's saddle. Instead, to her awe and relief, Myla watches as a man, entirely engulfed in blue flame, guides the dragon's direction. A proud smile steals over Myla's face, and as she sends a screeching strand of light at Joisvell, she finally breathes deep. Her lungs fill, and the anxiety falls from her body, replaced by a wave of assurance. As she turns her attention back to the mage who crafts another spear of ice, no doubt intended for her heart, Myla views her foe differently. Her body feels stronger, her mind feels clearer, and her limbs feel charged with magic again.

"It would appear—" Thyra leaps from the line of sharp ice slivers aiming for her belly, and with a relieved sigh, she continues. "The rumors about your husband are true."

"In his case," Myla replies, turning her eyes skyward to where the Gods no doubt cheer for her cause. "They usually are." Surely, the mage cannot withstand an attack from both the Gods and a dragon—not without the help of her enchanted boots, which are now soaked in blood. Surely a leg injury might do something to stunt her grounding.

Myla waits until Joisvell launches another attack before joining Thyra behind the wall of ice, where she closes her eyes. Born from need, from fervent prayer, from the hope that the Gods are always with her, Myla calls for their voice, feeling it ignite her lungs with the will to scream and be *heard*. No sooner has the trembling of her magic ensued, does the great claws of the beast grapple and bury themselves in a formation of ice overhead. Although the sky is black already, it somehow darkens with the canopy of the dragon's wings overhead, and the only visible light burns from Bryar's body in powerful waves of blue.

Through the chaos of the screaming dragon, the rumble of Myla's magic as it builds in her chest, and the relentless waves of ice, Myla can hardly find enough rationale to straighten and direct her wrath in any given direction. It is a frenzy of the senses bound to knock anyone off center.

At last, Myla watches as Bryar's feet find the ground, and he is barely able to stand upright against the quaking. Myla wobbles also, her legs nearly useless in keeping her upright. She glances at where Thyra was only moments ago, now finding the space empty, then she turns to Bryar.

"I think I know how to stop her. We need to get those boots off her!" Myla's voice is contorted already as she speaks, harnessing the wrath of the Gods until she is certain its ruinous power will not harm anyone save the mage.

Bryar moves to stand beside her, both hands elevated at his side as balls of orbing blue flames flash in his palms. "It is four against one. We will make it happen somehow," he shouts above the chaos, just barely dodging a frozen shard Joisvell aimed at his head. "Thanks for not dying," he adds breathlessly. "It was not looking great there for a moment."

Myla lets out a shaky laugh. "Thanks for coming back for me."

"Always."

They separate. Bryar to the mage's right, and Myla, to her left. Wherever Thyra is, Myla cannot see her, so she decides not to rely on the Skaldra's help any further. Overhead, Skuggi circles, no doubt waiting for a command to attack.

When the command indeed comes, Myla is surprised to find it is Brynja's order. Navigating the frigid maze, the child, followed by Vigdis, Imogene, Ivan, and countless soldiers carrying the Elspire banner, join the fray. It is only then that Bryar directs his wave of scorching flames at the frozen wall. The ice a dragon could not thaw melts easily beneath Bryar's blue flames.

Joisvell's face twists with rage as her glacial confinement transforms into rivers of boiling water all around them. The battlefield begins to clear, making way once more for the swarm of soldiers. Her distraction leaves her open to attack. From behind, Thyra stands now, and with a clean swipe of her blade, she kindly separates Joisvell from her boots in a sickening spray of blood. Bone peers from severed flesh, a sickening sight.

Myla untethers her hold on to the mighty, celestial voices. As they pass through her, Joisvell wails in pain, clutching her ears, and shrieking in agony as she quivers in a puddle of her own blood.

To Myla's awe, her soldier's helmets throb, purple orbs of light reflecting off them, and the warriors stay upright, unaffected by her cry. While the enemy cowers, her soldiers annihilate their distracted enemies effortlessly.

Bryar, also protected by an enchanted helmet, hurdles a blue flame at the mage. It consumes her. Her true weakness—an Ashborn flame with the blood of dragons—is her ruin.

And as she writhes on the ground, seizing from the burns which move through her flesh and the rapid loss of blood spraying from the severed arteries of her legs, Myla's army has regrouped, ready to face the final wave of battle.

Together, the soldiers of Old Falkmere, the rough and wild Aetherwing warriors, the valiant and flaming Ashborn, soldiers led by the Lady Elspire, and Myla with Bryar beside her, lay ruin to what remains of Maverick's army. Brynja the Menace can be found in the very center of the battle, reckless and fearless, skillfully hacking with her blade, rendering her enemies entirely useless against her. Her battle cry is ominous and powerful at once, and anyone damned to be on the receiving end of it undoubtedly dies a terrified death. Unified in their cause, the air of war changes to a wind of victory. Those who do not retreat fall to their knees in surrender. And those who still fight, no doubt afraid of Maverick's wrath should they cease, are cut down, until Myla stands, once more, toe to toe with her father.

He bears very few signs of combat. His blade is clean, his armor unscathed. He has stood by and allowed others to fight his war. Across from him stands his daughter, covered in her enemy's blood, panting with exertion, and ignoring the multiple cuts across her body. Her unwavering eyes bore into him, and she does not break the gaze, though he examines her warily. When angry daughters become angry mothers, they scream louder for the injustices of their upbringing, and today, Myla is certain Maverick will answer for his crimes with the highest price possible: blood.

"It appears I have miscalculated," he says, trying to reason with her. He casually leans against his gleaming blade, which sinks slowly into the mud, forcing him to readjust. As he does, his blade slips and falls with a splat into the mess at his feet. A rumble of laughter erupts from her army. "What can I say to appease your wrath?" he asks, looking at his weaponless hands.

Myla joins her soldiers in laughter now. "Maverick Alerys, a man whom the Gods never saw fit to grant magic, a man who has known not a shred of honor in his life, asks now what he can offer *me*? Tell me, father, beyond a few coins, what do you have left?" Myla gestures toward his fallen army. "*Nothing*. You will take only your cowardice to the grave and leave nothing behind to be remembered by. Now, *pick up your sword*."

His dark eyes swell with fear, and Maverick hesitantly crouches to retrieve his blade. When he straightens, he does not wait for honor. He swings.

As his blade flashes, glinting against firelight, Myla responds quickly, raising her blade to parry the attack. "How much coin did you spend on Sir Roderick's lessons?" Myla asks through gritted teeth as she and Maverick lean into the clash.

"More than your dowry," he hisses, his snake-like eyes, hollow and hungry for power, meeting hers.

Myla pushes into the burn of her muscles, shoving her father backwards. He staggers to catch his footing before bracing his feet in the mud once more. "I imagine it was much more to buy me a spot at the institute, yes?" She lurches, lowering her blade, which is met with a clank of metal as he blocks her attack.

"What are you getting at, daughter?" Maverick jabs his blade, and the tip contacts her breastplate, but Myla leaps backwards, deflecting his blow with a violent crack of steel on steel.

"I am simply ascertaining how much you were willing to pay for a position of power," Myla growls angrily. Then, as Maverick winds into another vicious swing, Myla drops her sword, allowing the fizzling energy of justice at her fingertips to spring free. Strands of stars, light, liquid gold travel faster than a blink, slicing Maverick's sword hand from his body. With a cry, his hand and weapon fall into the blood and mud at his feet.

Though quick and clean justice is likely the most honorable approach, the apparition appears in Myla's mind. The Goddess of

Vengeance stands just behind Maverick, and across her form are memories of Elenore, dripping from her skin like a painting.

Yes. Vengeance for Elenore.

With a glance sidelong to where Bryar stands, Myla drops her chin in a nod, and watches as Bryar moves toward the man who murdered his daughter. The steps are frightening, intentional, final. Instead of killing Maverick, however, Bryar reaches for his axe, which he is quick to lodge in the back of Maverick's thighs, bringing the man to his knees with an agonizing cry for mercy.

"You shall *kneel* when you speak to my wife. Haven't you heard? She is taking her throne back. That makes her *your queen."* At this, Bryar kneels until he is eye level with Maverick. For a chilling moment, the two men stare at one another. Myla wonders if Maverick looks at Bryar and sees the unraveling of his wicked plans. At least, she hopes he does. At last, Bryar breaks the silence. "For years, I thought the worst thing a father could do to his daughter was make her feel small, to treat her as less significant than currency. I thought that because I watched you tear her down, piece by piece."

Bryar stands now, the flames off his shoulders casting an eerie blue glow on the hollow fear on Maverick's face. "But then I watched her grieve after you took her child. And I realized the worst thing a father could do to his daughter is peel the skin of her humanity from her body, leaving nothing but a grieving shell. Not only did you kill your daughter's child..." His voice wavers momentarily in the stillness of the battlefield, with every man and woman watching. "You killed *my* child. You killed my son's sister. And the punishment for that leaves no room for honor." Bryar reaches down, grasping at the tip of Maverick's breastplate to pull the incapacitated man upright before swinging his free fist into Maverick's face. Again, and again, and again. Until his gauntlets leave cuts in Maverick's skin, and swelling in his jaw and eyes.

Then, with an angry cry, he throws Maverick's wounded body into the soiled ground.

The man whimpers as crimson seeps into the ground.

"I would kill you," he spits in Maverick's direction. "I *want* to kill you. But that is not for me to do." At last, he turns back to face Myla, offering her a nod. As he passes to stand behind her, he mutters quietly. "For Elenore, for your mother, for *you*. Finish this."

Myla chews on her words for a moment before finding the green of her husband's eyes. They are neither soft, nor hard. They just are. They are hollow, and an idea takes hold.

"I will kill him," she spits, careful to watch the horror pass over Maverick's face as she speaks, turning to Bryar. "Burn his eyes out first. He does not deserve to see either of their faces, Elenore's or my mother's, in the afterlife."

Dutifully, Bryar bends, fingers glowing a heated blue to obey his wife's wish. He leaves his mark, a sloppy, melted mess of flesh on a face, split eyes smelted into the orbital bones, that cruel gaze that spent so many years scowling at her completely destroyed. The high-pitched screams, and the evident pissing of himself accompanying this punishment, should haunt her memories, but Myla knows she will only revel in it, for his agony is but a fraction of hers, his loss miniscule to the lives he ended, and in some incomplete way, that feels like the start of justice.

Now, for the end of it.

At first, Myla's steps feel wobbled, shaking as the adrenaline of the fight, the tension of the past several years, and the grief of her upbringing collide. When she finds herself standing over the beaten, burned and faceless body of her father, a warm peace washes over her as she realizes this is the last time she will ever look on the wretch. Steadily, she reaches for the dagger sheathed at her thigh. Though the hilt is worn with years of use, the fox still gleams in the light of day, which slowly restores as her magic returns to her body. She kneels now before her father, her knees sinking into the ground oozing with his blood. "Tell me, father. If I cut your heart from your chest and looked inside it, would I find humanity there?" The silence behind her, the stillness of the massive army, which is the last thing Maverick Alerys will ever see, is chilling, and Myla shakes her head. "I think not."

Maverick's mouth twists in a grimace, his trembling palms splayed before her as he surrenders. "I never meant to hurt anyone," he says, his voice distorted with sobs of pain in his wounded state. Myla feels the heat radiating off her husband's body, and she knows if she does not kill Maverick soon, Bryar will return to finish the job.

"Tell that to my daughter," Myla hisses, grabbing at Maverick's throat. The blood on the fingertips of her leather gloves leaves sickening traces down his neck as she finds a firm hold, pulling him to his feet. "Tell that to your *wife*. And tell that to all the coin you spent to train me well. To teach me to fight. You spent a lot of coin to be killed, father."

Myla spits, moving her hand to Maverick's jawline where she grips until his mouth falls open, and the gargled sound of his protests slips between his lips. "What an expensive death. You were right about one thing. The Alerys name will be written in history. My name, the names of my children. Yours, however, shall be written *out* of history. You, Maverick Alerys, will be the nameless man, the *faceless* man, the man who never existed."

In one fluid motion, Myla plunges the dagger into his gaping mouth, severing his flapping tongue, and pushing deeper until the blade cuts through the back of his head. She feels nothing. No guilt, no grief, only justice for her murdered daughter.

You shall taste atonement when the raven eats the fox.

The labored breath of Maverick Alerys, the breath of a murderer, ceases as death finds him. His body grows heavy, and he collapses to the ground, freeing himself of his daughter's hold, and her blade from which his severed tongue dangles. Myla looks at the grotesque sight and scowls, "So you cannot torment my mother in the afterlife as you did here on earth." And with a flick of her wrists, Myla flings his tongue to the ground where it will be left to rot.

Suddenly, the sting of his slaps seems only a distant, irrelevant memory.

There is a unanimous inhale.

The air calms.

Awoken only by a slow, and savored inhale.

It is not relief. It is vindication.

CHAPTER 35

PAST: MYLA, TWENTY-TWO

MYLA STANDS IN AN exquisite gown, framed by the entry to the wedding aisle. If she were wearing it for any other occasion, she might describe it as magical. The bodice is an intricate embroidery of white lace in the design of peonies, peeking out from beneath an ivory ribbed corset. The wiring of the bodice, concealed by fine ivory satin, curls across her breasts like the framing on a stain glass window, delicate, and purely decorative. Satin material is bunched and stitched with precision to form a full row of peonies at each shoulder, serving as draping straps to the gown. Beneath many flowing layers of sheer, iridescent ivory tulle, is a sheath skirt of the same white peonies embroidered down her legs. She trembles, fingers wrapped around an exquisite bouquet of white hydrangeas and peonies.

All she can think of is how she wishes the peonies were black. They would suit her better.

On her neck, Myla wears a row of sparkling diamonds. A gift from her new husband. They feel heavy, like a collar or an anchor, dragging her beneath the surface of the sea. To drown. Lest she drown in her tears, or suffocate in the gown's tulle, or even strangle herself with the diamonds at her neck, she looks forward, willing her eyes to see, and her body *not* to feel.

To Caius's right, slightly behind him, ever the dutiful king's guard, stands Bryar, his eyes fixed on something in the distance and lips pressed into a firm, expressionless line.

He does not look at her, and for that, she is grateful.

But she keeps her eyes fixed on him. His face is the only stabilizing force in the room. He is the only reason she does not crumple to the floor right here for everyone to watch her shame.

Then, his lips twitch, and his fist tightens around his axe. His green eyes flicker to where hers are, and for a moment, they find solace in their quiet understanding.

He nods, and those soft, green eyes seem to say, 'Well, this is bullshit. Is it not?'

Myla's heart shatters.

The resolve she has carefully formulated with deep breaths and lies of *'this is ok'*, fractures. Tears form once more, and the pounding of her heart sounds like an angry battering ram on wood, or an urgent knock at a door. She may very well surrender. Here, for all to see, raging at her own wedding to the king. How satisfying it would be. But regardless, he would marry her. He would have children with her. He would count on her to carry the blame should this prophecy prove false. Perhaps she will marry this lonely king and find that their reign is spent nurturing ideas of defeating the Blood Stealer, all while their people grow to loathe them. As her mind spirals into visions of dying at the hands of angry citizens for all the things she cannot do, Elsa fades into view. And she remembers what she can do.

Myla straightens, loosening her grip on Maverick's arm. Gods forbid he is fooled into believing he is the one leading her toward her reign. No. She all but lets go of her hold and steps forward, pulling him for a moment behind her until he is able to fall back in stride. If this is to be her fate, she will walk on her own two feet, dragged by no man, and her chin will be held high.

Oh, how she hopes to make these men miserable someday.

As the throne grows nearer, Myla's eyes find Caius's. He wears a proud smile and extends a hand to her. Maverick, pressing a kiss to her cheek, releases her hold on her, passing her off to the king before him. Alas, his plot has proved successful, as Caius takes hold of her hand; his grip feels a bit too firm. It is not the hand of a gentle husband, guiding his wife into their marriage with love and respect. It is the grip of a man who knows he has done wrong, but will continue to do so, as long as the outcome promises to benefit him.

Now, standing beside Caius, the royal couple turns to face the crowd, and between them, a priest speaks.

"On this most fortuitous day, we gather to honor the Gods with a long-awaited marriage." A unanimous nod of agreement seems to pass over the crowd, but Myla ignores it. She ignores the way Caius strokes her hand with his thumb, as if to soothe her, and the way he smiles with his eyes. At her. As the priest speaks on, rambling about the curse which stains the land of Myrnith, and how Myla and Caius together will heal their realm. Myla drowns his voice out. Her eyes fall out of focus, and she allows her mind and body to step away from the moment entirely. She drifts to a more peaceful place.

A log. Fallen across the river. Sitting across it are five youths, dangling their feet into the cold water. Shoulder to shoulder, they sit, laughing, enjoying the heat of the summer day and the carelessness their youth allows. In her mind's eye, she sees a constellation of freckles beneath a pair of soft, green eyes, made brighter by the glow of the sun. She pictures a young blonde standing in the water, goading a boy to kiss her. She hears the splash of water droplets pelting her hot skin as they play in the water, and the crickets chirping as day wanes into night. She lies beneath the stars, watching them dance. And suddenly, the hands gripping hers soften until it is a gentle touch, not belonging to a greedy king, but to a blacksmith boy as he nervously holds her hand for the first time.

This sanctuary will save her. It is an escape she can fall back on when the days feel dark. She can remember the sun, and the stars, and the freckles, when the weight of the king's body presses against hers and she no longer wishes to be there.

As the priest looks to her, asking if she will accept the king's hand in marriage, Myla feels her eyebrows arch in defiance, and turning to look into the eyes of her intended, she asks, "If I should say no?"

A gasp rolls across the crowd, but nearest her, Elsa's face cracks in a broad grin, and Myla can almost hear her whisper, "*Give him hell*".

While saying 'no' is not an option, Myla finds satisfaction in the question regardless, and as her words betray her, mumbling a barely audible "yes", she realizes this is the first of many "yeses" she will not mean.

Of all the heavy things Myla has held in her life, from swords far too large for her stature, to the weight of her father's expectations, the delicate diamond tiara which is placed on her brow is the heaviest. She shrinks beneath it, sick with its gold against her skin, and the way it tangles in her hair as she pushes it to the center of her head. Somewhere, echoing in the back of her subconscious, she hears the priest announce her as the rightful queen of New Falkmere, and loyal wife to King Caius. But even further, tucked safely in the nooks of her most cherished memories, is the voice of Rhyland.

"Your secret is safe with me, girl who bleeds stars." And for a while, it was. For the longest time, many, herself included, resisted her path to the throne.

Resistance is beautiful and surrendering hurts.

Sunshine gleaming off the spines of thousands of books, white candles adding a sparkle to the already well-lit room, beautifully dressed ladies, and an arguably handsome king before her cannot silence the voice inside, which urges her to unleash her magic. And so here, resistance is once more painful. The vibrating of her palms as they close around a scepter feels volatile. The ache in her lungs to deliver a message from the Gods is overwhelming. Resisting it all feels like a betrayal.

On instruction, Myla stands from her place of kneeling, a feeble tiara, her symbol as ruler, and a heavy white cloak placed on her shoulders, which seems to drag her backward. As Caius guides her to turn, facing the crowd again, Myla watches while lords and ladies in attendance raise their own crowns, placing them on their heads, and in unison, the rulers of Myrnith stand, recognizing Myla as the rightful, Gods-ordained queen.

But in her heart, she is still just a girl.

CHAPTER 36

PRESENT

WITH STEADY HANDS, FALKMERE's most coveted artist dabs the final stroke of paint, a white fleck in the gleaming eyes of the little girl. Though the finished painting is framed already, and perched beside the Raven Throne, the commissioner insists that the girl's eyes sparkled more. So here the artist stands, hours after completing the painting, bringing even more life to the face of a child who has been dead now for months. It feels sickening, and somehow sweet.

"If I am to paint such a sad thing," he says, wiping his brush on a stained apron tied around his waist. "Will you at least tell me the name of the child?"

Examining the painting, feet set apart and hands crossed in reverence before him, is a severe-looking man. His thoughts seem rudely interrupted as he turns his attention from the picture to its painter. "Her name was Elenore."

"A fine name," the painter says halfheartedly, studying the curls which coil about the girl's face. He has painted many beautiful portraits. Sometimes, pretending to care about anything more than the cost of the painting is exhausting, but today, he feels something. "Who was she to you?"

The man chews on his bottom lip for a moment, deliberating over his answer before speaking. "She was the perfect culmination of a little girl who was afraid of herself, and a little boy who was afraid of fire. Together, they realized that fear was just power trying to break free."

The painter looks up at the commissioner, shaking his head in confusion. "I did not catch your name, sir."

The man turns slowly on his heel to walk away, resting an old hand upon the hilt of a blade at his side. "I am the man who taught your queen how to wield a sword." Sir Roderick stops to look over his shoulder, nodding at the painting of Elenore. "Their daughter should be here today. Leave the painting there so her mother might see her face at the coronation."

"How very surreal," Myla says, looking at the reflection of her husband through the vanity mirror.

As always, he is the inventor of handsome as he absently hums, *"Hmm?"*

To which she answers, "Winding up in the very same place I was over ten years ago. But today, I am almost totally content."

"One should never underestimate the power of having a choice," Bryar says with a casual grin while buttoning his fitted black vest, before leaning down to press a kiss to her neck. "I have a gift for you." He turns to the bed, lifting from it a black box.

Myla shivers as he places it on her lap. It feels heavy, familiar. Heavier still when unruly and purring, Prince Gourdy leaps atop the box to nuzzle beneath Myla's chin.

"Off with you," Myla laughs, gently lowering the fat cat to the ground. Tugging at the black ribbon securing it, Myla watches in awe as the box falls open, revealing her crown. Black peonies, dried with time, tastefully shroud spears of obsidian and smoky quartz. Raven feathers peek subtly from the folds of the black petals. It is the same crown she wore when she hated ruling New Falkmere. It is the crown she wore as a dowager. And it is the only crown she would want to wear while saving the throne for Caspian. She may wear it as a regent now, but it is the lightest burden she may ever carry, holding her son's birthright safely until he is of age.

"We spent many years waiting for this moment," she whispers once the emotions of the beautifully painful fruition of her journey passes. "Now it is here, and I feel like I do not know what to do."

Bryar takes her hand, helping her stand amidst the brilliant blue folds of her gown. The skirt looks plain until one examines it closer. Embroidered there, in a nearly identical blue thread with a subtle blend of gold, are flames which match her husband's tattoos, dancing across the material and lapping at her bodice. Beneath the sun, the gold threads will catch the light and set her dress ablaze. It feels only right, as he said, they are one.

They are unbreakable.

"You shall do what you have always done, so gracefully. Take it one moment at a time and listen to your intuition. It has yet to fail you."

Myla smiles, leaning into his sturdy frame and wrapping her arms around his neck. He links his hands at the small of her back, playing with the ends of her hair as it curls near his fingertips. "I have a gift for you, too."

"We do not have time for that, my love." He insists as a beastly hunger passes over his war-weary features. "My gift shall have to wait until tonight."

Myla grins into a slow, soft kiss, savoring the warmth of his lips as they simmer with passion for her. "Oh," she whispers. "In that case, I have two gifts for you." She rolls back onto her tiptoes, pushing off his body before moving to the chest on her side of the bed. "*That one* will have to wait until tonight," she agrees. "But this one..." The room stills as Myla crouches; creaking open the lid to the chest and reaching inside to retrieve something precious. "This one I need you to have now." As she stands, the blue cloak nearly blends in with that of her gown, and Bryar is quick to miss it. When she holds it at arm's length, the material shows wear and signs of war, years of resting with honor on his shoulders. His eyes focus on the offering, and his strong jaw tenses, an old hurt resurfacing.

"Myla." Bryar steps back in protest, but her soft smile melts his resolve.

"*Husband.*"

"Yes?" he asks, eyeing the cloak skeptically.

"I cannot rule our son's kingdom without you." Myla's eyes light with sincerity, and she takes a deep breath, continuing her argument. "I need you to wear this."

"It is Rhyland's now," Bryar argues as she steps closer, holding the cherished garment close to her chest.

"Rhyland stepped down this morning," Myla says with a soft smile. "Something about taking a posting as the new blademaster. After the incident with the ice spear, there was nothing more than a 'yes, dear' that would satisfy Elsa."

The corner of Bryar's mouth twitches in a smirk, and he eyes the cloak with hesitancy. For so many years, that cloak was the reason he could not love the woman before him. Now, it is one of the many reasons why he might be able to love her in peace. Finally, his sharp jaw tilts in agreement, and he turns his back to his wife, allowing her to fasten it to his shoulders once more. It is weightless, like the feeling he felt on the back of Brynja's massive dragon.

Destiny, when chosen, has a funny way of feeling like an extension of oneself, a perfect fit. Be it a cloak, a crown, or a dragon.

"Besides." She steps closer, whispering in his ear. "You will have three very unruly children, requiring your most attentive protection."

Bryar stills, his eyes traveling from his wife's moving lips to that place at her belly where her hand rests. A surge of exhilaration pulses through him, and when he looks back up to meet her gaze, he finds she is glowing. Her lips curl in a radiant smile, and tears of joy brim in her eyes.

"Another one?" he nearly laughs, pressing a hand to her stomach, reverently warming her belly where the young life grows.

"Yes. So it would seem." She rolls onto her toes, kissing his rough cheek tenderly. "Look at you. My Captain."

Bryar takes hold of her hips possessively, pulling her close before placing the crown on her head. He leans down, pressing a kiss to her forehead, and whispers, "My beautiful Raven Queen."

The throne room is not silent as the doors swing open, ushering Myla in. It bellows with celebratory cheers. Faces of joy and hope at last are a blur to her as she takes a step inside, breathing deep the smell of the early summer breeze which drifts through the open windows. This trip down the aisle is not guided by Maverick Alerys. At her arm is her captain, dressed in freshly polished crucible steel, wearing the queen's blue, and for the first time within the walls of the New Falkmere palace, he looks at her. Not only as her bodyguard, but as her husband. As her equal. As the father of her children, and as her best friend.

There is nothing to hide. There is no fear. He smiles at her, beaming with pride as he leads her toward the Raven Throne, a seat which has long craved the presence of its rightful ruler.

Standing, wearing tunics to match their mother's dress, are Caspian and Aidan. And between them is a sight which stops both Myla and Bryar.

It is a perfect likeness. It radiates childlike joy, and if they were to stare at it long enough, it might laugh back at them and tell them a silly secret.

Dangling from the corner of the ornate frame is a tiny aquamarine bracelet, no doubt put there by her twin brother, his own way of keeping her memory alive today.

A sob catches in Myla's throat, and her eyes pass over the room. They are all here. Elsa stands between Henry and Rhyland, the latter slouching slightly with the still-healing wound to his abdomen no doubt causing pain. Her new allies, the Skaldras, and many of their clan, Brynja the Menace included, smile at her with a respect only women who have fought together might share. Lenore is nearby, exchanging looks of pride with Imogene and Ivan. And between her strong, brave, handsome sons, is the beautiful, immortalized face of her daughter. Elenore.

From behind, as the doors of the throne room close, the master of ceremonies calls the room to attention, and all rise to welcome the Queen Who Bleeds Stars.

The End.

THE CONSERVATORY HAS NOT changed in the decade since she last stood here. It feels frozen in time, still holding sacred space for that scared young woman. At the very back, tucked away now, collecting dust and cobwebs, is her altar to the Spirit Mother. Today, Myla places her crown on it, an offering which can sit here a while, honoring the hairbreadth divide between herself and the Gods, a space she hopes to breach less and less as the years pass. In the serenity of her old sanctuary, without the identity of her crown, she looks soft and simple, and beautiful. The lanterns overhead glow gently with white candlelight, casting a golden ripple across her loose hair. She might be mistaken for just a woman, to those who don't know better.

"The last time we stood in this room, the Blood Stealer was on his way, and you were absolutely terrified." Her husband's voice breaks the silence from behind, and Myla turns, smiling at the sight. His freshly polished armor fits just right, and the way the queen's blue cloak frames his sturdy shoulders is the most comforting familiarity. He smiles back at her, those soft green eyes, creased in a smile, and a little less heavy than they have appeared in recent months, observing every detail of her simple beauty.

"You were equally terrified," Myla retorts playfully, moving down the path and into the open seating where her green sofa still sits, a little aged now.

"Terrified doesn't cover it," Bryar whispers, snaking a hand around her waist, his touch reverent with the humbling glory of his wife and queen before him now, a vision of victory. "But now, I feel pride. And gratitude."

"Gratitude?" Myla asks, letting her lips whisper a kiss against him before leaning back to await his answer.

"Yes," Bryar continues as his hands find a firm hold on her waist, drawing her closer to him, his body warming with passion. "I thank the Gods every day I wake up and find you beside me. For they looked inside my heart and knew what it needed to be whole."

A breath slips from her lips, and her heart swells in her chest. *Gratitude*. What an intentional word. Myla reaches for his face, running delicate fingers across his rough cheeks until she brushes the curve of his mouth, drawing him to her. "Kiss me again, the way you did that night in the monastery."

"I kissed you as if I would never see you again," he says, kissing her jawline slowly as his words continue. "And I very much intend to see you over and over and over again until we are gray, and it is our children looking after us." His lips find hers briefly, a sample of what is to come. "I'll kiss you instead with a mind to nurture you, so *when* we are old, you will want to kiss me even then." He moves to make good on his promise as she melts against him, fully intending to *nurture* his every inch, when the doors to the conservatory open and Elsa, followed by her dutiful boyfriends, enters.

"*Gods—no room is safe!*" Elsa merrily screams, turning to shield her eyes, no doubt exchanging amused grins with Rhyland and Henry. Both men brush past her, joining hands before sitting on the sofa. For a moment, Elsa pauses, her hands clasped before her, and a memory washes over her. She looks from Rhyland to Myla, and finally, Bryar. Myla wonders if behind the soft, sweet smile, and cheerful blue eyes, there is a passing moment of sadness. Elsa's eyes flicker to Myla's, and they share a knowing smile. At the end of this upheaval, they both know there is someone missing, someone who would have loved to see this conclusion to their decades-long struggle.

They both pause and feel the ache, knowing Callum should be here in this moment of peace, reveling in their long-awaited victory.

"What are we going to do without dooming problems to solve?" Rhyland asks, wearing a coy smile, which he flashes at Elsa. His words pull her from her moment of silence, and a flicker of joy washes over her face. She smiles at him. He smiles at her. Myla watches the exchange with a sense of warm satisfaction. Despite the pain of their past, Rhyland and Elsa also made it. Together.

"Considering you are the new blademaster, and we now have an entire estate to run—" Elsa says matter-of-factly, quickly interrupted by Henry, wearing a gracious smile.

"—Thank you," he interjects, looking at Myla sincerely. "We are thankful for a place to call our own."

"I have no use for that old house," Myla replies, thinking specifically of the study where Maverick struck her. And the many times she cried in her room or listened around a corner as her mother cried. Its history feels dark, but the walls are redeemable still. It is best they give her father's old estate new life and purpose. "I hope it is a refuge for you all."

At the conclusion of the War for the Raven Throne, Elsa insisted that there would be no more fighting in her future and asked that Henry and Rhyland step away as well. Some scars, like the loss of a loved one, can never heal, and should only be protected, acknowledged, and honored from a distance. Myla appointed Rhyland as the new blademaster and opened a new wing in the Institute for Healing Arts, a program Elsa will lead. Henry is to remain on Myla's council, and they will live happily, free from the hungry jaws of war, in Myla's old estate.

"Oh," Elsa says cheerfully, settling atop Henry's lap and casually linking an arm around his neck. "It already has." Her tone is suggestive, and the trio exchanges subtle smiles.

"Gross," Bryar grumbles, trying and failing to hide a smile. With a deep breath, he turns to Myla, examining her with reverence before speaking again. "What is next, my love?"

All eyes turn to their queen and friend now, awaiting her response. One she deliberates over before looking toward the door where a row of children run past before darting down the hall. As their laughter fades with distance, a small, sweet giggle echoes in the memories of her mind, or perhaps it is real. Perhaps *she* is here too, her spirit chasing after them, trying to keep up, still ready to play. The hairs on Myla's neck prickle as the giggle sounds back by her altar now, and the warmth of Elenore's presence fills her. A little laugh that could never be forgotten, echoes here now in the deepest parts of a mother's memory. With a deep, healing breath in, Myla looks to her companions with an answer.

"We do everything we can to prepare them," she nods toward the backs of the departing children. Tenderly, her hands find her belly, hoping to infuse the child with peace. Something none of her other children have yet known. "We must nurture something worth inheriting." With a final glance at the faces of her loved ones around her, Myla's breath hitches. That word- *gratitude.* She feels it deeply, something so ingrained in her, piece by piece, gifted in the loyalty and love of each person who shares the room with her now. A gift, she hopes, each of her children will find as they learn to navigate the world.

"We must beg the Gods for their wisdom as we heal New Falkmere. For this is no longer our story." Myla gestures outward to where the sound of laughter rings, lighthearted and hopeful. "It is theirs now."

A thundering of steps, followed by eagerly flung open doors, reveal Caspian and Aidan, who cradles Prince Gourdy like a baby. The eldest son wears a smirk of pride, and the youngest, shock and disbelief.

"Dad," Aidan asks, flashing his brother a look that says, '*you better not be lying*'.

"Did you ride a dragon?"

www.ingramcontent.com/pod-product-compliance
Lightning Source LLC
Chambersburg PA
CBHW071221250626
47163CB00001B/65